BORROWED

ROPES

Jim Fairchild

Jim Fairchild

Copyright © 2018 by Jim Fairchild

photos © by the author

Published by
James H. Fairchild
P.O. Box 7485
Missoula, MT 59807-7485

ISBN 9781980253617
Library of Congress data pending

For Art Green
(Camp Sloane, 1968 – 1969),
who started me down the trail:
whether you're in Tibet or in Cleveland,
I hope these have been shining years for you

AUTHOR'S NOTES

For the historical record: a rousing pro-democracy movement did, indeed, blossom in Kathmandu during early 1990, culminating in a brutally repressed demonstration on April 6th. An account of those events was written by Jeff Long. His article, "Dark Days in Shangri-La," appeared in the December 1990/January 1991 issue of Climbing Magazine. According to Long, between 50 and 200 demonstrators were killed, depending on whose estimate one wishes to believe. The Sherpa rebellion described in this novel is fictitious. A Sherpa strike in 2014 did, indeed, shut down climbing on Everest for the rest of that season. After an avalanche killed sixteen of their numbers, Sherpas struck for better compensation and safer work conditions. It didn't take prescience to see that the Sherpas were being taken advantage of by guide services and wealthy clients for decades, and that self-respecting Sherpas would eventually react.

For the semantic record: two names are used interchangeably throughout this book for the world's highest mountain. While much of the world has finally adopted the Tibetan *Chomolongma*, or Goddess Mother of the World, many climbers still used the English-imposed name. The less politically-correct name Everest still bears historical connotations of mythic proportions. With apologies to those offended, I use both names.

I began work on this story at the tail end of the 1980s, when it was already clear that guide services were not just changing, but destroying, the nature of Himalayan mountaineering. Many guides—and no doubt any owner of a guide service—will argue otherwise. But I believe that facts speak for themselves. Please read *High Crimes: The Fate of Everest in an Age of Greed* by Michael Kodas (Hachette Books, 2009).

Like the characters in this story, as a boy I spent my free time in the school library, reading every book I could find about the early years of Himalayan climbing. It was an incredible thrill to meet Willi Unsoeld and Lute Jerstad (members of the successful 1963 American Everest expedition) when I was still a young teenager.

While attending a mountaineering seminar on Mt. Rainier in 1987, I had the honor of tying into a rope behind Nawang Gombu, who summited Everest with Jim Whittaker on that 1963 expedition. Gombu summited Everest again in 1965 with an Indian team. He was the first person to climb the world's highest peak twice, a distinction that would not be bested for two decades. I recently unearthed a photo (see below) of Gombu, descending Rainier's Disappointment Cleaver in brilliant June sunshine, bent under his huge Jansport frame pack, a yellow rope connecting us. It seems like a dream now. Unsoeld and Jerstad died in the mountains; Gombu lived a long life and died at home in Darjeeling, India.

I completed this novel in the early '90s and had no luck placing it with a publisher. Nobody was interested in an Everest novel. Then, in 1996, after a storm that killed eight climbers on the mountain, the publishing world couldn't get its hands on enough Everest manuscripts. Mine had already been relegated to a garage shelf, where it sat for decades. I've dusted it off for you.

Jim Fairchild

* * *

Lose your dreams and you will lose your mind.
--"Ruby Tuesday," Mick Jagger and Keith Richards

When men climb on a great mountain together, the rope between them is more than a mere physical aid to the ascent; it is a symbol of the spirit of the enterprise. It is a symbol of men banded together in a common effort of will and strength—not against this or that imagined foeman of the instant, but against their only true enemies: inertia, cowardice, greed, ignorance and all weaknesses of the spirit.

--George Bell, in *K2: The Savage Mountain*, by Houston and Bates et al

The Mountain is the bond between Earth and Sky. Its solitary summit reaches the sphere of eternity, and its base spreads out in manifold foothills into the world of mortals. It is the way by which man can raise himself to the divine and by which the divine can reveal itself to man.

--Rene Daumal, *Mount Analogue*

Jim Fairchild

TABLE OF CONTENTS

Prologue:
The Fall

To tell you this story, I must begin with the fall.

Dave Porter and I were on the southeast ridge of Alaska's Mount Foraker. The date was June 17, 1974—almost sixteen years before our Everest foray. Since Everest, I've had an awfully hard time with numbers, even though I used to make my living as an accountant. But that date is one set of numbers that will never slip from my memory.

Foraker, the 17,400-foot neighbor of Denali, was our first real expedition. Mid-June is late in the climbing season for the Alaska Range. The weather becomes unstable. But school had forced the timing—I had just finished my freshman year in college, and Dave had graduated from high school the day before our flight to Anchorage.

Although the sixth highest peak in North America, Foraker is unfamiliar to many climbers. Most going to Alaska head for Denali, lured by its status as the highest peak on the continent. Even back in 1974, Denali's traditional route, the West Buttress, was being overrun each season by hundreds of climbers. During our early planning, I, too, had wanted to give the fabled Denali a try. But Dave worked on me incessantly, recounting tales of climbers on Denali catching dysentery at 19,000 feet because the snow used to make water at the usual campsites was so plastered with turds. Dave

Jim Fairchild

came up with the idea of Foraker, and I gave in. Foraker, it seemed, would give us the chance to have a large Alaskan mountain to ourselves.

It was a letdown to find upon flying into the Kahiltna Glacier that we would be sharing the route with a party of fifteen from the Tokyo University Mountain Club. During the first week of route-finding and load-ferrying on the narrow ridge, we played leap-frog with the Japanese team. Our private mountain had become a rush-hour freeway. We would be seeing a great deal of the Japanese, decked out in identical orange windsuits, humped over beneath identical orange backpacks, identical Nikons around their necks.

I began to warm to the Japanese. I especially grew to enjoy the company of their soft-spoken, purposeful leader, Naomi Yokomura. He, too, was a Cardinals fan. And Naomi was also in accounting: ten years my senior, he was an associate professor. In addition to our mutual Cardinals obsession, there was something special about him that drew me: a wiseness, a gentleness of spirit, which went far to ease the tension of the first cramped days on the route.

Getting to accept the presence of the Japanese, let alone like them, was harder for Dave. He had run-ins with them: trivial outbursts about stepping on each other's ropes, or the digging of latrines too close to each other's tents. Suffice it to say that—after a week of back-breaking work—Dave and I and seven of the Japanese found ourselves sharing a confined campsite on the ridge at 12,500 feet. The hardest climbing was behind us; perhaps two more days of climbing remained to the summit. It was then that a storm swooped in from the Gulf of Alaska.

The storm, the worst of the season, kept us pinned in our tents for five days. The wind screaming across the ridge threatened to knock us off our feet the few times we ventured out to tighten a tent guyline or search for stove fuel buried under the snow. The constant roar was deafening.

We spent the time trapped in the tents reading. Dave had brought two books: *Soul on Ice* and Mao's Little Red Book. I was studying *Robert's Rules of Order*. I planned to run for president of the Accounting Club that fall semester.

The Japanese had set up two four-man tents on cramped snow platforms barely wide enough for them. They had a radio with which they received weather forecasts from park headquarters. Once a day Dave and I would crawl over to Naomi's tent to listen. The forecast only got worse each day. Both teams's caches of food and fuel steadily dwindled. We soon pooled supplies.

On the fifth day of the storm, I lay in my soggy sleeping bag with a paperback copy of *An Annotated History of the Saint Louis Cardinals*. Naomi had loaned it to me. The text was in Japanese, but at least I could enjoy the pictures. My sleeping bag smelled like a chicken had died in it; the wind hammering the tent sounded as if fifty madmen on meth were taking turns whacking at the fabric with two-by-fours.

Dave had long ago finished his books. I would have offered him Naomi's book, but Dave was convinced organized sports were one more manifestation of a corrupt culture. Richard Nixon was an enthusiastic sports fan, Dave reminded me; that apparently proved his point. I realized Dave had been silent for hours, intently staring at one spot in the tent canopy above him. Finally, I followed his gaze.

"There," he said, pointing. "I've been watching that seam for four days. It's been stretching. I can see light through the needle holes now. The tent's going to blow apart before morning."

I sat up and looked. Sure enough, the constant battering of the wind had taken its toll on the stitching. There was no way to repair it; the entire tent was on the verge of disintegrating. It was time to make a decision.

We crawled to Naomi's tent and talked things over. Yes, he agreed, it was time to plan our retreat. But it was too late to leave

Jim Fairchild

that day; we would have to hope the tent could hold together until morning. While it would have been safer to wait a day for the new snow to consolidate, our caches were almost empty. We would all head down as one group at first light. Naomi graciously offered us the lead.

"You move faster," he explained. "And we owe this much at least to you. I'm sure you feel we've turned your mountain into Discount Day at Disneyland." He dug around in the rear of tent. "Now," he said, beaming beatifically. He held a bottle in one hand, a deck of cards in the other. "Sake for the spirit. Pinochle for the mind."

We spent the rest of that day in Naomi's tent. I took to pinochle quickly, although Dave had a hard time with the rules. It could have been the sake, or the victory joint Dave had been saving for the summit but which he now brought out and passed around. Since the Japanese and I declined, Dave smoked the whole joint. Or it could have been what was eating away at each of us, but which we did not discuss: the next day's descent through deep, unconsolidated snow, howling wind and whiteout. We were committed, and there wasn't any more to be said about it.

* * *

Dave and I were abruptly woken early the next morning by the simultaneous ululations of seven wristwatch alarms in the nearby tents. Both teams hastily broke camp. The tents were frozen; they threatened to blow away as we fought to pack them. Dave and I couldn't find my crampons or our rope. Both had been placed neatly near our tent six days earlier, but were now lost somewhere beneath four feet of fresh snow. Naomi lent us a spare rope and crampons out of his team's extra gear. As we roped up, unsteady on our feet after so long confined to the tents, we discussed being back in a few days with more supplies for another try. But I doubt there was anyone who—down deep—would have cared if we never saw the cramped little spot again.

Dave led off that morning of June 17th. I followed, tied in at half the normal interval. And yet, even at sixty feet, the only way I knew he was ahead of me in the whiteout was by the steady slithering of the red rope and the occasional tug when I paused to squint ahead or to adjust a pack strap.

Our progress was nerve-rackingly slow. The ridge, dangerously corniced even in good weather, was now a nightmare. With the fresh snow and the whiteout, it would be easy to wander off the route and fall through an overhanging cornice. The ridge plummeted shear on both sides to glaciers 5,000 feet below.

The Japanese followed, first a rope of three and then a rope of four. Naomi brought up the rear of that last rope. The Japanese tried to keep well behind Dave and me so they wouldn't trigger an avalanche onto us. I could tell the Japanese were somewhere behind us only by the faint muffled clinking of climbing hardware.

Hours passed, slogging slowly downward, peering into the wind-driven snow, keeping my eye on the red line that disappeared ahead of me into the whiteness. I concentrated on keeping that line taut—on feeling, through my mittened hand, any changes in Dave's speed and direction, much as a fisherman feels his line with bare fingers to sense the nibble of a fish. Though we were young, we had spent several seasons climbing together; merely by the motion and feel of the rope I could usually tell what Dave was up to. The rope was more than mere protection. It was a conduit that allowed us to communicate without words.

Despite the wind and whiteout, by noon we had dropped to a fork in the ridge at 9,000 feet, some 3,500 feet below our previous camp. The ridge below us split into two spurs. To our left—to the southeast—was the spur we had come up. To our right, somewhere in the whiteout, was the southwest spur. I could feel Dave come to a halt ahead; he began to coil in the rope. I knew it was time for a consultation.

When I reached Dave, he looked like a stranger. His eyebrows and sparse whiskers were caked with ice; the lines in his face looked like they belonged to a man three times his age. He pointed a mitten toward the left.

"There's our spur," he said. "I'm worried about the snow." Because of the overhanging cornices on the spur's crest, we would have to traverse across its steep flank. We could easily trigger an avalanche, Dave argued. "I'm thinking about the southwest spur," he said. "It's flanks aren't as steep."

I felt an internal alarm go off. The idea of descending unknown terrain in bad weather seemed against common sense. "No way," I said. "Let's stick to our route. We can be eating dinner in Base Camp by four o'clock."

Dave wiped his icy nose across the back of his mitten. He looked skeptically at the spur we'd ascended without speaking. He gave in.

He led downward again as I paid out the rope. I scanned the slope above for the Japanese team. They were nowhere in sight, but I thought I could hear the hushed clinking of their gear. I followed Dave.

We traversed our spur far beneath the corniced crest. Below us, to our right, the spur's flank plunged 2,000 feet to a glacier bowl. Although I could not see the bowl, I could feel violent updrafts from it every few seconds. They alternated with the equally violent downdrafts spilling down from the main ridge. The unpredictable winds made it difficult to keep my balance.

Yet, despite the buffeting of the wind, despite the steepness of the traverse, I was finally beginning to relax. I felt awash with lightness. I could feel it in my feet, in my shoulders. I could even begin to see lightness: slowly but steadily, the contradictory winds were helping to dissipate the whiteout. I could make out the lower reaches of our spur from time to time where it met the glacier below.

I was just now beginning to realize how trying the last six days had been, how joyful it would be to get back down to warmth and safety, to the world of living things, to my family.

The rope went slack. Dave had stopped. I could see him sitting against the steep slope, coiling in the rope.

"What's up?" I asked cheerfully, when I had reached him and sunk my axe into the snow. I was certain our problems were over.

"Look behind us," Dave said, taking in a final coil.

I turned impatiently. All I could see was our steadily descending track across the face of the spur. The very angularity of the track, its unwavering descent, spelled progress.

"Look below our tracks," Dave said.

I looked again. A tight knot grew in my stomach. Our tracks had acted like a knifeblade drawn across a surface under tension. The fresh snow was slowly peeling downward from the older, harder crust beneath. The entire slope was ready to avalanche.

"We have to go back," Dave said. He was calm; panic was inundating me.

"I'm sorry," I said. "It was my idea to come this way." I felt so stupid, and so worn out, that I thought I might cry.

Under the layers of ice, a smile worked across Dave's face. "It's nobody's fault." He stood up and handed me the coiled rope. "But we have to take the other spur. We need to get back before Naomi's guys follow us this way." He edged past me, careful not to knock me over with his huge pack. "Easy does it, pal," he said. "We'll make it yet." He squeezed my arm as he passed.

Now that we were headed back, we could glimpse the southwest spur through the clearing mist. Its flanks, did, indeed, look less steep. To reach it, we had a choice. We could follow our tracks back to where the two spurs came together, requiring three or four hundred feet of climbing through deep snow. Or we could cut directly across the couloir between the two spurs. Climbing our old tracks might dislodge the snow that had begun to slough off—and of course, would be exhausting. Dave and I decided to cut directly across the couloir.

We found ourselves wading through shallower snow as we got closer to the center of the gully. At first, this was a relief. But as Dave reached the center of the gully, I realized why the snow was getting thinner. The knot in my stomach tightened again.

The center of the gully was bare, swept clean by frequent avalanches. There was nothing but glare ice beneath Dave's boots. He faced the slope, kicking his crampon's front points into the ice. I tried to stomp a meager belay platform in the last of the snow beneath me. I took up the slack to give Dave tension as he edged across the ugly ice, knowing full well that I had no chance of stopping him if he fell. It was useless to try to set up an anchor. All I had were pickets; I would need a hammer to drive them in. Dave had the only hammer. He was just now gingerly lifting it from his harness. He swung its pick into the ice; I could almost see his nerves calm, now that he had both his axe and the hammer to anchor him as he inched across the gully.

It's funny, looking back sixteen years later. I see it clearly now: as clearly as if I were watching it on a movie screen in some suburban cineplex, my hands rancid with popcorn butter. I looked across that gully at Dave from my useless belay stance and knew we would never reach the other side. It was a simple fact, obvious and irrefutable. Its very incontrovertibility was strangely comforting. For a fraction of a second, I understood the utter waste of energy in fearing something out of my control; the knot in my stomach began to relax. And that's just when I heard the distant, rumbling boom from above.

Looking toward the top of the gully, I could see tendrils of cloud whipping off the higher ridge. I could see traces of brilliant blue sky. How wonderful, I thought. It's clearing. And then I looked halfway down. A churning cloud of snow was roaring down the gully toward us.

I fell against the slope and tried to sink my axe pick in a preparatory self-arrest. The pick glanced off the black ice just below the snow veneer. Although I didn't realize it then, the adze bounced back and gashed me over the eye. "*Dave!*" I screamed. "You've got to hold us!"

Dave had seen the avalanche as soon as I had. He swung the picks of both tools into the hard ice. I could see him kick his front points, trying for a secure placement. "Jeff!" he shouted. But then his voice was swallowed by the roaring from above. I could see him tuck his head into the slope, as if he hoped to hide beneath his pack.

"Dave!" I screamed again, flailing once more at the ice with my axe. But the word was smashed back down my throat by the wall of compressed air blasting down on us. I fought for breath. I squinted up one last time at the roiling cauldron of snow. It's advance edges ricocheted into my face like a thousand tiny razor blades, then hissed around my ankles.

And then the full force of the avalanche was upon me, like a team of thundering white horses pulling me downward.

I tried once more to self-arrest even as my downward acceleration registered in the pit of my stomach. The effort was useless. Stunned, disbelieving—as if it were happening to someone else—I was pulled under. The snow pushed down on my shoulders, then reached my face. I couldn't breathe.

I flipped onto my back and tried to swim upward, to stay on top of the roaring white mass. I flailed my arms wildly, losing my ice axe. I kicked my legs upward, but the snow kept grabbing them and pulling them under. I began cartwheeling. The snow yanked at me. And there was another yanking, this one at my waist: the yanking of the taut red line that ran somewhere to Dave.

The gully steepened. We must have been swept over a cliff, for we were now airborne, tumbling, weightless in a cloud of snow.

Jim Fairchild

Falling, falling, the red rope twisting around me. Fearing not the fall, but the end of the fall.

And then there was the first impact. I don't remember it, although I know it happened. I've since looked at the Bradford Washburn photos of the route, and have found what must have been that first cliff, and the spot below it where I must have hit. After that blow, all fear was gone, knocked out of me like my breath. I continued to fall. The slope again steepened; I was again airborne, tumbling in slow motion, weightless, surrounded by infinite whiteness.

And then there was the second impact. I remember this one. I remember the blinding flood of pain at the base of my skull. I have found this spot in the Washburn photos, too. The second impact was almost 1,000 feet from where our fall had started. Another steep 1,000 feet remained to the glacier bowl below.

I was tumbling when the rope snagged something. The cascading snow pulled me downward. But the rope, though stretched like a rubber band, held. The snow pounded me as I bounced and twisted. I tried to shield my face, but my nose and mouth filled with snow.

And then, as suddenly as it had overtaken me, the avalanche passed me by. The rope recoiled. I bounced upward across the rock-studded ice. I finally came to rest upside down, the rope twisted about my midsection. My axe was long gone, my mittens and hat and pack were gone, and one of my crampons had come off. The last tardy bits of avalanching snow hissed past, filling my parka. My head had taken a good blow. I could taste blood from the gash over my eye. My hands were numb. And my belly was getting numb, too, from the snow filling my parka. I reached upward and tried to shake the snow out of it. That's when I heard Dave.

"*Easy!*" he shouted. "Don't move." I looked around, but couldn't see him. Everything was upside down. Then I could hear the strong *whack-whack-whack* of his axe from above. I twisted my

18

body to look. Forty feet above me and on the far side of the gully, Dave leaned against the slope, anchored by his ice axe and hammer. He looked the same as he did before the fall, when he was edging his way toward the far spur. I shook my head in disbelief.

"Dave!" I shouted. I coughed, feeling a sharp jab of pain in my ribs. "Down here." I kicked at the slope with my one remaining crampon and tried to twist myself upright.

"I know!" he yelled. *"Stay still!"*

And then I could see what hadn't made sense at first. Dave was surrounded by a tangle of rope. I could see our red rope running upward from Dave to a rock nubbin around which it had caught. From the nubbin, it ran down to me. The nubbin looked like it could pull out any moment.

But there was a second rope, also. A blue rope. It was snagged around a picket sticking out of Dave's pack. Both ends of the blue rope ran down the slope past me. I struggled to look downward. I almost threw up.

Below me were three Japanese climbers. They had triggered the avalanche. Later, I would learn that they had reached the branch in the ridge just as Dave and I were in the middle of the gully. They assumed the best route would be straight down toward us. The unstable snow in the top of the gully peeled off, carrying them down on top of us.

The first of the Japanese lay fifteen feet below me. He hung limply, his head, too, downhill. His orange windsuit was shredded and bloodied from the fall. He looked like a tattered rag doll. Below him, on one end of the blue rope, hung a second climber. He was rightside up, curled against the rope, moaning faintly. He wore a mask of blood. On the far side of the gully was a third. The rope ran up from the first two, around the bent picket sticking from Dave's pack, to this man. One leg was twisted grotesquely. He flopped and kicked frantically with the other leg, trying to gain a foothold against the ice. He was screaming upward at Dave in

Japanese. His flailing was useless; he slipped again and again farther down. The rope jerked each time. Each time Dave cried out.

I craned my neck upward again toward Dave. I could see the thin red line between us stretched tenuously over the tiny rock nubbin. I could see the blue line holding the Japanese climbers pulling harder and harder down on Dave's pack. I could see the strain in Dave's shoulders, could see the tendons popping in his neck like braided wire cables, could see his legs and arms shake as he tried to hold the weight of both ropes. I knew something had to give. I knew that someone was going to die.

"Cut the rope!" I screamed. I forgot about the pain at the back of my head now, forgot about my freezing hands. I grabbed at the rope tied to my harness and tried to right myself. "Cut it, dammit! You can't hold them!" I kicked against the ice with my one crampon. I could feel the rope bounce on the nubbin, threatening to slip.

Dave's legs were shaking more wildly from the weight on his back. I could tell they were ready to buckle. The Japanese climber on the far side of the gully was hollering even more frantically at Dave. The climber thrashed about madly; with each motion Dave slipped a bit more. Any moment Dave would be yanked off the face. Any moment, all five of us would be dead.

"Cut it!" I pleaded. I tried to right myself one last time and failed. Tears flooded my eyes. I had a hard time seeing. I was hyperventilating, on the verge of passing out.

And then there was the sound of steel against ice. Again. And again. *Whack. Whack. Whack.* I looked upward. Dave hung from his hammer and swung wildly with his axe. I thought the arm clutching the hammer would be pulled from the socket.

Finally, on the fourth blow, the axe bit rope.

The blue line parted with an explosive report. Both ends whipped past me. Hanging upside down, I watched the three orange-clad figures plummet downward. They bounced once, then again, then disappeared where the gully steepened. Somewhere below me, 1,000 feet down in a glacier bowl, they would come to rest.

The sound of metal banging on metal took my attention upward again. Dave had pulled the bent picket out of his pack and was trying to hammer it into the slope. His arms spasmed so wildly that many of the hammer blows missed. At least once he hit himself with a sickening thud. I thought he would cry out. He didn't. And then, at last, I could feel the rope tug as he pulled a bight upward, clipping it securely to the anchor.

It was not until then that he finally let go. He slumped against the ice, shaking uncontrollably. He allowed himself a single sob of pain, a single sob of grief. It echoed downward through the bare gully; it echoed off the ridges on either side.

I knew I would live now. I, too, slumped against the ice. A queer feeling began to fill my insides. I suppose it was shock. I looked upward at Dave, then past him. The gully was scoured bare by the avalanche. It was like a gleaming path upward into the brilliant blue sky. The two ridges closed in on both sides of the gleaming path. Far up that shining path I could make out four orange dots. They were moving swiftly down toward us. Higher up, even beyond them, the shining path and the two ridges converged.

Yes, I thought, hanging there upside down, feeling myself grow faint. Something seemed most odd. Just when you think you understand a game like pinochle, the rules start making no sense. A tiny cloud passed in front of the sun, then was gone; the gully again shone blinding silver. I had to squint. High above, where the gully met the two ridges, there was a small notch. From my upside down vantage, it looked like a gate. A cloud passed once more in front of the sun. The gate closed. I lost consciousness.

* * *

PART ONE:

Beginnings

Chapter One:

On the Bitterroot

Dave and I grew up in Missoula, Montana, near the heart of the Bitterroot Mountains. The central Bitterroots run north to south for a hundred miles, paralleling the gently looping river of the same name. The range is regularly transected by deep canyons running east to west which provide access to the wilderness interior: high, crumbling cirques that hide vestiges of winter's snow, pristine alpine lakes teeming with cutthroat trout, and dizzying spires of tawny granite. Driving down Highway 93 along the Bitterroot River, one alternately sees huge, brooding mountains that look like sleeping, snow-dusted giants, and crazily tilted rock fangs with ridges as ragged as the rusty teeth on some old logger's rip saw.

It was under the shadow of these mountains that Dave and I grew up. It was under their spell that we fell.

We both went to DeMarinis Elementary School. I was a year ahead, so my memories of Dave in those first few years are vague. I do remember seeing him standing in the hallway outside his classroom almost every day with his forehead pressed against a molding strip that ran at a conveniently brutal height along the wall. He spent so much time up against that wall it's a wonder he didn't have a permanent groove in his forehead. He always seemed to be in trouble for something, and proud of it, grinning fiercely sideways

23

Jim Fairchild

at anyone walking past. I was always afraid to make eye contact with such a rebel, but secretly ached with jealousy.

I moved on to Kittredge Junior High, and had long forgotten the mop-haired kid with the frayed blue jeans and the untied Chuck Taylors. This was 1969, remember: a kid with mop hair, frayed jeans and untied basketball shoes was clearly a subversive. I was starting the eighth grade that fall, and my life was busy: class treasurer, president of the Business Club, Second Class Boy Scout one merit badge away from First Class. My life became a great deal busier when Dave reappeared. When I sit back nowadays and search my memory for the important events of 1969, they come up like this: Manson, My Lai, the moon landing, meeting Dave.

The school library was where it happened. My library period was just before lunch. Most of my classmates would spend the hour shooting spitballs, or ogling last year's Sports Illustrated swimsuit edition filched from behind the checkout desk, or spreading gossip about the latest hot couple in school. I spent my library hour hidden in a back reading room. There was a round table surrounded by four frayed chairs, and nearby were the Dewey Decimal 915s: geography and exploration. I had been led there after seeing a re-run of a National Geographic special, "Americans on Everest."

The television show told the story of the 1963 American Mount Everest Expedition—the first American climb of the world's highest peak. I had been mesmerized by the solitude of the high places: by the vast expanses of rock and ice, by the whipping winds and drifting snows. The Himalaya seemed of dimensions utterly alien to this planet—so much so that I immediately lost interest in my earlier passion, space exploration. Instead of memorizing the orbital radii of the planets and the names of the moons, instead of memorizing the names of Mercury and Gemini crews, I was now memorizing the heights of the world's tallest peaks. But there was more to it than alien geography. I had been drawn to the odd struggle of human beings to surmount such inhuman heights. There

24

was something that I couldn't put a finger on: a sense of higher unknowns, higher mysteries.

When library period was over, I would often remain in the library and read through lunch. I would forget about eating. There were so many good books, and so little time. I read all of them that year. Maurice Herzog's *Annapurna*, of course: a moving tale of suffering and transcendence (decades later, its veracity would be questioned). And there was Ralph Barker's *The Last Blue Mountain,* the story of four young students in the company of an older Himalayan veteran who try to scale a virgin 24,000-foot peak in the Karakoram, and find themselves in a grim battle for survival.

My favorite, though, had to be James Ramsey Ullman's *Americans on Everest.* It was the official account of the 1963 American Everest expedition, led by Norman Dyhrenfurth. A massive volume, it not only gave an inside view of a huge, well-oiled Himalayan expedition, but also included tediously detailed appendices of gear, food, finances, medical supplies and logistical plans. I studied those appendices—and the appendices in the journals of other historic Himalayan expeditions—paying minute attention to how many pairs of socks, how many rolls of toilet paper, how many pounds of freeze-dried pork an expedition needed to scale a Himalayan giant. Before long, I was compiling equipment lists for my own imaginary Everest expedition.

This new passion was my own little secret. I hid the three-ring binder holding my prospectus and gear lists from my parents. They thought I was in my room working on homework each night, when I was really tallying the weights of balaclavas and carabiners and cans of freeze-dried chili con carne: spinning my circular pocket slide rule with the fervency of a Buddhist monk spinning his prayer wheel. My passion was a secret from the rest of my class, too, who thought I was back in that reading room perusing old National Geographics for pictures of bare-breasted Tahitians. The mountaineering books in that library were my own private sanctum.

Jim Fairchild

Until, one day, I started to read the checkout cards tucked into the pockets inside the front covers. I was the only student who had signed most of the cards in years. But, before the fall semester was half over, another name started appearing: Dave Porter. An intruder had slipped into my private sanctum.

*   *   *

Shortly after Christmas break I sat in one of the frayed chairs in the reading room, perusing, once again, the appendices of *Americans on Everest*. I had come to an impasse on my own expedition packing lists. I couldn't decide how many cases of sardines in mustard sauce would be needed, and was searching Ullman for guidance. I had been poring over the appendices, ardently spinning my circular slide rule, when I was distracted by a sound. Somebody had farted. I peered over my glasses.

"Sorry," the kid sitting across from me said. "I cut the cheese." A book lay in his lap. I hadn't seen him come into the reading room. He was obviously a seventh grader, judging by his size: his feet barely met the floor as he sat back in the seat across from me. The joys of full-blown puberty were still several months away for him. His scraped knees protruded from holes in his jeans.

I recognized him. He was the subversive who was always standing out in the hallway in grade school.

"I believe I detect the fine balance of a Poo Valley Gorgonzola," I said, doing my best Julia Child.

The kid across from me glanced at my circular slide rule, and at my glasses, and at my plastic pocket protector. He didn't seem impressed. He lifted his book and began to read again.

I could see the cover. He was reading *Four Against Everest*.

"Are you Dave Porter?" I asked. I was face-to-face with the dastardly intruder. I was also face-to-face with the only other kid in school who shared my passion.

He put the book down again, exasperated. "Actually, no. My name is Spiro T. Agnew. Judging by your slide rule, you must be Albert Einstein."

Within seconds, we were arguing about the two books we were reading. Dave derided the book in my lap. He insisted that Dyhrenfurth's 1963 Everest expedition had been too big, too expensive, too beholden to corporate sponsors, too well-equipped—in other words, too assured of success.

I pointed to the book in his lap: *Four Against Everest.* It was the story of four novice climbers, led by Woodrow Wilson Sayre, a grandson of the President, who made an unauthorized, lightly equipped attempt on Everest from the north—i.e., Chinese-controlled—side in 1962, just months before Dyhrenfurth's big expedition on the Nepalese side. Although the Sayre team reached 25,000 feet, they fell far behind schedule, ran out of food, and were given up for dead. When they finally straggled back across the border into Nepal, thin as scarecrows, they were told by Cold-War-obsessed U.S. diplomats that they could have triggered a serious confrontation with Communist China.

Dave told me Sayre was his hero. I parroted the usual line embraced in the American climbing community in those years—that Sayre's attempt was foolish, even crazy, and had almost resulted in Nepal cancelling permission for Dyhrenfurth's attempt the following spring. We were soon shouting at each other so loudly that I took off my spittle-splattered glasses, certain blows were imminent. An assistant librarian had to come in and tell us to lower our voices. Dave and I were instant best friends. He taunted me with the nickname "Norman"; I taunted him with the nickname "Woodrow."

* * *

That next spring marked membership drive time for my Boy Scout troop. My father was an assistant Scoutmaster, so I was

Jim Fairchild

expected to bring in more than the average headcount of recruits. Dave seemed an obvious candidate. The head Scoutmaster wasn't thrilled with Dave's shenanigans. Dave had a tendency to fart the first several notes of "The Star-Spangled Banner" when we opened each meeting with the Pledge of Allegiance. He also despised uniforms. His Scout shirt was always untucked and misbuttoned, so that one tail hung longer than the other. It wasn't an accident. But we needed new blood—or more precisely, more membership dues— so Dave was tolerated.

On the flip side, Dave, too, was not favorably impressed. Studying for the Home Repair merit badge or practicing drill-and-ceremony for the Memorial Day parade was not his idea of a groovy Friday night. He told me exactly seventeen minutes into his first meeting that he was quitting. He ripped off his neckerchief and handed it to me.

"Wait until we go on our first camping trip," I said. "We're going up to Enchantment Lake in two weeks. Once you've been up to the mountains, you'll change your mind."

* * *

Enchantment Lake lies in the southern Bitterroots. A rough three-mile road leads to it, but four-wheel-drive vehicles can make the trip easily. Our troop never hiked in. By driving in, the Scoutmasters could haul in their huge canvas wall tent, a portable generator, several cases of Highlander beer and the direct-current black-and-white television with which they kept up on the weekend games. Once the spring snows were gone, our troop would head for the lake every other weekend.

While most of the Scoutmasters spent the weekends at the lake in their mildewy tent swilling Highlanders and Lewis and Clark vodka, smoking cigars, telling World War II and Korean War stories and watching the games, there were two adults who attempted to

28

make good use of the time with the kids. My father was one of them. He was not a drinker, was disgusted by the smell of cigars, had not gone off to war, and didn't follow sports. At the time, I wished he did even one of those things.

My father was a soil scientist at the local university. Until long after I left home, he always wore the same uniform: short-sleeved white shirt and red paisley bow tie, bristly Brylcreemed crewcut and horn-rimmed glasses. He wore a plastic pocket protector bearing the logo of some new fertilizer. I always got my new pocket protectors from his cast-offs, which he kept neatly alphabetized in a desk drawer. My father wore this invariable uniform even on our Scouting excursions, pulling on his Scout shirt over his white shirt and bow tie like a jacket. The pocket protector would be transferred to the outer shirt for easy access.

Once camp was set up by the lake, my father would round up the Scouts and take them on a nature walk. He knew botany, geology and entomology in addition to soils. He would lead us through the woods, spouting out Latin names of trees, pointing out rocks from the Jurassic and Triassic periods of the Mesozoic era, hushing us when a dragonfly would suddenly rise up from a lily pad and skim over the lake's mirror-perfect surface. He carried his expandable bullhide briefcase in one hand, weighed down with his old grad school textbooks for ready reference if the name of a particular genus eluded him. The kids would traipse along behind him, making faces to his back, addressing him as Professor Parson when they asked a question, but calling him Poindexter when he was out of earshot. Bringing up the rear, I was mortified to be his son.

As I said, there was one other adult who spent time with us on those weekends at Enchantment Lake. His name was Art Brown. He was a young man, perhaps 25. And yet, strangely, he seemed far more mature than all the other war-story-telling adults combined. Art was a man of long, intense silences. But when he spoke, his spare words rang true. He was a small man, but with broad, muscular shoulders, and legs as bulky as a bull elk's. He had a head of flaming red hair kept almost as closely cropped as my father's, and pale skin so deeply freckled it looked like a dark tan from a distance. Art was missing the top two joints of his left ring finger. The missing finger was a source of endless speculation amongst the Scouts, but none of us was brave enough to ask him how he had lost it. We knew only that it had happened during his tour of duty with the Navy SEALs in Vietnam, from which he had returned the previous fall. Although Art had no children himself, he had volunteered his services to the troop soon after his return from the war. He was the only leader who was an outdoorsman, unless you wanted to count drunken car camping and drunken road hunting. Art became my idol.

Each weekend at Enchantment Lake Art would organize day hikes or overnight backpack trips. But, as with the leaders, most of the Scouts were not terribly interested in the out-of-doors. Art had a coterie of four who followed him out onto the mountain trails. It became five with Dave. We would leave camp before the sun was up, while the snores of the other leaders still shook the canvas walls of their boozy tent, and head up the trail, surprising browsing deer.

Art could walk all day and all night without stopping. He moved up the trail ahead of us with an economy of motion that was matched only by his economy of speech. No movement was wasted. At first, we struggled to keep up with him, huffing and puffing and cussing far behind him, trying not to lose sight of him. But he was patient with us. He started us out on six- or seven-mile day trips, increasing the mileage each weekend. Before that summer of 1970 was half over, we were covering twenty miles a day. The size of Art's coterie had an inverse relationship to the mileage we covered. By July, only Dave and I were left. Churning up some dusty trail, switchback after switchback, Dave and I would compete with each other to stay on Art's heels.

While the rest of the troop spent the day fishing or working on their Citizenship merit badges, Art would take Dave and me off on some crosscountry hike, bushwhacking into a glacial cirque to practice orienteering. In bits and pieces, while stopping to sip water from an icy spring or while eating gorp in some sunny meadow riotous with the gold of blooming glacier lilies, Dave and I pried stories out of Art. He had been an accomplished climber before being drafted—the first real, live climber Dave and I had ever met. Art had been caught on El Capitan's Nose in a hailstorm once, sitting out the storm while hanging from a single rusty piton that buzzed with electricity. When the storm passed, a rainbow was seemingly close enough to reach out and poke. Art had been to Alaska once, too, climbing half a dozen unnamed peaks in the Alaska Range,and once dreamed of going to the Karakoram to climb nameless rock spires 20,000 feet high. We asked him if he was planning to climb any big mountains now that he was back from Vietnam.

He explained quietly that he was thinking about one mountain—although his goal was not to reach it summit. He dreamed of going to Tibet, to the sacred mountain of Kailas. He dreamed of joining the pilgrims who make the 32-mile circuit around the holy peak, many crawling on their hands and knees. Dave and I laughed. Art smiled softly, then didn't speak again for an hour.

We continued to learn from Art the true economy of movement: how to dance across boulder fields, how to climb scree slopes without slipping, how to kick steps across crusty midsummer snowfields. He taught us the arcane map skills of section and resection, back-azimuths and magnetic-to-grid conversion. Soon we were covering 25 miles a day entirely off-trail. Art was now letting us lead him across pathless divides and into hidden valleys that might not have seen a human visitor for decades. We didn't dare to ask him yet to teach us to climb, but soon we'd surely find the courage to do so. Dave and I beamed with pride as we followed Art back to camp after each excursion, our calves caked with trail dust, the canvas straps of our old Trapper Nelson packboards stained with salt. We could sense the awe in the other Scouts, who had spent the day learning how to properly construct a trench latrine. My skin was turning dark brown from the sun, my legs were displaying hard muscles I hadn't even known existed before. I was feeling a confidence in myself, thanks to Art, that I'd never, just a year ago, dreamed possible. My life was changing in mysterious and wonderful ways.

* * *

The Labor Day weekend came. Summer was drawing to a close. The troop took its last trip to Enchantment Lake before school started again.

All that summer, Art had been teaching Dave and me the essentials of high mountain travel. But we had never done any real climbing. That would change on the second afternoon at the lake. While the rest of the troop sat around the campfire studying for the Personal Hygiene merit badge, Art surreptitiously took Dave and me for a walk toward the lake.

At the far end of Enchantment Lake, half a mile from our camp, there rose a tawny granite tower named Ghost Spire. Its rock soared 200 feet above the lake below. Art said nothing during that half-mile, but when we reached the sun-baked cliffs, he turned and grinned. When he dropped his rucksack and opened it, Dave and I both dropped our jaws. Inside the pack was a shiny new three-strand Goldline rope.

Art taught us the merest basics that afternoon on Ghost Spire. He left the troop and the town a few weeks later for whereabouts unknown. He had a war to get out of his system. We never heard from him again. But he left Dave and me infected with his dream.

* * *

Dave quit the troop that fall, disgusted with the interminable meetings spent practicing drill-and-ceremony in the overheated school gym. Without both Art and Dave, Scouting seemed like a chore to me now. Feeling some sense of duty to my father— terrified to admit to him my desire to quit—I continued to make the meetings, grimly earning one merit badge after another, just a few short of Eagle rank. Although my father didn't understand it all, he knew that something had changed. We kept our distance.

That distance grew even greater near the holidays. I'd written away for a brochure from a climbing course at Mount Rainier. When it arrived, I summoned the courage to show it to my father. I promised to pay for the course myself if he would just sign the parental consent form. One look ath the cover photo of a climber rappelling off a teetering serac on the Cowlitz Glacier and my father made up his mind. The answer was *No*—not until I was old enough to pay my own hospital bills, too.

I was crushed. I had made elaborate mental lists of all the mountains I could climb by the time I went off to college if I could get started at the age of fifteen. I knew that many colleges had climbing clubs, many of which sponsored expeditions to large mountains. If I got a good climbing background while still in high school, I would be ready to go off on expeditions the minute I got to college. Now, that dream seemed down the pipes.

* * *

That next April, I was awarded my Eagle Scout badge. I never attended another Scout meeting. I started spending weekends at Dave's house in the Bitterroot Valley. Dave's father, Emmett, had offered me an open invitation, and I did my best to wear out his

Jim Fairchild

hospitality. Although my father was obviously upset by my absences both from home and from the Scouts, he knew something was missing from my life, and recognized Emmett's generosity and wisdom.

Dave and I began spending our weekends backpacking up the still-snowy canyons of the Bitterroots. My father was worried about us going by ourselves, but Emmett assured him that if any two boys knew how to take care of themselves in the mountains, it was Dave and I.

* * *

I should tell you a little about Emmett. He was a short but very muscular man, with long, wild hair and a shaggy beard. He owned a run-down Harley Davidson repair shop down Highway 93, across from Castle Crag in the Bitterroots. He usually wore black Harley T-shirts and a leather vest, and, during the warmer months of Dave's brief Scouting career, had brought Dave to meetings on the back of a mufflerless Harley trike.

The Scout leaders had never taken a liking to Emmett. It was more than his black biker T-shirts and long hair and beard. It was, I believe, Emmett's tattoos that turned off the leaders. You see, Emmett—like most of the leaders—was a veteran. But, unlike the others, Emmett was not a sentimental patriot. He did not join the others in wistful, pleasingly embellished remembrances of his time in uniform. Emmett had gone to Korea as a healthy young man. He had returned a cripple. It had been an experience that filled him with bitterness. And his tattoos expressed that bitterness.

Emmett had been an eighteen-year-old motorcycle courier with the 1st Marine Division during the early, dark days of the Korean conflict. It was his job to run messages from the rear lines to the front of the advancing column. It was work he loved: he was assigned his own motorcycle and .45 pistol, and he spent the bulk of the time on his own, racing up and down the rough road the Marine engineers had been building from the coast up through the mountains. For a young private, it was Heaven. When he was on his own, the throttle full out, there was just the open, climbing road, and the bracing bite of the winter air, and only a dim rumor of Chinese in the high hills to either side.

Emmett was at the front when the infamous Chinese attack started. Emmett's motorcycle was shot out from under him during the first night of that desperate withdrawal back along the Chosin Reservoir. Leaving his expired mount in the icy ditch beside the road, he was forced to continue on foot along with the infantry units. Most of the Marines at the front had been issued heavy galoshes. The galoshes were universally despised, but Emmett's boots were even less adequate. Because his courier job required a sensitive touch to shift gears, he was wearing only his standard-issue leather combat boots. By the time he reached the rear, he had frostbite on his left foot. He bade a fond adieu to all five toes at the Army hospital in Japan. As a result, Emmett now walked with a lopsided limp.

Aside from the limp, Emmett was a powerful, well-built man—more so than any of the Scout leaders, Art included. But it was that limp that ate away at his insides, filling him with bitterness. He knew his war (like most wars) had been inconclusive and stupid, and he despised all men who would send children off to fight and die. Across the base knuckles of both hands he had tattooed the letters FTMC—short for *Fuck The Marine Corps*. On his heavily muscled right bicep was the message, *FROZEN AT CHOSIN—1950.* On his left arm was the refrain:

> *I ANSWERED THE CALL OF DUTY*
> *THE MARINE CORPS STOLE MY BOOTY*

And, below his navel, just above the waist of his jeans—

visible whenever his T-shirt rode up on his beer belly, which was often—was a red arrow pointing downward, beside the historical postscript, *MACARTHUR ATE HERE*.

But Emmett's best tattoo was one the Scout leaders had never seen. It was on his left shoulder. I had caught a glimpse of it that summer. Emmett had parked his trike across from the school, waiting for Dave to get out of a troop meeting. It was a warm evening, and the sun had not yet gone down. Emmett had taken off his sweaty T-shirt, and was kneeling over the trike, making adjustments to the carburetor jets, when Dave and I emerged. The tattoo, its shimmering reds and golds and blues glowing in the light of the summer evening, filled me with such awe that I stood transfixed.

On Emmett's shoulder, a huge eagle soared far above an icy mountaintop. The eagle's left talon was crippled. In its right, it gripped an olive branch. A tear ran from the corner of the eagle's piercing eye. Below the mountain, in small, elaborate letters, was the question:

I SHALL LIFT MINE EYES UNTO THE HILLS FROM WHENCE COMETH MY SALVATION?

Across the flank of the mountain itself was the word *KOREA*.

As Emmett worked on the engine, adjusting the idle with a screwdriver, his shoulders flexed. For a fleeting moment, I would have sworn that the eagle's wings were beating, that it clenched the olive branch harder, that it tucked its head down into the wind in grim determination. Even though I knew it was a trick of the evening light and Emmett's thick muscles, I'll always remember the sight of that tattoo as a magical revelation. When Emmett heard Dave and me approaching, he turned. He saw me staring. Embarrassed, he grabbed his T-shirt. I never saw the tattoo again.

* * *

One Saturday morning in May, Dave and I lay on our packs in the back of Emmett's bouncing pickup. As usual, Emmett was taking us to another trailhead to drop us off for the weekend. The morning was already warm, and the sun glinted off the Bitterroot River beside the highway. Off to the west, the improbably jagged ridgeline of Castle Crag was still deep in winter snow. Dave and I craned our necks in awe, shouting over the noise of the wind, trying to pick out routes up the soaring cliffs. The sliding window at the back of the cab was open, and I could see Emmett look back every so often at us, grinning, his wild hair and beard blowing.

At the trailhead, while Dave and I lifted our packs out of the truck, Emmett dug behind the rusting toolbox. He pulled out a huge cardboard box: a good four feet long, a foot wide and a foot deep. He handed it to us. Inside the box were two shiny new ice axes and a stiffly coiled Goldline rope, just like the one we'd climbed on with Art.

Emmett had found the items circled in a dog-eared climbing catalog Dave kept around the house. Emmett had secretly mailed off an order. "You fellas ought to know what to do with them," he said, wagging one bushy eyebrow.

Dave and I each grabbed an axe. They were hand-forged Stubai Aschenbrenners from Austria. The gleaming steel heads shone in the morning sun. I gingerly ran my thumb along the edge of the adze. It was almost as sharp as a knife. I gripped the smoothly sanded ash shaft and hefted the axe. The glide ring and cotton web wrist strap slid smoothly down to my hand.

"*Boss!*" Dave said. I was speechless.

"I know real climbing is what you fellas are itching to do," Emmett said. "You two are smart. I know you'll be careful." Beaming a broad smile through his beard, Emmett hitched up his belt loops with his thumbs. "One more thing, Jeff. Let me take care of your father."

* * *

That Sunday afternoon, Emmett met us at the trailhead at the usual time. When we pulled up the gravel road to Emmett's house, my father's black Volvo was already parked by the house. He was running even earlier than usual. Dad was at the screen door, talking with Mrs. Porter.

Emmett was out of the truck and headed for my Dad like an appliance salesman on commission, his hand out, almost before the truck's last backfire.

"Walt! Walt Parson! Nice to see ya." Emmett grabbed my father's hand and shook it vigorously. My father was so surprised by the warm welcome that he looked scared. Dave and I climbed out of the truck and lifted our packs. We should have left them where they were, since our ice axes were strapped to them. Although Emmett tried to block my father's view, he saw them instantly.

"That's it, young man!" My father began to bounce up and down on the toes of his Hush Puppies. "Those are ice axes. I told you what I thought about climbing. Get in the car."

"Hold on, Jeff," Emmett said. "Why don't you two boys get your gear unloaded while I talk to your father?"

"This is between Jeff and me," my father told Emmett. "I'd appreciate it if you'd stay out of my family business. You've already apparently been helping Jeff make a fool of me behind my back."

Emmett put a hand on my father's shoulder. He glanced past Dad toward Dave and me, and motioned for us to get lost. Dave and I took our gear to the shed. We hid there in the darkness, breathing hard. We could still hear.

"*Now, Walt*," Emmett said. "Nobody's been made a fool. Let's talk."

"There's nothing to talk about."

"Let's talk about our boys," Emmett said. "Every dad has time for that."

My father looked down at his tightly laced Hush Puppies. He looked at his Timex. "I've got time. But not too much."

Emmett took my father by the shoulder and led him toward the sagging porch. They sat on its edge a diplomatic distance apart.

"Now, Walt." Emmett crossed one buckled engineer's boot over the other. "Let's be reasonable. These kids know as much about the mountains as you know about soil. As much as I know about Harleys. You should hear them talk. They love those damned hills. What more can you ask for, Walt, but that your son finds something he truly loves, that he sticks with it, that he *excels* at it? I have no doubt but that some day you and I will be reading about these two kids, climbing some big mountain somewhere. Maybe even Everest."

"I'm responsible for my son's safety," my father said. "People get killed climbing. I may not be able to stop my son from doing it. But I *can* tell him he has to wait until he's no longer living under my roof to do it."

Emmett shook his head. "Walt, Walt, Walt." He reached down and took a swipe at the dust on a boot. "Wasn't there something *you* dreamed about when you were their age? Something that you never got the chance to do, but that might have changed your life if you had?"

My father put one foot across a knee. He picked at the thin waxed shoestring on his Hush Puppy. "Sure," he said. "Didn't everybody?"

Emmett laughed. "Sure. What was it for you?"

"I wanted to fly," my father said. Peering through the cracks in the shed, I was shocked. I had never heard him admit this before.

Jim Fairchild

"I wanted to be a barnstormer. When I was in high school, they used to fly into town and put on shows. I wanted to run off and learn to fly in an aerial circus."

"What ever happened to the dream?" Emmett asked.

"My father told me I wasn't being practical," Dad said. "He said I had too much intelligence to run off and get killed barnstorming. That I should go to college and get a real profession."

"He didn't understand," Emmett said, scratching his beard, "that it wasn't a matter of a career. Your Dad didn't understand that it was a matter of the *heart*. In your heart, you were already pulling barrel rolls. Coming in over the deck full-throttle, upsidedown in an open cockpit, your scarf whipping in the wind. Hell *yes*, brother. You just wanted to follow your heart: to become one with the wind, to fly like an eagle. You just wanted to 'kiss the sky,' to quote the immortal Doctor Hendrix."

"Right," my father said. "That's it. Exactly."

"Look at me, Walt," Emmett said. "What do you see? A bearded yahoo with a beergut and a greasy Harley T-shirt. But inside of me beats the heart of a violinist. When I was a kid, I dreamed of playing first violin in some famous orchestra somewhere. When I told my old man, he laughed like hell and called me a pansy. Then he beat the snot out of me. He knocked out a tooth with a two-by-four.

"When I hear a bow drawn across strings, I still get all choked up. I love Mozart. Strauss. My wife likes Canned Heat and Hot Tuna. But when she and Dave are gone, I put *Death and Transfiguration* on the turntable. I fall to pieces. You tell my kid that, and I'll slap the living piss out of you." Back in the shed, Dave and I giggled.

My father adjusted his pocket protector. "I don't want Jeff to get hurt."

Emmett put a hand on my father's shoulder again. "The greatest hurt we can inflict," Emmett said, "is to stand in the way of our boys doing what they love. Let them follow their hearts, come what may."

My father and I headed home. At first both of us rode along in silence. But soon, for the first time in many months, we had a long, animated conversation. As we drove northward along the gently looping Bitterroot, the late afternoon sun glinting off the water like a mirror, my father told me about old barnstormers like Jimmy Angel and Bessie Coleman. I told him about Herman Buhl and Nanga Parbat. The next day, my father mailed off an order to a climber's co-op in Seattle. Two weeks later, a stiff new pair of German climbing boots with bright red laces arrived on the doorstep. Finally, with my father's blessing, Dave and I began climbing in earnest.

*   *   *

Dave and I spent those next few years before I went off to college honing our skills. We taught ourselves, learning from books, perseverance and sweat. During the summers, we spent our days between odd jobs on warm Bitterroot granite. Our shredded knuckles were badges of honor. During the winters, we snowshoed into the wilderness, climbing steep couloirs and corniced ridges, sleeping in wind-whipped tents or dripping snowcaves by night.

In the summer after my high school graduation, we made a road trip to the Cascades in Dave's rusty '63 VW Bug. We raced up Hood, Adams, Baker, Shuksan, Glacier Peak. We went to Rainier, of course. But at the ranger station at Paradise, we were told Dave was too young to climb without a parental consent form. We sneaked up the snowfields to Camp Muir that night under cover of darkness. Then, at two in the morning, when a guided group headed for the summit, we followed in the dark, our headlamps off. We reached the summit right behind the guided group, stopped long enough to guzzle some water, then beat the others down before they

Jim Fairchild

could report us to the rangers.

We schemed about much greater things. We talked about Everest, of course: the Holy Grail of climbing. Two expeditions had recently attempted the peak's fierce Southwest Face. Despite the efforts of some of the most talented names in climbing, both efforts had failed. We dreamed of our own try at the face. I, of course, envisioned an attempt on a grand scale, and promptly compiled a phonebook-thick prospectus with minutely detailed equipment and food lists. Dave, however, dreamed of scaling the face's steeply tilted rock and ice in a radically different manner, almost unheard of in the Himalaya at the time save for visionaries like Tilman and Shipton: just the two of us, on our own, carrying everything we needed on our backs, the mountain to ourselves.

And we talked about Alaska. As I've said, I pushed for Denali, but Dave finally sold me on Foraker. Just like Emmett, there was a bit of a salesman in him. Forgetting, for the time being, about the distant Himalaya, we focused on Foraker. I drew up the equipment and food lists while Dave studied the Washburn photos. The next year, we were on our way.

* * *

Chapter Two:

The Stranger in the Mirror

W hen I regained consciousness, Dave and Naomi were anchored to the ice beside me, bandaging the gash over my eye. The other three Japanese climbers who had been on Naomi's rope were rigging a rappel anchor for the coming descent. Dave and Naomi took turns watching the slopes above for more avalanching. I tried to speak, tried to point out where I had seen the gate open above. But the words did not come out coherently.

The descent seemed endless. After a series of rappels to get us down the couloir, we still faced a long slog across the glacier to Base Camp. I was tied into a rope with Dave ahead of me, Naomi behind. Several times I passed out, slumping into the snow. Naomi would snap an ammonia inhalant under my nose and rub my shoulders. "This shall soon be just a memory, Jeffrey-san," he would assure me. The gentleness of his voice would revive me like a cool breeze, and I would find the power to get up and move again.

Dave had little to say on the long slog to Base Camp. He was in agony. His back had been brutally wrenched when the picket in his pack snagged the other team's rope. He hobbled down the glacier like an old man.

Naomi had radioed ahead to the rest of his team. As we plodded around the final turn of the glacier, Base Camp in sight, we could see them headed swiftly our way, small orange dots against blinding white. I collapsed again. When I came to, three smiling Japanese were gently helping me to my feet.

We spent that night camped on the glacier. I slept in Naomi's tent, where he could keep on eye on me. He was concerned about the blow I'd taken to the back of my head. Dave slept alone in our tent. He wanted it that way.

I was already feeling better. Naomi and I talked late into the night about the Cardinals. Naomi had once met Stan Musial in Saint Louis and spoke glowingly of the kind, humble man. He told me about Japanese baseball. Finally, unable to avoid the subject any longer, I asked him about the three climbers who had plummeted to their deaths. "There will be time for that later, Jeffrey-san." he said. "For now, it is important that we talk baseball."

I awoke in the middle of the night. It was eerily still. A full moon cast its blue light through the tent canopy. Trying to get back to sleep, I concentrated on the sound of the soft, sighing wind. I thought about Dave and the horrible decision he'd had to make. I wanted to go to his tent, to tell him how much I owed him. But fatigue won out. There would be time to tell him later: a whole, precious lifetime. After a few minutes, I felt myself drifting downward again. Then, just before sleep had me, it dawned on me that it wasn't a soft wind I was hearing at all, but something much closer. It was the sound of soft crying. It came from Dave's tent.

* * *

The glacier pilot arrived early the next morning. It took him several flights to get us all back to Talkeetna. Naomi, Dave and I rode out on the first sortie. We flew low under a thick cloud ceiling. Foraker was hidden in swirling mist. I tried hard for a glimpse of our route, for a glimpse of the couloir where we fell, for a glimpse of the ungained summit. But I had no luck. Dave never looked back. He was silent the entire flight, hidden behind his glacier glasses.

When we landed at Talkeetna, the pilot dropped us off and, without cutting the engine, took off again for the glacier. A doctor had been waiting for us to arrive. He checked my head. He judged it a minor concussion, although he recommended an x-ray in Anchorage. Naomi and I went into the open hangar and collapsed on a pile of old sleeping bags.

Outside, the doctor looked for Dave. He was sitting stiffly on a crate beside an ancient wingless Cessna. The doctor gave Dave some muscle relaxants for his back, scribbled him a prescription, and left. A light rain fell. Dave remained outside, his injured back up against the old plane. Before the rest of the Japanese climbers had even arrived back in Talkeetna, Naomi hired a local driver to take us to Anchorage so I could get my x-ray. I wanted Dave to come with me, but he said he should wait for our gear.

When the driver showed up, I said goodbye to Dave. I finally tried to thank him for what he had done on the mountain. But the words that came from my mouth were pathetically inadequate. He said little, barely looking at me. We shook hands. It was almost as if he recoiled at my touch. Then Naomi and I climbed into the truck beside the driver. When we left the landing strip, Dave was still sitting on the shipping crate, his back against the wingless old plane's fuselage, his face lifted into the cool rain.

*   *   *

When Dave got to Anchorage, he didn't stop at the hospital to check on me. He flew directly home. When I got back to Missoula, I called Dave's house. Emmett told me Dave had packed up his Bug and headed out on the road for a few days. Dave's parents invited me over for dinner. While they treated me—as usual—as if I were their second son, they could cast no light on

Jim Fairchild

where Dave was headed. Dave's departure for "a few days" stretched into weeks, then months. I didn't see Dave again—not until Nepal, sixteen years later.

I went back to college that fall. I was only a sophomore, but I felt decades older than most of the other students. Never a casual student, I began to work even harder now.

I wrote a letter to Naomi that winter. I had been having problems sleeping. I kept dreaming about the three Japanese climbers who had died. I realized that I couldn't even remember their faces. I asked Naomi if he had any photographs of them. I also told Naomi about Dave. I had called Emmett in November, and he still hadn't heard from his son. I told Naomi I was afraid the accident was eating Dave up inside, wherever he was.

A month later, I received a reply. Naomi sent me a copy of the announcement from a memorial service held at Tokyo University for the three lost climbers. He carefully wrote English translations in the margins. The announcement had biographies and black-and-white photos of the three: Akiro Yoshimura, Yoshiki Aoti, Hiroshi Sasahara. They all looked young and gregarious, dressed smartly in dark suits and skinny ties for what must have been their college yearbook pictures.

I stared intently at the photos, studying the lines of the bright faces. Slowly, comparing those grainy, poorly printed images to those in my memory banks from Foraker, I began to connect names and faces. I stayed up late that night, drinking heavily, which is not my custom. I began to piece together snippets of conversation on the mountain, casual encounters, gestures. I remembered Akiro: Dave had once yelled at the Japanese early on the climb when one of them stepped on our coiled rope at Base Camp. One of the Japanese had yelled back in his own language, shaking his fist, flipping Dave the middle finger—apparently the only Americanism he knew. Akiro, unable himself to speak English, stepped forward between the two combatants. He did a splendid Japanese Groucho Marx imitation, complete with imaginary cigar. Dave was soon laughing wildly. According to the biographies, Akiro had left behind a wife and two twin baby girls.

In addition to the memorial service announcement, Naomi sent me a short handwritten note. I read it that night, read it again, read it until I had it memorized.

Dear Jeffrey-san:
Enclosed you will find materials as requested.

It was a true delight to hear from you. You have been much in my thoughts and dreams lately. At the risk of sounding like a stale fortune cookie from a bad Chinese buffet, you and David-san must not take blame for what happened on Foraker. A greater wheel was turning. David-san, in particular, must be content in knowing that he behaved with grace, compassion and courage when confronted with a terrifying choice. That is all that can be asked. My colleagues and I shall always be thankful to him for that.

I pray that David-san finds the answers for which he is apparently searching. Wishing the best for the both of you in all future endeavors,

Your friend,
Naomi Yokomura

* * *

During my junior year I began dating Jennifer, a junior in English. She dressed in Indian gauze skirts and beads, and seemed universes apart from me. My Accounting Club friends thought I

47

was crazy. But Jen was my perfect balance: where I was somber, she was light-hearted. Where I was analytical, she was intuitive. Despite our vast differences—or, precisely because of them—I was finally able to feel a certain amount of peacefulness I hadn't known since the fall on Foraker. Jen even convinced me to stop wearing a sport jacket to class. We were engaged before the end of winter quarter.

My father had retired from the university. He'd opened up his own lawn care franchise. He seemed much happier. I'm not sure why, but he even retired his bowties and white shirts. It may have been the friendship that had grown between him and Emmett. The two played golf together. If Dave had known, I'm sure he would have reminded everyone that Nixon was a golfer. Emmett, my father told me, was a real smash on the golf course in his black Harley T-shirt and kelly green polyester golfing slacks. Both men, along with their wives, had season tickets to the university symphony orchestra. As a result of a promise made to each other soon after that Sunday afternoon discussion on Emmett's porch years earlier, my father began to take flying lessons. Emmett began to study the violin.

Early in my senior year word came from my father that Emmett had been arrested for his role in a major marijuana-growing scheme. He faced multiple federal charges: possession, conspiracy to distribute, resisting arrest. It was now obvious how Emmett had managed to survive all these years, even though his Harley repair shop never seemed very busy.

My father took it upon himself to organize Emmett's defense. He scoured town for an aggressive lawyer and took a loan against his lawn care franchise to raise Emmett's bail. Dave's mother left Emmett and moved to California. The Feds confiscated Emmett's house and shop. When Emmett was released on bail, awaiting trial, my parents took him in.

Emmett still hadn't heard anything from Dave. He hadn't

been home yet, more than two years after the fall. There had been a postcard from Big Sur, a short, almost illegible letter from Mexico, then an edgy phone call from Seattle. Dave said he was working at a climbing shop. He reluctantly gave Emmett an address. Emmett drove 500 miles through the night to surprise his son. Nobody at the climbing shop had ever heard of Dave.

Jen and I were married right after graduation in June 1977. I went to work as a junior accountant at EarthCorp, an up-and-coming conglomerate based in Missoula with interests in mining, trucking, railroads and construction. I was proud of my job; I put in long hours. Jen worked for a year as a teacher, but then opened her own business: a job placement service. Her Indian gauze skirts and beads were replaced by navy wool gabardine suits and pearls. At first, the change didn't seem important.

After a long, drawn-out trial, Emmett was convicted only of the possession charge. He served eighteen months at a federal facility in South Dakota. He was given charge of the warden's flower garden, where he honed his green thumb. When his parole hearing came up, my father drove to South Dakota to speak on his behalf. When Emmett was released, my parents took him in. He became second-in-command at the lawn care franchise.

Because of my commitments to job and marriage, I found less and less time to climb. I tried to stay active in the local mountain club. But on the few weekends I was able to get out with the club, something essential seemed missing.

I quickly advanced upward at EarthCorp. Before I could catch my breath, I was corporate controller: the righthand numbers man for the president/CEO. It was everything I'd dreamed of since junior high school. And yet, on many a morning sitting in my corner office in the tallest building in town, I'd find myself staring absently out my window southward toward the Bitterroots, their deep snows glowing pink in the early light. The tight starched collar of my button-down Oxford cloth shirt represented everything that

Jim Fairchild

was wrong with my life. Success was choking me.

I tried to explain to Jen what I was feeling. I told her that something basic—something essential—was slowly slipping from my heart, and that I had to recapture it. She said she understood, and was behind me all the way, whatever I should decide. She was my best friend now—as far as I knew, my only friend.

Despite the consternation of EarthCorp's president/CEO, I arranged to take six weeks off in May 1979. I led a group from the local mountain club to Denali. We did the standard West Buttress route. Remembering Dave's arguments against the route six years earlier, I tried to push for something else: Mount Deborah, perhaps, or Mount Hunter. But the others were eager to add Denali to their climbing resumés.

Yes, we reached the summit. Every one of us. But, just as Dave had warned years earlier, the campsites were deep with frozen crap. We spent our nights in hand-me-down snow caves, the walls stained yellow with piss, the claustrophobic interior thick with cigar smoke and stale farts from four Texas oil engineers who had asked to share our caves after their tents were destroyed by the wind. Sitting out three-day storms, I slipped into a black depression, listening to my companions argue about the merits of open-cell versus closed-cell sleeping pads, down versus synthetic sleeping bags. They seemed so wrapped up in the minutiae of the means that they were utterly incapable of appreciating the essence of the ends. I found myself frequently exiting our snowhole, crawling out into the raging storm, simply to merge with the hissing of wind against snow, to feel its sting on my face, to watch the spectral refraction of light through the prism of a million perfect crystals.

After our descent from the summit and our flight out to Talkeetna, the rest of the group flew back to Missoula. I stayed an extra day, renting a pilot and a plane for a quick visit to Foraker. Although the weather had been poor on Denali, it was a spectacular, sunny day for my return to Foraker. The pilot—the same one who

50

had flown Dave and me in five years earlier—circled the mountain several times. Unlike the morning Dave, Naomi and I had flow out, I could now pick out our route, the steep couloir down which we had fallen, and the summit that had eluded us.

I took a roll of photographs. But I had come for another purpose. Before departing on the flight, I had scoured Talkeetna for a flower shop. Finding none, and short on time, I jumped into the backyard of a small house. I had wrenched up a fistful of scraggly flowers from a pot on the back porch: violets and daisies, a marigold or two. I left a twenty-dollar bill in the flower pot, hastily hid the purloined flowers inside my parka, then jogged back to the airstrip.

Now, circling over the glacier bowl where the three Japanese climbers had likely come to rest five years earlier, I slid open the plexiglass window beside me. While the pilot was busy gauging wind shear and altitude, I dropped the wilted flowers out the window. The pilot circled one last time so that I could watch the flowers drift lazily downward. Disoriented, I lost sight of them. But then, just as we banked for Talkeetna, I spotted them: out beyond the tip of the wing, a fragile splash of color coming gently to rest on the sterile ice below, marking the spot where three men's lives had ended so that mine might go on.

* * *

Back home after Denali, I became more immersed than ever in work. EarthCorp had become the largest private employer in the state; Fortune Magazine ran a cover story about its founder. When EarthCorp snapped its corporate fingers, the state government jumped: whether with another tax break or by looking the other way when environmental laws were violated in our mining operations.

As frequently happens in the business world, cash flow problems occurred just as EarthCorp was growing fastest. The

51

president/CEO called me into his office suite the fall after my trip to Denali. He had never quite seemed to forgive me for taking time off for the West Buttress climb. We were facing tax time, and, despite the corporation's vast wealth on paper, sufficient liquid assets weren't on hand for immediate needs. The president/CEO suggested that I be "creative."

When I asked him precisely what that meant, he outlined a plan to postdate the invoices for millions of dollars of purchases made by our subsidiaries. It would entail an intricate web of deception between us and the many suppliers which, in the poor business climate of Montana, so desperately depended upon EarthCorp for their survival. It wouldn't be cheating, exactly, my boss insisted: we would eventually declare all of our acquisitions, but just at a later time more conducive to our cash flow. It was time to grow a pair and play like the Big Dogs, he said.

As I stood before his antique mahogany desk, listening to the unfolding plan, my shirt collar pinched tighter than ever. The president/CEO's voice became a thin drone. I looked past his shoulder, out the window, toward the snow-dappled mountains to the south. I felt light-headed. I realized that I had come to a crossroad in my life. It was the same feeling I'd had on Foraker as I stood in my feeble belay stance, watching Dave inch gingerly across the icy gully moments before the avalanche.

Although I knew better, I agreed to the plan. I scheduled meetings with our suppliers. I strong-armed them into cooperating. If they refused to go along with the charade, they would lose our business. In Montana, that might mean bankruptcy. I carried out my duties with grim efficiency. I was rewarded for my efforts: a gleaming jet-black BMW with a red bow on the hood sat in my driveway the morning after the company's taxes were filed. My salary jumped by thirty percent.

And yet I felt utterly empty. I knew that this was just the start; I knew that we would keep putting off declaring the acquisitions. I knew that, despite all the money, all the fancy cars and perquisites in the world, my soul would forever be poorer for what I had done. I was too ashamed to share my secret with Jen.

With both of us so immersed in our careers, Jen and I had put off starting a family. Finally, in 1984, we had our first child. Gretchen, an exuberant blond, brought a sense of lightness and purity that had slipped from my life. Not content to stop with one, we were blessed with the arrival of Robin, another blond-maned girl, the next year.

Robin was, at first, diagnosed with autism. She lived in her own private world, content to remain silent. At the age of four, she finally began to speak—but only in whispers, and only with her lips pressed to the ear of her big sister. Gretchen served as Robin's interpreter to the outside world; Gretchen gladly took on the role. She taught her little sister her favorite songs; soon, Robin and Gretchen were singing and dancing together in the yard. Jen and I thanked every conceivable god for the change.

In time, Robin began to whisper into her mother's ear, too. She would whisper her secrets, then burst into giggles, and then run away. It was from me alone that Robin remained a stranger. Ever since she had been born, whenever she looked into my eyes, I could see her distrust. It was an accusatory glare: as if she knew from the moment of her conception that I was destined to abandon her. As much as I wanted to be close to her, her gaze made me feel intensely guilty of some crime I hadn't even yet contemplated.

As I've told you, Jen had become quite a businesswoman. While once, when we'd first met, she had served as my perfect foil, she was now my perfect reflection. When I saw her each morning, dressed in crisp navy gabardine, briefcase in hand, I saw myself. I wanted to flee in horror from this alien creature.

When we had first met, I'd shared with her my dreams of the higher mountains. I'd explained to her how central to my existence those dreams were, how they gave form and meaning and mystery to

Jim Fairchild

my life. I'd told her that those dreams would have to come before any relationship: that whatever happened between us, I would need time to pursue those dreams. She'd said she understood; she'd said she would never trammel that pursuit.

And she hadn't. I'd done it to myself. I'd placed upon my shoulders a mantle of responsibility: as employee, as husband, as father, I'd convinced myself tht my place must now be at home, and that climbing was a selfish, adolescent pursuit.

It was a ridiculous Moebius strip of logic, but I turned that self-assumed burden of responsibility back around on itself and focused it into a searing blast of resentment against Jen and the girls. Everything my life had become, everything I had lost from my life—even though I couldn't even explain exactly what it was I'd lost—I blamed on them. Jen and I grew distant. Our love life became abysmally irregular. On the weekends, even though we'd hardly seen each other all week, I'd find excuses to go back to work. I'd sit in the office on the top floor in the highest building in town and gaze southward, toward the snowy Bitterroots.

It's stupid, of course. I could have been out there climbing right then, my boots crunching upward over virgin windpacked snow on some distant ridge, instead of sitting behind my big desk staring ruefully at the mountains. But I had lost something essential: not my dreams, but the will to pursue them. I knew I needed to make a radical mid-course correction. But I didn't know where—or how—to begin.

* * *

The chance for that mid-course correction came the morning after April Fool's Day, 1990. It was a Monday, and I was going through the mail at work. My secretary had already opened the business correspondence; each letter was neatly adorned with a yellow sticky note explaining what action she'd already taken. As

54

usual, she was so efficient that I had little to do.

But, at the bottom of the stack, there was one piece of mail that had puzzled her. The sticky note on it simply had a red question mark drawn on it.

I pulled the note off and dropped it into the trash can. I read the letterhead. It was as if an icy blast of air had just blown in through the windows.

Dear Mr. Parson:

We are in receipt of your deposit and payment in full for our upcoming expedition to Pumori.

Enclosed you will find a suggested equipment list. Also, you will find enclosed medical and biographical questionnaires. Please complete them immediately and return them via fax. If you have questions, feel free to call.

We are looking forward to our climb with you. A member of our Nepalese staff will meet you at the Kathmandu airport upon our arrival on April 6th. Hotel accommodations have been arranged.

An attempt on a famous Himalayan peak is, for many, a once-in-a-lifetime experience, and we look forward to making it a successful one for you. We believe you will find life takes on a fresh, new meaning from the vantage of 23,442 feet.

Best regards,
Big Mountain Guides, Inc.

I felt as if I had been made the brunt of some malicious April Fool's joke. I dialed the phone number from the letterhead for Big Mountain Guides, Inc. *Pumori*: I had known of this mountain since

Jim Fairchild

I was a kid. It was a haunting, snowy pyramid rising into the sky at the very foot of Everest. Its name meant Daughter Peak. A woman picked up the phone on the other end.

"This is Jeff Parson," I said. "I just received confirmation for my trip to Pumori. Funny thing is, I don't remember applying."

"*My*," the voice responded. "That's certainly a sign it's time for a vacation." I could hear the hurried tapping of fingers on a keyboard, the shuffling of papers, then a muffled giggle. "Oh, yes. Jeffrey Parson. The Pumori climb. Here we are."

"How did I pay for that?"

"You didn't pay for it," the voice answered. "Your friend did."

Which friend is that?"

"Here's a note," she said. "Dave Porter. Says he'll see you in Nepal."

I felt the blood drain from my face. "Do you have a phone number or an address for him?" I grabbed a pen.

"Sorry," she said. "It only says he wired the money from Kathmandu."

I dropped the pen. "Thank you," I said. I hung up. I loosened my tie and unbuttoned the collar of my starched shirt. I pushed the chair back from the desk. Outside the windows of my office, to the south, the morning light was glowing red on the higher snowfields and couloirs of the Bitterroots. I pulled off my tie and dropped it into the trash can.

* * *

"Don't you think this is a little out of the blue?" Jen asked. She sat at one end of the dinner table, I at the other. At either side sat our daughters, shooting peas and carrots across the table at each other when they thought we weren't looking.

"I think it's great that you're interested in climbing again.

You need *something* back in your life that kindles some modicum of passion. And I know how much seeing Dave would mean to you. Do you think I've forgotten about your accident in Alaska? I'm just not excited about you disappearing for almost two months with just a few days' notice."

"It's taken me off guard, too," I said.

"Imagine, if you will," Jen said, in her best Rod Serling: "you come home after a trying day at EarthCorp and find the kids running wild in the house with sharp knives in their hands. A note is hastily scribbled on the mirror in lipstick saying, 'Sorry, Jeff: I've just gotten a letter from an old friend today. I'm joining her in the Amazon for two months to catalog tree frogs. My flight leaves in thirty minutes. I'm not sure I'll be able to write. There's leftover meatloaf in the microwave. Tootle-loo."

"It's not quite that bad," I said.

"Allow me some artistic license."

"I'll make it up to you," I said. "If you want to run off to the Amazon when I get back, I'll understand. I'll even understand if you come back with Tarzan's sweaty loincloth in your luggage."

Jen chuckled acidly. "Let's stay out of Tarzan's loincloth for the moment. Although it *is* an interesting visual. You've always been my best friend. But even the best of friends can let you down so badly you have to reconsider your friendship. We're not kids any more. We have kids of our own. We have *responsibilities*. The way I see it, you have two paths you can take. If you take one, you choose your family. If you take the other, you go to Pumori. You choose."

Don't you think you're over-reacting?" I asked.

"Do you think you've cornered the market on snap decisions?" Jen paused. She considered the lace hem on the tablecloth. Then she looked up, smiling gently. "Anyway, this isn't snap. It's not even about you going to Nepal. I've tried, all these years, to help you with your hurt. We've managed to have a decent

Jim Fairchild

run. But maybe it's time to just let go. The girls and I have the real world to contend with. We can't get dragged back down with you into the distant past, back down into this ancient Dreamworld of yours." She patiently spooned more peas and carrots onto the girls' plates.

I played with the silverware on the table before me, with the linen napkin in my lap. Their very smoothness, their lack of texture, represented what was missing from my life. I dreamed of eating with callused, skinned hands, my food in my lap, cowering down out of the howling wind behind a boulder at the foot of a glacier half a world away, countless, nameless, unclimbed icy peaks soaring upward around me toward the very belly of Heaven.

"I have to be able to live with myself," I said. "I'm sorry."

"I'm sorry, too," Jen said. She put the spoon down carefully. Still, it clanged against the china. The note echoed hollowly. Robin giggled at the sound. "We had some damned fine years together," Jen said. "Maybe, one day, we'll at least still be friends." She stood; she tossed her napkin onto her plate. And then she left the room.

* * *

PART TWO:

The Abode of Snow

Chapter Three:
The Team

I was somewhere over the Pacific: west of Hawaii, east of Asia, lost in limbo. I had been flying for what felt like years. Out the window beside me, out past the graceful arc of the plane's wing, silver light reflected back blindingly off the clouds. I pulled down the shade and closed my eyes.

I replayed—for the millionth time—my departure for the airport from home. Jen and I hadn't kissed or hugged. She watched from the front door as I got into the cab.

Gretchen, sobbing, had tried to climb into the cab with me. While Robin waited silently behind her, I held Gretchen until she calmed down. At last, Gretchen forced a smile; she said goodbye and stepped back.

And then Robin stumbled forward. Climbing up onto the doorsill, she hugged me hard. She pressed her cool lips to my ear. For the first time in her life, she spoke to me. "Don't go," she whispered.

It was as if I had spent eons asleep in a dark forest, dreaming of a voice that might wake me and make my world whole. Suddenly, I had heard that very voice; the wait had been so long I couldn't believe my ears. I pulled back and looked at Robin. Just as our eyes met, she giggled and leaped down from the cab. She darted into the house.

Gretchen was still standing near the cab. She had seen her little sister whisper in my ear. Gretchen knew her crucial role in the family had just changed forever. A dark cloud descended over her face. I reached once more for her. She stepped back, scowling.

Something unearthly had just happened. I felt as if my heart had been ripped out of my chest. I was so paralyzed that for a moment I wanted to die. "Let's go," a cold voice told the cabbie. The voice had come from my own throat. I fell back in the seat. All the way to the airport, all through the flight, I could still feel the coolness of Robin's lips on my ear.

Halfway to Asia, to take my mind off Robin, I focused on my job. The president/CEO at EarthCorp was flabbergasted that I was leaving for six weeks with just a couple of days' notice. I think he suspected I was having a nervous breakdown. I didn't know if I'd have a job when I got back.

I lifted the manila envelope from the seatback pocket in front of me. It was from Big Mountain Guides, Inc. I'd read its contents a dozen times. It contained a detailed flight itinerary and biographies of the other team members. I pulled out the information one more time.

BUTCH TUCKER
Chief Guide, Pumori Climb

Home: Ashford, Washington

Personal Statistics: Age 36, 6 ft. 4 in., 180 lbs., single

Occupation: Professional Mountain Guide

Jim Fairchild

Education: A.A. Outdoor Recreation, Seattle Community College

General: Chief Guide for Big Mountain Guides, Inc., America's oldest guide service; youngest Eagle Scout in Washington State history; all-state high school basketball center; technical adviser and stunt coordinator for numerous climbing movies; personal trainer for Clint Eastwood in "The Eiger Sanction." Fluent in Khowar, Balti, Ladakhi, Hindi-Urdu, Nepali and Tibetan languages.

Mountaineering: Climbing since 1967. Member, American Alpine Club. Professional guide since 1971; multiple certifications through American Mountain Guides Association. All major peaks and routes in Washington and Oregon Cascades. 532 ascents (and counting) of Mount Rainier, including 8 new routes. Set speed record on Disappointment Cleaver route (2 hours 27 minutes round trip in running shoes).

Expeditions: Too many to count, but includes: 27 ascents of Denali (20,320 ft., highest peak in North America)—five different routes; 7 ascents of Aconcagua (22,961 ft., highest peak in Western Hemisphere)—three different routes; 14 expeditions to Nepal Himalaya over 7,000 meters; 1989 Big Mountain Guides Everest Expedition. First American solo ascent via north side.

* * *

JOHN FUP
Assistant Guide, Pumori Climb

Home: Renton, Washington

Personal Statistics: Age 20, 5 ft. 9 in., 170 lbs., single

Occupation: College student; apprentice guide, Big Mountain Guides, Inc. (seasonal position)

Education: B.S. in progress, Electrical Engineering, University of Washington (junior year)

General: Second season with Big Mountain Guides. Amateur radio operator. Volunteer, Big Brothers. Baritone, University of Washington Glee Club.

Mountaineering: Since 1986.   Leader, ascents of Mount Hood, Mount Baker, Glacier Peak. Assistant guide on 14 ascents of Mount Rainier. Thousands of ascents, Muir Snowfield, humping groceries to Camp Muir for Big Mountain Guides.

Expeditions: Denali via West Buttress, 1989 (assistant guide for Big Mountain Guides trip). Pumori is my first Himalayan climb—the first of many, I hope.

* * *

SARAH SCHWENNESSEN
Client, Pumori Climb

Jim Fairchild

Home: Houston, Texas

Personal Statistics: Age 28, 5 ft. 2 in., 112 lbs., single

Occupation: Attorney for major petrochemical firm

Education: B.A. political science/economics, Columbia University; J.D. Harvard Law School (magna cum laude)

General: Specialist in leveraged buyout theory; marathon runner; record-holder for class, Badwater 146 Run, Death Valley; writer/producer of video, "Creative Defenses: How to Shield Your Firm From Product Safety Litigation" (more than 8,000 copies sold).

Mountaineering: Rock climbing since 1985. All major routes at Shawangunks, Eldorado Canyon, Joshua Tree. Participant and semi-finalist, various indoor wall climbing contests nationwide. Ice and snow climbing since 1988. Ascents of Mount Rainier (1988), Denali (1989); both led by Big Mountain Guides, Inc.

Expeditions: Other than Denali, this is my first. I consider this a training expedition. My goal is to be the first American woman to climb all fourteen 8,000-meter peaks by the age of thirty. I am signed up for Big Mountain Guides, Inc. trips to Manaslu and Cho Oyu this fall, both to be led by Butch

Tucker.

* * *

LASLOW ABRAMOWITZ
Client, Pumori Climb

Home: Muttontown, New York

Personal Statistics: Age 41, 5 ft. 8 in., 195 lbs., married, three children

Occupation: Gynecologist

Education: B.S. Zoology/Pre-Medicine, City College of New York; M.D., University of Michigan

General: Internship, University Hospital, Baltimore, Maryland; Residency, gynecology, Bellevue Hospital, New York; Boy Scout leader, Syosset Council, since 1977 (advisor for Hiking, Camping and First Aid merit badges); amateur videographer; wine connoisseur. Volunteer caregiver in various African countries, Doctors Without Borders.

Mountaineering: Since 1987. Graduate, Big Mountain Guides, Inc. Snow and Ice Seminar (included ascent of Mount Rainier), 1987. Guided ascents of Mount Hood and Mount Baker, 1988. Hiking/backpacking since 1962. Winter hiking, Adirondacks and Catskills, since 1967.

Expeditions: Denali, 1989 (with Big Mountain

Guides, Inc.). Didn't summit due to mountain sickness. I promise not to let anyone down this time.

* * *

EUGENE DAVENPORT
Client, Pumori Climb

Home: Tuscaloosa, Alabama

Personal Statistics: Age 36, 5 ft. 10 in., 180 lbs., married, one child.

Occupation: Sales representative, farm tools distributor

Education: B.S. Agricultural Science, University of Alabama

General: Backpacking since 1970. Appalachian Trail thru-hike, 1975. Avid 10K runner. Past president, Tuscaloosa Jaycees. Former high school football halfback (state championship runner-ups). Voted one of Alabama's Top Ten Junior Businessmen, 1981. Author, "The Will to Succeed" (brochure published by Alabama Chamber of Commerce).

Mountaineering: Since 1984. Rock climbing, New River Gorge, Seneca Rocks. Graduate, Mount Rainier Snow and Ice Seminar (1985), conducted by Big Mountain Guides, Inc. Led ascents of Mts. Baker, Hood, Adams (1986); Mts. Shasta, Whitney

(1987); Popocatepetl, Iztaccihuatl, Orizaba volcanoes, Mexico (1988). Business Manager, Alabama Alpine Club.

Expeditions: Big Mountain Guides trip to Denali (1989) led by Butch Tucker. Successfully summitted. Am mighty pleased to be climbing with Butch again. Have no doubt we can kick Pumori's butt without breaking a sweat.

* * *

CHRISTINA SIMPSON
Client, Pumori Climb

Home: East Grinstead, England

Personal Statistics: Age 36, height and weight average (I fail to see the relevance, as I haven't signed up for a sumo wrestling match), married with no children of which I'm aware (I've been told I'd remember if I'd had any)

Occupation: Co-owner (with hubby) of butcher shop

Education: Usual public school rut. Went to art school for two years, convinced I was the next Botticelli. Found painting wasn't my medium. I do better in lamb chops than in oils. Still, there's a fine art to a well-executed chop—and, I dare say, I am no minor master.

General: I still paint on the side. Have sold a few pieces to tight-trousered lads from London. Enjoy poetry. Have gone to bed often with William Blake. "Songs of Experience," not "Songs of Innocence."

Mountaineering: Rock climbing since age 11. Major routes throughout United Kingdom: Lands End, Isle of Skye, Pembroke, Cairngorms, Lake District. Put up first ascents in Cheddar Gorge, including Hell Bent. Ice and winter climbing since age 17. Most major peaks and routes in Scotland. Led climbs in Alps: Jungfrau, Monch, Matterhorn, West Flank of Eiger, Mount Blanc.

Expeditions: This shall be my first true expedition. I've dreamed of a pilgrimage to the Himalaya, and in particular to the goddess Pumori, for years. I've cleft a mountain of lamb chops for this chance, and shan't have another opportunity in a long spell. I shall give this beautiful mountain, and the rest of you, my best.

* * *

And then there was my own biography:

JEFF PARSON
Client, Pumori Climb

Home: Missoula, Montana

Personal Statistics: Age 35, 5 ft. 11 in., 180 lbs., married, two daughters

Occupation: Corporate controller/accountant (as of this writing)

Education: B.A. Accounting, University of Montana

General: In love with mountains since the age of 13. Backpacking since 1968. Eagle Scout. President, Montana Certified Public Accountants Association. Board member, Montana Chamber of Commerce. Past member, Montana Governor's Economic Advisory Council.

Mountaineering: Since 1971. Most major routes, including first ascents, Bitterroots (Montana); most major peaks in Cascades (Rainier, Hood, Adams, Baker, Glacier Peak, etc.); Exum Ridge and North Face, Grand Teton; past president, University of Montana Alpine Club; past president, Missoula Mountain Club.

Expeditions: Mount Foraker, Alaska, 1974. Co-leader. Failed to summit due to weather. Denali (West Buttress), 1979; leader (all members summitted). This is my first trip to the Himalaya, although it's been my dream since I was a kid. Things that have been lost, I hope, will soon be regained.

* * *

Finally, I read Dave's biography for the seven-hundreth time:

DAVE PORTER
Client, Pumori Climb

Home: An interesting concept.

Personal Statistics: Age 34, 6 ft. 1 in., weight lean and getting leaner. Unmarried; no kids

Occupation: Professional mountain bum

Education: Master of B.S.

General: My choice would be Dwight Eisenhower, who warned us of the military-industrial complex, and put the sexy in bald *way* before Telly Savalas

Mountaineering: Since 1971. Some darned good rock climbs on Montana granite. The usual snow slogs in the Cascades. Got around Europe one summer. Did some north faces with whomever happened to be hanging around the climber's camps. Did the standard Matterhorn route solo. Local guides didn't appreciate it; they kicked rocks down on me. Split my noggin open. Bummed around the Andes, too: Huascaran (North Face); Aconcagua (South Face); Illimani; Fitzroy; sundry volcanoes in Ecuador and Bolivia. Most of these done solo. I've had a bad time with partners. Have been living in Nepal the last couple of years, hanging out with Sherpa friends. Been climbing lots of 6,000ers: the usual trekker's peaks, plus solos on Ama Dablam, Kangtega, Thamserku. Last year I did some soloing in the Annapurna group.

Expeditions: Got a taste of them as a wee lad. Didn't care for the flavor. Went to Foraker in 1974 with my old pal Jeff Parson. Ran into bad weather. Lost some folks. Since then, I've tried to go light. Thought I'd give expeditions another try, though. Invited Jeff along. Sort of. This trip is going to be a surprise for him. He could thank me by bringing me a new toothbrush.

* * *

Chapter Four:
Paint It Black

I stood in line at the Kathmandu airport, waiting for my turn with the Nepalese customs officer. His crisp khaki seemed impervious to the withering humidity. The heat was a rude shock. Montana had still been shaking off the grasp of winter when I'd left. My shirt was soaked with sweat.

Despite the crackling loudspeaker announcing arrivals and departures, I thought I could hear firecrackers and horns and bells outside. It sounded as if I had arrived in Kathmandu in the midst of a holiday festival.

When the customs officer had finished pummeling my papers with his inked stamps, I dragged my pack out into the main terminal. It was as if I'd stepped into an asylum. The lobby was aswirl with tourists, policemen and cabbies. The tourists—mostly Americans and Japanese—clamored around the ticket counters, shouting excitedly at the airline agents. They waved fistfuls of cash, bidding for tickets, offering bribes. It seemed they hadn't enjoyed their stays in Nepal much. A platoon of policemen, old Enfield rifles slung over their shoulders, swept through the lobby, checking passports and identity papers. The heavy police presence wasn't welcoming.

Long before I got to the terminal entrance, I was besieged by a mass of cabbies offering me their services. The guide service had said I would be met by the expedition sirdar, a Sherpa named Chotari. Some of the cabbies were waving hand-printed placards bearing the names of trekking or guide services. I searched for a sign bearing the name of Big Mountain Guides, but saw none.

I had read about Chotari in climbing journals. The sirdar is the man who keeps an expedition moving: he hires and supervises the porters, keeps track of the loads, picks out the campsites on the approach march. A good sirdar can make an expedition function like a well-oiled machine; a bad sirdar can turn an expedition into an exercise in chaos. Chotari's services had been sought out by dozens of expeditions. Before his career as sirdar, he had been an energetic high-altitude Sherpa, with a dozen major Himalayan summits under his belt, including an ascent of Everest without oxygen. Now that he was a sirdar, he could have spent each climb ensconced in the relative comfort of Base Camp. But he didn't. He still carried a full load, racing the other Sherpas up the mountain, keeping their spirits high. I tried to picture Chotari. If he was like the sirdars in many expedition tales, he would be an older man, perhaps a bit wizened.

Finally, I saw a cabbie waving a Big Mountain Guides sign. He was a small, quick, brown-skinned man with black hair that swept back and fell down on his shoulders. He sported Vuarnets, pressed Levis and an Ocean Pacific shirt. A toothpick dangled from his mouth. I dragged my pack toward him.

"Jeff Parson?" he asked, pulling the toothpick from his mouth. He scoped me out from over the top of his Vuarnets as he reached for my heavy pack.

"I thought Chotari was supposed to meet me."

"Later, brother," the driver said, already turning and striding briskly for the doors. He carried my pack over one shoulder as if it weighed nothing. "For now, let's haul ass."

I followed him outside, into the din of idling and departing taxis. I had trouble keeping up. The air was thick with exhaust. The cabbie opened the Checker's trunk and easily tossed in my huge

Jim Fairchild

pack, then opened the back door for me. As I climbed in, I heard, once again, the sound of firecrackers and sirens in the distance.

"What holiday is this?" I asked, shifting my butt off a broken seat spring.

The old engine growled to life. The cabbie propped his Vuarnets on top of his head. "No holiday, Jeff. The army's dropping the hammer on democracy protesters."

There was another round of muffled claps. "That's guns, not firecrackers," the cabbie said. "Look." He pointed with his toothpick at two soldiers sitting in a jeep at the entrance to the terminal. They were dressed in crisp camouflage fatigues and helmets. Both held shiny new automatic rifles between their knees.

"Ghurkas," the cabbie said. "Trained by Israel. Their pals are busy in the city center using women and children and old monks for target practice."

"Let's get out of here," I said. I slid down in my seat.

"No, no, Jeff. *I* sit low. *You* sit high. The army shoots only at brown skin. Your tourist money buys ammo for their Galil rifles and starch for their uniforms." He slid low behind the steering wheel and shoved the ancient Checker into gear.

*   *   *

The old taxi raced down avenues and careened around corners, its bald tires screeching. My driver handled the wheel like Mario Andretti, his toothpick glued to the corner of his mouth, defying centrifugal force.

We were headed for the Royal Hotel. We had to stop at countless roadblocks manned by camouflage-uniformed Ghurkas. Finally, my driver began to avoid them, careening down sidestreets and trash-clogged alleys. We gradually made our way toward the city center. I could still hear the sharp report of rifle fire over the roar of the Checker.

74

"When do I meet Chotari?" I asked.

"At the hotel."

"Do you know him?"

"*Everybody* knows Chotari," the cabbie said. "Chotari is a legend."

"He's quite a climber, isn't he?"

"Gotcha. One big tiger. Chotari has climbed many mountains. He climbed Chomolongma without oxygen. Sherpas and Sahibs all love Chotari. The sweet Sherpanis fight over Chotari like rock candy."

We swerved onto a dirty boulevard lined with tea shops and guesthouses. The street seemed eerily empty. We sped past an overturned car. I began to notice broken windows in the shops and houses, and shards of glass and chunks of concrete in the street. Oily smoke hung low in the air.

Up ahead was another roadblock. But this one was not manned by soldiers. It had been erected by protesters. Two rickety sedans had been overturned in the street, their tires set on fire. My driver came to a halt.

From somewhere in the smoke came the sound of hundreds of chanting voices. There was the sound of shattering glass, and the chilling crack of rifle fire. Through the black smoke on the far side of the roadblock, I could make out the figures of children marching past on a cross-street, their arms linked. Then came a phalanx of maroon-robed monks, arms likewise linked. Their fluttering robes looked like a wall of flame through the thick smoke. The rifle fire became more rapid. The wall of maroon wavered. Screaming children scurried back in the direction from which they had come.

"Let's get the hell out of here," I said.

"Gotcha." The cabbie slammed the Checker into reverse; we zipped back toward another cross-street. Before we turned down it, I looked back. The rifle fire was now a heavy fusillade. A maroon robe collapsed to the ground as if a magician had just waved a wand

Jim Fairchild

and made the man beneath it disappear. A child darted past.
Another burst of gunfire rang out. The child—no bigger than
Robin—crumpled to the ground, beside the maroon robe. A
bloodied arm rose from beneath and tried to pull the child under the
robe. But I could tell it was too late.

* * *

The Royal Hotel had once been a palace owned by the ruling
Ranas. I was ill from the heat, the smoke of burning tires, and the
sight of monks and children being gunned down. My driver pulled
my pack out of the trunk; with one powerful arm around me, he
helped me inside. He got me checked in at the front desk, then
helped me to my room. A ceiling fan turned lazily above us in the
dark. The gentle breeze helped to clear my head.

The cabbie drew back the curtains and threw open the
windows. Down on the street, it was getting dark. There were few
streetlamps. "Don't leave your room tonight," he said. "I will be
here in the morning to take you back to the airport. You catch the
early flight to Lukla, where you meet your group."

"I thought we were supposed to spend a day touring
Kathmandu."

"It's not safe," he said. "The others arrived here this
morning. They have already flown to Lukla. It's safe there."

"When do I meet Chotari?"

"You already have."

"*You?*"

"Gotcha. I am Chotari, Tiger of the Snows. Our regular
driver is gun-shy."

We shook hands. "You're much younger than I expected."

"It's from good living," Chotari said. "Exercise. Fresh air.
Regular cholesterol screening. And more sex than a mountain
goat."

76

"I thought sirdars are older."

"I'm thirty-two," Chotari said. "I have been climbing for seventeen years. That makes me an old fart by Sherpa standards." He took the pulpy toothpick from his mouth and tossed it out the window. "I have read your biography. You have never climbed with a guide before?"

"Never."

"Ah, then. A *true* climber. We will have a splendid time on Pumori. So many clients just come here to prove something—to beat the mountain. I enjoy climbers such as you who understand that climbing a mountain is an act of love."

Chotari told me he would have dinner delivered to my room. I told him that after what we'd witnessed on the way to the hotel, I wasn't hungry.

"I still don't believe it," I said, collapsing onto the edge of the bed.

A muscle twitched in Chotari's face. "You are an accountant?"

"That's right."

"When you go home, you must make an account of what you have seen."

"I do my accounting with numbers," I explained. "Not with words."

"Do what you can, then," Chotari said. He pulled the curtains shut. He turned toward me, and grasped my arm so strongly it hurt. "I have stood on the Roof of the World, my friend. I have been humbled by the rush of the wind there. It was as powerful as the very breath of the gods. But I tell you: the wind I felt on the Roof of the World is nothing compared to the winds blowing in the streets of Kathmandu tonight."

* * *

Chapter Five:
Flight to Lukla

Chotari banged on my door before the sun was up. We were booked on a Royal Nepal Airlines flight to Lukla at eight. I'd overslept. We sped to the airport—this time driven by a real cabbie—and climbed into the tiny Twin Otter, only to sit for two hours, delayed by fog at Lukla.

My legs cramped. Chotari sat beside me, oblivious to discomfort. He wore climbing knickers now, with a fleece jacket and hiking boots, and his ever-present Vuarnets. He had his head back, napping. His hands were folded in his lap. A huge gold Rolex weighed down one wrist.

Finally, the two engines thundered to life. The smell of exhaust filled the leaky cabin. Climbing swiftly, we left behind the bustling valley of Kathmandu. Beyond its edges, fields bordered by ancient stone walls spread toward mist-laced foothills. As we began to climb over the hills, the fields became terraced. The steepest hillsides had been tamed for cultivation. I wondered how many centuries ago the first terraces had been built.

We sped eastward. The plane labored up over steep, jungled ridges, zoomed close over their crests, then dropped dizzyingly down into the mist-shrouded river gorges beyond. From time to time, as we crested a ridge and were above the mists, we could see, off to the north and east, high, blinding walls. It was mostly cloud, and it amused me to see the tourists onboard excitedly point and tape with their camcorders. And yet, once or twice, high above the blinding cloud, there would appear the unmistakable profile of some nameless, snowy summit.

As we soared over the ridges, I could look down and see signs of serious erosion. When the first European and American expeditions had walked in over these hills—before the construction of airstrips nearer their destinations—they were lush with moss-draped forests and rhododendron thickets. Now, after three decades, the hills were showing wear. Some of the expeditions had employed as many as a thousand porters; those throngs were like a small, roving city, pulverizing the trails into dust, ransacking the forests for fuel for their campfires. While the Nepalese government had in recent years taken measures to cut down on this abuse, the damage was already done.

Although the 200-mile flight took only ninety minutes, it seemed endless. Finally, though, we began to descend for the last time. Chotari woke up on cue. He wiped a string of drool from his mouth, pulled off his Vuarnets and peered out the window. "Ah," he said, pleased. "Next stop: Lukla. Soon, to the mountains." He slapped me on the knee.

We circled once tightly. Then, as we plummeted downward, I spotted the rusting wreckage of two old planes to the south of the runway—a confidence-builder. As we made the final approach, the runway looked askew. The odd angle twisted my stomach.

With a screech of rubber, we were on the ground. Steeply terraced hills raced past as brakes squealed and tires smoked. The plane lurched to a stop.

Before the attendant had the cabin door open, Chotari was out of his seat, adjusting his jacket smartly, pulling a Big Mountain Guides baseball cap onto his head. He pushed his Vuarnets into place. The moment the door was open, Chotari sprang out, leaping down onto the tarmac. He was immediately in command, barking orders to two porters waiting at the edge of the apron. Chotari reminded me of DeGaulle returning to Paris.

I ducked low and climbed down from the plane. It was overcast; a light mist fell. Although we were only a day's walk from Namche Bazar, the heart of the Sherpa homeland, it was too cloudy to see the nearby mountains.

A crewmember unloaded luggage from the tail of the plane. Chotari, his back as rigid as a bronze victory statue, pointed out our packs to the porters.

"The rest of the group is camped near the bank of the Dudh Kosi," Chotari told me. He pointed out a sparse path that wound from the airfield toward the river, hidden somewhere in mist below us.

* * *

The trail descended past the ghostly shapes of yaks grazing in the fog, then through a rhododendron thicket, redolent with pouting red blossoms. The roaring of the hidden river became deafening.

We broke out onto a flat. Ancient trees raised their leafless, moss-tangled limbs into the fog. We wound between moss-covered boulders. From somewhere up ahead, I could hear the clanging of pots, and then voices. Finally, we wound around a huge, overhanging boulder. Ahead, I could see the muted red of tents in the mist. We had reached camp.

Chotari strode toward a green tarpaulin strung amidst the trees. Beneath it, a Sherpa boy in a tattered poncho was busy behind a double-burner stove. The porters put our packs down. Chotari handed them a few rupee notes, and, in the Tibetan dialect common to Sherpas, told them to come back in the morning. Steam rising from their backs, the porters departed, waving.

I was chilled by the walk in the mist. Chotari noticed.

"Grab your pack, Jeff. I'll find a tent for you." He checked his Rolex. "Dinner should be ready soon."

As we stepped out from under the kitchen fly, a tall, blond-maned figure approached through the mist: thin bordering on gaunt, moving from the waist-down only. One weathered, long-fingered hand outstretched, the other buried in a parka pocket, it was Butch Tucker, the head guide.

"Better late than never," he said, gliding toward me. "Butch Tucker. You must be Jeff." Butch strode toward me with the rolling, fluid, almost slow-motion movements of a praying mantis. He shook hands like a candidate midway through a campaign: he barely squeezed.

He motioned to Chotari. "Thanks. I'll get Jeff situated." Chotari headed back to the kitchen fly for a cup of tea. I followed Butch toward the tents, my pack over one shoulder.

"How was your flight from Kathmandu?" he asked.

"Beautiful," I said. "Couldn't see any major summits, though."

"You'll see them soon enough. I'll get you a tentmate assigned, and introduce you to the rest of the team."

As we approached the tents, I could see feet sticking out of the flaps. People were busy sorting gear or unrolling sleeping bags inside. "I thought Dave and I would be sharing a tent," I said.

Butch turned toward me as we walked. "Dave's apparently up in Namche Bazar. We got a note from him at our Kathmandu office a few days ago."

"How soon to Namche Bazar?"

"You can walk there in a day from Lukla," Butch said. "But in order to give everyone a chance to acclimate, we'll take two days. We'll camp tomorrow night at Phakding, just before we cross the river."

"Dave surprised me with this trip," I said.

"Dave seems to be *full* of surprises. We don't get many

clients who arrange to meet us in Khumbu. It doesn't give us much time to get acquainted before we start up a mountain together. We like a little time to assess a client's skill sets."

Butch stepped up to one of the tents. He kicked a boot sticking out of the flaps. "I'll introduce you to your tentmate for now. Later, in Namche Bazar, you and Dave can tent together."

Two boots, toes down, backed hastily out of the tent. It reminded me of a scurrying dung beetle. A body followed. The body belonged to a short, overweight, middle-aged man wearing bifocals. The glasses slipped down his nose as he rose to his knees. "Yes?" he asked. His nose wrinkled. He poked the glasses back into place.

"Laslow," Butch said, "this is Jeff Parson. Jeff, this is Laslow Abramowitz. You two will be tentmates until Namche Bazar."

"My pleasure, surely," Laslow said, reaching up to shake hands. "Hope you don't mind my snoring. I'm afraid the problem is polyps. My head feels like a Long Island sewer drain at these altitudes."

"No problem. If you don't mind my farting, I won't mind your snoring."

"If you'll excuse me," Laslow said, "I've got to get my gear sorted. I would've had this done in Kathmandu, but that darned insurrection threw a monkeywrench into things." He opened the tent and pointed to the chaos inside.

"I keep all my clothing and personal items sorted and labelled by day and by altitude," Laslow explained. "I use an interlocking system of color-coded Ziploc pouches. Socks, for instance, are sorted by the day they are to be worn for the first time. One pair is marked for Day One, one pair for day Five, one for Day Nine, and so on. Same with pre-moistened facial towelettes. Except that I have one marked for each sequential day. The towelettes are an essential daily item. Dental floss, too. I cut it into two-foot lengths, one for each day, coil it and put it in a Ziploc, along with one towelette, a disposable dental stimulator and a packet of foot powder."

"I spent the three most laid-back weeks of my life with Laslow on Denali last year," Butch said drily.

Laslow rolled his thick eyebrows skyward, then continued. "It gets deceptively complicated. Some items are sorted by both day *and* altitude. For instance, I have to sort rectal wipes and throat lozenges by both day and altitude, since they will be used every day, but only above Base Camp. Hence, I call it an interlocking sorting system."

"On Denali," Butch said, "he switched the rectal wipes and the throat lozenges. He had a calm ass and clean lips. He was a popular tentmate."

"*Funny*, Butch." Laslow hefted a small black notebook, a ballpoint pen and a half-dozen colored grease pencils. "I keep track of my system in this book. I keep master lists by day and altitude, as well as cross-indices by nomenclature. I didn't do that on Denali last year, and I think it hurt my performance. If the altitude affects me this time, I can refer to my notebook."

"Exceedingly impressive," I said, glancing at Butch. I was already having serious doubts about our chances for success on Pumori.

"Laslow was a real tiger on Denali," Butch said. "Until he ran into some altitude, anyway. But I think Laslow will excel on Pumori."

Laslow glanced upward from his work. "I'm going to kick Pumori's butt." He thrust a grease-pencil-smudged thumb confidently skyward.

"Good attitude, Laslow," Butch said. "Come on, Jeff. I'll introduce you to the rest of the team."

I dropped my pack in front of Laslow's tent and followed. I hoped that Butch wouldn't be around when I unpacked my gear. I, too, used Ziploc pouches. At least mine weren't labelled.

From within the next tent came the sound of furious filing. Another pair of boots was sticking out from the flaps. Butch kicked a toe. "*Hey!*" somebody yelled inside. "Who's the numbnut?"

A man close to my age thrust his head outside. He had a thin ginger moustache. He'd been filing his crampon points so energetically that his fingers were festooned with bloodied Band-Aids.

Butch introduced me to Eugene Davenport. Eugene thrust a hand upward. Metal filings clung to the Band-Aids. "Glad to meetcha, partner. I've read your bio. You sound like a crackerjack climber." After I shook his hand, I wiped metal filings onto my trousers.

Butch looked down at the crampon pinned precariously between Eugene's knees. The filed points glistened menacingly. "Be careful you don't get those *too* sharp, Eugene. Looks like you could skin a polecat with your front points."

"My Daddy always said, 'The man who don't keep his tool in shape is anybody's fool.'" Eugene smiled with pride at his handiwork.

"Words of wisdom," Butch said. He led me toward another tent. "I get a lot of good ol' boys on these trips," he said when we were out of earshot. "A century ago, Eugene would have gone off to fight for Dixie, hoping to come home with a manly saber scar or two. Nowadays, guys like him go off to kick some poor mountain's ass. You can always tell the Southern boys on top of a mountain: they're hootin' and hollerin' and waving their ice axes over their heads like they've just clubbed a 50-pound possum to death and can't wait to drag it back home to toss on the Weber."

When we got to the next tent, a face appeared through the flaps. It was a much younger man, with short hair and a few freckles. Although he hadn't shaved in days, he sported only a few stray whiskers. We'd caught him in the middle of writing a letter home. The young man set down his pen and smiled at me. Butch introduced me to John Fup, his assistant guide.

There was an instant connection between John and me. Although he seemed so young, it dawned on me that I was even younger when I went to Foraker. I envied John's chance to climb in the Himalaya at such a young age.

"This is John's second season with Big Mountain Guides," Butch said. "He's studying electrical engineering. He's not much of a climber, but at least when a headlamp goes on the fritz, he's usually good at troubleshooting the problem."

Thank you so much, Butch," John said. "If modern science learns to generate electricity from the human ego, we'll be able to electrify all of Nepal from Butch's alone."

"John," Butch said, "why don't you see if the cookboy needs a hand?"

John groaned. He put down his letter and clambered out of the tent. "Time to pay penance peeling potatoes again."

"What kind of a name is 'Fup'?" I asked. "German?"

John zipped his parka tightly. "It stands for 'Fucked-Up Peon.' That's what Butch calls *all* his assistant guides. Last trip, it was Brian Fup. Next trip, it'll be George Fup. My real name is John McGifford."

"Glad to make your acquaintance, John *McGifford*," I said. I shook his hand once more. Butch studied the toes of his boots, as if he were bored, and wanted me to know it. I wanted to tell him what I thought of the nickname he gave his assistant guides.

"I think I see Christina under the kitchen fly," Butch said. "She's our token limey. Or perhaps that should be token limette."

I followed Butch back to the kitchen fly. Chotari was still standing under it, huddled out of the mist, sipping a tall mug of steaming tea. Christina was joking with the cookboy. She sampled something simmering in one of his two dented kettles. After a theatrical bout of gagging, she dropped the wooden spoon back into the kettle with a splash and tousled the boy's hair. The giggling Sherpa boy—perhaps fifteen years old—tried to shove her out of his kitchen.

"Christina," Butch said, stooping low to get under the fly. "I want you to meet Jeff Parson. Jeff, this is Christina Simpson."

"Ah," she said, as I stepped under the fly. She lifted her nose to study me; her old wool balaclava threatened to fall off her head into a kettle. "We'd given you up for a goner, what with all the bloody fighting." Her hand was the first thing warm and dry I'd found since arriving at camp. "How inhospitable of these Third World wogs to be thinking of trivial matters like justice and democracy when we have a mountain to climb. The bounders! Well, at least the fabled team is closer to being fully assembled. We're just missing your mythical friend now. I trust you had a comfortable flight to Lukla International Airport?"

"Simply splendid, Christina."

"Call me Chris." She reached past the cookboy's shoulder to grab the wooden spoon again. "You can at least address me with more familiarity than the tax man."

She stirred the second kettle, then lifted the spoon and took a long, loud slurp. "Pasang, our fine young executive chef, will be teasing our tastebuds tonight with a sumptuous repast of yak soup, yak stew and boiled potatoes. To wash it down, we shall have a bottomless pot of Darjeeling tea, topped with a film of rancid yak butter. Versatile creature, the yak. I've been entreating upon Pasang to save me the tail bones and a hock or two for a bedtime snack, but apparently haven't offered a sufficient bribe yet."

John had stepped up under the fly. He, too, stood behind Pasang, peering over the boy's shoulder at the simmering kettles. He began to reach for the spoon. Chris slapped John's hand away. "How dare you invade the chef's sanctum? *Out.* Be gone with you!" Pasang, peeling garlic, giggled.

"I hate to break it up," Butch said, "but I want Jeff to meet

Sarah, too." We stepped from under the fly. I followed Butch toward the large overhanging boulder I'd passed coming into camp. "There she is," Butch said. He nodded toward the boulder.

Up ahead, through the mist, a wildly colored spider seemed to cling to invisible holds on the rock. As we got closer, I could see that it was a young blond-haired woman with the build of an Eastern European gymnast. She wore a slim purple parka and Lycra tights. She moved diagonally up the seamless granite overhang, perhaps a dozen feet off the ground: hanging from two-finger holds, swinging her heels up to footholds almost as high as her head. The rock was splotched liberally with white chalk. Sarah dipped her hands into the chalk bag behind her back between moves.

Butch motioned for me to stay back. "She's pretty intense," he whispered. "She doesn't like to be distracted."

Sarah hung just a couple of feet from the top of the overhang. She searched the final stretch for holds. I could see tremors in her arms. She would have to move upward soon, or back off.

"She's good," I whispered.

"She's *great*," Butch whispered back. "But she knows it."

Sarah focused on a spot two feet above her at the very lip of the overhang. She summoned her reserves for a leap upward—not necessarily for a hold that would get her to the top, but at least to slap the highest possible point on the route before backing down. She was used to the arcane rules of competition climbing on artificial walls. To me, indoor climbing was about as interesting as high school gymnastics and had nothing to do with mountaineering.

Sarah's shaking legs tensed. Her rock-climbing prowess was magnitudes better than mine had ever been, and that was before the rust set in. She began her leap. I began to applaud.

In mid-leap, Sarah glanced down at me. I'd broken her concentration. She slapped the rock near its lip; she had planned to drop back onto her last footholds, but—thanks to yours truly—she

Jim Fairchild

was out of control. She dropped free of the rock to the mossy ground below, mysteriously—elegantly—landing on all fours, like a Lycra-clad cat.

"Good move, Jeff," Butch muttered. Sarah seemed unhurt. She stood up, fastidiously brushing off her hands.

"I don't appreciate being distracted while I'm climbing," she said, walking over, glaring icily at me. She was still breathing heavily from her fall. She had fine, sharp features, and dark eyes that bore into me like a half-inch-drive Bosch drill.

"I apologize," I said. "I was so impressed that I wasn't thinking."

Butch saved me. He introduced me to Sarah Schwennessen. Her shake was as firm as a vise. She left chalk on my hand. She picked up a notebook from a nearby boulder and began to jot notes.

"Sarah's working on a bouldering guidebook for the Khumbu region," Butch said.

Sarah spoke without looking up. "It should be of use to world-class climbers trying to stay in condition on the way into the mountains."

"Sounds like a worthy project," I grovelled.

"I've read your bio," Sarah said. She clicked her pen emphatically, then stuffed it and the notebook into her parka. "Pretty light on rock experience."

I realized I was under inquisition by someone I'd just met. "Actually, I got started on backcountry granite in Montana."

"But nothing like a multi-day wall climb with 5.10 pitches," she said.

"No," I said. "But I've always considered rock just one means to an end. The end is attaining the summit."

"You're a *generalist*," she said.

"You could say that."

"And I'm a specialist," she said. She reached into another parka pocket and pulled out a yellow Walkman. "As long as you

88

realize where each of our strengths lie," she said, putting on her headphones, "we'll get along just fine on Pumori."

Butch tried to play peacemaker. "Jeff has a solid climbing background going back almost twenty years. He's led trips in the Alaska Range."

I'm aware of that," Sarah said. She adjusted the volume on her Walkman, then turned toward the kitchen fly. Butch walked beside her; I followed.

"But I have some questions for Jeff," Sarah said without looking back. She was unconsciously shouting to compensate for the Violent Femmes tune blasting through her earbuds. "First: about Dave. His record is impressive. But most of it is solo work. There's no way to verify any of it, other than the one foray to Foraker."

Butch cleared his throat. "I've got some questions about Dave, too."

"Did you hire a detective to check out the team?" I asked Sarah's back.

Sarah turned, smiling tightly. "Let's just say I had backgrounds checked. I have plans that depend upon my reaching the top of Pumori. I can't afford unreliable partners."

"What do you call Laslow?" I asked. "What do you call Eugene?"

"I call them *known quantities*," Sarah said. "Dave, on the other hand, is a wildcard. He has no climbing club or guide service references. If the climbing bio he submitted is accurate, he's a prima donna who, despite having allegedly bagged an impressive array of summits, has spent little time tied into a rope with other climbers. He's not a team player. If the bio is a fabrication—which, of course, I'm not suggesting—he has no business on Pumori with us."

My face felt on fire. "I can't vouch for what Dave's done the last few years. But I *can* vouch for his integrity. I would stake my life on it."

"Fine," Sarah said. "I realize you haven't seen him in sixteen years. But let me ask you something you should know about. Dave's bio seemed to say that lives were lost on Foraker. Your bio mentioned nothing."

I felt as if a total stranger had stepped up on a street corner and slapped me across the face. "It's a long story."

"It was an accident in a national park," Sarah said. "It was a matter of public record."

"We've got time after dinner," Butch said. "I've been wanting to ask you about your accident myself. As chief guide, I have a need to know."

"I don't want to seem harsh," Sarah said, walking briskly ahead. "But I have to be able to trust my partners. And I don't think I'm being unfair in inferring that some error in judgment was made on Foraker."

"All right, folks," Butch said. "We're going to be spending the next several weeks together. We need to keep it civil. The three of us can sit down quietly after dinner and talk about it."

* * *

We sat under the kitchen fly in the light of Pasang's lantern. Beyond the circle of light, darkness had swallowed the mossy woods. Butch and Sarah listened closely while I tried to explain what happened on Foraker. I spoke softly, not caring for the rest of the team to overhear. There were parts that I left out, because I will *never* be able to talk about them. When I was done, Butch and Sarah sat silently and shook their heads as if they understood. The last time I'd discussed the accident in detail was shortly after I'd met Jen, a year after the fall. Both Butch and Sarah apologized for making me recount it; Sarah even patted my arm. But apologies didn't help. I felt savaged.

Butch stood up by the makeshift table to address the whole group. He gave a quick run-down on our schedule for the next few days. Although it was possible to walk from our current campsite to Namche Bazar in one long day, we would take two. We would be climbing from 8,000 feet to almost 11,300 feet at Namche Bazar. We would spend one night midway near the village of Phakding.

Once at Namche Bazar, we would lay over for five days for further acclimating. Our plans were flexible for those days: we could hike into the surrounding mountains to strengthen our legs and lungs; we could scramble up some of the nearby lower peaks; or we could simply lie on our bellies in our tents—whichever each of us had the energy to attempt.

After leaving Namche Bazar, Butch explained, we would hike to the famous monastery of Thyangboche—a day farther up the trail at 12,700 feet. There we would acclimate a couple more days. Then, finally, we would proceed northward along the Imja Khola and the Khumbu Glacier toward our base camp.

Butch opened the floor for discussion. He was assailed with a torrent of questions about how the first summit team would be picked. Chris and I, sitting at the rear, sat astounded. Sarah and Eugene were suspicious of any method Butch suggested. They didn't like the idea of drawing lots; they didn't like the idea of Butch making the decision based on our physical conditions when the time came. The two were soon arguing heatedly with Butch. It sounded like an argument over a car accident, rather than a discussion amongst fellow climbers. Chotari stood in the shadows behind us, sipping a mug of tea. He shook his head sadly at me, then turned toward his tent.

Chris finally spoke. "Get off Butch's arse, you two. When all is said and done, *Pumori* will decide who has first crack." Eugene and Sarah looked glumly at each other, but fell silent.

"Thanks for rescuing me," Butch sighed to Chris. He raised his hands in prayerful thanks.

* * *

I fell asleep quickly that night. I never heard Laslow's snoring. I dreamed of spring snow in the Bitterroots, and of three orange figures hurtling down a slope in Alaska. I dreamed of Dave after the fall, holding me on that tenuous belay, and of Dave's sob that echoed off the surrounding ridges. I dreamed of my daughters, rollicking in a meadow beside a river, the summer sun glinting in their hair. I dreamed of cool lips and whispered words that could heal the world, and of unspoken promises I knew I had to keep.

* * *

We were on our way an hour after dawn. The trail wound in and out of the gorge of the Dudh Kosi, or Milky River. The Dudh Kosi's precipitous gorge is the primary pathway into the Khumbu. Its headwaters are just a few miles west of Pumori and Everest.

We camped that night just past the village of Phakding in an ethereal, moss-draped magnolia grove overlooking the foaming river. Right after dinner, exhausted by my first day on the trail, I crawled into my sleeping bag.

Laslow kept me awake. He knelt in the tent for hours, his headlamp on, sorting through his Ziploc pouches. He was frantically trying to remember his packing scheme; although he had his black notebook laid open, the system eluded him. Sweat broke out on his upper lip. He talked out loud to himself, confused. He was missing two pairs of longjohn bottoms. A chink had already appeared in his system; he clearly feared it might forbode a complete collapse of the precarious dike he'd built to hold back the black churning waters of chaos. His headlamp began to fade about eleven o'clock. Muttering loudly to himself, he dug into a Ziploc marked BATTERIES (SPARE, APPROACH MARCH).

I tossed and turned. By midnight, Laslow had still not repacked his gear to his satisfaction. I sat up and reached for my trousers.

"Did I wake you?" Laslow asked, blinding me with his headlamp.

"Not at all," I said, shielding my eyes. "I've been sleeping like a babe. I just need some fresh air."

Outside, the fog had lifted. High above, a crescent moon stood watch. It cast sharp shadows through the stark tree limbs. Below, I could make out the moonlit foam of the tumbling river. Out here, Laslow's sorting was just a dim rustling, like a mouse in a wall. As my ears adjusted, I became aware of the sound of singing. Off through the woods, I could make out the glow of a campfire. I stumbled through the brush, curious.

I stood behind a crooked magnolia ten yards from the fire, mesmerized by the snaking flames. Several of our porters circled the fire. A few were already asleep, curled on their sides, covered by threadbare blankets. But a few remained awake, legs crossed, facing the flames. They sang some ancient Tibetan folk song, rocking gently with the music. The only instrument was a set of thumb cymbals wielded by a toothless old man.

I didn't understand a word of their language. But, watching the light dance in their eyes, listening as their voices rose with hopefulness and lowered with trepidation, I believed their song was about the journey ahead: a timeless song about leaving behind loved ones, about facing terrifying uncertainties. I wanted to enter their circle of light, to learn their song. But, ashamed of my spying, I did not.

When the song was over, I crept back to the tent. Laslow's headlamp still glowed through the canopy. Without speaking, I crawled in past him. While Laslow fretted over his sorting system, I drifted off to sleep.

* * *

I awoke the next morning to the sound of clanging pots. Laslow was already awake, on all fours in the tent, once again going through his interlocking series of Ziplocs. He had dark pouches under his eyes.

Today, we would reach Namche Bazar.

Today, I would see Dave again.

We descended to the Dudh Kosi. We crossed a fragile suspension bridge to the west bank, then continued northward through the gorge. After an hour or two, we recrossed again via another shaky foot bridge. The air was crisp and clear, the morning shadows stark. The mist was rising; tattered wisps of clouds clung to the higher ridges on either side.

A huge brunch was awaiting us just up the trail. Pasang had left camp before the rest of us with a couple of the porters and raced ahead in order to have it ready. Standing with his Big Mountain Guides ballcap cocked sideways, he served us the greasy feast spread out on three flat table-cloth-clad boulders. We dropped our packs and headed for the chow line. The porters dropped their huge loads and clustered around small fires, cooking chapatis on hot stones. Laslow finally straggled in, far behind even the oldest of the porters, muttering to himself.

I sat against a boulder to eat. Chris sat against a nearby magnolia. Chotari walked my way, his steaming tea mug and heaping plate reflected in his Vuarnets.

"Good chow, Chotari," I said. "Pass the word to Pasang."

Chotari groaned. "Killer stuff. But I'd trade my Rolex for a sausage McMuffin right now." He plopped down on a stump between Chris and me. He lifted his mug in a toast. "Today, Jeffrey: Namche Bazar. Today, you see David."

"I'm not sure I'll even recognize him."

"Expect the unexpected." Chotari sniffed one of his boiled

eggs. He tossed it to a skinny dog belonging to one of the porters.

"Have you ever met Dave?" I asked.

"I know David well. He's living with my second cousin, Ang Dorje."

"*Ang Dorje?*" I asked. "You're kidding. He's climbed Everest five times—four without oxygen. He holds the world record."

"Make that *six* times. *Five* without oxygen."

"How'd Dave end up living with Ang Dorje?"

"Ask David," Chotari said. "It's a small, small world."

* * *

We crossed the river once more, then climbed steadily up the far side. Kangtega and Thamserku played hide-and-seek through the clouds. The sun broke through finally, bathing us in shimmering light, igniting incandescent hues of jade in the deeper pools of the seething river far below. We were nearing Namche Bazar. It wasn't just seeing Dave I was looking forward to now. If the clouds would only lift, we might have our first closeup view of Everest.

We climbed past steep terraced hillsides. We climbed past mani walls, their rock faces etched with Buddhist prayers. We climbed past a stone chorten adorned with fluttering prayer flags and brass prayer wheels. I watched our porters spin the prayer wheels without looking up as they passed. As I came to the chorten, I gave the nearest prayer wheel as good a spin as my heavy pack allowed.

The trail climbed onward. We were walking in the late afternoon sun; tufts of ragged grass on the rocky hillsides cast long shadows. Butch had stopped ahead on the crest of a ridge, and had dropped his pack. Sarah was already there, too, digging out her camera. Chris and I labored up to them.

"*There.*" Butch pointed across a final drainage and up the next hillside. "Namche Bazar." Sarah, her motor drive whirring,

Jim Fairchild

shot a whole roll of film.

It was just as I'd always pictured it. Dozens of stone-and-timber houses clung to the side of a steep, boulder-strewn amphitheater, separated by dusty streets. Countless ice-covered peaks loomed nearby. To the northeast rose the awesome spire of Ama Dablam. Midway up its slim neck, Ama Dablam is adorned by a precariously hanging glacier. When the light hits it just right, it resembles a piece of turquoise and silver jewelry worn around the neck by Sherpa women—hence the name of the mountain, which means Mother's Charm Box.

And yet the one peak I had come so far to see, the one peak I had dreamed of as a child, was still hidden. Everest, and its subsidiary peaks of Lhotse and Nuptse, lay less than fifteen miles to the northeast. A wall of swirling clouds blocked them from sight.

Waiting for the rest of the group to catch up, I stared at the wall of cloud. Occasionally the wall would part, as if a curtain fluttering before an open window, and I could glimpse black rock and pristine snow. But never the top. John arrived, then Eugene. Both dropped their packs and frantically dug out their cameras. Our porters filed past, eager to get to the village and secure lodging for the night, perhaps with relatives. Finally, Laslow toiled up the hill, mopping his forehead with a sweat-soaked handkerchief. He clutched his video camera under one drooping arm.

"Hang in there, Laslow," I shouted. "Namche Bazar is just ahead."

"*Just ahead*," Laslow sputtered. "Just around the next bend. Just one more mile. That's all I've been hearing the last two days."

I watched the clouds swirling in the direction of Everest. They grew more turbulent. "If you get up this hill," I said, "you might get your first glimpse of Everest on video."

Laslow's glasses slid down his sweaty nose. "Sure, Jeff. Anything to motivate Laslow. It won't work. I've had it." He collapsed twenty yards down the hill.

The rest of us laughed. We watched the clouds and waited. They were slowly breaking up into horizontal bands. Within a moment, we could glimpse the long escarpment of Nuptse. Nuptse formed a wall almost five miles long, much of it over 25,000 feet. The wall's fluted top peeked through the clouds, its rock aflame in the afternoon light. Our mountain, Pumori, though nearby, was too low to be seen.

Then, as a higher band of cloud dissipated, I could follow the curve of Nuptse's ridge to the summit of Lhotse. At more than 27,900 feet, Lhotse was the fourth-highest peak in the world. If it had stood alone, it would have been considered a formidable goal in its own right. And yet, because it stood in the shadow of Everest, it had been almost ignored until recent years.

And then the highest clouds finally unravelled. It was as if a mischievous child had grabbed an errant thread in his mother's skirt and run off, the entire garment suddenly dissolving behind him. Camera shutters and motor drives began whirring around me like locusts.

There, peeking over the top of the Nuptse-Lhotse wall, bathed in the fiery glow of late day, was the Roof of the World. I was gazing at Everest—known to the Sherpas as Chomolongma, or Goddess Mother of the World. Only its final slopes were visible: the South Summit, and the final summit ridge. Its precipitous Southwest Face was almost totally hidden by Nuptse.

Even the normally reserved Butch sat in awe. He had trodden Everest's summit only a year earlier. The view obviously stirred deep emotions.

"You're missing it, Laslow," I shouted. "We can see Everest!"

"Sure," Laslow said, slumped against the hill below us. His video camera lay in the dust by his feet. "Tell me another good one. All I want right now is a hot shower, a cold martini, and a soft bed— with a Magic Fingers and a huge pile of quarters."

Eugene, sprawled against his pack, lowered his camera and stared at the highest point on Earth. "Man, I sure would love to kick that mother's butt."

Chris—who had brought no camera on the trip to keep her load light—sneered at Eugene. "Nobody kicks a mountain's butt. Especially *that* mountain. If you're extremely fortunate, she will let you visit her and then go home with your scrawny chicken-butt in one piece to tell the tale."

High up, the jetstream blasted across Everest's summit. The fabled snow plume was like the hair of a goddess streaming back in the celestial wind.

"You'd better hurry up," John yelled down at Laslow. "This view won't last forever."

Laslow furrowed his brows. "This better not be a joke," he huffed. He grunted as he wrestled his pack onto his shoulders. He bent over, gasping, and retrieved his video camera from the trail. Then he trudged upward.

Another bank of clouds was spilling in over Everest's West Ridge from Tibet. "Hurry, Laslow," I shouted. "The clouds are coming again."

"Shake your tail, old man," Eugene said. "The show's about over."

Laslow lunged the last few yards uphill. When he reached the crest of the ridge, he collapsed by my feet in the dust.

"*Where?*" he gasped, reaching for his camera. "*Where?*"

"There," Butch said. "Where all those clouds are. You just missed it."

Tears came to Laslow's eyes. He gasped for air. "You guys," he finally said. "What a bunch of pals."

* * *

Chapter Six:
Namche Bazar

We made camp on a dusty, stone-terraced field at the low end of town. We went through the usual drill setting up camp: the porters checked their loads with Chotari, Pasang started dinner in his dented kettles under the kitchen tarp, John issued tents. It was hard for me to keep my mind on simple tasks. Dave was perhaps just a stone's throw away. I kept an eye on the nearest street, hoping that I might glimpse him.

Chotari had promised to take me to Ang Dorje's house, where Dave was staying. I badgered him to hurry. "A sirdar's duties are never done, my friend," he said, starting another inventory or rechecking the porter payroll. I kept forgetting that Chotari was eager to get done at camp, too. After all, he had a home with a wife and children a few blocks away. They would be sitting up waiting for him. I could see the lines grow in his face as the night fell. I realized how selfish I was being. I offered to finish his payroll so he could get home to his family. His eyes lit up.

"I can still drop you off at Ang Dorje's house, Jeffrey," he said, handing me his clipboard.

"Nonsense," I said. "Give your sweet-pea a hug for me. You can take me to see Dave tomorrow."

I finished Chotari's paperwork by the light of Pasang's

Jim Fairchild

lantern, then crawled off to bed. Laslow's snoring lulled me to
sleep. I dreamed of flowers falling from a cobalt sky. And I
dreamed of my daughters dancing beside the river back home,
daisies in their hair. In the dream, Robin finished a pirouette, then
reached a hand toward me. And then she spoke, clearly and sweetly.
"Come home, Daddy. It's time to play by the river."

I sat up in my sleeping bag so abruptly that I briefly awoke
Laslow. I was certain I had felt Robin reaching out for me from half
a world away. Just as when I sat in the taxi in front of my house, I
felt as if my heart was being torn out of my chest. I got up and
rechecked Chotari's payroll by lantern light until three in the
morning.

*   *   *

Three hours later, Chotari and I climbed through the dusty
streets and up the worn stairs that linked them, headed for the
highest reaches of Namche Bazar. It was Saturday; already the
streets were teeming with people headed for the weekly market.
Men and women, some of whom had walked for days from remote
villages, carried bulging baskets of goods on their backs: green
vegetables and potatoes, handknit sweaters and brass cookware.
Chotari walked briskly ahead of me, his hair slicked back, his
Vuarnets on. Although he'd gotten no more sleep than me, you
wouldn't have known it.

We reached the village's uppermost tier of houses.
"Bigwigs," Chotari said, pausing to push his Vuarnets back up the
bridge of his nose. "Village elders, rich businessmen. And Ang
Dorje." He pointed out an imposing two-story house at the far end
of the street.

"Ang Dorje must do very well," I said. As we reached the
house, I noticed the elaborate hand-carved scrollwork around the
shuttered windows.

100

"Ang Dorje is the Don Corlione of climbing Sherpas," Chotari said. "In a nice sort of way, of course. Nobody's ever woken up with a severed yak's head in their bed—at least not that I know of. But without his blessing, a young Sherpa will never get work on big expeditions."

Chotari tried the wooden door at street level. It wouldn't budge. "Only rich people lock their doors," he said. He bent down and picked up an egg-sized rock. He took aim at a shuttered window on the second floor. The rock smacked so hard against the shutter I thought the wood might split.

"*Ang Dorje!*" Chotari shouted, cupping his hands to his mouth. "Wake up, you dried-up yak turd! Shame on a rich man who sleeps late on market day."

The shutters flew open with a crash. A muscular Sherpa without a shirt leaned out and scowled down at us. "Who is this in the street below," he roared, "bellowing with the breath of a ripe yak fart?" I began to laugh.

"It is I, humble Chotari." Chotari pulled off his Vuarnets and bowed grandly. "I bring David's friend to see him. But perhaps we'll come back. I forget that old goats sleep late."

Ang Dorje stepped back from the window. When he reappeared, he had a mug in his hands with the remnants of last night's chang. He poured the brew down at us. We jumped aside. Stale chang splattered my trousers.

"A toast to the mountain goddesses," Ang Dorje shouted. "And a toast to my bellowing old friend, Chotari." Unlike most of the other climbing Sherpas, Ang Dorje still wore his hair in the ancient Tibetan style: long locks fastidiously pomaded with yak butter, then braided down the back.

Chotari stomped his feet, trying to shake off the chang on his boots. He laughed. Then he and Ang Dorje exchanged a few words in their native tongue. I could hear Dave's name mentioned; Ang Dorje studied me carefully.

Jim Fairchild

"David lives in the shed behind the house," Chotari explained. "He's been shacking up with Ang Dorje's daughter. Enjoy your visit. I better get my butt back to camp. I'm sure Butch has a list of things for me to do."

"Thanks for everything, Chotari."

"Nothing to it. Later, alligator."

I stepped around to the back of the house, avoiding the yak and goat turds in the dusty yard. A stone shed with a single shuttered window and a crooked wooden door stood in the shaded corner. Smoke curled up from a chimney. I stepped to the door. Summoning my courage, I knocked three times.

The door creaked open. A Sherpani, perhaps sixteen years old, looked up at me with bright almond eyes. She wore a scarlet wool blouse with a black wool vest, and a rainbow-colored wraparound skirt. A large silver medallion engraved with Tibetan inscriptions was tucked into a waist sash. Jade and silver earrings dangled from each ear.

"Is Dave home?" I asked. My heart raced. The girl motioned me inside. I peered into the dark doorway. I could barely make out the profile of a tall Sherpa standing by a table, his face in shadows. He was emptying out an old daypack. I stepped through the doorway; the Sherpa turned. The orange glow of the breakfast fire lit his face.

It took me a moment to realize it was Dave. His dark hair was braided into a ponytail that reached midway down his back. Three Tibetan brass hoop earrings hung from one ear. He was wearing an orange wool tunic with holes at the elbows, and a pair of knee-high yakskin boots, and a pair of moth-eaten wool knickers. They were the same pair he'd worn on Foraker.

"*Jeff,*" he said, dropping the pack onto the table. "Look what the yak dragged in. I've been expecting you."

I stepped farther into the smoky hut, blinking. *Yes*, I told myself. *This is not a dream.* Despite his week-old beard, I could

102

see the same old laugh lines around the mouth and eyes—deeper now, of course. His face was weathered to a burnished bronze.

"It's been a long time," he said, striding toward me. He ignored my outstretched hand. He gave me a bearhug that almost knocked the glasses off my face. "Looks like you've been living pretty well," he said, pinching the fleshy handle on my side. "We'll get that burned off on Pumori."

There was a giggle behind me. Dave looked past my shoulder. "Pardon my manners. I can be as rude as a yak in rut. I want you to meet Karma."

Karma bowed graciously. She shut the door, then began to clean up the remnants of breakfast.

"You have a beautiful name," I said. "Doesn't it mean destiny?"

"*Right path* would be closer," Dave said. "In Tibetan, it also means star."

"Does she understand much English?" I asked.

"Not yet. But she's learning. She knows more cuss words than anything else. So far, I've been learning more from her than the other way around."

I put my hands in my trouser pockets and caught my breath. "There's a lot to talk about. I don't know where to begin."

"We can begin by walking to the market," Dave said, shouldering his pack. "I need to pick up some groceries. We can talk along the way." He gave Karma a kiss.

*   *   *

Dave strode briskly through the streets toward the village center. I almost had to jog to keep up. We passed Sherpas and Sherpanis doing their morning chores. Some leaned out windows, shaking out woolen blankets; others stood in doorways, brooms in hand, sweeping out clouds of dust. When each saw Dave, they stopped to wave. Some shouted "Tashi delay!" Others shouted "Hello" or "Good morning, David." At each greeting, Dave smiled mischievously and waved, never breaking stride.

"Thanks for signing me up for the trip," I said, trying to figure out where to begin. "I'll pay you back, of course."

"Did you bring my toothbrush?" Dave asked, jogging down stone steps.

"I thought that was a joke. I've got a spare back in camp you can have."

Dave stopped. He turned and gripped my shoulders. "I don't really need a toothbrush, Norman. We actually can buy them here. But I figured one of the first things you'd want to jabber about is silly ancient debts. I figured you could bring me something just as silly, and then we'd be even." His words stunned me. His casualness slashed me to the core.

We reached the bazaar at the center of town. Each side of the square was lined with stalls where Sherpas peddled their goods. The customers seemed an even mix of locals and foreign visitors: trekkers and climbers decked out in new "adventure travel" clothes, cameras in hands, floppy sunhats on their heads. They milled about, gawking, attempting to drive bargains for handmade sweaters and Tibetan jewelry with vendors far more savvy than themselves.

"Over here," Dave said, pointing to an old Sherpa woman selling vegetables. Dave picked out bundles of onions and carrots and chili peppers. The old woman, sitting cross-legged on the cobblestones, handed the vegetables up to Dave. After he paid her, they both bowed, exchanging thanks.

"Namche Bazar is the wealthiest village in Khumbu," Dave said, as we looked for a stall selling millet. "But the economy's based on tourism these days. A Sherpa can make more in a week as a porter for a bunch of fat trekkers than he can all spring tending the fields. The old barter system has been replaced by a hard-cash economy, so a lot of what's grown is carried out to Kathmandu or

India to sell. You can find all kinds of wild stuff here in the market: Romanian condoms, Pop-Tarts, Marlboro 100s, Bee Gees T-shirts. But sometimes it's hard to find a decent onion." He bit into one he'd just bought.

We pushed through the crowd, looking for decent rice. I cleared my throat. "There was a message I was supposed to give you sixteen years ago."

"From whom?" Dave asked, inspecting an open burlap sack of rice.

"Naomi Yokomura."

"*Naomi.* I remember." Dave sifted the rice doubtfully through his callused fingers.

"He sent me a note the winter after Foraker. He wanted you to know that there were no hard feelings. He said you did what you had to do."

The vendor weighed out a kilogram of rice in his ancient brass scale. Dave watched carefully to make sure the scale's needle was centered.

"There was another message I've been waiting to deliver," I said.

"Shoot, pardner," Dave said, paying for the rice. He snugged shut his pack. He turned to face me, squinting. He wasn't making this easy.

I dug my hands deeper into my trouser pockets. "This message is from me. I never got to thank you for what you did on Foraker. I know it's been hard on you."

"Hard on me. Hard on you. Take your hands off your hard-on and carry this." He handed me the pack full of groceries. "It's good to be together again."

* * *

We turned a corner in the market and came face-to-face with

Butch. Behind him, moving in a tight wedge, was the rest of our team, cameras at the ready.

"I've been looking for you," Butch told me. "I didn't know what your plans were for today."

"I assumed Chotari had told you," I said. I introduced Butch to Dave. The two shook. They were like two junkyard dogs sniffing each other.

"I've been looking forward to meeting you," Butch told Dave. "I realize you and Jeff will want to spend some time together. But I'd appreciate it if you'd be at our camp tonight with your gear. I need to check it out."

Dave snapped to attention. "Can do, sir."

"Thanks," Butch said drily. He turned to me. "And Jeff. I'd appreciate it if you'd keep me informed of your plans when you're away from the group. I can't read minds."

"I had a problem with authority figures in the Boy Scouts," Dave said. "I thought I'd gotten past it."

"This isn't the Boy Scouts," Butch said. "We're here to climb a Himalayan mountain. There's a big difference."

"Right-o," Dave said. "The Boy Scouts had adult leaders."

Butch didn't smile. "See you two in camp." He departed, the group in tow. Sarah eyed Dave as if he were a vagrant sleeping on a sidewalk. John and Chris both winked after shaking Dave's hand.

I looked at Dave. "Diplomacy was never your strong point."

"I couldn't help myself," he said. "I've never met a swollen ego yet that didn't need puncturing."

* * *

When we had climbed back up to the highest level of the village, Dave and I parted ways. He went home with his groceries; I headed back to camp. Some of our group was still in town. After a quick lunch, John, Chris and I went for a hike toward Khumjung, a village a little over 13,000 feet a couple of miles up the trail. We found it a pleasant change from tourist-infested Namche Bazar. We found a high, rocky knoll and sat back against our daypacks. Before us, Everest's upper reaches, bathed in the warm glow of the late afternoon sun, peeked over the massive wall of Nuptse.

We got back to camp just in time for dinner. Dave still hadn't arrived. After eating, Butch held a short meeting under the kitchen tarp. He would be leading a hike in the morning up the lower flanks of Khumbila, a sacred mountain just north of Namche Bazar. The plan was to reach 15,000 feet, giving those who went a taste of altitude. After the meeting, most of the team wandered toward their tents. John remained to help Pasang with the dinner dishes. Chotari and I remained, too, sitting on cardboard supply boxes, sipping tea. Chotari regaled me with tales of the famous climbers with whom he'd shared a rope: Haston, Scott, Uemura, Mauri, Hiebeler, Mazaud, Boardman. Even Unsoeld. It was a Who's Who of Himalayan mountaineering.

Finally, as darkness fell, Dave walked into camp. He strode up to the kitchen tarp just as Pasang was lighting the lantern.

"Namaste, y'all," Dave said, dropping his bulging rucksack to the ground.

Butch was reading in his tent. When he heard Dave, he walked over, clipboard in hand. He offered the other hand to Dave. They shook. "I'm sorry our first encounter wasn't more upbeat," Butch said. "I apologize. We have a beautiful climb ahead of us. I hope we can become good friends."

I shouldn't have been shocked by the apology. Butch made his living largely on his ability to keep groups of diverse people working peacefully together under trying circumstances toward a common goal. Unlike Dave, he was adept at the art of diplomacy.

"I apologize, too," Dave said. "I was out of place. I know you have a lot of weight on your shoulders. I don't want to make

Jim Fairchild

your job any harder than it already is."

"It's history, then." Butch smiled. He put a foot up on a crate and propped his clipboard on his raised knee. Pencil in hand, he said to Dave, "Let's take a peek at your gear. I inspected everybody else's back in Lukla. It just needs to be safe and serviceable."

Dave emptied his pack onto the crates that had been arranged to make the kitchen table. Butch read down the list as Dave held up each item. Eugene and Sarah wandered over to the kitchen fly, curious.

Dave was carrying the same old rucksack he'd taken to Foraker. it was a big French model made of blue cotton canvas. Its like hadn't been made in decades. It was faded and frayed, with holes that looked like mice favored the taste of it. Everyone else but Chris and the guides had spent a small fortune on new gear for the climb.

Butch lifted the rucksack skeptically. "Do you think there are enough threads left to make it up Pumori and back?" He stuck a bony finger through a hole. Sarah and Eugene snickered.

"It's been up a few hundred mountains with me," Dave said. "We're old amigos. We take turns carrying each other. I'd be lost without it."

"I suppose it's serviceable," Butch said, raising an eyebrow. "But you can find plenty of good, slightly used gear in the bazaar."

They worked down the list until they came to wind parkas. Dave held up a faded orange anorak. The cuffs were so frayed they looked fringed.

Butch frowned. "This is cotton. We suggest a synthetic waterproof, breathable parka. Something made in the last decade. It's not too late to find something in Namche Bazar."

Dave dropped the anorak onto the table. "Ang Dorje gave it to me," he said. "He wore it on his very first Everest climb, with the Japanese in 1970. It has major mojo."

108

Butch cleared his throat. He returned to the checklist. While much of Dave's gear was old, certain items were not: his double boots and sleeping bag were the finest available. He'd bought them for pennies on the dollar from destitute climbers trying to raise airfare to get home.

Butch went down the list until he came to ICE AXE. Dave reached under the pile of gear. I grinned. It was the Stubai Aschenbrenner that Emmett had given him. Its steel head was still shining, the shaft rich with oil. Dave had taken immaculate care of it. I'd lost mine during the fall on Foraker.

Eugene chortled. "That axe belongs in a museum."

"An ice axe with a wooden shaft doesn't belong on a Himalayan mountain," Sarah said. "It's not strong enough for a belay."

"Tell that to Pete Schoening," Dave said.

"*Who*?" Sarah asked.

"Probably another airhead hippie we'll meet up the trail," Eugene suggested.

"On K2, in 1953," Dave explained, "Pete saved five falling friends with an axe like this. It's probably the most famous belay in the annals of climbing."

"Thanks for the history lesson," Eugene said. "I'll go to my tent now and do my homework. I have a lot of studying to do to keep up with Professor Porter." Sarah glared at Dave, her arms crossed. Then she followed Eugene.

Butch hefted the old Aschenbrenner. "This is a beauty. I started out climbing with one exactly like it when I was a kid. My Dad gave me mine, too." He put the axe on the table, then laid down his clipboard. "Dave, I sense that you know the strengths and weaknesses of your gear. Both of you are experienced climbers, from what I can tell."

"I sense doubts," Dave said.

"In your case, Dave, I couldn't really check references.

Most of your climbs have been solos."

"Check with Ang Dorje," Dave said. "I've been living with him for two years."

Butch took his foot off the supply box. "I guess I will, Dave. Not that I doubt your word. But back to what I wanted to say: you're both experienced climbers. You know how important cohesiveness is on a team. Let's make this a safe and successful climb. Let's work together—*not* against each other."

"Fine," Dave said.

"Fine," I chimed in.

"Good enough," Butch said. "I'll see you two in the morning for our hike, then?"

When Butch had departed for his tent, Dave repacked his gear. "By the way," he said, stuffing his old French down parka into his pack. "Ang Dorje's having a party tonight. He's headed up to Everest Base Camp in a few days. That big *Summit 8000* expedition is paying him ten grand to climb with them. He's having a few friends over before he leaves. Chotari will be there. Wanna go?"

"As long as it doesn't run too late. I want to make the hike tomorrow."

"No sweat," Dave said. He cinched shut his pack, then swung it onto one shoulder. "I'll make sure you get your beauty sleep."

* * *

We stopped at Dave's home first. He dropped off his pack and kissed Karma goodbye. The party was in full swing by the time we climbed the ladder to the main floor of Ang Dorje's house.

The room was packed with Sherpas stomping to Tibetan music blaring from a boombox. Chotari sat in one corner behind his Vuarnets, sipping chang. When the Sherpas saw Dave, they shouted "Namaste!" and "What's shaking, brother?" and "Look what the yak dragged in!" Mugs of foamy chang were hoisted, and a chant arose: *DAY-VID, DAY-VID, DAY-VID!*

Accepting a mug of chang thrust at him by Chotari, Dave put an arm around me. He spoke in the native dialect, then in English: "I'd like you all to meet Jeffrey Parson. He's come a long way to climb with Chotari and me."

Mugs were hoisted again, and another chant arose: *JEFF-REY, JEFF-REY, JEFF-REY!* A mug of chang was thrust at me, too, and I was bearhugged by everyone in the room. It seemed as if they were all betting on whom could crack my ribs first.

Everyone hugged me, save one. At the far end of a massive wooden table, his back to a blazing fire, sat Ang Dorje. While the others finished greeting me, Ang Dorje sized me up. Finally, he raised a mug: "To David's friend." All other mugs were raised. Chang dripped down dozens of chins.

The party returned to a chaos of conversation and music. The room was hot; the fire blazed high in the central fireplace. The wall behind me was covered with dozens of framed photographs, some color, some ancient black-and-white. They were pictures of Ang Dorje and the men and women with whom he'd shared a rope. It was a veritable picture history of Himalayan climbing since the mid-'60s. He had climbed with the best.

"Most of them have died in the mountains," I said to Dave.

He lowered his mug. "Each death took a little piece of Ang Dorje's heart."

"He's been at it a long time," I said. "He looks good for his age."

"He's forty-three. Not exactly a spring chicken by Sherpa standards."

"Why was he so stand-offish with me?" I asked.

"Don't worry. He knows you're my oldest friend. He just takes time to warm to Westerners. He doesn't care for most of the climbers coming to the Khumbu nowadays. He feels they have no reverence for the mountains. It's all about ego: pushing absurd new unnatural routes, setting speed records, making first hang glider or parapente descents. They're all looking for bogus firsts to drum up sponsorship money. And he's *really* grown sick of guided climbing, and the kind of people it is attracting to his mountains."

"Then why are *we* going with a guide service?" I asked. "Sounds like you already know your way around the Himalaya by now."

"Convenience," Dave said, shrugging. Chang foam clung to his whiskers.

A commotion came from the trap door in the floor. The goats and chickens downstairs were raising a ruckus. At the top of the ladder a small Sherpa boy appeared, perhaps five years old, dressed in a knee-length wool coat. He was bare-footed, a wool balaclava rolled up and perched on his head.

"David!" he shouted, clambering up. He ran over and jumped onto Dave.

"I want you to meet my buddy," Dave said. He hoisted the child onto his shoulders. He introduced me to Mingma. The boy was busy scratching Dave's beard. "He's fascinated with whiskers. Most of the Sherpa men don't have heavy beards."

I tried to say hello, but Mingma was so busy scratching Dave's face that welts were rising. "I didn't imagine you as the fatherly type."

"I think I'm in the fatherly way," Dave said. "At least, I think Karma is in the motherly way."

"Congratulations," I said, lifting my mug. "It will change your life."

"I don't know if I'm ready." Mingma pulled at Dave's earrings.

"Is Mingma Ang Dorje's child?" I asked.

"Naw." Dave wrestled Mingma's hands away from his earrings. "All of Ang Dorje's kids have grown up and moved away, except for Karma. Mingma's his nephew. He lives here. Here, and with Karma and me." Dave swung Mingma down. The boy went to check out the hors d'ouvres.

"Where's his family?" I asked.

"His father was Phu Dorje, Ang Dorje's little brother. Phu Dorje died last fall on Chomolongma. Ang Dorje hasn't been the same since." Dave took me by the elbow and led me to a corner across the room with more privacy.

"It was a Franco-German expedition on the South Col route," Dave explained. "They'd just established Camp III, a little shy of 24,000 feet on the Lhotse Face. Ang Dorje and his brother were making a carry to help stock the new camp. The Sherpas were shuttling back and forth on their own. The route was old hat. The two of them had both been up the Lhotse Face hundreds of times.

"Just as they approached camp, Ang Dorje heard a deep creaking, like a tree limb bending. There was a groaning noise from above. Before he could look up, a huge ice serac above the camp had collapsed.

"When the roaring stopped, Ang Dorje was still alive. One leg was pinned under an ice block, but he dug himself out. His brother was tied in somewhere behind him. He followed the rope down the slope. The rope would disappear under blocks the size of pianos, then reappear on the far side.

"He finally found his brother. Phu Dorje was buried up to his neck. Avalanche rubble kept slipping downward, threatening to bury his face. His face and scalp were laid open to the bone. But he was still breathing.

"Ang Dorje dug with his bare hands to clear a hole around his brother. The larger the hole he dug, the more the ice threatened to cave back in. He stopped from time to time to scream for help from the Europeans who'd been climbing above the camp. It took them an hour and a half to descend to help. They found Ang Dorje sitting in the snow, his dying brother's head in his lap.

Jim Fairchild

"One of the French climbers was a doctor. He dropped his pack and felt Phu Dorje's pulse. *Finis*, he said simply, and walked away. He said Ang Dorje should just bury him in place, and get down the mountain.

"Ang Dorje sat cradling his brother's head until it grew dark—until he could be sure, at last, that his little brother had expired. Phu Dorje had held onto life tenaciously. Ang Dorje recited Buddhist prayers as the light waned. All but one of the European team had long ago headed down. Only the French doctor remained, pacing back and forth in the avalanche rubble and smoking a cigarette, impatiently slapping his mittens together to keep his hands warm.

"Finally, as night fell, the doctor checked Phu Dorje for a pulse. The doctor told Ang Dorje to bury his brother and be done with it.

"Ang Dorje carefully packed snow with his bare hands around his brother's battered face. But, before he completely covered him, he pulled his brother's ponytail from the ice. He took his knife and cut it off as a reminder. He's carried it with him ever since." Dave pointed toward Ang Dorje, sitting quietly by the fire. "Look at that sash tied around the waist of his tunic. Look at that braid of hair hanging at his side."

"I thought it was hair from a yak's tail," I said.

"He carries that ponytail as a reminder," Dave said as softly as the music allowed. "A reminder of everything great that climbing once was, and of everything vile that it has become."

* * *

It was past midnight. Chotari and most of the other Sherpas were gone. A few remained to help Karma and Ang Dorje's wife, Nima, clean up the party debris.

Mingma sat in my lap. He should have been to bed hours

114

ago. I had made the mistake of showing him my keychain Rubik's Cube. He had watched, mesmerized, his grape Fanta in his hands, while I worked the cube the first time. I had often entertained Robin on my knee this way when she couldn't sleep. Something about the rotating colored cubelets had seemed to hypnotize her.

Mingma set down his Fanta and took the cube from me. Although we couldn't speak each other's language, he knew what to do. His tiny hands worked so swiftly—and I had imbibed so much chang—that they were blurs. I had once been a minor master of the Rubik's Cube, and had read a mathematical study of its solution. At one time I could solve the puzzle in only 52 moves. I was only two moves behind the mathematical genius Morwen Thistlewaite.

I tried to count Mingma's moves. Perhaps, thanks to the chang, I missed a move or two. In a few moments he handed the cube back to me, each side a different solid color. I swear to you that he solved it in eighteen moves. Thistlewaite had once hypothesized that the ultimate "clean solution" would require at least twenty moves.

I tried to ask him how he'd done it. Of course, he didn't understand a word I said. Mingma had already climbed off my knee. He reached for his can of grape Fanta. Finally, he looked up at me.

"Magic," he said simply. Dave had been teaching him well.

* * *

Dave and Ang Dorje sat by the fire on the far side of the room, talking quietly. The stereo played softly now: baleful horns and resonant cymbals. The flickering flames reflected in Ang Dorje's dark eyes. Dave motioned for me to sit with them. I took a seat by Dave's side.

A bottle sat on the table. Beside it were three filled shot glasses. "*Arak*," Dave said. "Like Schnapps." Ang Dorje turned from the fire and watched me. "He wants to have a drink with you," Dave said, sliding me a shot glass. "He likes the way you got along with Mingma."

Ang Dorje lifted his glass. "To the brotherhood of climbing," he said, in English far better than he presumed. "To the rope that connects all souls. And above all, to the mountain goddesses who allow us to come home safely after each journey." He tipped back the glass.

I followed suit. I almost gagged. Ang Dorje grinned, then refilled the glasses. Dave spoke. "There are things happening in the Khumbu that Ang Dorje wishes to share with you."

"Oh?"

"You've heard about the *Summit 8000* expedition that Ang Dorje is leaving for in a few days," Dave said.

"Sure. Rich clients paying big bucks to get dragged up all the 8,000-meter peaks by star climbers being paid megasalaries. They hope to reach all fourteen summits within three climbing seasons."

"Right," Dave said. He took a sip of arak. "They warmed up on Annapurna and Dhauligiri last spring, then knocked off Nanga Parbat and Manaslu last fall. Because of the luck of the draw with climbing permits, they're doing Chomolongma and Lhotse this season. They're up at Everest Base Camp right now, waiting for a break in the weather to begin climbing. Forty-two clients, fifteen paid climbers, fifty high-altitude Sherpas, 1,500 low-altitude porters and a herd of yaks to get all their gear to Base Camp. They've got two leased helicopters to help shuttle loads and a BBC film crew in residence. They've got a SurroundSound entertainment tent, three Jacuzzis, two Swedish masseuses, a master Italian chef, and a partridge in a pear tree."

"I'll stick with Master Chef Pasang," I said.

Dave continued. "Ang Dorje and some of the other Sherpa elders feel that expeditions have gotten out of hand. Too much money, too much greed, too little heart. It's time to do something."

"How so?"

"It's time for a Sherpa strike."

"Strikes have happened on lots of expeditions," I said. "The Sherpas are famed for impromptu strikes over insufficient pay or the quality of the climbing clothing they are issued. The Sahibs always cave in and the expedition quickly gets back to work."

"We're not talking about striking one expedition," Dave said. "We're talking about shutting down *every* expedition in the Khumbu region at once. Every climb, on every peak, throughout the entire Khumbu Himalaya, for the duration of the season."

"Sounds like economic suicide," I said. "And what do you mean by *we*?"

"It would be economic suicide, if provisions hadn't been made. And by 'we,' I mean just that. I've been helping Ang Dorje raise funds to offset the effects of the strike. And we've formed a cooperative to help Sherpa families readjust their ways of making a living.

"Historically, the Khumbu supported itself through farming and herding. It was a hard life, but at least the Sherpas were self-sufficient. All that changed in 1950, when Nepal opened its doors to Westerners. More and more Sherpas gave up full-time agriculture to work as porters. They could make more loot in a couple of months humping loads for trekkers and climbers than they could make in a whole year of farming and herding. Problem is, you can't eat cash. With fewer Sherpas farming or herding full-time, all that cash is just so much fuel for cooking fires under half-empty kettles."

"What are you suggesting?" I asked. "Going back to scratching for a living in the soil? There's been a population explosion since 1950. A strike sounds like a prescription for starvation."

"Sentencing the Sherpas to a future of toting bags for sunburned tourists is a prescription for hopelessness," Dave said.

117

"Sure, there are risks. But we've done well with fundraising. The co-op has enough stashed away to help the Sherpa families get through the first rough season or two. We'll be able to bring in experts to teach the Sherpas how to farm more effectively—not for cash crops to be shipped elsewhere, but to fill their own needs."

"What if most of the Sherpas actually like their newfound wealth? What if they like the Vuarnets and the Levis the tourists give them? What if they don't go along with the plan? 'How you gonna keep them down on the farm,' as an old song goes? It's one heck of a dangerous gamble. If it fails, a Khumbu-wide strike might chase off tourists and climbers for years."

"It won't be a failure," Dave said, "if it draws the world's attention."

"To what?"

"To the need of the Sherpas for self-determination. For dignity. For freedom from the ultimate vestige of colonialism: the 'adventure travel' industry."

"So you've become the Che Guevera of the Himalaya," I said. "I wish the Sherpas luck. They're playing with powerful historical forces."

"Finally," Dave insisted, "they'll be able to shape those historical forces with their own hands."

I looked at Ang Dorje. He had been listening to Dave. Although he didn't seem to trust his own English, it was clear that he understood every word and concurred. "Why have you let me in on your plan?" I asked the Sherpa.

"He wants you to bear witness," Dave said, answering for Ang Dorje. "He knows that a precise mathematical mind must inherently be open to greater truths."

"Does the strike mean our Pumori climb is down the drain?" I asked.

For once, before Dave could open his mouth, Ang Dorje spoke. "You will have a shot at the Mountain Daughter, as we call

118

Pumori. The strike will be called when *Summit 8000* starts to stock its high camps, and it needs Sherpa help the most. By then, you and David should already be back down from Pumori. Chotari knows this."

"Chotari sits on the co-op council," Dave explained. "He's on the strike-planning committee."

The conversation had made my head spin as much as the chang and the arak. "Well," I said. I filled my glass one last time and raised a toast. "I'm honored that you've taken me into your confidence. Here's to your final trip to Everest, Ang Dorje. It's a pity you won't be capping your career with one last climb to its summit."

I waited for the others to raise their glasses. They didn't.

Dave spoke. "Ang Dorje has already received $10,000 to go on the *Summit 8000* climb. There was a time when he might even have climbed for free, so long as he shared a rope with good friends like Chris Bonington and Doug Scott. Now, for the first time in his life, he doesn't care about reaching the summit. No amount of money can make a difference. He dreads returning to the mountain where he buried his little brother."

"I'm sorry for everything that happened," I told Ang Dorje.

Ang Dorje filled our glasses one more time, then took a drink. "Thank you, Jeffrey," he said. "When one buries a little brother before his time, one's world changes. A light in one's heart is extinguished." We drank until the fire died to embers. We drank until the bottle was empty. Sometime shortly thereafter—*very* shortly thereafter—my forehead crashed to the table.

* * *

When I awoke, I was on the floor beneath Ang Dorje's table. My head felt like an oak spike had been hammered between my eyes. When I opened them, I could see Dave. He was curled up on

119

the floor in front of the cold fireplace. It was a quarter before seven.

Dave sat up gingerly, running his fingers through his hair. "I don't think I'll be making the hike today," he said. "Please extend my apologizes to General Tucker. Tell him I'm fogged in."

* * *

We hiked far up the flanks of Khumbila. From 15,000 feet, Everest seemed close enough to reach out and touch. But I was too tired to lift my head to enjoy the view. As soon as we stopped for lunch, I collapsed in the rocks, sick.

I was the last into camp that evening, staggering far behind Laslow. When I got there, Dave was sitting under the kitchen fly sipping a mug of tea, his bulging old pack beside him. Butch was already reciting the Riot Act to him. Dave, freshly shaved, his hair still wet, was putting on a convincing show of contrition.

He spent that night at our camp. He wanted to show Butch he could be a team player. I thought it a magnanimous gesture, since his home—and Karma and Mingma—were just a few dusty streets away. Dave said it was just as well. It was time for him to meld with our Pumori team. He wanted to join us in the morning on our next training hike.

Dave and I set up a tent together. Laslow was glad to have a tent to himself again. It would give him more room for sorting.

Dave and I exchanged pleasantries before rolling onto our sides, facing opposite walls of the tent. It was silent now, except for the occasional crackle of an exploding ember in the dying fire outside, and, from somewhere in the village, the soft drone of a Tibetan chant.

I stared at the tent wall, unable to drift off. The thin ripstop fabric flickered orange from the last of the fire. I felt lost in a time warp. Sixteen years after the accident on Foraker that had changed my life, I was again sharing a tent with Dave. It was as if the years between had never existed. There were so many things I needed to ask him. I knew how one's memory plays tricks with facts.

Just when I found the courage to speak, Dave began snoring. I closed my eyes. There would always be tomorrow.

* * *

We set out after breakfast for a hike up the flanks of Kangtega, to the east across the Dudh Kosi. Sarah and Eugene remained behind. Sarah had found some promising boulders near the river and wanted to chart routes on them. She asked Eugene to come along to belay.

By early afternoon we'd reached a spur at almost 16,000 feet. Dave pointed out snow-clad peaks, reciting their climbing histories, and recounted Sherpa myths that had grown up around them.

After lunch on the spur, we headed downward. By four, we were back at the Dudh Kosi, just below Namche Bazar. We took a break before the final uphill. The river clearing was bustling. An Italian expedition headed for Lhotse was taking a break. The clearing rang with the cheery voices of its hundred or so porters, happy to be nearing Namche Bazar, where many of them lived.

From nearby, audible even over the jubilant porters, came the sound of hammering. Sarah was placing bolts on a tawny 25-foot boulder just down the river. The rest of us grabbed our packs and wandered over to kibitz.

Sarah had set up an anchor at the top of the boulder. She was rappelling down the rock, preparing clip-in points before attempting the climb. She hung from the rope, her feet splayed against the rock. She held a drill bit in one hand, a hammer in the other. As she swung, her arms bulged with braided muscles.

Below her, Eugene leaned back against a smaller boulder, watching her progress, pointing out possible bolt positions. Eugene turned to Butch, who'd just sat down nearby. "Heck of a route," Eugene said. "Sarah figures it could be one of the first 5.13s in the Khumbu."

In the woods around us, porters from the Italian climb stoked small fires, brewing an afternoon pot of tea before the final climb to the village. Most turned their backs to Sarah and the insistent pounding of her hammer.

One young boy, however, seemed fascinated. Barely a teenager, perhaps thirteen years old, he wandered over from a nearby fire. He stood beside me, barefooted, mouth agape, watching Sarah.

Her final bolt hammered into place, Sarah rappelled to the ground. She tied into one end of the doubled rope running down from the top anchor. Eugene took the other end and ran it through a belay device on his harness.

Sarah studied the sheer rock above her, studded with shiny new bolt hangars. Eugene handed her a stiff wire brush. She scoured the rubber on her smooth-soled rock shoes, roughing it so it would adhere better to the rock. She approached the boulder. She dipped her fingertips into her chalk bag.

"Belay on?" she asked, wiping her chalky hands together.

"Belay on," Eugene confirmed, taking up slack.

"Ready to climb," Sarah said.

"Climb away." Eugene braced himself.

Sarah began to glide gracefully up the rock. As she approached each bolt hangar, she pulled a quickdraw sling from her gear rack. The sling had a carabiner clipped into each end. She would clip one carabiner through the bolt hangar, then pull the rope at her waist upward and swiftly clip it into the sling's lower carabiner. She moved with ease toward the top third of the wall.

Then, with only eight feet to go, Sarah became stymied. The rock above her was subtly concave. At the bottom of the boulder, the young porter pushed back his wool balaclava, squinting upward.

His eyes lit up.

"Meek tang!" he shouted, one hand on his balaclava, the other pointing above Sarah's head.

Dave translated. "He said *look*. He sees a hold."

Sarah clung to paper-thin holds, searching for a passage to the top. She tested a few fingerholds, but backed off them, unimpressed. I saw the first tremors in her tensed legs and arms.

The Sherpa boy stepped to the bottom of the boulder. He took Sarah's wire brush and vigorously scrubbed the leathery bottoms of hs bare feet.

"Ouch," I said, imagining the brush against my own feet.

"He sees something that Sarah doesn't," Dave whispered.

The boy began to climb toward Sarah. Where Sarah's moves had been the product of intensive training and gymnastic ability, the boy's were the product of sheer tenacity and intuition.

"Get that kid off the rock!" Eugene shouted, holding the rope.

"Let him try," Dave said. "The Khumbu is his home."

Sarah's concentration had been broken. She glanced down and saw the boy rapidly ascending toward her. Her face grew flushed. "Get him off the rock!" she sputtered.

One by one, porters from nearby fires wandered over to the boulder. Soon, a score of them stood amongst us, enraptured by the contest above.

"Get him down!" Sarah shouted, her voice wavering, her face scarlet. "He'll get killed if he falls!" Already, the boy was nearing Sarah's heels. He would have to find a way past her. The rock began to overhang above him. I felt a knot in my stomach; he was far past the point of safe retreat.

"*Ka lee ka lee!*" a porter beside me shouted to the boy.

"Careful!" Dave shouted.

Sarah tested a handhold to her right. Above her, just beyond reach, was the final gleaming bolt hangar. "Tension," she shouted.

Eugene gripped the rope tightly.

The boy—his leathery feet somehow adhering spider-like to invisible holds—skittered to the left beneath Sarah, then lunged for a fingernail-deep crack above him. Somehow, ignoring every rule of physics, he moved up the concavity until he was even with Sarah.

"Get him down!" Sarah hollered.

The boy turned to Sarah and grinned. Then, peering upward, he detected a flaw in the seemingly smooth overhang.

If the boy peeled, he would freefall almost twenty-five feet. I turned to Chris and John. "We have to be ready to break his fall," I said, knowing that anyone trying to catch him would be seriously injured. Nevertheless, we moved below him. Even Butch—spilling his bag of peanuts—ran over, positioning himself directly below the boy, his outstretched hands far above the rest of ours.

Dave stood amongst the porters. "I think he's got it," he whispered.

A foot from the top of the rock, the boy looked up. His balaclava fell from his head and sailed downward. Chris caught it, gasping. A porter standing beside me—an old man in his fifties missing several teeth—gasped also. The gasp became a whistle. He pulled the moth-eaten cap from his head and wrung it in both callused hands.

And then the boy lunged.

He threw one arm over the top and found an invisible handhold. A bare foot slipped off the rock. Then his other foot slipped. The boy exhaled mightily. Hanging by one arm, he lunged again. The other hand found another invisible hold. Finally, he hauled himself up and over the lip of the overhang. He waved once toothily, then disappeared somewhere above.

The porters cheered wildly. They threw their hats into the air. An old man near Dave, missing several fingers and all of his teeth, danced a wild jig, banging his cookpot with a smoking stick carried over from his fire.

"My God," Chris shouted, clapping her hands until they were red. "The little scamp did it!"

"*Son of a bitch*," Sarah muttered. "Falling!"

Eugene held the rope tightly. Sarah peeled from her holds. She dropped past the last bolt she'd clipped into and bounced on the stretchy rope. Hanging free, she began to spin. "Let me down," she barked. Eugene fed the rope through his belay device. In a moment Sarah was on the ground, yanking angrily at the locking carabiner at her waist.

"Somebody could have been killed," she fumed. Untied now, she flung the rope into the dirt. She sat down, shaking, and yanked at the laces of her rock shoes so hard I thought they'd break. Eugene coiled the rope.

The porters jumped up and down, chanting *SONAM, SONAM, SONAM!* Soon, the young boy, Sonam, reappeared. He had scampered down the gentle backside of the boulder. The porters cheered him wildly. Blushing, he took a broad bow.

Dave motioned to the old man beating on the kettle. He took the kettle from him and stepped beside the boy. "I crown thee Sonam, King of the Tigers!" Dave crowned the boy with the upsidedown kettle, then knelt before him.

The porters cheered hoarsely. They surged forward and grabbed the boy, lifting him above their heads. A burly porter hefted the boy onto his shoulders; a procession was formed. It snaked toward the clearing beside the river. Sonam, bouncing up and down on the big porter's shoulders, looked overwhelmed. The kettle crown threatened to slide over his face.

Sarah put her hiking boots back on. Lips clenched, she packed her climbing gear. Finally, she directed her fury at Dave. "You let that boy risk his life. You made a joke out of it—at *my* expense."

Dave replied calmly. "Not at all, Sarah. Nobody goaded Sonam on. He did what came naturally. I'm sorry if you felt people were making fun of you. The Sherpas are thrilled by Sonam's success—*not* by your failure."

"Don't tell me they weren't laughing at me," Sarah insisted. "You encouraged the whole thing. You even crowned the kid with a cookpot."

"Listen," Dave said. "You want to know how Sonam found his way up that rock? The old Sherpa with the kettle told me."

Sarah put her pack on and tugged at the shoulder straps. "Sure."

"Sonam's been a porter since the age of seven," Dave said. "At an age when the rest of us are watching cartoons and being told how special we are, he was humping 65-pound loads ten miles a day barefooted for the price of a couple of candy bars. He carried his loads alone, because his parents had to stay home, tending their potato fields. He's rested a dozen times in the shade of that rock you wanted to climb. He's cooked chapatis beside it, sitting close to it, trying to keep out of the rain. He's watched the smoke from his fire curl up along the rock. Dreaming of his home and his family, he's watched the smoke slowly darken flaws otherwise invisible to the eye, revealing to him the secret path to the top."

"Cut the hippie bullshit," Sarah snapped.

"Take a look," Dave said. He pointed to the higher reaches of the boulder. Sarah's angular route was marked by white chalk and gleaming bolt anchors. Sonam's variation followed a series of thin black curls, where smoke had traced a subtle, curving path around otherwise imperceptible bulges and microflakes.

"I see it," Sarah said, peering upward. "I'll be damned. I apologize."

"What happened here will be talked about for years," Dave said. "The rest of his life, other Sherpas will call Sonam *Smokechaser*. And you should be proud. You played a part in it. Every time the tale is told around a campfire, the Sherpas will fondly remember you."

* * *

Long after the others had gone to bed, Dave and I sat silently and poked at the fire with sticks. I could remember the nights we'd spent camped by Enchantment Lake as kids, sitting around a fire much like this one. But, on this third night of our reunion, I could see that, in many ways, we had become strangers. We had spent sixteen years following vastly divergent paths.

Chotari stepped up to the fire. He wore his knickers and wind parka. His Vuarnets were propped on top of his ballcap. "Evening, brothers," he said. I detected a slight wobble. He had been partying in the village.

"What's the word?" I asked.

He buried his hands in his parka pockets and put a boot up on a rock near the fire. "You dudes haven't seen Ang Dorje, have you?"

"Not since night before last," I said. "I'm still hungover from it."

"I haven't been in town since yesterday," Dave said. "Although I might sneak home tonight to check on Karma and Mingma. Is there a problem?"

Chotari rubbed the tip of his nose. "I was just at Ang Dorje's crib. His old lady hasn't seen him since this afternoon. He's supposed to split tomorrow morning for Everest Base Camp."

Dave scratched a knee through a hole in his old knickers. "Has Nima checked the teahouses?"

"Yep. This isn't like the old fart. When he goes out, he always tells Nima where he's headed. She has him trained like a pet goat."

"Tell her not to worry," Dave said. "He'll show up in the morning just in time to grab his pack and blaze up the trail in a cloud of arak fumes."

"Right thinking," Chotari said. "I'll tell Nima. Have a good one, boys." Chotari gave Dave a high-five. He did a wobbly about-face and headed back into the village. I went to bed. Just as I was falling asleep, Dave followed. But he didn't stay. He grabbed his parka from the tent and headed home.

* * *

When I awoke in the morning to the clanging of Pasang's pots, Dave was back in camp. He sat under the kitchen fly with Chotari. Both of them were quietly sipping mugs of steaming tea.

I got dressed and packed my gear for the daily training hike; then I joined them under the fly. "Did Ang Dorje make it home?" I asked.

"No sign of him," Chotari said. "He'll have his butt in a bind if he doesn't show up at Everest Base Camp on time. He's already cashed his check."

"He'll show up," Dave said. "It's been a tough time for him. He doesn't want to see where he buried his brother. But he'll honor his agreement."

* * *

We headed up the trail after breakfast. Our destination this day would be the lower reaches of the Gokyo Valley. The trail climbed briefly, then leveled out above the raging Dudh Kosi. This early in the morning, fog shrouded the higher peaks.

We came to a junction. Here, we would take another trail northward, leaving the main path that heads for Everest. We'd covered two or three miles already, but I still felt almost as fresh as when we started. While the others sat for a break, I stalked around the clearing, taking in the view.

Dave, squatting on a rock, ripped huge pieces from a

buttered chapati that Karma had made him and stuffed them into his mouth. He looked at me and laughed. "You should remember to take advantage of a break."

A lone man suddenly appeared ahead on the main trail. The middle-aged Sherpa came grinding up the switchbacks from the river far below, his hair matted by sweat to his forehead. Without speaking or even looking up, he jogged toward Namche Bazar.

"Not very sociable," I said.

"A runner," Dave said, stuffing the last of his chapati in his mouth. "They carry news back and forth between villages. Like a telegraph system with problem perspiration."

* * *

Butch signalled that it was time to saddle up. We had to wait for Laslow to finish sorting his gear. Suddenly, from Namche Bazar, the sound of blowing horns and clanging gongs and cymbals floated clearly in the morning air.

Dave peered toward the sound. "Funeral dirge. Somebody important."

A commotion came from below, on the main trail. Dave and I walked to the edge of the drop-off, where we could look down at the approaching switchbacks.

Below us, moving slowly, were six men. They climbed awkwardly up the narrow trail, two abreast, three on each side of a litter. On the litter was a sleeping bag. It was obvious somebody was zipped inside it.

"Could be an injured climber," Dave said. "Or a sick villager from up the valley being brought to the clinic in Namche Bazar." As the men laboring with the litter reached the final switchback below us, Dave shouted to them: "Namaste! Dee ming la?"

The six men, exhausted, ground to a halt. The oldest man

wiped his brow and caught his breath. "How is brother David today?"

"Fine," Dave said. I heard rising tension in his voice. "What's going on?" He asked more questions in the native dialect.

The old man answered, pointing toward the gorge below. The old man's face was etched with sorrow. Then, the men inhaled deeply and climbed onward. Before I could ask Dave for a translation, he was running down the switchbacks to meet the litter. I followed.

"It's Ang Dorje," he said to me over his shoulder. Dave's face was ashen, the same way he looked after the three Japanese fell to their deaths on Foraker. "They found him in the river, hung up in a logjam. Sometime last night he must have jumped off the bridge on the way to Thyangboche."

When we met the litter bearers, they came to a halt again. Dave tore open the sleeping bag. Inside was Ang Dorje. His face was swollen and blue, his arms folded across his chest. Dave put a hand to Ang Dorje's face. A tear ran down Dave's cheek and splattered in the dust.

I felt like a clown. I put a hand on Dave's shoulder. "What can I do?"

Dave turned to me—and the rest of our group, who had now joined us. "I have to go back with his body," Dave said. "I have to be the one to tell Karma. And Mingma. Ang Dorje was the closest thing he had to a father."

"Let me go with you," I said. I looked at Ang Dorje's swollen face, and remembered how his voice had been both strong and sweet—like whiskey and honey. I thought about the night I'd spent with him, and the sense of honor I'd felt when he chose to confide his secrets to me. I, too, was crying.

"It would be best if you went ahead with Butch for the day," Dave said. The litter bearers began climbing again; Dave took a place in their ranks. "This changes things."

* * *

We scrambled up a rockpile of a peak whose summit was just over 16,000 feet. Returning to our camp at the edge of Namche Bazar, we should have been a light-hearted, if tired, bunch. But even the rest of the team who hadn't known Ang Dorje were somber. Ang Dorje was a legend. The town reverberated with the beating of drums, the wailing of horns, and the spiralling ululations of chanting monks.

Pasang, busy with dinner preparations, didn't lift his head when we arrived. Normally, he would have greeted us and proudly recited the evening's menu. I could see that he had been weeping. Chris gave him a silent hug. Chotari was off paying his condolences to Ang Dorje's widow.

After Pasang had served us our yak Parmesana, he hurriedly untied his apron and handed it to John. John had volunteered to take over kitchen duties so Pasang could go into town and pay his respects, too. We all ate quietly—from equal parts fatigue and the mournful feel in the air.

The others went to their tents after dinner. I sat alone by the fire, listening to the doleful music from the village. Shortly after ten—just as I was thinking about my sleeping bag—someone walked up to the fire. It was Dave. He squatted on the far side of the flames. He wore a crisply pressed black tunic and his old knickers. His eyes shone red in the light of the fire.

He told me that Ang Dorje's funeral would be in the morning, and that he would be bowing out of the next day's hike to attend. He asked if I wanted to go to the funeral with him. *Of course*, I said. Dave thanked me for my decision; he gave me a hug that startled me. Then he went home to Karma and Mingma.

* * *

In the morning, I told Butch of my plans. "Pass on my condolences," he said. "There will never be another Ang Dorje. It was an honor to climb with him on Everest last year." He told me he'd try to get into town after the day's hike to pay respects.

After the others had departed, I dug through my duffel bag for my travel clothes. They were musty and crumpled—khaki trousers and a polo shirt. They still carried the acrid scent of burning tires from Kathmandu. But I figured Ang Dorje wouldn't mind. I shaved. Finally, I walked into town. I knocked on the door to Dave's hut.

Mingma met me at the door. He was freshly scrubbed, and wore a finely starched white shirt buttoned to the collar under his wool coat. Dave and Karma stood by the table, both dressed in black. Dave stood behind her, his hands loose on her hips.

"Thanks for coming," Dave said. "It means a lot."

"It means a lot that you asked," I said. We sat at the table. Mingma sat on my knee. I pulled out my key ring and showed him my miniature Rubik's Cube. Karma put a cassette tape of Tibetan chants in the battery-powered boombox on the mantle, and a pitcher of chang was brought forth. Stories were told about Ang Dorje; subdued jokes were exchanged. Dave translated.

At ten, we joined the procession forming in front of Ang Dorje's house. Twelve monks with shaved heads, dressed in maroon robes, led the way. Each carried a horn, a gong or cymbals. The monks not blowing horns chanted sonorously. Then came eight men bearing Ang Dorje's litter. He was wrapped in a simple wool shroud. Nima, his widow, followed behind the litter. Dave, Karma, Mingma and I stepped behind her.

We were followed by perhaps two hundred residents of Namche Bazar and nearby villages. Every Sherpa who made a living climbing and who wasn't on a mountain at the moment seemed to be in the procession. Some had come down from Everest

Base Camp for the funeral. Many were accompanied by their wives and children—some in Western jackets and dresses, but most in colorful Sherpa garb, the women weighed down with heirloom silver and jade.

The procession snaked up the barren hill above town. It reached the top of a rocky knoll, where it came to a halt. The litter was lowered onto a smoke-streaked rock bier. Dave explained that it was a *ghat*, the traditional place for cremation. In the native language, ghat also meant a river crossing. A rough-hewn pole had been erected beside the ghat. Multi-colored prayer flags fluttered from ropes guying the pole.

An elderly monk swinging a smoking censer performed the service. He delivered a melodic prayer for Ang Dorje's spirit. We filed past the ghat when the monk was done. The shroud had been pulled back. As I shuffled past, I noticed the sash around Ang Dorje's waist. His brother's ponytail was still there, hanging off the edge of the litter, ready to accompany Ang Dorje into the afterworld. The ponytail had been freshly plaited and pomaded.

Each of us then tied a prayer flag to the pole. By the time the last mourner had bade Ang Dorje farewell, the pole was festooned with hundreds of prayer flags. Their colors fluttered lightly in the morning breeze. It reminded me of a carnival Maypole that had somehow come to life.

And then Nima, Karma and Mingma stepped forward with huge brass flagons of clarified yak butter. They soaked the bundles of brush piled under the body. Mingma, struggling to lift his flagon, almost spilled it, until Dave stepped forward to lend a hand. When the brush was soaked, Nima lit the fire. The flames leapt quickly; we had to retreat. I turned in time to see Phu Dorje's ponytail vanish in a flash of white vapor.

At Dave's hut, I said goodbye. I bowed wordlessly to Karma. She hugged me. Mingma lurched forward and hugged my leg. I tousled his hair. Then I realized he'd reached into my pants pocket and pulled out the Rubik's Cube.

"Magic," he said, his eyes gleaming.

I began to take the cube off my key ring for him. And then I looked at the collection of keys: one for the BMW, one for the Trooper, two for the house, one for my club locker. There was one for my office, one for my file cabinet, one for EarthCorp's executive washroom. It dawned on me how absurd it was that I'd carried them halfway around the world, and how meaningless they were now. I handed the entire key ring to Mingma.

He jangled the keys in his hand, mesmerized by the sound.

* * *

I spent the afternoon in camp, helping Pasang get dinner ready. He put me to work where I couldn't do any damage—peeling potatoes.

After the team—minus Dave—ate dinner, we sat by the fire. Butch got out a map of Pumori and sketched out our route. He pointed out where we'd set up camps. As had happened before, an argument arose about the selection of summit teams. Butch threw up his hands. He folded his map and went to bed.

As night fell, the others headed for their tents. I tossed wood on the fire until it leapt high. Despite the light it cast, I could see the glow from the top of the knoll, where the embers of the funeral fire still burned. Lulled by the heat on my face, I put my chin on my knees and drifted off.

A hand on my shoulder woke me. "Thanks for waiting." It was Dave. He squatted to stir the fire. His tunic was unbuttoned; a bottle of arak was on the ground between us. It was almost empty. Satisfied with the fire, he sat.

Dave watched the flames rekindle. He reached for the arak and took a swig. A drop rolled down his chin. "It's been a heck of a party. Ang Dorje had a lot of friends." He offered me the bottle.

I declined. "How are Mingma and Karma?"

"Mingma's okay," Dave said. "After the funeral, he told Karma he hated the river for taking Ang Dorje. I took him for a walk along the gorge. We kicked big rocks down into the deeper pools. We climbed down and skipped pebbles across the shallows. I told him that if he listened carefully to the river, he would always be able to hear the music and the wisdom of Ang Dorje's voice in it.

"As for Karma: she lived her whole life afraid that her father would die on some high mountain, like his brother. It's a relief to her that at least he died close to home, so that she could see him one last time, and so that there could be a proper funeral."

"I'm glad I met him," I said.

Dave poked at the fire. "So am I. He treated me like a son."

My shins were getting hot. I tucked my knees closer to my chest. "So tell me, stranger. What have you been doing with yourself since Foraker?"

Dave stared into the fire. He finally wiped the arak from his chin with his sleeve. "It's a long story. I've forgotten half of it myself."

"Try."

"Remember the 1969 television season?"

"I remember *Mod Squad*," I admitted. "I had a crush on Peggy Lipton."

"I had a thing for *Then Came Bronson*," Dave said. "Jim Bronson was a newspaperman. His best friend died, and Bronson's life fell apart. Bronson sold everything he owned, jumped on his dead friend's Harley-Davidson Sportster and took off on the road looking for answers."

"I remember," I said. "Starring Michael Parks. Lots of shots of Bronson in his watch cap tooling down Highway 1 through the redwoods near Big Sur. Each episode he stops along his journey, working odd jobs, touching people's lives."

"The show flopped," Dave said. "Lasted one season."

"So what's this got to do with anything?" I asked.

"After Foraker, I played *Then Came Bronson*. I loaded some clothes and food and a little bit of climbing gear into my VW and took off. A stranger asked Bronson in one episode where he was headed. Bronson answered, 'I don't know. Wherever I end up, I guess.' That was my philosophy."

"Where'd you end up?"

Dave told me how, after Foraker, he didn't want to see snow again. So he headed south. He spent that first summer camping on beaches up and down Baja California. In the fall, wanting to see the sun *rise* over the ocean instead of set, he headed for Veracruz. Just as he got to the city limits, his transaxle broke. Low on food and lower on cash, he was forced to look for work. Luckily, he had done well in high school Spanish; it got him work in a sardine cannery. It took until the following summer to save enough to fix the car; he rented a shack made of cardboard and hubcaps on the beach.

A vacationing American businessman strolling along the beach came upon the shack. Dave shared a pot of coffee with him. Before he left, the man gave Dave the business card of a banker in Mexico City. Once Dave's car was fixed, he found himself in a secondhand suit and tie, working as a bank teller.

Dave spent three years in Mexico City. Living simply, he was able to save his pesos. Some weekends he would drive to the beach. On the few clear days in Mexico City, though, something would draw his attention: the nearby snow-capped volcanoes of Popocatepetl and Iztaccihuatl, both nearly 18,000 feet high.

The first couple of years, he forced himself to look away. But, one day, digging through the back of his car, he found his rusting crampons and the ice axe Emmett had given him. Soon, he had climbed both volcanoes more than twenty times.

His self-imposed exile from the United States had worn thin. He pawned his suit and tie, loaded the VW with lentils and rice and peppers, traded his pesos for dollars and headed north. He spent a month on foot in the Sierras, bagging peaks, staying off-trail to avoid backpackers. He drove north along the Cascades, slogging up volcanoes. He made a solo climb of Rainier's Liberty Ridge without a Park Service permit, and—still in his climbing clothes and boots—led rangers on a car chase clear out of the park before shaking them.

"Then I figured I'd give Alaska another try," Dave said. "I sold my Bug and bought a one-way ferry ticket."

"What year was this?" I asked.

"Must have been '79."

The same month I was on Denali's West Buttress, Dave was on the south side, soloing the Cassin Ridge. He made the summit two days after me. We had just missed each other. Our bootprints on the summit had probably crossed. Once again, he was climbing without a Park Service permit. This time, there was no escape. Park rangers nabbed him as he climbed out of the glacier pilot's Cessna in Talkeetna. He was driven to the Federal Magistrate's office in Anchorage, where he posted a $500 bond. He never appeared for his court date.

"There's still probably a bench warrant with my name on it in Alaska," he said.

"Then what? Onward to the North Pole?"

"I hitched down the Alcan Highway to Seattle," Dave said. "I joined the Army, and ended up in Grenada. I got shot in the ass."

I laughed so hard that I had to reach for the arak to calm myself. "That's a good one: *you* in a uniform."

"Yeah. It's a good one. And it's true."

I put the bottle down. "You're *serious*."

"I can't explain why I did it. Maybe military service is like substance abuse: a habit handed down from father to son, afflicting mostly working-class families. Maybe I was tired of wandering. Maybe I still needed to prove something to myself. Or *disprove* something to myself. I ended up in the 82nd Airborne. The recruiter

Jim Fairchild

told me that anybody crazy enough to climb mountains by himself was crazy enough to jump out of perfectly good airplanes."

"I can't imagine you in the Army," I said. "I remember how you hated your Boy Scout uniform. I remember how bitter your Dad was about Korea. Did you find what you were looking for?"

"I did," Dave said.

"And what was it?"

"That I wasn't as bad a person as I'd thought."

"Because of what happened on Foraker?"

"Naomi had it right. I took the accident pretty hard. There wasn't a night those first few years when I didn't dream about chopping that rope. There wasn't a night I didn't see those three bodies flying down that gully. I needed to talk with someone about it so badly sometimes that I'd find a place on the beach to myself and scream at the ocean."

"I wish you'd stayed in touch," I said. ""I know how much it must have hurt. It was a hell of a choice for an eighteen-year-old to make."

"It's okay now. I realized that hanging on a fence in Grenada."

He told me how his battalion had jumped onto the island the second day of the operation—an American invasion nearly forgotten to history now. Most of the fighting was already over; his unit was assigned mop-up. Although they could hear small firefights in the distance, that first day they didn't have to fire a single shot. They took a few prisoners: pathetic middle-aged Cuban laborers who had been working on a new airstrip, and who had been ordered to carry rusting old rifles that in many cases weren't even loaded.

On the second morning, on the outskirts of St. George's, his platoon was detailed to secure a Cuban motorpool full of rusting backhoes and bulldozers. It was surrounded by a sagging chainlink fence. Dave was a buck sergeant, with less than three months to go before his discharge. He had already had enough of the Army, and

138

had no interest in being a hero. And he had no interest in killing sad Cuban laborers to make a geopolitical statement for Ronald Reagan.

While the rest of the platoon covered them from across the street, Dave's squad reconned the motorpool. They circled its perimeter. It was dead. Dave and his radioman went back to tell the lieutenant, hunkered down behind a cherry '65 LeMans parked on the street. The lieutenant told them to open the gate.

When Dave and the radioman were halfway across the street, he heard a loud crack. A sniper round had just blown out the windshield of the LeMans. For a split second, Dave thought about how upset the car's owner would be.

In the next second, Dave realized his predicament. There was a second loud crack. His radioman fell facefirst onto the pavement beside him. Brains and blood oozed out of the back of his helmet.

Time dilated. The M60 gunner behind the LeMans opened up. Dave now had rounds zipping past him in both directions. Rounds were smashing into the pavement all around him. Rounds sparked off the chainlink fence ahead of him.

People shouted at him to move. But Dave didn't know where to go. It was a long way back to the Pontiac, and he would have to turn his back to the sniper to get there. The fence was eight feet high, but if he could get over it, he could take cover behind a bulldozer.

"I tried to get over the fence. I jumped halfway up and grabbed the barbed wire on top. Rounds sparked on the fence a couple of feet from my hands. I closed my eyes. Then I did this beautiful sideways roll up and over the wire.

"My feet never made contact with the pavement on the other side. I opened my eyes. Everything was upsidedown. My back was against the chainlink. The bulldozer was right in front of me, where it should be, but it as 180 degrees out of whack. I had snagged my load-bearing harness on the barbed wire when I rolled over the top.

Jim Fairchild

I tried to reach behind me, but I couldn't lift my weight off the harness to unsnag it. I dropped my rifle and tried with both hands, but still couldn't budge it. I unfastened my pistol belt but my harness was still hung up.

"I started screaming at the top of my lungs. Blood started draining to my face. I thought I was going to have a brain hemorrhage from screaming. I could hear the LT somewhere behind me yelling orders, and could see that the platoon was starting to maneuver.

"I finally stopped struggling. I realized how ridiculous it was. I was stuck upsidedown on a fence on an island most people have never heard of, bullets whizzing past me like hornets in both directions, and there was nothing to do but relax and enjoy the show. A round slammed into one of my canteens. Water cascaded into my nostrils. I thought it was blood. I started to choke. When I realized it was water, I started laughing, even as I choked. I could see the headline: *HOMETOWN SOLDIER DROWNS ON FENCE DURING FURIOUS FIREFIGHT.*

"In front of me, behind the dozer, I saw movement. Through the dozer's suspension, I saw a pair of huaraches. I could see a straw hat. I glimpsed the weathered face of an old Cuban. I remember his silver whiskers. He was hiding behind the dozer, shaking and praying, as afraid of the firefight as me. He had laid a rusty AK-47 on the dozer's tracks, afraid to use it. It was obvious the old man was not a threat. The sniper fire was coming from somewhere else.

"I caught a glimpse of someone running into the compound. It was the LT. He'd come through the gate—the way I should have gone. He was firing his weapon on full-auto. He had no clue what he was shooting at.

"I saw him run between two lines of dozers and start to work his way down, searching for the sniper. A round slammed into the fence again, bouncing me around. I didn't realize it then, but one of

140

my M60 gunner's rounds had actually just nailed me in the butt. The blood ran down my back and dripped into my helmet. I thought it was still water from the ruptured canteen.

"I could see my LT's jungle boots between the dozers, coming down the line toward the old man, who was still crouched behind the dozer in front of me. His back was toward the lieutenant. And then the LT yelled something. I couldn't make out the words over all the firing, but I know it was in English.

"I saw the old man stand up. I saw his hands above his head. They trembled like dead leaves on a tree. I could see his face through the dozer cab. He was scared to death.

"There was a burst of automatic fire. The old man flew back. I didn't see him hit the pavement, but I could hear it. It was as if someone had just tossed a sack of beans to the ground. His straw hat sailed out past the dozer blade. It rolled on the edge of its brim. It wobbled toward me and came to rest upsidedown in front of me. The sweatband was soaked.

"And then I heard a weapon clatter onto the pavement. The lieutenant had grabbed the rusty AK off the dozer tracks and tossed it onto the ground near the old man. The LT waved at the rest of the platoon. He hollered for them to cease fire. Somewhere in the distance, the real sniper who had been shooting at us disengaged, too.

"I was beginning to feel weak. I finally realized I'd been hit. I could see my blood pattering onto the pavement. But I was clear-headed enough to know I'd just seen a terrified old man gunned down in cold blood. That little West Point prick got himself a Silver Star for 'neutralizing a sniper position that had inflicted harsh losses on his unit.' It was fucking murder. I thought I'd known something about guilt. I had no clue until then."

"The bastard should have gone to Leavenworth," I said.

"I had the last laugh," Dave said. "I blackmailed him."

"What did you shake him down for?"

"A ninety-percent medical disability."

"For getting shot in the *ass*?"

"No. The lieutenant had a friend in the Medical Corps write the evaluation. A fine piece of fiction. Panic disorder. Post-traumatic delayed stress syndrome. The VA has sent me a check every month for more than six years. I'm a member of the leisure class now."

"I've always dreamed of retiring young," I said. "What did you do after the Army?"

"I almost went home," Dave said. "But the idea of telling my old man I'd been in the Army scared me more than the memories of hanging on that fence upsidedown. So I headed to Seattle. I thought about working in a climbing shop. But I didn't feel like dealing with people. And I didn't need the money."

"That's when you called Emmett," I said. "He drove all night to Seattle to find you. You really took a dump on his heart. He loves you."

Dave told me how he headed south again—farther this time. He climbed the volcanoes of Ecuador, then headed for the Peruvian and Chilean Andes. On Aconcagua's Polish Route, he met a young Chilean named Carlos Abrego. Abrego's father owned a chorizo factory and a huge hacienda; he bankrolled his son's climbing ambitions, hoping to become the father of the first Chilean to climb Everest. Dave and Carlos became inseparable. Dave even had his own room at the hacienda. Finally, though, Carlos left for the Himalaya. Dave stayed behind.

"I wasn't ready to commit to being part of a team," Dave said. "Carlos was a great friend, but I felt suffocated being around one person for too long."

"But you ended up in the Himalaya anyway."

"Carlos kept writing," Dave said. "Telling me stories about his climbs in Nepal. He soloed Annapurna's South Face guerrilla-style—no permit. He did Kanchenjunga with an embittered ex-

142

partner of Messner. He told me about the great routes that still hadn't been touched. At first, I wouldn't take the bait. But I got tired of the hacienda and stuffing chorizo. I got tired of having to regale Carlos' father with climbing stories after every dinner. I finally bought a plane ticket for Kathmandu. That was two years ago. I've been here ever since."

"Where's Carlos?" I asked.

"Sometime between the time my plane left the ground in Santiago and the time I landed in Kathmandu, he fell on Makalu. He was soloing the West Face. The first climbing I did in Nepal was going to retrieve his body. That's how I met Ang Dorje. He and Carlos were good friends. Ang Dorje and I buried Carlos on a moraine overlooking the Barun Glacier."

"That was a rough start," I said. "But you seem at home here now."

"It feels like the place I was always meant to find. My own Range of Light, as John Muir would have called it. Especially after I'd met Ang Dorje. There was powerful chemistry between us. We could both hear the whispering of the mountain spirits. Before I knew it, he'd invited me to live with him."

"What's happening to the Sherpa co-op and the strike now that Ang Dorje is gone?"

"We've had an orderly succession." Dave dropped a branch on the fire. "Chotari has been promoted to Supreme Burrito."

"Are you sure he's the right choice?" I asked. "He's so Westernized."

"Don't let the Vuarnets fool you. In his heart, Chotari loves tradition as much as Ang Dorje ever did. Maybe *more*. Because Chotari understands Western ways better. That makes his contempt for Western ways even deeper."

"Listen, Dave," I said, crossing my legs. "I've been thinking about this co-op. I've got contacts in Fortune 500 boardrooms. They're always on the lookout for good charities. It's about tax deductions as well as about their public image. I'd be surprised if I couldn't raise a million dollars the first year. It would just take a few phone calls once I get home."

"Thanks," Dave said. "But we are flush with cash."

"How could you beat a cool million?"

Dave grinned. "We've launched a speculative trading venture with the cooperation of certain government authorities."

"Why do I detect the odor of illegality?"

"We're marketing Kashmiri hash. Tibetan yakherders pick it up at Tashigong, on the border of Kashmir and Tibet. They bring it down the highway from Tibet into Kathmandu. Then it's flown west: Ankara, Rome, Berlin."

"Like father, like son," I said. "I can't believe you'd get the Sherpas involved. Your father spent almost two years in prison for the same sort of high jinks."

"Ang Dorje didn't know where the money came from. Actually, nobody in the co-op but me knows. I'm sorry if it offends your delicate sense of morality. But morality isn't always black and white. I wish it were, but I've encountered thousands of shades of grey. Speaking of my old man: how's he doing?"

"Fine," I said. "After he got out of prison, he went to work for my Dad at the lawn care business. Emmett might buy him out. My Dad's finally bought his cropduster. Emmett's playing third fiddle in the orchestra."

"He used to hide his classical albums from Mom and me," Dave said. "I found them hidden in his closet, behind the *Playboys*. I used to sneak them out when my parents were gone."

"The *Playboys*?"

"Well, yeah. But also the records: Rachmaninoff. Strauss. Chopin."

"He's quite the horticulturist," I said. "He's got a huge greenhouse. He's working on a new strain of the state flower, the Bitterroot. He's hoping to present a bouquet of them to the governor on Statehood Day."

I couldn't stop myself now. I cared too much about Emmett. "He was devastated when you didn't keep in touch. Especially when he was locked up. What do you think he'd say if he found out you were trafficking drugs?"

"He'd say that at least I'd greased the right palms."

"How so?" I asked.

"When the Tibetans reach Kathmandu with the hash, they rendezvous with Nepalese Army trucks. The army stores the hash in government warehouses and delivers it to the airport. The generals and colonels take half of the profits. They love the extra pocket change so much they've been pestering me to increase the shipments."

"I saw the Nepalese Army in action," I said. "I saw them gun down old monks and little children."

"It's a sad time," Dave said.

"You've entered into a pact with murderers. I don't know you any more."

"We've got time to change that," Dave said. "I'm sorry you're disappointed with what you've found so far." He stood and put a hand on my shoulder. I ignored the gesture. He disappeared into the dark.

* * *

Jim Fairchild

Chapter Seven:
Thyangboche Monastery

When Pasang's clanging cookpots awoke me the next morning, Dave's sleeping bag was empty. We were scheduled to depart that morning for our next step toward Pumori: the monastery at Thyangboche. I wondered if Dave would go. Ang Dorje's death might change his plans. After the previous night's conversation, I could live with any outcome.

Under the kitchen fly, I poured a mug of tea, then filled a wash basin from Pasang's kettle. Chotari stood in the gloom, clipboard in hand, assigning porter loads.

Someone sat on a crate next to Chotari. His back was dimly illuminated by the blue flame of Pasang's stove. I could make out steam rising from a mug of tea, and a pomaded ponytail.

"Dave?" I asked, water dripping from my face.

"Namaste."

"How's Karma?" I dried my face.

"She's with friends."

"And Mingma?" I zipped shut my toilet kit.

"It's been hard for him," Dave said. "He lost his Dad, and now he's lost his uncle. But he still has Karma. And he's got your Rubik's Cube."

"And he's got you." I found a vacant crate and sat down,

juggling toilet kit, towel and tea mug.

"When I get back from Pumori, I'll have a family to take care of. Karma, and the kid she's carrying, and my buddy Mingma."

"So you're going on to Pumori with us?" I asked.

In the greyness, I could dimly make out the outline of Dave's hands rising to his face. I could hear him sip his tea, and could see the blue glow of rising steam. "I'm afraid you're stuck with me, Norman."

"Will Karma be okay?"

"She *wants* me to go," Dave said. "She understands that greater wheels have been set in motion."

"Don't you think Mingma needs you?"

The steam from Dave's tea curled up around his face. "I told him that when I get back, I'd be honored to settle down and be his father. I told him this will be my last climb."

I lost grip of my mug and slopped steaming tea into my lap. "*What?*"

"I don't have anything left to prove. If you climb hard enough and long enough it's just a game of Russian roulette. And the people left behind are the *real* victims. I don't want to do that to Karma and Mingma."

I dabbed at my lap with my towel. "I'm glad we'll have this last climb together, then."

"So am I, old friend," Dave said. He took a final sip from his mug, then splashed the tea leaves onto the ground. "Great things lie ahead."

* * *

We moved out at a gentle but steady pace. It looked like we might see rain before the day was through.

We followed a ridge overlooking the river. The first three

miles were familiar territory—we'd hiked it the day Ang Dorje had been found in the river. We stopped for a break at the same junction where the litter bearers had appeared. Even the normally chatty porters were silent during this break. It was as if the very ground beneath us was drenched with sorrow. Lifting our loads again, we headed down the switchbacks into the gorge, knees creaking.

Finally, we reached the roaring river. Ahead of us lay the fragile suspension bridge from which Ang Dorje had leapt to his death. Its rusted cables were festooned with fresh prayer flags left by mourners. They fluttered in the perpetual breeze of the gorge. We moved gingerly across the bouncing bridge. We regrouped on the far side.

Chotari brought up the rear. I watched as he reached the middle of the ancient swaying span. He reached into his parka and pulled out a white prayer flag. He tied the flag to a cable already bedecked with streaming silk. He said a prayer, his eyes tightly shut. The river swallowed his words.

When he was done, he headed toward us. He ran his fingers through the fluttering silk beside him like a child dipping its fingers into an icy stream. When he stepped onto the bank beside me, he pointed up the trail. "Let's boogie," he said, shaking his hips like John Travolta in *Saturday Night Fever*. But his Vuarnets failed to hide the tears running down his face.

* * *

As we climbed toward the Thyangboche monastery, snowflakes began to fall. An icy wind began to blow; snow stung our faces. The monastery sits atop a spur just below the icy peaks of Thamserku and Kangtega. By the time we approached the crest, we were walking through a foot of wet snow. I worried about the porters. Chotari had issued them all new canvas tennis shoes in Lukla for the march to Base Camp. But many porters chose to walk barefooted. They strapped the new shoes to the tops of their loads, planning to sell them for cash when they got back home.

We finally crested the top. The full fury of the wind-driven snow lashed our faces. I leaned my head into the wind. Off to the right, peering through frozen eyelashes, I could make out a stone chorten, decked out in whipping prayer flags, the grey stone plastered with snow.

The column ground to a halt. I could see Butch gesturing to a monk. The monk held the hood of his wind-whipped robe over his shaved head to protect it from the icy blasts. He pointed to a low stone hut where we would be staying.

One by one, we squeezed through the door. Before I followed, I squinted into the blowing snow. I could see numerous stone houses and outbuildings. But I couldn't spot the famous red-walled gompa at the center of the monastery. It was one of the most photographed sights in the Nepal Himalaya. It was within the gompa that climbing teams heading for the highest peaks sought the blessing of the resident abbot. While it was merely a pleasant tradition for most of the foreign climbers, their Sherpas took the matter with the utmost seriousness. If an expedition neglected to seek that blessing, untold woe could befall it higher up.

I tapped the ice-glazed pack in front of me. Dave turned around. His eyebrows and ponytail were shrouded in ice. "Where's the gompa?" I asked.

Dave stomped the snow from his boots. "It burned down last year."

We stepped into the hut. Pasang already had a smoky fire blazing in the fireplace and was starting dinner. The hut smelled of burning juniper and searing yakmeat and wet wool. We dropped our packs and brushed the snow from our clothes.

"Was the gompa a complete loss?" I asked Dave.

"Almost." Dave pulled his old cotton anorak—the gift from Ang Dorje—over his head. "The monastery lost 600-year-old texts

Jim Fairchild

documenting the history of Buddhism in the Khumbu. Most of the statues and frescoes were destroyed. The frescoes were famous throughout the Buddhist world." He hung the anorak on a rusty nail near the fire.

"What caused the blaze?" I wiped melting snow from my face with my bandanna.

"Maybe a spark in a sooty chimney. Maybe a leaky kerosene heater. Most of the monks were in Kathmandu for the funeral of a heavyweight lama. Those that were here had to stand back and watch the flames. There wasn't enough water to fight the fire. After the monks returned, some of them developed a theory about the fire."

"What's that?" I pulled off my wet windpants.

"They think the gompa burned because the Sherpa people have abandoned their faith." Dave sat on an ancient bench and pulled off his wet boots. "They believe that the Sherpas have sold their souls to the tourism industry. They believe that the monastery defiled itself by selling blessings to climbers. Karmic justice necessitated that the gompa be cleansed by fire."

"What's that mean for us?" I asked. I wedged myself between Eugene and Laslow in front of the fire. "Will *we* receive the abbott's blessing?"

"I have no idea," Dave said. He wrestled into dry socks. "Things have changed since the fire."

I wriggled my butt in front of the delightful flames. "I'm not superstitious," I said. "But I've read that porters have second thoughts about carrying loads for an expedition that hasn't received the blessing. Some expeditions consider it essential."

"Call me a cynic," Eugene said. "But getting up a mountain depends more on climbing ability than the blessing of a voodoo doctor."

I ignored Eugene. He was a walking argument for eugenics. "It doesn't matter if you believe literally in the blessing," I said.

150

"It's a simple matter of good labor relations with the Sherpas."

"We'll just have to see how it shakes out," Dave said, tugging on his dry yakskin boots. "What we want and what we receive are usually two distinctly different things." He yanked the leather laces so tightly they squeaked.

*   *   *

We were scheduled to spend two days at Thyangboche. It would give our bodies more time to adjust to the altitude. We huddled together that first night in the stone shelter, glad for the warmth of the fire, more than willing to put up with the crowding. Our porters had found shelter in a nearby hut. As we sat about enjoying the steaming curried yak with lentils Pasang had prepared, I could hear—even through the stone walls and the howling wind— the chanting and singing of the porters next door, and the stomp-shuffle of their dancing. We had encountered our first nasty weather, and it had drawn us together.

In the morning, after breakfast, we took a tour of the monastery. What was left of the burned gompa was covered with tattered translucent tarps. The charred beams were visible through the plastic. The smell of soot still hung heavy, fifteen months after the fire.

A novice monk led us into an outbuilding that now served as a temporary gompa. The few tapestries and paintings that had been rescued from the conflagration covered the walls. The room danced with flickering shadows cast by yak butter lanterns and candles. A thirty-inch gold Buddha—the only one rescued from the fire— reclined on a shrine at the front of the room. The Buddha lay propped languorously on one elbow, his head resting on his hand. He smiled blissfully, no doubt pleased to have escaped the fire.

Before we left, the novitiate led us past a wooden box. It had no lid. Inside, it was fat with crumpled dollars and pound notes,

Deutschmarks, traveler's checks, tarnished rupee coins. Someone had dropped a cat's-eye marble and a child's troll doll into the box. The young monk simply stated that the gompa could not be rebuilt without the generosity of those who passed by.

Each of us filed past the box. Butch dropped in a thick fold of bills—although much of it was a routine donation from the guide service, a great deal of it was his own. The rest of us—even Eugene—emptied our pockets of rupee notes and coins that would serve no use on Pumori.

Dave brought up the rear. He came to the box. He looked at the smiling Buddha, and then at a flock of French trekkers who'd been led into the room after us. The French had just returned from Everest Base Camp, their faces windburned. They joked garrulously. One heavy man with a thick beard and a tweed hat knelt beside the Buddha and put his arm around it, mugging for a friend with a video camera.

Dave reached inside his anorak. He pulled out a roll of currency as thick as my wrist. I could see American greenbacks and Indian notes. A piece of rough twine held the roll together. He dropped it into the box. He noticed my raised eyebrows. "It'll just be dead weight on the mountain," he said.

*   *   *

We took a steep hike up a snowy ridge after lunch. When we tromped back down that afternoon in our heavy double climbing boots, Thyangboche was aswirl with people stomping through the melting snow and mud. The Italian Lhotse expedition had caught up with us, along with its hundred porters. A smaller American and British group headed for nearby Ama Dablam had just arrived, too. They had a mere two dozen porters. Two large trekking groups had also arrived. Each was accompanied by its attendant army of porters. The Italian expedition was busy pitching tents in the mud.

The other groups were attempting to find lodging in the dormitory or nearby houses and huts.

The jewel box of Ama Dablam, which had shone an eery turquoise in the shadows of morning, was now a fiery gold in the light of evening. We made plans for the morning to once again venture onto the nearby ridges.

* * *

Laslow's digital alarm chimed at four in the morning. Butch went to the door. When he pried it open, a blast of wind-driven snow slammed him in the face. A cornice of snow over the door lintel fell and just missed his head. He shut the door and brushed the snow from his eyebrows. "I don't think we'll be going high today," he said. Nobody seemed disappointed. Butch told a grateful Pasang to go back to bed and not to worry about fixing an early breakfast. It was a luxury to sleep late in our warm bags.

Only Chotari made the trip out into the elements. He wanted to check on our scantily outfitted porters next door. When he returned, he said he'd broken out the expedition's spare sleeping bags for the porters to share. Butch fretted about lice. Chotari, holding his temper, reminded Butch of the porter's moth-eaten blankets. The high-altitude Sherpas were all issued warm climbing clothing and sleeping bags at the start of the expedition, and ate the same food as the Sahibs. But the low-altitude porters had to provide their own clothes, blankets, food and cook gear. The only items they were issued were the tennis shoes, which many still declined to wear, and cheap sunglasses, which Chotari had issued them once we hit the snowline.

By mid-afternoon the wind had calmed. Another foot of wet snow had fallen. Soon, the sun was beating down from a crystal blue sky, and a steady dripping could be heard from the eaves. I spent the afternoon sharpening my ice axe and crampons, taking care not to get carried away like Eugene. Dave wandered off to visit with the Italian Lhotse expedition. He knew some of the team's Sherpas. Most our our group was sprawled around the hut. Eugene had his headphones on, listening to a Tony Robbins tape on "life mastery." Laslow cleaned his video camera. John wrote a long letter home. Sarah edited the notes for her Khumbu rock-climbing guide. Chris was reading the last pages of *The Tibetan Book of the Dead*. She planned to start a Jackie Collins novel next—for spiritual balance, she said.

Dinner was almost ready. Even from inside, I could hear the chanting and drumming and horn-blowing of the monks. I could hear singing and dancing from the porters next door. But just as Pasang began to set up the serving line, I became aware of an odd stillness. The monks had stopped playing their instruments. They had stopped chanting. Even the porters next door had stopped dancing. Then I could hear shouting, and the sound of people racing past through the melting snow. I stepped outside.

As I zipped shut my down jacket, I could see monks milling around frantically. Porters talked agitatedly, pointing toward the gompa.

Dave approached from the Italian camp. His hands were buried in the pockets of his anorak.

"What's going on?" I asked.

"Someone snuck into the gompa last night and stole the Buddha," he said. "The old abbot collapsed with chest pains when he was told. He's beginning to believe the monks who think the monastery is doomed."

"The thief is probably one of the trekkers or climbers," I said. "Can't they all be searched?"

"The nearest constable is in Namche Bazar. The monks have sent a runner for him, but he won't get here until midday tomorrow at best. There must be eighty foreigners here, and a couple of hundred porters. And a mountain of baggage. Even when the constable gets here, a search seems like an impossible task for one man."

Heart-rending chanting and wailing came from the gompa. It was accompanied by the beat of a single drum. "Nobody would steal the Buddha unless they're getting ready to head home," I said. "Nobody headed up to the mountains would want to lug it with them." And then I thought of the French trekkers who'd visited the gompa after us. "What about—"

"I looked for the French trekkers," Dave said, reading my mind. "They left this morning for Namche Bazar. I told the monks about them. But the runner going for the constable had already left. The constable's probably going to walk right past the French without thinking to search them."

"There's got to be something we can do."

"Karma takes strange paths," Dave said.

Chotari approached through the melting snow.

"Bad news," he said. He pulled the Vuarnets from his face. I could see the deep lines around his eyes. "I spent the whole day working a deal for the blessing: a hundred bucks, ten pounds of soap flakes and a case of kitchen matches. Then a monk ran in and said the Buddha was stolen. I'm afraid our climb won't receive a blessing. *No* expedition will receive a blessing."

* * *

Dave barely touched his dinner. He set his plate down and walked over to his rucksack. He pulled out a motheaten sweater, a pair of mittens, a wool cap and a curved Ghurka kukri knife, strapped into an ancient leather sheath. He dropped them into his smaller daypack, then lifted it onto his back.

"I've been sitting all day," he said. "The weather's clearing. I thought I'd take a short walk."

"Would you like company?" I asked.

"I think I need a few hours of solitude. A little John Muir time." He cinched the pack's shoulder straps, then stepped out the door.

Chris looked up from her Jackie Collins novel. "A tad late for a stroll in the country, wouldn't you say?"

* * *

I tried to stay awake until Dave returned. At midnight, fatigue won out. I was awakened at 3:30 by Laslow's snoring. Dave's sleeping bag was still empty. I drifted off again.

I awoke once more, coughing. The hut was filled by a low-hanging cloud of smoke. Somebody was crouched by the fireplace, blowing on a pile of tinder.

I looked at my watch. It was 5:30. The figure was on one knee, breaking twigs and placing them on the tiny flame. I could see a ponytail.

"Dave?" I asked.

"*Shhh*," he said, a finger to his lips. Soon, the fire was raging. The thick smoke began creeping up the chimney as the hut warmed. Dave climbed into his sleeping bag. He pulled off his anorak and laid down. He looked exhausted.

"Where have you been?" I whispered over Laslow's snoring.

"Been partying with Yetis," he said. "I'm bushed. Talk to you in an hour or two."

Soothed by the fire, I drifted off again. I was awakened too soon by the clanging of Pasang's pots.

On a bench behind me, Chris laced her double boots. "Morning, lovie," she said. "Wind's dropped. We're headed up the trail to Pheriche today."

I fished around in my sleeping bag for my pants. Then I noticed Dave, sitting on the bench beside Chris. He was having difficulty lacing his boots.

"A little hungover this morning?" I asked.

He looked up dourly at me, silent, struggling with his laces.

And then I looked at his hands. The knuckles were bloodied and swollen. I watched him try to yank his boot laces; pain shot instantly across his face. I began to say something, but his glare silenced me.

A tumultuous clanging of cymbals and bells broke out, and then dozens of joyous voices. I could hear doors and shutters flying open, and the sound of people running through the snow. I looked at Dave, and at his hands. I understood. I fastened my pants and jumped up.

The door to our hut burst open. Chotari stood there, the brilliant light of morning glinting like a halo behind him. It was too bright to see his face, but I could see his hand rise upward and remove his Vuarnets.

"What's going on?" Chris asked.

"The Buddha," Chotari said, beaming. *"He's back.* A monk was doing morning housekeeping, and found him back in his usual place. The abbot sees this as a sign. He will give us his blessing."

Pasang's face lit up with joy under his sideways ballcap. He began to bang his steel ladle against an empty kettle, keeping time with the gongs and bells and chants outside. Everyone but Eugene jumped up and began to dance. Chotari put his Vuarnets back on and joined our dance.

* * *

Chotari was busy organizing the porter loads. We had packed our personal gear, and had dragged our packs outside, leaning them against the hut. We were just waiting for our meeting with the abbot. Then we would head up the trail toward Pheriche.

A commotion broke out toward the trail from down-valley. I thought I was having a flashback: six men headed our way, carrying a litter bearing someone in a sleeping bag. The litter was followed closely by a Nepalese constable in crisp khaki and knee-high rubber boots. Behind the constable came a thin man in a baby-blue running suit. He looked familiar. He was the leader of the trekking group that had visited the gompa immediately after us.

Dave sat against the hut's stone wall. His closed eyes were lifted to the sun. His hands were in his lap. Wool mittens hid the damage.

I sat down beside him on my pack. "You rescued the Buddha."

Dave's eyes remained shut. "I'm pooped. I took a tumble in the dark."

As Chotari checked off another porter load, the constable approached. He touched Chotari's elbow; Chotari put down his clipboard. The two men walked quietly toward the gompa. I could see Dave open one eye and glimpse in their direction.

In a few minutes, Chotari returned. He picked up his clipboard. He pulled his felt-tip pen from beneath the strong metal clip.

"Looks like somebody got hurt pretty bad last night," he said to nobody in particular. He cleared his throat, then scanned the clipboard. "One of the French trekkers. They were halfway to Namche Bazar, camped near the river. A wild beast crept into their camp. It dragged one of them into the woods. Broke his nose and jaw. Hung him by the feet from a tree with a piece of climbing rope. The poor soul almost choked to death on his own blood."

Chris crossed her arms tightly. "Do you think we're safe?"

Chotari made a correction to a column of numbers on the clipboard. "I doubt the demented beast will return. I believe its work is done. It has probably already disappeared back into the high mountains."

"Will the Frog be okay?" Chris asked, aghast.

"If weather allows, a helicopter will come today for him,"

Chotari said. "He should be in the hospital in Kathmandu by nightfall, getting his jaw wired shut."

Dave and I glanced silently at each other.

We still had almost an hour before our appointment with the abbot—when, if all went well, our expedition would receive its blessing. We had time to burn. Some of the others read. I sat beside Dave, soaking up the sun, suspecting we hadn't heard the last of the night's events.

Chotari had almost finished assigning the porter loads. He came to one box, and checked the stencilled number on its side against the number on his clipboard. His eyebrows raised past his Vuarnets; he looked at the box again. He put down his clipboard and knelt for a closer look.

A hole had been cut in the box. Chotari pushed back the neatly cut cardboard flap. Even from where I sat, I could see inside the hole. It was the bright blue of climbing rope, destined for the slopes of Pumori. Chotari dug around inside the hole with two fingers. He pulled out the end of the rope. It had been cut.

Chotari tucked the rope end back into the box, then stood. He assigned the last of the loads, then walked over to Dave and me.

"Well, brothers," he said, tapping the clipboard against his thigh. "Ready to head upward today?"

"Let's blow this popsicle stand," Dave said, opening one eye and squinting.

"Just want to warn you," Chotari said. He kicked at the melting snow with his double boot. "Something broke into our rope last night and stole a piece. If I had rupees to bet, I'd say the missing piece was used to hang the Frenchman from the tree. Keep your eyes open for a Yeti. They are tall, have long hair, and smell." He stared hard at Dave, then headed into the hut.

When he was gone, I sniffed toward Dave. "I think I smell a Yeti."

"I gave that trekker's karma a gentle tweak in the right

159

direction," Dave said. "He'll thank me some day."

"Was it hard finding the Buddha?"

"Easy as peach pie," Dave said. "They were all sitting around their fire, sipping Boujolais. The big guy with the beard was sitting with the Buddha in his lap. He kept trying to pour wine into its mouth. His friends thought it was hilarious. One of them tried to feed it a baguette. The others finally went to bed. Paté-Ass passed out by the fire. It didn't take any effort at all to liberate the Buddha."

"Except for getting Paté-Ass up into a tree."

"Simple mechanics," Dave said. "I used a climbing pulley."

* * *

We filed into the gompa. It smelled of juniper incense and burning yak butter, used to fuel the flickering brass lanterns. Lantern smoke curled up around the high hewn rafters. A young novitiate greeted us, bowing deeply. He asked us to be seated on mats along the walls. At the front of the room lay the gold Buddha, back from his escapade. Banks of candles burned around him; he had been sprinkled with pink blossoms.

The abbot entered from a door beside the shrine. We rose. The abbot was a small man of indeterminate age, although I'd guess mid-fifties. He wore thick glasses. We all exchanged bows. He smiled so broadly his eyes were shut.

He began to speak. His voice was like an ancient string instrument, the sound of which had long ago been forgotten by the modern world: neither high nor deep, its tone took a delicate middle road. The novitiate translated: "The abbot wishes to inform you that you begin your undertaking at an auspicious time. The disappearance and subsequent return of our Buddha mark a turning point for both Thyangboche and the Sherpa people.

"In recent years, our timeless ways of life have been

corrupted. The fire that consumed our monastery was a sign that our faith was in imminent peril.

"When the Buddha vanished, it was a test. He retreated to the sacred summit of Khumbila, and watched for the reaction of the Sherpa people. From his mountaintop vantage, he observed the earnestness of their sorrow.

"If the Buddha had decided the Sherpa people had abandoned their faith, he would have stayed upon Khumbila forever. The swiftness with which he returned is a sign that the Sherpa people still have strong faith. It is a sign that the future holds great things for them. This event will live on forever in the history of the Sherpa people. It will be a story passed down through time." Then the abbot stepped up to each of us, reached into a box held by his assistant, and draped a white prayer scarf around each of our necks.

The abbot came to Laslow. Laslow bowed so deeply that his glasses slipped off his nose and clattered to the ground. Mortified, he lunged after them. At the same time, the abbot bent down to retrieve them, too. They collided midway: Laslow's balding head, and the shaved head of the abbot.

"*Oh my God*," Laslow gasped, rising, a hand on top of his head. He turned to the novitiate. "I'm so sorry. Tell him I'll never forgive myself."

But before the novitiate could translate, the abbot—like Laslow, with one hand to the top of his head—began to laugh. He took his hand from his head, then grasped Laslow by both shoulders. Laslow began to laugh, too. Soon, both men were laughing so hard that their faces were scarlet. At last, the abbot stooped down and retrieved the fallen glasses. He opened them gingerly and wiped the lenses with the hem of his robe, inspecting them for scratches. Satisfied, he placed them carefully on Laslow's face. Then he clasped Laslow's hand. Their smiles would have thawed a glacier. The abbot spoke a few words to his assistant.

As the abbot moved down the line to Eugene, the novitiate

whispered to Laslow. "He says that within you is the power to heal great wounds—both those of others and those of your own." Laslow grew pale.

Finally, the abbot came to Dave. He placed his last silk scarf around Dave's neck. The abbot took Dave's hand in his. Dave was still wearing the mittens. As the abbot squeezed Dave's hand, I could see Dave flinch.

Then the abbot reached inside his robe. A leather thong hung around his neck, and he pulled it over his shaved head. A small charm hung from it. It was a tiny Buddha, crafted of gold. The Buddha sat in the lotus position, palms raised upward, eyes closed, smiling blissfully. The abbot looked tenderly at the Buddha, then lifted the thong. He placed it around Dave's neck, over the silk scarf. The abbot spoke.

The novitiate translated. "Some spirits are shaped by this world, while other spirits shape this world. This man is of the latter. It is a perilous role, and requires much wisdom. May the wisdom of Buddha guide him through his world-shaping duties." The abbot winked at Dave. They hugged tightly. Then the abbot let go of Dave and stepped back. The abbot lifted the hem of his robe and danced a few steps of a private little jig of joy. Then, just as abruptly, he turned and left the room, the novitiate in tow.

"We've just witnessed another myth being born," Eugene muttered.

"Don't be a dick," Chris whispered.

Once outside, Chotari rounded up the porters. Soon, I was lost in my walking mantra, the monastery at Thyangboche a magical memory.

* * *

Chapter Eight:
Pumori

We passed the small village of Pangboche, with its own gompa, red-walled and pagoda-roofed—much as Thyangboche's gompa must have looked before the fire. Then we crossed boulder-strewn pastures, bisected by ancient crumbling stone walls and dotted by an occasional stone hut. In the summer, when the grass was green, these pastures would be home to grazing yaks, the huts home to Sherpa families faithfully watching their herds. But for now, the pastures and huts were bleak and empty and silent, buried in snow.

This was a hushed place: white snow and grey rock, the sigh of the wind, the tickle of a snowflake, the rhythmic scraping of boots and ice axes on the trail. We walked silently. We were now traversing a world of three elements: rock, snow and sky.

The grey of day was blending into the grey of dusk when we crossed the Khumbu Khola, just upstream from its junction with the larger Imja Khola. This would be our final major river crossing before Base Camp. As I crossed the delicate suspension bridge, I looked down into the foaming waters. The milky torrent rushed from the Khumbu Glacier, which tumbled from the southern flank of Everest and passed our mountain, Pumori. We were so close now.

We camped that night near Pheriche, one of the higher Sherpa summer settlements. We were at 14,000 feet—just shy of the elevation of Mount Rainier. The wind blew bitterly as we struggled by headlamp light to set up our tents.

In the middle of the night, my bladder woke me. I didn't want to wake Dave with my headlamp, so I stuck it in a pocket. Outside, the clouds had cleared. A half-moon bathed the surrounding peaks in silver and blue and violet.

I stumbled across our campsite toward a stone wall, where I figured I could relieve myself. When I reached it, I realized it wasn't stone. I took out my headlamp at last and switched it on.

The wall was a mountain of garbage: spaghetti cans, aluminum foil, butane cannisters, soiled underwear. There was enough debris to fill a five-ton truck. A cardboard box lay crushed nearby. Something was stencilled on its side. I bent closer with my headlamp to read the words: *SUMMIT 8000 EXPEDITION 1990.*

* * *

When I awoke the next morning, the tents were covered by a dusting of snow, and we had to shake them off before packing them.

We wound our way upward through the highest of the walled pastures. Soon, the last of the ancient walls were behind us. The open valley was littered with snow-covered boulders. We were slowly climbing the terminal moraine of the Khumbu Glacier: the broad heap of rocky debris that the advancing ice had been bulldozing ahead of itself for millennia.

The route was marked with rock cairns, yak turds, foil Capri Sonne pouches and PowerBar wrappers. We had lunch when we crested the terminal moraine. Ahead of us lay the gravel-covered tongue of the famed Khumbu Glacier.

* * *

We set up our tents that night at Lobuche, at 16,200 feet. We made camp much earlier than the previous night, and dined on yak entrail soup and freeze-dried turkey quiche. John and Sarah, feeling the altitude, were unable to hold down their dinners and went to bed early. The rest of us rhapsodized about how lucky we were to have the entrail soup to ourselves.

But the joking was mostly subdued. Even Eugene was less abrasive than normal. We were all starting to feel a bit nervous about what lay ahead. If all went well, we would be establishing our Base Camp the next day. We would be ready, at last, to begin climbing. The yak entrails roiling in my stomach had to share space with butterflies. Dave retired to our tent and fell asleep quickly after dinner. I sat up long after he'd started snoring, checking my gear.

I slept fitfully. I dreamed of a boat ramp on the river back home, and a game I used to play with Robin. I would put her in her red Radio Flyer wagon and lower her down with a length of rope tied to the handle. I had once played the game with Gretchen, and it had terrified her. But Robin was mesmerized by the river, and when the water lapped over the bed of the wagon, she giggled so hard that spit ran down her chin. In the dream, though, our roles had been reversed. *I* was in the wagon. Robin held the rope. I was terrified that she would let go. But her grip was steady.

*   *   *

The next morning, I was awakened by a hand in our tent door. Pasang thrust in two mugs of tea. As I sat up and took them, he said: "Today, Jeffrey-sahib, we reach Base Camp. Tomorrow, you climb like tiger."

After dressing, I poked my head out of the tent. The clouds had lifted. The gentle light of morning cast long shadows, making ridges look steeper, crevasses deeper. The snows were a soft pink, the ice an ethereal blue.

Jim Fairchild

Straight ahead, up the glacier, the jagged pyramids of Lingtren and Khumbutse soared to almost 22,000 feet. To their right was the Lho La, a notch in a fluted wall of ice and rock. George Mallory had climbed to the Lho La from the Tibetan side in 1921, and had been the first known white man to peer down upon the mountains that now spread out ahead of us.

Finally, my eyes rose to a stately pyramid to the left of the Khumbu Glacier: *Pumori*. Although I had studied every photo of the mountain I could find before our departure, I wasn't prepared for the real thing.

Mallory, upon that first glimpse almost seventy years earlier, had named it Pomo Ri, or Daughter Peak—appropriate for its spot beside and below Everest. The account of an early German expedition to Pumori had been entitled unabashedly "Der Schönste Berg Im Welt": The Most Beautiful Mountain in the World. Rising to 23,442 feet, Pumori was dwarfed by nearby Everest, Lhotse and Nuptse. And yet, though smaller, it had a symmetry, an economy of lines, that the others lacked. I followed its soaring ridges and steep faces to the narrow point of its summit. My heart raced with joy and fear.

The clouds blew in again. I would have to wait for days for another glimpse.

We followed the western lateral moraine of the glacier after breaking camp. I stumbled over the shifting rocks, unable to find a comfortable rhythm. I suspected altitude was partly responsible for my clumsiness. But it was also the enormity of what lay ahead.

We reached Gorak Shep by mid-afternoon. Large snowflakes drifted down onto the ice-bound lake. We pulled on down jackets and set up tents. This would be our Base Camp. Our porters, their teeth chattering, some still stubbornly barefoot, stacked their loads near the kitchen fly and—after being paid by Chotari—hurried back down the valley. I wanted to go after them and thank them. But they had no time for sentimental partings.

166

* * *

After breakfast the next morning, we sat under the kitchen fly. Sarah and John had both been sick all night and were still unable to eat. At least they were able to drink endless mugs of tea forced upon them by Chotari.

This would be a rest day—mandated both by altitude and by weather. Butch, standing at one end of the fly with a boot up on a crate, discussed our route, the East Ridge. He gave us a rundown of the timetable for route-finding, the stocking of camps and summit attempts. If the weather cooperated, we could be on top in ten days. We had enough food and fuel for twice that.

Butch brought up the touchy matter of summit teams. "There'll be two," he said. "I'll lead one, and Chotari and John the other. I'd like to get input as to who you'd all prefer to climb with. It's important that each of us feels comfortable with, and confidence in, our rope partners. I'll throw the floor open."

Eugene, sitting on a box, spoke up. "I can tell you who I *don't* want to climb with."

"And to whom do we refer?" Butch asked, drumming a pencil on his clipboard.

"Dave," Eugene said. He looked at Dave, then at me. "I've got to be sure anyone I tie in with is all there. And—excuse me for my bluntness—but I think ol' Davie Crockett has spent too much time in the ozone."

Dave, sitting between Eugene and me, grinned. "Thank you, good buddy," he said, mimicking Eugene's Tuscaloosa drawl. "I appreciate that rousing vote of confidence." He slapped Eugene's knee affectionately. Eugene flinched.

"Fair enough," Butch said. He jotted Eugene's name under his own on the left side of his clipboard. "Eugene, you can climb on my team. I'll put Dave on Chotari's and John's team. Anybody else

Jim Fairchild

have a strong preference?"

Sarah cleared her throat. "I have to admit that I initially felt the same way about Dave. I don't any longer. But, at the same time, it's important to me to get up this mountain. I need to know I'm climbing with a team as motivated as I am. I'd like to climb with Butch and Eugene." She smiled apologetically at Dave. "We just seem to come from very different worlds. I hope I haven't offended you." Dave nodded silently.

Butch wrote Sarah's name under his own. "Anybody else?" He swung his pencil in an arc. It came to rest pointing at me. "What about you, Jeff? I imagine you have a preference."

"I started climbing with Dave when I was a kid. When I'm tied in with him, I know what he's doing just by the feel of the rope. Put me on Chotari's team."

"Aw shucks, big guy," Dave said. He poked me in the shoulder.

"Moving right along," Butch said, scribbling. "What about you, Laslow?"

Laslow squirmed on a cardboard box across from me. His forehead was furrowed. He looked at Sarah and Eugene, then at Dave and me.

"I'd like to climb on Chotari's team," he said.

Butch raised an eyebrow, then his pencil. "Okay." He jotted Laslow's name under mine. "Just remember that once we pick teams, they won't change unless someone gets ill."

Laslow wore a transparent smile. It dawned on me why he'd chosen to climb with Dave and me: Laslow was afraid of succeeding on Pumori. Certainly he thought he stood a greater chance of success on Butch's team. But by climbing with Dave and me, he would have a ready-made excuse for failure.

Butch studied his clipboard. "That leaves you, Chris. Chotari's team has five members. Mine has three. Want to climb with Sarah, Eugene and me?"

"Actually," Chris said, "I'd rather fancied climbing with Dave and Jeff."

"I'm afraid that won't work," Butch said. "As a matter of safety, each team should have at least four members. My team's looking pretty darned strong. You stand a good chance of summitting with us."

"The summit isn't everything," Chris said.

"To be honest, Butch," Eugene said, "I'd just as soon have her on the other team. I think ol' Chris has spent too much time breathing too little oxygen, too. And I don't appreciate her British sarcasm."

"Bugger off, Eugene," Chris snapped.

"I apologize for Eugene's remark," Butch said. "I doubt he meant it."

"I sure as hell did," Eugene insisted. "I need to bag this summit so bad I can taste it. I want to climb with people who are gung-ho team players, who climb to *win*. The Himalaya is no place for wimps."

"Thank you for your subtle perspective," Butch said. "The fact remains, though," he said, looking back at Chris, "that I have to consider safety. Chris, I'm going to pencil you down for my team. You'll have a couple of days to adjust to the idea before we start climbing in earnest. I promise you I'll do everything to make you feel comfortable on my team."

"I respect that sentiment," Chris said. "But I've cleaved far too many chops to get here. Eugene resides on too low a rung of the evolutionary ladder for me to trust him on my rope."

Butch put his clipboard down. "I promise that neither Eugene nor I will drag our knuckles on the ground. What do you say?"

Chris held up her nose. "I say that you may suckle my hairy arse and call me Madame Shorty." She stormed off to her tent.

* * *

It was snowing hard the next morning; the wind whipped the snow past the tent flaps and shook the taut walls violently. It reminded me of the way the tent shook on Foraker, the night before the fall. I ventured out to the kitchen for breakfast, followed by Dave. The weather was so bad that only Laslow joined us. We wolfed down biscuits smeared with half-frozen yak butter, washed down hastily with tea, then ran back to our tents.

In the afternoon, the clouds broke. Brilliant sunshine poured down on Gorak Shep; the tent became insufferably hot. Dave and I crawled out.

The sun reflected off the frozen tarn like a mirror. It would have been a great day for ice-skating. High up, Pumori's ice sparkled like jewels. Sarah and John each sat against a boulder, as still and as white as marble statues. Both were still sick from the altitude.

Pasang started dinner under the kitchen fly, sagging low with snow. Butch and Chris stood nearby. They spoke quietly, intently, studying the toes of their boots.

"Nothing's set in stone yet," I could hear Butch say. "We have two very sick climbers right now. Teams could still change."

"I didn't mean to come off as a snot-nose," Chris said. "Lord knows we've got enough of that already. Please just bear in mind my preference if you *do* shuffle teams."

"You have my *promise*," Butch said. He patted Chris warmly on the shoulder. She returned the gesture.

After dinner, as darkness fell, we gathered under the kitchen fly around Pasang's bright lantern. Butch discussed plans for the next day. If weather allowed, he would lead the route toward our first high camp astride the East Ridge. He would establish an equipment dump halfway, and those on the other team would relay loads to the dump.

"What about our teams for tomorrow?" Eugene asked.

"We'll stick with what was agreed upon last night," Butch said. "Each team will be missing one person. Sarah and John have both agreed with me that they need another day to acclimate."

We had quickly split into an "A-Team" and a "B-Team": the former invariably enjoying the glories of route-finding and first crack at the summit, the latter invariably given the thankless support tasks: ferrying load after load, supporting the first team on its summit try. Eugene seemed relieved—assured, for now, of his place on the A-Team.

*   *   *

The next morning, the sun was shining on the peaks around us, the air was crisp, and there was only the slightest of breezes. Before breakfast, Dave and I dragged our gear out of the tent and packed for the day's carry.

Chris had her pack propped against a nearby rock. "Morning, lads," she said. "With any luck I'll muck up and get myself demoted to the B-Team yet."

Eugene joined us, his fleece cap perched jauntily on his head, a red bandanna around his neck. He was still ecstatic that he'd made the A-Team.

Laslow had finally awakened, and stuck his head out of his tent door. He had his video camera trained on us. "Come on, guys," he moaned. "Smile for the camera." Dave bent over and dropped his knickers.

The flaps of the tent beside Laslow's flew open. John's head appeared. He was on his belly, too weak to lift his face from the ground. "How's this?" he asked Laslow, and started retching. He'd been at it all night, and had now progressed to dry heaves. Laslow captured it on video.

Chris adjusted her crampons. "I'm rather worried about

John. He isn't taking to the altitude. Far worse than Sarah. He can't even keep fluids down. He's becoming dehydrated. He's got one foot across the line toward pulmonary edema, and he's kicking himself in the arse with the other."

"We'll have to keep an eye on him," Dave said. "Another day or two will tell."

The flaps to Butch's tent rustled. A pair of sock-clad feet appeared, then hands tugging on boots. Finally, a head emerged.

It wasn't Butch. It was Sarah. She was clad in longjohns. She rose, testing her balance, then wobbled toward the kitchen fly.

"Whoa, doggies," Eugene said. "What's *that* all about?" He watched as Sarah got a mug of tea from Pasang, flipped back her morning hair and drank.

"She was really doing the old heave-ho last night," Chris explained. "Butch took a look at her, and was worried about her condition. He suggested she spend the night in his tent, so he could keep an eye on her."

The tent flaps rustled again. Butch climbed out. He wore longjohn bottoms, inner boots and glacier glasses. His bronzed chest was narrow but muscular. He began to brush his teeth beside the tent. Realizing Laslow was taping him, he waved with his foamy toothbrush.

"Looks like Sarah just bagged her first 8,000-meter prick," Dave said.

"They've been spending a lot of time together," Chris said. "I have a feeling they haven't been discussing front-pointing technique."

* * *

Our route up Pumori would be entirely on snow and ice. We would wind our way upward from Base Camp and cross a broken serac field. The steep serac field lay under the precipitous East

Face, and would be exposed to avalanches.

The serac field would lead us to a broad snow shoulder halfway up the East Ridge, astride the Nepal-Tibet border. The near-level shoulder was a long climb from Base Camp, but was safe from avalanching, and was therefore a good site for Camp One. Above the shoulder, the East Ridge rose at a 45-degree angle to the summit. The first half of that length was broken by seracs, and we would have to thread our way through jumbled ice and crevasses. Once past the seracs, the last stretch of the route above the shoulder was a graceful, almost unbroken snow slope, rising at the same unrelenting angle straight to the summit. We would establish a final camp—Camp Two—just above the seracs, at the base of the final snow pyramid.

Butch's A-Team moved out shortly after first light. They would push as far toward the shoulder as their strength and conditions permitted. Butch was in the lead, with Chris in the middle and Eugene in the rear. Their packs were fairly light: they carried down parkas, water bottles and lunch, and the gear they'd need for route-finding: two spools of seven-millimeter rope for fixed line at tough spots, a dozen three-foot aluminum pickets to anchor the fixed ropes, and a few score bamboo wands to mark the path. Each wand had a strip of flame-red surveyor's tape tied to the end. The pickets and wands were strapped to their packs, and rose high above their heads. As the three waved farewell and departed Base Camp in the soft pink light of morning, the red tape on the wands fluttered above them like prayer flags.

The B-Team finally roped up at nine o'clock: Chotari in the lead, then me, then Laslow, with Dave in the rear. Although Chotari was quiet, concentrating on his duties as rope leader, his smile spoke of his happiness to be climbing at last. He looked as if a great weight had been taken off his shoulders. Our packs bulged with food and stove fuel, which we would cache at the dump midway to Camp One. Each of us was carrying at least sixty pounds. Chotari set a slow but steady pace, allowing us to synchronize our breathing with the rhythm of walking. We crossed the last of the rocky glacial debris past Base Camp and began traversing the serac field.

Laslow, unfortunately, seemed to have a hard time synchronizing. After an hour, at our first break, he collapsed on his pack in the snow. His chest heaved; his brow dripped with sweat. Dave tried to explain the rest-step and pressure-breathing, but Laslow insisted he already knew. He insisted his pack's suspension was the problem. The rest of us waited as Laslow tore apart the pack, puzzling over its straps and buckles, then tried to reassemble it. Finally, when we were all thoroughly chilled, Laslow was ready to move again.

By one o'clock we had gained 2,000 feet in elevation. We were midway to the shoulder. A hundred yards ahead of us, a cluster of wands marked the gear dump. The dump was in the lee of an ice wall, offering some protection from avalanches. At the dump, Chotari, Dave and I dropped our packs and sat down; Laslow collapsed nearby in the snow.

We were almost a thousand feet higher than the rocky spur known as Kala Pattar. It was from the top of Kala Pattar that many of the classic photos of Everest's south side have been taken. Our view was magnitudes better. We could look down onto the broad bowl of the broken Khumbu Glacier, the traditional site of Everest Base Camp. Chotari pointed out a sprawling cluster of red and orange and blue dots. They were the tents of the *Summit 8000* expedition, and the tents of half a dozen smaller groups. We could look across at the frozen chaos of the Khumbu Icefall, where the majority of deaths on the world's highest peak have occurred. Although most of the Western Cwm—the 20,000-foot-high frozen valley hidden between the walls of Everest and Nuptse—was still too high to be seen, we now had an awesome glimpse of the towering face of Lhotse, lying at the head of the Cwm. (Cwm, pronounced "coom," is Welsh for "valley.")

To the left of the Khumbu Glacier, beyond Lingtren and the saddle of the Lho La, soared Everest's West Ridge. This was the daring route pioneered by Unsoeld and Hornbein on Dyhrenfurth's 1963 expedition. To the right of the broken ridge soared the fierce Southwest Face: a complex of black cliffs, steep snowfields and rotten yellow rock bands. To the left of the West Ridge, in Tibet, I could see the snowy terraces of the Northwest Face, split high up by the scar of the Hornbein Couloir.

I was brought out of my trance by a deep boom. High up on Pumori's East Face, a serac had crumbled. We watched the debris roar down the face. For a few moments my whole body trembled, until I realized we were far from the avalanche's path. It fanned out across the fragile thread of footprints we'd stomped into the snow hours earlier, obliterating any trace of our passage for several hundred yards. I would be glad to spend as little time as possible on these slopes below the shoulder.

We hastily cached our loads. As we did, I looked toward the shoulder. I could see the three dots of the A-Team moving slowly but steadily up a broad snow dome below the shoulder. They were above the last of the serac field, and had only a simple but tiring slog remaining to their goal.

Our packs were nearly weightless now; I felt as if I were floating as we descended. Even Laslow seemed to enjoy our quick pace. The light-heartedness of our descent was soon blunted by thick clouds pouring over the shoulder from Tibet. Looking behind me, up toward the thick streamers driven by the jetstream, I worried about the A-Team. The winds higher up looked strong enough to blow the three of them off the shoulder like tumbleweed.

Halfway back to Base Camp, I looked ahead. In the distance, a figure was slumped in the snow. We drew closer. It was John. He leaned against his pack, bulging high with food and fuel. His face was ashen and drawn.

Chotari, coiling in the rope, chastised John. "You're crazy, little brother. You're still sick as a dog." John said sheepishly that he'd been directly in the path of the huge avalanche that spilled down the East Face, and had to sprint a hundred yards under his heavy pack to get clear. Dave asked him why he hadn't jettisoned his pack; John said he knew he'd be in enough trouble already without getting a whole load of precious food and fuel buried.

Chotari was angry that John had risked his health to attempt a carry. He made it clear that John was risking others as well: if a person were to fall ill high on the peak, rescuers would be in as much jeopardy as the rescued. We stashed John's load, marked it with wands, then helped him back to camp.

The sky boiled with angry grey clouds by the time we reached our tents. Sarah greeted each of us with a hug. I was surprised and yet touched. Pasang greeted us with a theatrical bow, then with scalding-hot tea and freshly baked sugar cookies. Dave and Laslow helped John into his sleeping bag. Chotari found Butch's binoculars and scanned the route for the A-Team. I stood beside him, squinting.

Finally, I saw one—then two, then three—dots emerge from the maze of the jumbled ice halfway down from the shoulder. "*Dynamite*," Chotari said. "First day rates a 9.8 on a scale of ten." He lowered the binoculars and clicked his fingers like Charlie Parker.

*   *   *

The A-Team stumbled into camp shortly after five o'clock. Their faces were windburned scarlet. They dropped their coils of rope in front of the kitchen fly and collapsed. The rest of us greeted them, hugging them until they cringed.

Pasang had prepared a high-altitude Surf and Turf: charbroiled yak T-bones smothered in onions and mushrooms, and freeze-dried shrimp scallopini. A carafe of Cabernet Sauvignon would have hit the spot, but we made due with a bottle of arak from Chotari's duffel bag.

John hobbled over from his tent to join us. He ate heartily, complimenting Pasang's artistry. But he had to leave abruptly to "worship the Boulder Goddesses." He returned as white as a sheet. He didn't touch his plate again, but found enough energy to laugh at Dave's arak-fueled jokes.

Butch, bone-tired after leading all day, hobbled off to bed after dinner. Eugene nearly fell asleep in his scallopini; Laslow helped him to his tent. Chris sat across from me under the flapping fly. By the light of the lantern, her burned cheeks glowed. She recounted for us B-Teamers what it was like to stand astride the very spine of the Himalaya.

"It was a mindless snow slog at first," she said. "And then we hit the top of the shoulder without warning. The brown Tibetan plain stretched out so far I could feel the curvature of the planet. If I get no farther on this mountain, I'll be a happy lass."

John listened closely, his arms over his aching stomach. More than anyone, he was enthralled by Chris's tale. Certainly he knew that—in his condition—he might never reach the shoulder, let alone the summit. Sarah, beside him, seemed almost as enraptured. She was still weak, too. Wishing us good night, she helped John up. The two departed for their tents.

I was eager for my own chance to spy the plain of Tibet. The bottle of arak made the rounds. The sky was black now, the wind blowing steadily. The fly over our heads drummed and snapped loudly. We had to shout to be heard over the din.

* * *

The next morning Dave and I were up before dawn. It would be the B-Team's day to climb all the way to the shoulder, while the A-Team—recovering from their push the previous day—made a

Jim Fairchild

leisurely carry to the dump.

When we were done packing, we headed for the kitchen. A steady wind blew, and the fly fluttered loudly. Chotari sat under the fly, finished with breakfast. He held a mug of tea in one hand; he was cleaning his teeth with a toothpick. He took the toothpick from his mouth and pointed with it toward Laslow's tent. Chotari shook his head doubtfully.

I could see Laslow's headlamp through the tent fabric. He was engaged in last-minute sorting. I could see his shadow: he was on his hands and knees in the tent, desperately digging through his Ziplocs.

"I'll be amazed if our friend reaches the shoulder, let alone the top," Chotari said. "You two help me keep an eye on him today."

Finally, Laslow was done packing. By the time he joined us, it was light enough to see ominous clouds hanging low over our route.

"Maybe we'll climb right through them," Chotari said. "Could be a beautiful day on the shoulder, and ugly as a runny yak turd down here."

As Laslow ate, a huge, jet-black bird swooped down out of the grey sky. It settled onto a mound of rubbish left by a previous expedition just beyond our tents. It flapped its wings once before folding them. Its wingspan must have been five feet. It grabbed old cans in its huge beak and crushed them like a vise, hoping to extract morsels. When it was done with the cans, the huge bird flipped them over its back. The cans clattered onto the rocks.

"Looks like a crow on steroids," I said.

"A gorak," Dave said. "One of the biggest members of the raven family. They've been seen at over 26,000 feet on Everest's South Col, picking through the remains of old camps."

"How do they survive the altitude?" I asked. I watched the huge gorak pick at an old beer bottle. The bird stuck its beak into

178

the bottle and lifted it over its head, testing to see if any of its contents remained.

"Who knows?" Dave asked. "The Sherpas consider them mystical creatures."

Chotari set down his mug. "The gorak freaks out Western climbers. It is a big, ugly camp robber. But we Sherpas are happy to share the mountains with the gorak. It is a wandering spirit."

I watched the gorak. Something was wrong. The beer bottle was stuck on its beak. It shook the bottle, trying to fling it off. It scratched frantically at it with one huge foot, then fell onto its side in the trash heap.

I walked cautiously toward it. The bird was back on its feet, shaking its head in a panic.

"*Easy*," Chotari warned. "Goraks can kick butt."

I approached the bird slowly from the front so I wouldn't startle it. I knelt down and spoke soothingly: "*Easy, gorak*." The bird answered by opening its wings and flapping at me. The gust almost bowled me over.

"You're friend Jeffrey is crazier than you," Chotari told Dave.

I reached out slowly. The bird took a step back, peering at me with one unblinking eye, its bottle-adorned head cocked sideways. And then I lunged for the bottle. The bird flapped its wings and raked at my hand with one taloned foot. It drew blood. I refused to let go.

The bottle suddenly popped off the gorak's beak. I rolled backward down the trash heap. When I came to a halt, I was looking up at Chotari.

The gorak flapped its wings. It was soaring my way. Chotari ducked. I could feel the rush of the air. I shielded my face. The huge bird passed over me so low I thought it was attacking.

But it didn't. Beating its wings mightily, the gorak swooped down the moraine. Lumbering upward, the bird finally disappeared into the grey sky. Just as it slipped from sight, it split the sky with a shriek. I gathered myself and stood up, tossing the beer bottle onto the trash heap. It crashed into shards. I brushed the dirt from my rump.

"It will be back," Chotari said. "You have been adopted."

"Maybe Pasang has a recipe for Kentucky-Fried Gorak," Dave said.

Laslow was at last ready. We hefted our packs. The A-Team was just rousing, and stuck their heads out their tents to wish us well. They would leave in a few hours to carry their loads to the dump.

John managed to stick his head out the door of his tent, too. His face was drained. But he gave us the most spirited send-off of all. "Onward and upward," he croaked. "Heaven awaits those who hump their loads."

*　*　*

Once roped up and in the serac field, we made steady progress. Laslow was our one weak link. He had a terrible time finding a breathing rhythm; we had to make frequent stops for him to catch his breath. Nevertheless, once he caught his breath, he was eager to plug upward—until the process repeated itself three or four minutes later.

The dark, roiling clouds loomed closer and closer over our heads. Finally, we were climbing upward into their very bellies. They were not as thick as I had thought: we could still make out the bamboo wands that marked our route. Soon, we had climbed above the clouds. They lay below us now like a soft silver carpet, blinding sunlight reflecting from their tops. The sky above was a pure cobalt blue: so clean and so clear I felt as if I were glimpsing the vacuum of outer space, and as if it were drawing me upward into it.

* * *

By midafternoon we were just below the shoulder. The winds must have been sixty miles an hour. They sucked the air from my lungs. All four of us were on our hands and knees, crawling over wind-crusted snow toward the final crest. Just ahead, I could see a half-dozen wands blowing wildly in the gale, bent over until the flagging whipped against the snow. The wands marked the cache left by the A-Team the previous day. We were almost on top.

The rope to Dave went slack. I fought forward on my hands and knees, my pack pressing down on the back of my head. For days, I'd dreamed of reaching the shoulder. Now, I just wanted to get the hell down.

And then I bumped into Dave. He was on his knees, hurriedly pulling sacks of food and bottles of stove fuel from his pack. Laslow had collapsed in the snow beside him, gasping for air, shielding his eyes from the wind-driven snow. His video camera hung caked in ice from his chest harness. He'd worn himself out trying to tape our climb. Chotari struggled with Laslow's pack, pulling out supplies to be cached.

Dave cupped his mittened hands to his mouth. "We need to get Laslow down fast. If we wait too long, he won't make it down on his own."

I wrestled off my pack. I added my load to the supplies Chotari was caching. He tamped snow over the buried treasure, then helped Laslow sit up.

"*Wait*," I shouted, and pointed to the crest of the shoulder. I unclipped from the rope; my figure-eight knot slithered away. Dave and Chotari were busy with Laslow; I crawled past them.

I didn't know whether the shoulder was corniced. I didn't know when the snow below me might give way, sending me plummeting thousands of feet to some glacier in Tibet. But I also didn't know if I'd ever make it back to the shoulder again.

Jim Fairchild

The snow beneath me stopped rising. I lifted my head into the gale. The wind blasted me with millions of tiny ice crystals. They worked their way behind my glacier glasses. I couldn't see. I felt my way forward.

The snow began to slope downward. I was now crawling into Tibet. I couldn't tell how much farther it was before the dropoff. Indeed, I might be over the dropoff already, on an overhanging cornice.

And then, just as I decided to turn back, the wind relented. *I could see.* Ahead of me, to the north, the wind-blown ice had parted. I looked out and down into a crystalline abyss.

Spreading out before me was the dusty plain of Tibet. On every horizon distant white mountain ranges beckoned.

The wind began to pick up again. I searched the horizon, trying to remember my Tibetan geography. I tried to spot the mountain named Kailas—the object of Art's dreams, the mountain he hoped would bring him—at last—some glimmer of peace. The ground blizzard slapped me in the face. My view of Tibet disappeared as suddenly as it had appeared.

I crawled back to the others, my lungs fighting for air. I reached the knot in the rope where I belonged, and struggled with the locking carabiner on my harness. My fingers had long ago gone numb; I had trouble catching the knotted loop in the carabiner. Just as I finally succeeded, and the carabiner gate snapped shut, a shadow caught my eye. Sitting in the snow, I looked up.

High above was the gorak. Its head bent into the blast from Tibet, the big bird hovered in place, tacking into the wind.

Dave and Chotari shouted at me to get my pack on. When I looked up, the bird had banked hard into the wind. It shot off sideways, disappearing east, toward the flanks of Everest.

"Did you see it?" I asked.

Dave shouted at me over the roar of the wind. "Get your goddamned pack on! We have to get down!" I looked at his face. I

182

couldn't understand why he was so angry. I couldn't believe he hadn't seen the bird.

This time, it was Chotari who shouted. *"Let's boogie, dammit!"* He stabbed downward with his mittened hand. Shocked by the urgency in his normally gentle voice, I pulled on my pack. I looked at Laslow, sprawled against the snow, his face blue. I came back to the here and now.

*   *   *

We stumbled into Base Camp in mid-afternoon, the wind still pushing at our backs. I could barely see. I remembered pulling my glacier glasses off to look at the bird high above. My eyes had been injured by the blast of ice crystals. Laslow was in even worse shape. Dave and Chotari helped him to his tent.

I crumpled into a heap against a crate near the kitchen fly. Pasang pulled off my mittens, checked my hands for circulation, then thrust a hot mug of tea into them. Chris knelt beside me now, staring curiously.

"I saw Tibet," I said. *"I crawled into it."* My lips cracked as I spoke. I tasted blood. I wanted to tell Chris about the huge bird that had hovered over us. But when I tried to speak again, only croaking noises came out.

Chris took the mug from my hands and put it down. She, too, examined my hands for frostbite. When she was satisfied, she tousled my hair. "It's okay, Jeffie." She put the mug back in my hands, wrapping my fingers around the handle for me. "Drink your tea, dear. The altitude has sapped you."

*   *   *

It was morning. Dave sat in the tent beside me, his sleeping bag around his waist. He was speaking through the open tent door

Jim Fairchild

with Chotari. Chotari told him that a low front had moved in from Tibet, nixxing climbing for the next few days. Dave told Chotari that I wasn't in any shape to climb today, anyway. Chotari said that Laslow was out of it, too, and would need rest. I rolled back over.

I finally crawled out of my sleeping bag for lunch. My eyes were windburned; I had to squint to see. Chris helped me administer eye drops. I was ravenous after the previous day's climb and after skipping breakfast. I inhaled the lunch Pasang had laid out. I wolfed down seconds, then thirds.

After lunch, Butch announced that those who were up to it could go with him on a short hike to Everest Base Camp, less than two miles away. The weather down low on the glaciers wouldn't be as bad as up on our mountain. I was eager to go. Although Dave thought I needed rest, I insisted I felt up to it. John and Laslow stayed back. We took daypacks.

We were soon strung out along the rocky debris of the Khumbu Glacier's lateral moraine. Before long, we were forced off the moraine and began ascending the glacier itself. We stumbled up the gravel-covered ice, skirting pools of meltwater, winding through forests of *névés penitentes*: pillars of ice carved by wind and sun into shapes bearing an uncanny resemblance to humans bent in prayer.

We reached a high point on the glacier. Below, on a rocky island in the midst of the ice, sprawled Everest Base Camp. Almost a hundred tightly packed tents spread out like a Boy Scout jamboree on the Fourth of July. Most belonged to the *Summit 8000* expedition. We dropped down and crossed the dirty ice.

We straggled onto the rock island. Like any other city, this one was dizzy with activity: a runner had just arrived, carrying mail from below. Porters had also just arrived with towering loads of fresh vegetables and live squawking chickens in wicker cages. High-altitude Sherpas, decked out in neon-green one-piece windsuits emblazoned with the *Summit 8000* logo, played hackysack by a shimmering meltwater pool.

Bearded Europeans who appeared to be clients sat about in similar neon-green outfits, sharpening crampons and sorting gear. Some mumbled to themselves as they sorted. *An expedition full of Laslows*, I thought.

A huge neon-green dome tent sat like a glowing pustule at the center of the city. Its roof was studded with television and radio antennae. Two satellite dishes were erected nearby; a snarl of cables ran back from them to the tent. The air reverberated with the cacophony of generators, from which cables ran underfoot in every direction, delivering power to the tent city. Behind the pustular tent sat two neon-green Alouette helicopters, bearing the expedition logo on their tail booms.

We passed a cavernous dining tent, its front flaps open. Inside, under glaring lights, we could see an Italian chef in sparkling white hat and apron put the finishing touches on linguini and clam sauce. It smelled from a distance like he wasn't holding back on the garlic. Two Sherpa assistants in identical white hats and aprons tried to unjam an industrial mixer. An Italian soccer match blared from a wide-screen color TV. I preferred the ambience of Pasang's humble but happy kitchen much better.

The next huge tent had a plywood patio out front. The patio sported tables with Cinzano umbrellas and a multitude of folding chairs. Sherpanis decked out in Bavarian Bierhaus outfits—low-cut white push-up corsets, lederhosen and pigtails—balanced trays of foamy beer steins ordered by impatient pretzel- and sausage-munching clients in neon-green. The beer steins, of course, were neon-green, and were emblazoned with the *Summit 8000* logo.

"I say," Chris chimed. "Has anyone seen the tennis courts?"

Dave pointed to four structures that looked like phone booths covered in black tiles. "Solar-powered outhouses," he explained. "They convert the gilded droppings of wealthy clients into methane and water. A sort of reverse alchemy."

Jim Fairchild

Up ahead, Butch had stopped in front of the central green pustular tent. He chatted with a neon-green man with a thick German accent and a greasy fleischwurst in his hand. Then Butch turned back to us.

"*Summit 8000* just paused route-finding higher up because of the weather," he explained. "They're holding a press conference inside the command tent. If we behave, we can listen."

We filed into the back of the tent. The interior was lit with harsh floodlights for camera crews from European, Japanese and American networks. They had flown by helicopter to Base Camp to cover the largest expedition in Everest's history. At the front of the tent, a long table sprouted a forest of microphones. Sitting behind the table were some of the climbers on the *Summit 8000* payroll. They came from Britain, the United States, Germany, France, Japan, Poland, Yugoslavia, Czechoslovakia. These superstars had been hired not just to short-rope clients up the mountain, but to lend credibility to the expedition. They squirmed under the glare of the lights, their folding chairs creaking. One chair remained empty.

The press conference started. The superstars, decked out in obligatory neon-green, were introduced. The questions were predictable: about the weather, the route, the chances for success. Dave began to fidget; he left the tent to look for Sherpa acquaintances.

Some of the reporters asked astute questions. One asked about the huge salaries paid the superstars. Another asked how many more monster expeditions Everest could suffer before it was turned into the world's highest landfill. Another asked whether— given enough money and leisure time—*any* talentless schmuck could get dragged up the world's highest mountain. The climbers were not comfortable being put on the spot. For all but the most famous of them, making a living as a full-time climber was tough. It required constant grovelling for corporate sponsorship and reluctantly taking occasional guiding gigs pulling clueless clients up mountains. The fat checks offered by *Summit 8000* had been too good to turn down, no matter the smell.

And then the press conference turned to inanities. A CNN reporter asked why they climbed. George Mallory had been asked why he wanted to climb Everest in the early 1920s during a tiresome lecture tour forced on him by his expedition sponsors. He snapped back, "Because it's there." The acid sarcasm had been lost to the multitude who have repeated the quote over the decades. What Mallory probably wanted to say was "Because it's there, *you blithering idiot.*"

A short man with a greying crewcut stumbled through a tent door behind the front table. He tripped over a microphone cable but caught himself. He carried a pipe in one hand, a mug of tea in the other. He apologetically squeezed past the others and took the last empty chair. My eyes still burned from Pumori's winds; I had to squint.

Another climber began to give her answer to the "why" question. Her words became a droning as I focused on the newcomer. He was a middle-aged Japanese man in a tattered turtleneck sweater instead of the requisite neon-green. As he settled into his seat, he relit his Meerschaum pipe.

It was Naomi Yokomura. I almost shouted his name.

I hadn't seen Naomi in sixteen years—not since he'd left me at the hospital in Anchorage, after the fall on Foraker. He had aged; he was still athletically built, but less stocky. His hair was salt and pepper.

I had frequently seen his name over the years in climbing journals. He'd lived a full life. He had climbed Everest via the South Col two years after Foraker, and attempted the first complete ski descent. The attempt—caught on film—had climaxed with a high-speed tumble down the Lhotse Face. A parachute brake halted his fall seconds before he would have plummeted over an ice cliff.

He returned to Alaska two years after that, making the first

Jim Fairchild

solo winter ascent of Denali. In 1982 he led a dog team to the North Pole. A polar bear killed three of his sled dogs and then ripped into his tent, inflicting serious wounds on Naomi before he jammed his rifle down the beast's throat and shot it. Naomi sutured his own wounds with the sailmaker's needle and thread from his repair kit, then continued northward. Still hungry for adventure after the North Pole, Naomi almost climbed K2 in 1986—the same summer thirteen climbers perished on the mountain. He had been one of the few wise climbers who retreated from the Abruzzi Shoulder when the weather turned bad.

And then, in 1989, he led a huge Japanese expedition that scaled both the Tibetan and Nepalese sides of Everest. Teams from each side rendezvoused on the summit. It had been the largest expedition in Everest history—until *Summit 8000*. Seven hundred yaks had carried loads to the Tibetan base camp on the Rongbuk Glacier, while 2,200 porters had humped loads to the Nepalese base camp. Some critics called the climb "Dust Clouds Over Everest." The trip had been underwritten by the Kirin Brewery and the maker of Japan's most popular seaweed soup.

Naomi had been on the first team to reach the top, and had made a live TV broadcast from the summit. I'd been transfixed by the broadcast. I had the impression that—despite all of its outward success—Naomi was uncomfortable with the huge scale of the expedition. It had been an eery experience to see on TV the face of the gentle man who had helped me down Foraker after the fall.

Now, the latecomer Naomi was being asked the "why" question. First, he apologized for being late. He said he'd been using one of the solar-powered outhouses, and the door had stuck. He'd been stranded until a passing Sherpa hacked off the latch with an ice axe.

When the laughter died down, Naomi grappled with the question. He crossed his ankles and took a long puff on his pipe. He blew smoke rings upward and watched them disappear. His eyes closed; I thought he was about to burst out laughing.

But he was too gracious to mock the reporter. He tapped his pipe against the table, then cradled its warmth between both hands.

"Why do I climb?" he asked. "A valid question, not deserving of mockery. I ask myself this often, when clinging to some rock face thousands of feet above a glacier—or when trapped in the midst of a crowded press conference." The audience roared.

He continued. "Why do I seek the heights? I seek the heights to remind myself of the *absurdity* of seeking the heights. I seek the heights to remind myself of the infinite wisdom of remaining home, before a warm hearth, beside my loving wife, in a room vibrating with the laughter of my children.

"When I reach the top of each new mountain—and find, again, only the same unearthly loneliness and relentless wind—I relearn this simple lesson. And then I descend carefully, and go home, laughing at my frail memory and grateful for all that awaits me. Until—in time—I once again forget this simple lesson. And then the absurd cycle repeats itself. And I once again find myself answering this same question in a press conference."

Naomi relit his pipe, blowing a cloud of smoke skyward— much to the consternation of the Czech superstar in neon-green beside him, who waved it away.

The press conference droned on. Staring at Naomi, I remembered the long days tentbound on Foraker's narrow ridge, the pinochle lessons, the copy of *An Annotated History of the Saint Louis Cardinals* he had lent me. I thought about the strange paths that had brought us together again.

The press conference finally concluded. The harsh lights were extinguished; news crews coiled cables and packed cameras. The audience began to file out. I remained behind.

Up at the front table, the superstars stretched their legs, then began to file out the door Naomi had entered earlier. Naomi stood, too, gathering his tea mug and tobacco pouch. He clenched his pipe stem between his teeth.

As the crowd filed past me, I shouted Naomi's name. He raised his head, peering. The tent was dark now; he couldn't see me behind the people leaving.

Finally, I was able to make my way past the last of the milling news crews, and weaved my way through the maze of folding chairs. "*Naomi!* It's Jeff Parson." I tripped over a folding chair and almost fell.

I reached the table behind which Naomi stood. He squinted at me blankly, still clutching tea mug and tobacco pouch, pipe between his teeth.

"Jeff Parson," I repeated. "Mount Foraker. 1974."

Naomi opened one eye wide. "*Jeffrey Parson. Mount Foraker.*" He opened the other eye wide. He dropped the tobacco pouch to the table, then the tea mug. It spilled. We both lunged for it. The pipe fell from Naomi's mouth and bounced off the table. I let go of the mug and caught the pipe midair.

It was red-hot. I juggled it, then gingerly passed it back to Naomi, who had by now righted his tea mug and was wiping up the spill with a press release.

"Thank you," he said. He put the pipe down and stepped around the table. "Jeffrey-san," he said. "You are no longer a boy." He took my hand and squeezed it tightly between both of his. His hands were wet with tea.

"You've changed, too," I said.

"I'm an old fart now," he conceded. There was a pause as he looked *through* me—at a memory, I assumed, of a day on a mountain far away in space and time, when three of his dearest friends perished.

And then he spoke. "How about those '74 Cardinals, Jeffrey-san!"

"How about those Cards," I repeated. I gave him a high-five. We laughed.

Naomi sighed. "Lou Brock set the record for stolen bases. It was a good season until we ran into the Pirates."

We both fell silent. Naomi straightened the cuffs of his tattered sweater. I cleared my throat. "I still dream about your friends," I said. As soon as I said it I realized it may have been too much, too soon.

Naomi gently patted my shoulder. It was obvious he didn't squander such endearments lightly. "That is ancient history. What happened simply *happened*. Accept it. Life is like my grandmother. Some days she invites you in for sweetcakes and tea. Other days, she chases you with a broom as if you were a cat that had just sprayed her bonsai. Did you get my letter?"

"Yes," I said. "I still have it somewhere."

"We shall not dwell on the past, then," Naomi said. "I shall add, though, that when I first climbed Chomolongma, in 1976, I left photos of all three of the boys in the summit snows. It was a sunny, windless day. That had been the dream of all three, to some day rest atop the Goddess Mother, with their faces lifted to the sun. And now they do. Their spirits are mirthful now. Of this I am convinced, with all my heart. Let your spirit be mirthful, too."

"Thanks," I said. I had dreamed of seeing Naomi again for so may years that it was a bit too much. I couldn't speak for a moment.

"And David-san?" Naomi asked. "Did you finally hear from him?"

"We're both here to climb Pumori," I said. "Our camp's just across the glacier. He was here in the tent awhile ago. He got bored and stepped out."

"Most understandable. How *is* David? I've heard the Sherpas mention his name. It seems they all know him."

"He's been climbing a blue streak. He's been living in Namche Bazar with Ang Dorje."

"Poor Ang Dorje," Naomi said. "I climbed with him on my

191

first trip to Chomolongma. David is honored to have been taken under his wing." Naomi rubbed a cramp in his leg. "Give my regards to David. After what happened on Foraker he carried himself with a dignity beyond his years. Tell him I would be most pleased to see him."

We shook hands. "Good luck on Everest," I said. "If the weather cooperates, maybe you'll make it to the summit a third time."

"I have no summit aspirations," Naomi said. "I'm not sure why I came this time, to be honest. I don't need the money. It's as if something drew me back here, despite my better judgment."

"What about the answer you gave the reporter?" I asked.

"Pseudomystical sophistry," he said, winking. "Good luck on Daughter Peak. Maybe we'll get a break with the weather, and we can get up our mountains and go home, where we belong." Then, juggling pipe and tea mug, he gave me a hug.

* * *

The rest of our group was waiting for me outside. They were impatient to get back to Gorak Shep for dinner.

"Dave," I said, pulling on my pack. "I just saw Naomi."

"It's a small world. Hope you said hello for me."

"He's working for *Summit 8000*. He'd love to see you. Maybe we could stay awhile."

Butch shrugged his shoulders in approval. But Dave waved a hand, motioning that we should leave. "Let's not keep Pasang waiting for us," he said. "We'll hold up dinner." We began to hike across the darkening glacier toward our Base Camp. I brought up the rear of the column, behind Dave.

"Maybe we can come back tomorrow," I suggested, "if the weather's still too bad to climb. Seeing Naomi might help you put Foraker into perspective."

Dave slowed. As we lagged behind the group, he turned. "What makes you think I haven't put Foraker into perspective?"

"I just mean that you were so damned young." I stumbled on the ice. "I know how you must have felt. I think you should speak with Naomi."

Dave saw the gap that had grown between us and the rest of the group and quickened his pace. "You don't have an *inkling* about how I felt. But Foraker was a million years ago. I live in the here and now."

Breathing hard, I tried to keep up with him. Before I could apologize, he continued: "If either of us has had a problem dealing with Foraker, it's *you*. You wake me up at night with your thrashing. My guess is you're still falling in your dreams. My guess is you still see the three of them falling down that gully. My guess is the guilt's still eating you alive."

I was stunned. "*Of course* I feel guilty," I stammered. I came to a halt. I tried to hold back my words, but they flew out. "Of course, it wasn't *me* who cut the rope."

Dave lurched to a halt and turned. We faced each other on the gloomy glacier, having finally, for the first time on the trip—for the first time in sixteen years—broached the subject that stood like a brick wall between us.

For a moment, I thought he might hit me. I didn't know him well enough anymore to rule it out. Instead, he hugged me. "I know it's been hard," he said, patting my back. "We're going to have time on Pumori to sort it out."

Night had fully fallen. A blanket of clouds hung low, but it was starting to break up. Far ahead of us, weaving across the glacier toward Gorak Shep, I could make out the comforting pools of light cast by our companions' headlamps. Dave and I ran through the moonlight to catch up.

* * *

The next morning the weather had relented. The A-Team—including a much-revived Sarah—headed back for the shoulder, intent on establishing Camp One. They carried two tents, stoves, cooking gear and more food and fuel. The rest of us bade them good luck, then slept a few more hours.

I awoke again at eight o'clock. I got dressed and met Dave and Chotari under the kitchen fly. Laslow was still in his tent sorting Ziplocs.

I groggily grabbed a mug of tea. "Looks like a great day to climb."

"Did you see your friend?" Chotari asked.

I looked around, expecting to see Naomi.

"In front of the tent," Dave said. "You walked right by him."

I looked back. There, perched imperiously upon a boulder, basking in the morning light, was the huge gorak. It flexed its jet-black wings, squinting as happily as a cat. It preened an errant feather.

"My Dad warned me about befriending strays," I said.

As soon as I spoke, the bird focused on me. It let out a shriek. It leapt in three mighty bounds to another boulder beside the kitchen fly, nearer us. It stared impatiently at me.

"It's found a soulmate," Chotari said, chuckling.

By the time breakfast was done, I'd given the gorak half my potatoes, two biscuits and a fried egg. It flipped the egg over a wing; it stuck to a rock and quickly froze in place. The egg was still there, mummifying in the thin air, when Dave and I finally left Pumori.

* * *

Our B-Team left camp at ten. John stayed behind. Chotari

was worried. If John didn't start to adjust to the altitude soon, he would have to descend. Pasang promised to look out for John today, but Chotari didn't seem much relieved.

We carried huge loads of food and fuel to the dump halfway up the serac field. The air was still, the sun brilliant. We stripped down to longjohn tops, the snow reflecting the sun's heat like an oven.

When we got back to Base Camp, Butch radioed. His team had reached the shoulder just after three o'clock. He said it was almost windless there; they were pitching the tents and starting dinner. In the morning—if the weather held—they would push toward the planned site of Camp Two, just below the final, graceful ramp to the summit. Our task, that day, would be to haul loads to Camp One on the shoulder, where we would spend the night. The A-Team, after getting as far as they could that day, would descend past us to Base Camp. The B-Team would have a chance to push the route higher the following day.

I was relieved to see, upon returning to Base Camp, that the gorak was gone. I hoped to hear that Pasang had it in a kettle. I took my stiff double boots off and lounged under the kitchen fly with the others. John, a towel hanging over his head, managed to hobble over and join us. Pasang served dinner. John took one look at the yak au gratin, then went to worship the Boulder Goddesses. We got to bed early, anxious about our long climb the next day.

* * *

We arose long before sunrise. Pasang already had his stove blazing, a big pot of tea awaiting us as we staggered to the kitchen.

John had been so sick that morning he couldn't even open the tent door when Chotari went to check on him. "Sorry, brothers," Chotari said. "But if he doesn't improve soon, I will stop climbing and help him hike out. John's a good boy with a big heart. I've

195

seen too many dead climbers." He said he had discussed John with Butch on the radio the night before. Chotari had suggested John should descend at least to Pheriche. Butch had insisted John would be needed for the summit push, and had urged patience.

Dave and I told Chotari we would support whatever decision he made. He thanked us. Finally, Laslow was ready, and we were on our way: climbing through the grey of pre-dawn toward the shoulder.

We were across the serac field before the sun broke over the jagged wall of Lhotse. One second we were bathed in a soft pink glow; the next second we were blinded, and had to dig out our glacier glasses. We continued upward at the slow but steady pace set by Chotari—two deep breaths, then one step; two deep breaths, then one step. Laslow alone seemed to struggle, unable to establish a rhythm.

Dave kept trying to explain to Laslow the basics of the rest-step, the basics of pressure-breathing. Dave was incredibly patient with Laslow. It dawned on me how Dave could have been a successful guide, had he chosen that path. Laslow, gasping, protested that the problem wasn't him. His clothing wasn't breathing properly, despite the manufacturers' claims. He kept forcing us to halt while he played with the armpit zippers on his expensive new parka.

"Concentrate on your breathing rhythm," Dave urged again.

"*It's not me,*" Laslow insisted. "My parka isn't breathing!" He yanked so furiously at a zipper that I could hear a seam rip. He flung a broken zipper pull into the snow. I had to marvel at the elegance of his self-deception: how he had devoted so much time and energy to his gear, and how that gear now provided him yet another graceful excuse for failure.

Despite Laslow's problems, we slogged onward. We passed the serac field safely and began the long climb up the bulging snow dome. I could never quite see the top. It was always just out of sight, hidden by the dome's bulge.

It was only when I'd completely forgotten about the top—my mind locked into a simple mantra of step-breath-breath, step-breath-breath—that we crested onto the last broad curve of the shoulder. The arching expanse was now home to two tents. Their taut walls drummed in the wind. Prow-shaped snowdrifts had already begun to grow in their lee. We crawled the last few yards across the windswept snow.

Dave and I shared one tent that night, Chotari and Laslow the other. After settling in, Dave and I crawled through the growing darkness to the other tent for dinner. Chotari fumed silently over the one-burner stove. Laslow was too busy sorting Ziplocs to help cook. Dave and I pitched in as best we could without tipping anything over in the cramped tent.

We discussed the whereabouts of the A-Team. It was now nearly dark, and they hadn't made it back down to the shoulder. Finally, after twice knocking over the kettle of melting snow, Chotari said it was time to try the radio.

While Dave took over the stove, Chotari began searching for the radio beneath sleeping bags and boot liners and rancid socks. A cackling arose from beneath a tall stack of Laslow's Ziplocs. Chotari knocked them over—much to Laslow's horror—and found the radio.

It was Butch. His team had made rapid progress up the ridge that day, establishing the final camp at 22,700 feet—a mere 742 feet below the summit. The route beyond looked straightforward: a beautiful, curving snow ramp that rose to a point in the sky where all ridges converged. If the wind had not grown, he said, his team could have nabbed the summit and dashed back down.

Butch announced a change in plans. His A-Team would stay overnight at the new Camp Two, or Ridge Camp. They had just enough food for one more day of climbing, he said; and, because the day's conditions had been so excellent, it would be stupid not to

Jim Fairchild

push a little farther the next day. They would then descend all the way to Base Camp that next evening.

"What if you make the summit tomorrow?" Chotari asked, hunched over the radio. He understood what was being pulled. The A-Team would consume all the food at the high camp, leaving nothing for the B-Team's turn at pushing the route.

Butch's voice oozed with sincerity. "The summit's not necessarily our goal tomorrow. We simply want to push the route a little farther while conditions are good and while we're feeling strong."

"And yaks fly out of my butt," Chotari muttered, his thumb off the TRANSMIT key. "Fine," he told Butch. "Climb safely." Disgusted, Chotari clicked off the radio.

* * *

I lay in my sleeping bag after dinner, listening to the howling wind outside the tent. The wind made me realize how alone we were. But it finally lulled me to sleep.

I was awakened from a bad dream at two o'clock by a heavy pressure on my chest. Panic-stricken, thinking I was having a heart attack, I tried to sit up, but couldn't. I was trapped. I ripped open my sleeping bag and reached upward. The icy tent canopy was only inches from my face. A pole had snapped in the incessant gale.

"Get your gear on!" Dave yelled, his headlamp shining in my eyes. He grabbed his boots. "We've got to move to the other tent before we're blown off the mountain."

The four of us spent an eternity waiting for dawn wedged together in the one undamaged tent. Nobody slept. We all knew that it was just a matter of time before this tent blew apart, too. I remembered that night on Foraker sixteen years earlier, when Dave and I laid awake and watched our tent's seams unravel under the onslaught of the hellish winds.

198

I wondered if I was doomed to repeat the same stupid mistakes over and over again in my life. I wanted off this mountain. I wanted to go home to the daughter I was just beginning to know. I made a silent vow, as Laslow farted against my thigh, not to forget that resolution in the light of day.

When the sun arose, we hurriedly dressed and packed. We crawled out into the wind—still unabated—and collapsed what was left of the tents so they wouldn't blow away while we were gone. We tied into our ice-encrusted rope and raced down the mountain. Even Laslow moved swiftly.

Higher up, in still more dreadful conditions, Butch's team was doing the same. When they met up with us that evening at Base Camp, it was clear that they had narrowly escaped with their lives. Sarah was so exhausted that Chris and Eugene had to help her across the final stretch of moraine. Chris's face was so red and swollen from the wind that I thought she was a Sherpa. Even Butch, bringing up the rear, looked wiped out. I hoped he realized that his greed for the summit had put his team in peril.

Dave and I helped Sarah to bed. She smiled up at Dave. "Thank you. I never told you how sorry I am about Ang Dorje." Dave was too stunned to speak. He helped Chotari check Eugene for frostbite—despite Eugene's protests—while Pasang poured Butch a mug of steaming tea.

Once we were sure the A-Team was okay, I took a walk. I walked past Butch, collapsed under the kitchen fly, tea mug in hand, his face battered raw by the wind. We stared silently at each other. I walked out across the moraine into the darkness and the wind. I walked until the glow of Pasang's lantern was almost hidden by the jumble of boulders.

And then, just when darkness had almost swallowed me completely, I realized how utterly alone I was without the others, regardless of how much they disappointed me. I steered back toward the light. Chotari sat alone now, his sad smile warming my

199

heart.   Finding Pasang's playing cards, I tried to teach Chotari
pinochle, but realized I'd forgotten all the rules.

*   *   *

The storm raged three days.   We waited two more for the
snow to consolidate, as Dave and Naomi and I had failed to do on
Foraker. During those five days in camp, I struggled with my desire
to go home, and with my responsibility to my fellow climbers.
Finally, I resolved to get the climb over with, to do my part to help
the others up the mountain—and then to get home safely again,
where I would start to sort out the chaos I'd made of my life. The
mountain hardly seemed to matter now. I wondered if I'd already
found what I'd come to discover, half a world away from where I
belonged.

On the sixth day, we arose to a brilliant, cloudless sky. The
air was cool and hushed, like an unexpected kiss. Not a trace of
windblown snow could be seen streaming from the ridges high
above. On that day, we set out—at last—for the summit snows of
Daughter Peak.

*   *   *

Chapter Nine:

Where Ridges Converge

We were not a happy lot that brilliant morning as both teams headed upward—the A-Team to begin their push for the top, the B-Team ferrying one last load of supplies in support before we began our own push for the summit the next day.

Of all the glum faces, Chris won the prize. Her face was scabbed from her team's harrowing descent six days earlier. But the windburn was only one source of her heat.

Chris and Butch had been locked in a fiery argument the night before, under Pasang's kitchen fly, before the dinner dishes had been cleared. Knowing we were finally headed for the top, Chris had once again asked to join the B-Team. She told Butch that she would feel more comfortable climbing with us miscreants. But Butch said that because nobody on the B-Team—meaning, really, Laslow—wanted to switch places, she was stuck on the A-Team.

Chris was indignant. She offered to sign a statement declaring her contract with Big Mountain Guides null and void: that, in effect, she was leaving the trip, and could then link up with the B-Team just as if she were a solo climber in the Alps who shares a rope with strangers on a crowded route out of convenience.

Butch examined the toes of his boots, then shook his head. He said she would still be eating Big Mountain Guides food and using Big Mountain Guides equipment. He reminded her that the contract specified that she would bow to the chief guide's judgment on all safety matters, and that the contract was in effect until she had safely climbed onto a departing jet at the Kathmandu airport. Then he added: "I'm sorry. You have two choices. You can climb on my rope. Or you can stay in camp and help Pasang nurse John."

"Nurse on this," Chris had replied, flipping him the middle finger. She stormed off, so mad she tripped over a tent guyline and fell, cutting her hands on the rocky ground. But she gave her final answer a few minutes later, when we could see her headlamp inside her tent, casting shadows as she packed. She would climb with Butch.

I suspected that Butch's true reason for keeping Chris on the A-Team was that he knew how vital she was to his *own* chance for the summit. Sarah and Eugene were motivated, but they were amateurs. Chris, on the other hand, had behind her two decades of hardcore unguided alpine ascents. Her credentials were unimpeachable. Her credentials were, in fact, far more impressive that those of many professional guides, who spend their seasons making dozens of slogs up the same handful of relatively easy tourist routes on mountains like Rainier. Butch certainly realized she was the strongest, most reliable partner on his rope.

Chotari, too, was incensed tht morning as we headed up the lower snow fields of Pumori. Minutes after Butch's argument with Chris, Chotari had confronted Butch about John's condition.

During the last week, while we were trapped at Base Camp by the weather, John had managed to get dressed each morning and join us for breakfast. He no longer projectile-vomited after each meal—but only because he had almost given up trying to eat. His once-boyish cheeks were now gaunt and sunken. He must have lost twenty pounds. Chotari told Butch that John was at risk for pulmonary edema. Chotari insisted that John should descend immediately: at least as far as Namche Bazar, and perhaps even to

Kathmandu.

Butch argued that John had weathered the worst of his mountain sickness. He said that John had no business above Base Camp, but that he had stopped vomiting, and could certainly hang on for the week or so that—given good weather—it would take both teams to get up the mountain and back.

"Hire two porters to take him down," Chotari insisted. "Radio Namche Bazar tonight. The porters can be here tomorrow."

"I'm sorry, Chotari," Butch said. "But you're out of line. John will be fine at Base Camp. Besides, you know that this expedition is operating on a slim profit margin. We can't afford unplanned expenses. You have a well-deserved reputation for taking care of your sahibs. That's why I asked for you. Don't worry. John will be fine."

"*Yak droppings*," Chotari had muttered. Then he, too, went off to pack.

Next in line to vex Butch's patience had been Eugene. He had walked with a nervous bounce to the kitchen fly and sat down in front of Butch. He wanted to talk about Sarah.

"What now?" Butch asked, rolling his eyes.

"She was worn out when we got down from the ridge," Eugene said.

"We *all* were," Butch said. "Me as much as anybody."

"Sarah wasn't just tired," Eugene insisted. "She was *shot*. She had to be dragged like a sack of spuds."

"She's had almost a week of rest," Butch said. "She looks as strong as anybody now. She just pushed herself too hard. In a couple of days, when we're going for the top, you'll be glad she's on your rope, helping you up."

Eugene cracked a knuckle. "She could get us into hot water."

Butch lost it. "*Listen*," he said, leaning so close that Eugene cowered back. "My job is to make sure that each of you gets a fair chance at the summit. It's fair that Sarah gets that chance. She's paid her dues. And it's fair that *you* accept that fact. If you can't, I don't want you on this mountain. You can stay here with Pasang, whistling 'Dixie' and peeling carrots. *Get off my nuts.*"

"Don't get me wrong," Eugene sputtered, raising his palms in surrender. He stood. "I respect your authority more than anyone. I figured it was a matter of safety. Sorry I said anything." He sprinted for his tent, tail tucked.

Butch rose. He drained the last of his tea, then handed Pasang the mug. He looked at Dave and me and groaned. "God," he said. "I *detest* ass-kissers." Then he, too, headed for his tent.

Laslow came from his tent and joined us. His nostrils were packed with gauze thick with burn ointment. On our last trip up the mountain he'd forgotten to put sunscreen in his nasal orifices, and sun reflecting off the snow had burned them beet-red. He carried a Ziploc in one hand.

Dave and I waited for Laslow to speak. He stood silently, fidgetting with his Ziploc. Finally, I had to ask. "Is something the matter, Laslow?"

Laslow pulled an altimeter out of the Ziploc and handed it to me.

"Nice," I said. "Swiss. Three hundred bucks." I handed it to Dave.

Dave squinted. "5,100 meters. Nice altimeter." He handed it back to Laslow.

"Don't you get it?" Laslow asked. "Gorak Shep should be 5,160 meters."

Dave grinned. "That's because of this beautiful high pressure system that's moving in. It throws off the altimeter."

Laslow rolled his eyes. "Thanks. I went to college for nine years. I know that. My point is this: wherever there's high pressure, there's low pressure right behind."

"Well, Doc," Dave said. "You zinged me. Yes, as a matter

of basic logic, good weather is eventually followed by bad. And bad weather is eventually followed by good. The yin-yang of meteorology."

"I'm worried," Laslow said. "We could be lulled into a false sense of security by this good weather. We could climb up onto that ridge and get trapped by what's coming in behind it. *WHAM. BAM.* We're history."

Dave motioned for Laslow to sit beside him. "Listen, Laslow." He put an arm around Laslow's shoulders. "You have every reason to be concerned. The weather should always be watched on any mountain—especially on a mountain this big. You can rest assured that Butch, as head guide, and Chotari, as our rope leader, will be keeping their very experienced eyes on it. They radio Kathmandu every day for the latest forecasts." He took his arm from around Laslow and reached for his tea. "And you can count on me, too. I've climbed and lived in these parts a fair bit now, and I think I've developed a good feel for the weather. I won't let anything sneak up on us."

"You think this good weather will last?" Laslow asked, poking at his glasses.

"*Nothing* lasts forever. But I suspect we'll have a solid week of good weather."

"Great," Laslow said.

"The weather's not *really* the issue, is it?" Dave asked.

"No."

"You're worried," Dave said. "About whether you'll fail. Actually, about how to *make sure* you'll fail—but gracefully, so you can go home and leave all this climbing stuff behind you once and for all."

A weight seemed to lift from Laslow's shoulders. "*I'm scared stiff.* I just want to get it over with and go home."

"Join the club," Dave said. "We all get butterflies. None of us will sleep well tonight. Except maybe Eugene. And if he knew half as much as he thinks he does, he'd toss and turn, too."

"*You* get butterflies?" Laslow asked.

"You're darned tootin.' Before every climb. I've got a proposition."

"Yes?" Laslow's glasses slipped down his nose again.

"We'll work together," Dave said, squeezing Laslow's knee. "You help me to the top, and I'll help you to the top. A deal?"

Laslow smiled. "A deal." They shook. Laslow stood. "Do you think John will be safe down here? I could stay with him. I'm a doctor, after all."

"I need you on the mountain," Dave said. "I'm going to be depending on your help."

"Thanks," Laslow said. He looked like a different person. He began to go.

"You forgot your Ziploc," Dave said. He handed it to Laslow.

*   *   *

Both teams reached Shoulder Camp shortly after two in the afternoon. The B-Team added our loads of food and fuel to the camp cache. The A-Team rehabilitated the two collapsed tents. They dug them out of hard windpacked snow and replaced the damaged poles.

Chotari stomped his boots in the snow and slapped his mittens together, impatient to head back down. Our team would be back up soon enough for own summit try; right now, we were in support of the A-Team. Laslow was impatient, too. He had his pack on and was clipped back into the rope. I was impressed with how strongly he had climbed today, despite the heavy video camera slung across his chest. He had finally listened to Dave's entreaties about pressure-breathing and rest-stepping.

Before roping up, Dave and I bade farewell to Chris. She

hugged each of us, slapping our backs. "Climb safely," Dave told her. "I want the first dance at our victory shindig."

Dave bade farewell to Sarah, too. She was inside her tent, inflating her sleeping pad. She lifted an arm to wave, but was wracked by violent coughing.

As I clipped into the rope, I watched Sarah. It was hard to believe that this was the same woman who had become unglued when the Sherpa boy surpassed her on the boulder. The mountain seemed to be changing her. The mountain was *humbling* her. It was teaching her that ego was dead weight up here. I hoped her awesome drive would see her safely to the top and back.

The rope tugged at my waist. "Good luck, Sarah," I shouted over the wind. I had a gut feeling she'd need it. She turned, surprised and pleased, and waved.

* * *

The B-Team was back in Base Camp by five o'clock that evening. Dave and I stumbled toward our tent; it had been a long day. John's tent was open. He was lying on his sleeping bag, his hands folded across his chest like a mummy, a towel tied over the top of his head with a piece of cord. He wore his glacier glasses, even in the shade of the tent's interior. He looked like a young, emaciated Yasir Arafat recovering from a hard weekend of Tunisian nightclubbing.

"Knock, knock," Dave said, squatting outside John's tent door.

John didn't move. "Hark," he croaked. "Methinks I hear an emissary of the living."

"You feeling that bad?" Dave asked.

"I've glimpsed the Stygian gloom." Ever so slowly, John rolled with a hiss onto his belly, coming to rest with his chin in his hands. "I'd like to eat just *one* cracker and know I won't have to look at it again shortly."

Dave said he might be able to help. He went to our tent and began digging through his things. When he came back, he carried a small oil-stained square of muslin. The corners had been tied together, making a palm-sized bundle. He set it down and untied the corners.

"Hash," Dave said. "I was saving it for a victory fandango. But humanitarian imperatives dictate immediate medicinal dispensation." He fished in a pocket and pulled out a small brass pipe. Sitting on the gravel and crossing his legs, he broke off a small chunk of the hash. He packed it into the burnished pipe and lit it.

Dave disappeared inside a thick blue cloud. Then he passed the pipe to John. "This does more for nausea than anything known to modern medicine," Dave said. John inhaled. I thought his chest would explode from the coughing.

"Try once more, Johnny-O," Dave said. "It shouldn't feel as harsh the second time."

True enough, the second time there was no coughing. After John handed me the pipe, he exhaled a thin stream of blue smoke. "*Whoa, dude,*" he croaked.

"I'll leave this with you while we're on the mountain," Dave said. He carefully reknotted the cloth and slid the hash inside John's tent. "Like any other medicine, use it judiciously. It won't do me any good up high. It'll do you more good, down here high." Then Dave saw the pipe in my hand. "Partakest thou?" he asked.

I hadn't smoked dope since a single episode in high school—sitting around a campfire while backpacking with Dave. I had been revolted by the acid burn in my lungs and the pungent smell. I don't know what possessed me to try it now. After the chest-splitting coughing subsided, I felt a profound dread that had haunted me for days suddenly *dissolve*—as instantly as frost sublimating in the first rays of the morning sun. I started giggling uncontrollably at my coughing. My face soon hurt from grinning.

"We'll be thinking of you up there, Johnny-O," Dave said, taking another hit. "If only some of our other compatriots had half your fair, young spirit. I feel like we're extras in a B-movie called 'Mountain of the Living Dead.'"

Soon, Pasang was clanging pots together, announcing dinner. We stumbled to the kitchen fly. Pasang had slaved all afternoon over a kettle of yak Carbonara with a steaming side of hot buttered chapatis. For the first time in weeks, John was able to eat and hold down his food. He wolfed down seconds, and then thirds. The rest of us, amazed and grinning, watched while John wiped the empty kettle clean with a chapati. Done at last, he wiped his mouth primly on a corner of his towel mufti. He burped; everything stayed in place. He thanked Dave for the "medication." Laslow, who didn't know the nature of the medication, raised an eyebrow but asked no questions. Chotari beamed. A great weight seemed lifted from Chotari's tired shoulders.

* * *

We were on our way the next morning, carrying one last load of food and fuel. By mid-afternoon we had occupied Shoulder Camp, vacated by the A-Team. They were on their way up to Camp Two, or Ridge Camp, which they'd established just before the storm that had blasted us all off the mountain. As we unpacked, I glanced up the icy ramp that rose into the sky. High up, almost indiscernible against the immensity of the ridge, I could make out four tiny dots. If I watched long enough, I could make out movement. They were too far away to see the rope that joined them.

Dave and I joined the others in their tent for dinner. At eight, Butch radioed Chotari and said the A-Team was safely ensconced at Ridge Camp. They'd dug out and repaired the tents and were melting snow for dinner. They were all raring to go for the summit the next morning. He said they all felt strong, and that the weather looked superb. Butch said they'd be on their way by three in the morning. Early starts were a wise tradition in mountaineering. Climbers could take advantage of firm snow before the midday sun created potential avalanche conditions. And climbers could be back down to safety before afternoon cumulus developed.

Chotari listened patiently to the radio. Finally, when Butch was done, Chotari replied. He said we'd be at Ridge Camp by the time the A-Team came down from their summit try. Then, the following morning, our team would make our own attempt on the top.

Butch signed off. Chotari, Dave and I crowded around the stove, melting another pot of snow for tea. It was imperative that we drink as many fluids as possible. Judging by my bulging bladder, we were succeeding.

Laslow was in the rear of tent, going through his Ziplocs. He had them stacked into teetering piles: one for the next day's climb, one for the following night at Ridge Camp, one for the summit day. In addition, he had piles for each possible combination of the aforementioned. I tried to remember the simple algebraic formula for the total possible number of Ziploc combinations. I was concerned when the formula eluded me.

Finally, I counted Laslow's stacks. There were six of them—each leaning against Chotari. Chotari seemed acutely annoyed, but said nothing. As he nursed the stove, he constantly had to push back a mountain of Ziplocs.

When the three of us had drained another kettle of tea, Chotari unzipped the tent door, empty kettle in hand. I assumed he was going to scoop more snow.

Instead, Chotari set down the kettle outside. Then he turned. He scooped up an armful of Ziplocs. Laslow flinched in horror.

"*Sayonara!*" Chotari yelled. He tossed the Ziplocs out the door. I could hear them skitter somewhere down the frozen slope.

Then, before the petrified Laslow could speak, Chotari scooped up more. These, too, flew out the door.

"*Oh sweet Jesus!*" Laslow sputtered, his face blanched. He lunged for Chotari. He tried to pin Chotari's arms. But Chotari swatted him away effortlessly.

Dave and I sat back out of the way, shielding the roaring stove from the melee. Finally, the last of the Ziplocs had been flung outside. Chotari leaned out of the tent and calmly retrieved the kettle. He scooped it full of snow and placed it on the stove as if nothing had happened.

I looked at Laslow. He was on his knees in shock, shaking. It was amazing that this hadn't happened earlier. Purple welts rose on his face. I thought he might have a seizure. He clutched a single empty Ziploc in both hands. "You've destroyed my system. Now I've got to start all over again."

Chotari turned to Laslow. "Sorry," he said. "I had no right to do that. I'll help you find your things, brother. You and I have needed to take a walk together for a long time."

"I know I'm a pain," Laslow said. "I'm sorry." He tossed the empty Ziploc into the back of the tent.

Chotari and Laslow bundled up in their down parkas and mittens and were soon out in the dark, working by the light of their headlamps to recover the Ziplocs. Some had slid fifty yards down the shoulder; the two donned crampons to go after them. They were gone half an hour. When they crawled back into the tent, Laslow was telling Chotari about his boyhood summers in Miami Beach. Chotari was telling about his three semesters at Florida State. He went there on a U.S. Agency for International Development grant to study animal husbandry, but told Laslow he majored in beaches and bikinis before homesickness brought him back to the Khumbu. I couldn't tell if they were listening to each other; it didn't seem to matter. They sounded like dear old friends catching up on the news.

Soon, Laslow was repacking. Chotari had apparently made a

few gentle suggestions outside. Laslow dumped his things out of the Ziplocs. Then he quickly crammed his things into two large stuff sacks. I was astounded. He had lithely switched from a differential to an integrative equation.

All this time Laslow had been so absorbed in his interlocking sorting system, and all he had needed was a friend to take him under a wing and remind him of the beauty of simplicity. This was the crux of Laslow's Ziploc conundrum: he had been too afraid to ask for help; the rest of us had been too afraid to offer it. Chotari, unbidden, offered help where help was needed.

It was a quarter to ten. Dave and I zipped our down parkas, readying to crawl to our cold tent. Just as I reached for the door, the radio crackled.

"Chotari. Roger. Chotari. This is Pasang. Over. Copy. Roger?"

"Who the heck is *Roger*?" Laslow asked.

Chotari dove for the radio. Before he could respond, Butch's voice cackled. "Pasang, this is Butch. What are you doing on the radio?"

"This is Pasang. I talk to Chotari, please, Butch-sahib."

Chotari stepped in. "This is Chotari, little brother. What's wrong?"

Pasang began to speak urgently in his native dialect. I could hear John's name spoken by both Sherpas. Again. And again.

Butch interrupted. "Let's keep the transmissions in English. Is something wrong with John?"

"Pasang's trying to explain," Chotari snapped. "Let him speak in his own tongue. Go ahead, Pasang."

Pasang continued in his own language. Chotari, clutching the radio with both hands, nodded gravely.

When he was done, Chotari translated for Butch. "Pasang says John is *very* ill. At dinner he seemed fine. He ate a big dinner, held it down, then went to his tent. Pasang took him tea before going to bed. John couldn't get up. His lips were blue. He had coughed up blood. When John breathes, Pasang says he hears a loud rattling."

Laslow looked alarmed. "Cyanosis. Bloody sputum. Rales."

Butch came back on the radio. "Chotari, give me Laslow." Chotari had to show Laslow how to key the mike.

"This is Laslow. Go ahead."

"Laslow," Butch's voice crackled. He sounded out of breath. "How does it sound to you?"

Laslow fumbled with the radio. Finally, he replied firmly: "John is in the advanced stages of pulmonary edema. He needs immediate attention."

There was a static-filled pause on the other end. Then Butch radioed back: "Chotari, listen up. I don't want anybody climbing down in the dark. But at first light, I want you to send Laslow down to Base Camp. Have Dave take him down. You and Jeff can head for Ridge Camp and your summit try if you want. If you don't, feel free to go down with the others. The A-Team's going for the top. But then I'll arrange for John's evacuation."

Chotari snatched the radio from Laslow. He struggled to channel his anger into constructive words in a language not his own. He closed his eyes and pressed the radio against his forehead. Finally, he keyed the mike.

"Two days ago, Butch, I asked you for porters to take John down. Today, he could be sitting in a teahouse in Namche Bazar, flirting with the Sherpanis. But *no*. You said *no*. Not enough money."

"That was then," Butch said. "This is now."

"Yes," Chotari said. "This is now. Right now, a good boy could die because of you. I'm climbing down tonight. If I can get a helicopter, I will have him flown to Namche Bazar at dawn."

"Now hold on," Butch said. "That's a decision for a doctor

Jim Fairchild

to make."

"Do not lecture me," Chotari said. He shook with anger. "I've buried enough climbers. I've read all the books on mountain sickness. There is one cure: immediate descent. By helicopter, if necessary. If not, the boy's death will be on your hands."

There was a long pause; then the radio squawked again. "Take Laslow with you," Butch said. "But please, Chotari: wait until first light to descend."

Dave grabbed the radio from Chotari. "This is Dave, Butch. Laslow is not going down the mountain. I repeat: Laslow is not going down the mountain."

"This is Butch. What the hell are you talking about, Slick?"

"We need Laslow on the mountain," Dave said. "Chotari has more hands-on experience with mountain sickness than the rest of us combined. He knows the treatment. He can go down tonight and arrange an evacuation. It's better to keep Laslow up here, where other climbers might need him."

Dave stared at Laslow. Laslow looked crushed and confused. It was obvious he'd already taken a liking to this honorable way of begging out of an attempt on the summit of Pumori.

I glared at Dave. He evaded my eyes. I was sickened by the dictatorial, manipulative way he was making decisions for Laslow. I wanted to say something. But the radio squawked again.

"Let me speak with Laslow," Butch said. Dave handed the radio back.

"Listen, Laslow," Butch said. "Dave's argument bears some merit. But John is seriously ill. You're our only doctor. You're the only person qualified to decide where you belong on the mountain. I want it straight from you: should you go down, or should you stay at Shoulder Camp?"

Laslow clutched the radio. He looked at the rest of us, desperately seeking someone to make the decision for him. He

214

looked at Chotari.

Still stuffing his gear into his pack, Chotari told Laslow: "This is how I see it: a young boy is very sick at Base Camp. He needs help. And you're the only doctor. But I'll be honest, brother-man: I don't want you on a rope with me at night. If you fall, I'll have no warning. We'll *both* get killed. It's safer for me to haul ass down on my own. Tonight, I'll take a good look at John. I can start him on Furosemide and oxygen. I'll call you if I have questions."

Chotari reached for his down parka. Cramming it into the top of his pack, he looked at Laslow. "I've seen enough mountaintops. But as for you, my friend: it would gladden my heart if you reach the top of Daughter Peak."

"Laslow?" Butch's exhausted voice asked. "You there?"

Laslow still hadn't heard what he wanted. He looked at Dave.

"We made a promise to each other," Dave said.

Dave's words made my blood boil. He certainly didn't need Laslow's help to get to the top of Pumori. I tried to fathom his motives for riding Laslow so hard.

"Laslow?" Butch squawked again. "*You there?*"

Laslow looked at me, his eyes pleading for one voice urging his descent.

"Dammit, Laslow," I said. "Don't let people play games with you."

"*Laslow*," Butch barked. "We don't have all night."

Laslow keyed the mike. "Sorry to keep you waiting. Chotari knows what needs to be done. I've got a bottle of eighty-milligram Furosemide in my large medical kit at Base Camp, and Chotari can start John on that. There's an emergency oxygen bottle in my kit, and Pasang should start John on it immediately. It's only good for a few hours, so if Chotari can send Pasang to wrangle a larger bottle from the *Summit 8000* camp, that would be excellent. While John is stabilizing, Chotari should arrange for a chopper.

Jim Fairchild

And I don't want to hear any more damned bickering about the cost." I was hearing a self-confident Laslow I had never before encountered.

"Sounds like a plan," Butch said. "But enlighten me, Laslow. Don't you think you might be most useful at Base Camp?"

Laslow looked at Dave, then at me, then back at the radio. "I belong up here, where I can help if any summit climbers need me. I belong up here, where I have a chance for the top." Laslow beamed at Dave. Then he frowned apologetically at me. Behind us, Chotari crawled out of the tent, dragging his pack after him.

Butch came back on. "Thank you, Laslow. I just wanted to hear it from you. Tell Chotari to call from Base Camp with an update on John's condition."

Chotari sat outside on the snow, tugging his crampon straps tightly. He'd been listening; he gave Laslow a thumbs-up. Chotari pulled his headlamp over his hat, then switched it on.

"Later boys," he said. "Time to boogie." The moon was climbing over Lhotse. Chotari focused his headlamp on the icy slope below.

"Be careful," I shouted.

"Thanks for everything," Laslow shouted.

"Wait until we're back in Namche Bazar," Dave hollered. "I'll toss a yak on the barbie."

Chotari bounded down the shoulder. He moved so swiftly and so gracefully that it looked like he was skiing. My eyes followed his circle of light until it disappeared far down the black, black mountain.

* * *

The wind was incessant that night. The constant drumming of the tent walls kept me from sleeping. Before dawn, we gathered for a quick breakfast in Laslow's tent. None of us were able to eat

216

much.

At last, at four in the morning, we began to pack our things. We drank some tea and filled our water bottles. We clipped into our rope, which Dave had left neatly coiled outside the night before. Dave led the way, with Laslow in the middle; I brought up the rear. The sun was still hiding behind Lhotse. It cast radiating fingers of soft light and shadow above the mountain's crown. The fingers brushed clouds streaming off Everest's summit.

The way to Ridge Camp led up an unwavering 45-degree slope. The first half was broken by crevasses and overhanging seracs. As each serac loomed ahead, I picked up the pace until I was past it, breathless but relieved.

Jumping the crevasses was even more exhausting. The uphill lip was often three to four feet higher than the lower. I had to leap, ice axe high over my head, and plant axe and crampons into the far wall. I would then scramble frantically over the edge while Laslow—strong and confident—belayed from above. Finally across, I would roll onto my side, gasping and wheezing, fighting the urge to vomit.

After six hours of climbing, we skirted a final serac. Ahead, tucked beneath an ice wall, sat the two tents of Ridge Camp. Beyond the ice wall, the final 742 vertical feet of ridge rose toward the summit—a gleaming ramp of ice, glistening in the midday sun like the edge of a knife.

We dropped our packs and fell on top of them. Laslow let out a loud *HARRUMPH* when he collapsed onto his pack. His chest-mounted video camera had knocked the air from his lungs. When we finally had the energy to move again, we dragged our things into the tents.

While I started to melt snow, Dave dug out the radio. He made contact with Chotari. It had taken Chotari only two hours to jog down to Base Camp the previous night. When he got there, he found Pasang kneeling beside John. The tent was thick with juniper smoke. Pasang, eyes closed, was chanting fervently, clutching the prayer scarf the abbot of Thyangboche had presented him.

Chotari had immediately retrieved Laslow's big medical bag and started John on Furosemide. John was already dehydrated; the drug would aggravate the condition. Chotari had Pasang dig out every package of instant Gatorade from the kitchen stocks. Pasang, trembling with worry, returned with a five-gallon jerry can sloshing over the brim. Chotari dug out the emergency oxygen bottle—good for a few hours—and fitted a mask to John's face. Pasang and Chotari had taken turns during the day, plying John with medicine and Gatorade, and monitoring his pulse and lungs.

"What about getting porters to take him down?" Dave asked.

"John needs to stabilize before he's moved," Chotari said. "But I'm splitting in a few minutes for Everest Base Camp. First, to round up a larger oxygen bottle. Second, to see if any extra porters are hanging out looking for work—big bulls who can haul ass. If so, I'll have them carry John down first thing."

"Sounds good," Dave said. "Have you heard from the A-Team yet?"

"Negatori. But I've been busy with John. I've been bad about monitoring the radio. Maybe you should give Butch a jingle."

"Gotcha," Dave said. "Take care of Master John."

"Gotcha," Chotari replied. "Climb safely. No accidents, please. I hate the paperwork."

Dave tried to raise the A-Team. Although they should have been at most 742 feet above us, he got no response. He turned up the volume, then tried again. He looked at me, puzzled. He climbed out of the tent. I followed.

Dave scanned the ridge above. He tried the radio again, speaking slowly into the mike. He took his thumb off and waited patiently. The only reply was the scratch of static. Dave paced the camp, stopping every few feet to transmit from a new location. Still, only static.

Dave collapsed the radio antenna. "I don't like it. It's two o'clock. They should be on their way down by now. If we don't hear or see anything by six, I'm heading up the ridge."

"I'll go with you," I said.

"Muchas gracias, amigo. Let's hope it doesn't come to that."

We took turns watching the ridge. I took first shift, wrapped in my down parka, huddling beside the tent, futilely seeking shelter from the wind. I watched frozen rocks high on the ridge so long that I convinced myself I could see them moving.

After two hours, just when I could focus no longer, Dave relieved me. I handed him my down parka and climbed into the tent. He had left a kettle of unidentifiable freeze-dried glop on the stove for me. I was too tired and worried to eat it. I collapsed onto my sleeping bag, listening to Laslow's snoring in the other tent. Dave and I had decided not to alarm him by sharing our concerns about the other team.

I was almost asleep. Suddenly, Dave's face was in the tent door. He clutched his old ice axe.

"The A-Team's on the way down," he said. "Get the stove cranking. They're going to need all the tea you can brew. I'm heading up."

"Let Laslow make tea," I said. "I'm going with you." I grabbed my boots. Looking past Dave, I saw that the last oranges of afternoon had faded; the bone-chilling reds of evening were bleeding across the ice-clear sky. It must have been six or seven o'clock.

I saw the look on Dave's face for the first time. Something was wrong.

"I can only see three of them," he said. "They don't answer the radio."

"Can you tell who's missing?" I laced my boots. My hands trembled so badly I missed the hooks.

"Only God knows," Dave said. "I'll tell Laslow to start the

stove."

* * *

As shadows closed in on us, the rope between us tugged so hard it nearly pulled me off my feet. Dave raced upward as if he were at sea-level instead of at almost 23,000 feet. I was near collapse. Somehow I managed to keep up.

The distance to the descending team narrowed. I could see that one of the climbers was staggering. The other two were fighting to keep the middle climber from falling off the ridge, pulling the rope tight from both ends.

I began to recognize the features. Highest up, providing the strongest belay, was Butch. I could hear his voice. The words were still unintelligible from this distance. The tone, though, was unmistakable: comforting, then cajoling, then short-tempered.

Narrowing the gap between Dave and me, I could finally make out the lowest figure. It was Eugene. I could make out his words: "If you give up now, we'll never get off this goddamned mountain." He yanked hard on the rope running back to the middle climber.

Dave had come to a halt above me. I coiled the rope while Dave stepped aside to let the descending team pass. I strained in the darkness to see which of the women was in the middle. My stomach knotted.

Eugene reached Dave. "What happened?" Dave asked.

"We could've bagged the top. We had to babysit instead."

As Eugene descended past Dave, I finally spotted Sarah's parka. I was frantic to know what had happened to Chris.

Eugene descended the narrow ramp until he reached me. I asked him about Chris. "Ask Butch," he muttered angrily. Eugene passed me, his crampons kicking the ice with unneeded force, sending ice shards downhill.

Dave shouted up to Butch. He asked what had happened to Chris. Butch shouted back down, but the words were swallowed by a gust of wind. Sarah, teetering, reached Dave.

"Glad to see you, Missy," Dave said. He patted her back. Her knees buckled. Dave almost fell under her weight.

Butch descended to her, coiling in the rope. He helped Dave get her back on her feet. Dave and Butch spoke gently with her; Butch rubbed her shoulders. It looked like Butch was explaining to Dave what had happened, but I was still too far down to understand.

The A-Team began to descend again. Sarah passed me, smiling weakly. Butch, holding a tight rope between them, passed next. He looked exhausted. He was concentrating too much on his belay even to look in my direction.

Then Dave descended toward me.

"Where the hell is Chris?" I shouted over the wind, as I took in more rope.

"*She's okay*," Dave shouted. He reached my side and plunged his axe into the slope. "Sarah started to get ataxic about 200 feet from the top. She took a header off the ridge and pulled the whole team with her. Chris was the only one who could self-arrest. She belayed the rest of the team until they could climb back up to the ridge."

"But *where the hell* is she?"

"Sorry," Dave said. "When they all got back onto the ridge, Chris told Butch she still wanted to try for the top, even if she had to do it solo. Butch told her to go for it. It was the least he could do— she'd just saved the whole team. She should be back down any time."

"Why didn't they call on the radio?" I asked, peeved.

"After the fall, Butch was helping Sarah. He asked Eugene to hold the radio for a second. The Tuscaloosa Terror dropped it down the South Face."

Dave and I plunge-stepped down to camp. Laslow had just

gotten his first look at Sarah. It was as if his worst fears had been born out. He ordered Butch to get her into the tent. Dave and I crammed in to help. Eugene remained outside, repacking his gear, muttering to himself.

Dave and Butch began pouring mug after mug of tea down Sarah's parched throat. Butch had to hold the mug to her lips for her. Laslow dressed a gaping cut on her chin, and another over her right eye. When he wiped off the caked blood with alcohol pads, Sarah winced, but didn't cry. He closed the jagged wounds with butterfly closures.

Laslow checked Sarah's pulse. It was elevated. He checked her eyes for tracking ability, her lips for color. "I was worried about you," he said gently. His professional manner moved me. "How do you feel, dear?"

"Better than before."

"Before *what*?" Laslow asked.

"Before the fall," Sarah said groggily. "I had an incredible headache. I couldn't see straight. I thought I could see someone off to the right of the ridge, waving at me, telling me to hurry up and follow."

"She stepped right of the ridge into space," Butch said.

Sarah turned to Butch. She began to weep softly. "I'm so sorry. I could have killed somebody." She looked around the tent. "Is this Shoulder Camp?"

"We're at Ridge Camp," Butch said. "It's still a long way down."

Sarah looked out the open tent door. Her eyes grew wide. "Where's Chris?"

Butch handed Sarah more tea, then said: "Chris went for the top. She should be back any time. Finish your tea. You need to get some sleep."

"*Wrong*," Laslow said. "She has to get down the mountain immediately."

"She's exhausted," Butch protested. "It's dark. She'll fall again."

"She's showing all the symptoms of cerebral edema," Laslow said. "If she doesn't go down now, she'll be dead by morning. End of story."

Butch cleared his throat. He took the mug from Sarah. "I know you're right, Laslow. I'm not thinking straight."

We helped Sarah out of the tent. It was a struggle; she wanted to burrow into a sleeping bag. We got her back into her harness and crampons and clipped into the rope. Eugene, ready long ago, his headlamp on his head, watched with disgust. Butch pulled on his gear, while Dave fetched fresh batteries for the A-Team's headlamps.

"Do you want our radio?" Dave asked Butch.

"It should stay with the highest team," Butch said. "Call us at Base Camp if Chris is late."

"Will do."

"Good luck tomorrow," Butch said. Although his face was badly windburned, I could see his tired smile. "If Chris didn't make the top today, it's up to you guys. Make me look good."

"We could've bagged the top," Eugene said, scraping at the ice with the spike of his axe, "if a certain unfit climber had been left in Base Camp."

"*Chill out*, Eugene," Butch snapped. He turned back to Dave. "Radio Chotari and tell him to keep a light burning. I'm gonna keep the pedal down and get this truckload of cattle clear to Base Camp tonight."

"Gotcha," Dave said.

"Thanks, guys," Sarah said, her voice hoarse.

"You get down this mountain right now, young lady," Laslow scolded.

Sarah hugged Laslow. The bright beam of her headlamp reflected off his smudged glasses. He looked embarrassed. Then

223

Sarah hugged Dave, and then me. I squeezed her tightly. She wobbled in my arms. She felt as frail as an autumn leaf. I wondered how she would make it down the mountain in the dark.

"Enough smooching," Eugene drawled. "We still have to evacuate the sick, lame and lazy."

It was too much for Butch. He threw down his ice axe. He unbuckled the waistbelt on his pack. "Eugene," he said, taking a step forward. "Open your piehole one more time, and I'll kick your butt out into 22,000 feet of Tibetan airspace. You'll be the first Alabama Airways flight to land in Lhasa."

Eugene backed away. His neck retracted turtle-like into his parka. "Okay." He held up his mittened palms. "Okay, okay, okay. I respect your authority more than anyone else on this mountain. I'm just disappointed, is all."

Butch glared at Eugene. Their two headlamps locked in a silent contest of light and will. Finally, Butch's beam bent. He picked up his ice axe. "Don't kiss my ass anymore, Eugene." He thrust the spike of his axe less than an inch from Eugene's burned, runny nose. "Not *ever* again. My ass is tired enough without your cornpone-caked lips hanging onto it like a leech."

The tension had cracked like an icicle on an overhanging serac. We all hooted hoarsely. The A-Team headed downward in the dark. Dave, Laslow and I watched their tiny pools of light bounce down the mountain.

* * *

Dave and I returned to our tent. Dave radioed Chotari at Base Camp and informed him of the day's events. Then Dave asked if Chotari had found porters to carry John down to Namche Bazar.

"No luck," Chotari answered.

"What do you mean?" Dave asked. "There should be *dozens* of them over at Everest Base Camp eager for work."

"Seems like a labor problem has erupted."

Dave looked confused. He took his thumb off the radio and looked at me. "The strike wasn't supposed to start yet. And it wasn't supposed to involve the low-altitude porters."

I shrugged. "Ask Chotari."

Dave was afraid to ask for clarification over the radio, not knowing who might be listening. Then he remembered that Butch didn't have a radio. "Tell me, Chotari," he said. "Are you talking about a *strike?*"

"Gotcha."

"But I thought—"

"Seems like some of the low-level porters didn't dig seeing their sisters working in low-cut blouses at the *Summit 8000* Bierhaus tent. They torched it last night, then called a strike. They aren't asking for more money. They just want to show the *Summit 8000* bigwigs who really runs the show. Nothing goes up to or down from Everest Base Camp."

"What about higher up?" Dave asked. "Are the high-altitude Sherpas still working?"

Of course," Chotari said, hamming it up. "We Sherpa tigers are consummate professionals. We would *never* dream of a strike."

"Keep trying to snag porters for John," Dave said. "Radio Namche Bazar if you have to. Pay them whatever it takes. If you need it, you know where I keep my scratch."

"Roger-dodger," Chotari said. "But if it takes a day or two to find porters, I think John will be okay. A Sherpa friend at the *Summit 8000* Base Camp pinched two 800-liter oxygen bottles for me. I'm giving John two liters a minute as needed. The oxygen and the Furosemide seem to be doing the trick. John's chest sounds better. He's been asking for more of Doctor Dave's Miracle Cure."

"Tell him Doctor Dave says that's a no-no for his lungs until he's out of the woods. I've gotta go. We have to keep an eye out for Chris."

* * *

Dave and I took turns scanning the ridge above. It was pitch-black now; the moon was just a hint of light behind Lhotse. Surely we should be able to see the beam of Chris's headlamp. Dave took over from me at ten; I crawled into the tent to warm up. I got into my sleeping bag, but couldn't sleep.

Just as I finally got comfortable, Dave shouted outside. "I think I see something!" I jumped up and grabbed my boots, then dove outside.

Dave pointed up the ridge with the spike of his ice axe. The moon, nearly full, was above Lhotse's crown now; the icy ridge glowed blue in its light. "*There,*" he said, pointing midway up. "About 300 feet up—where the ridge snakes a little to the right."

"I don't see anything," I said. "Did you see her headlamp?"

"No," Dave said. "But I know I saw something moving."

And then, in a moment, I saw it, too. It was the unmistakable shape of someone moving down the icy ridge inches at a time, feeling her way down with her ice axe like a blind person with a cane: without headlamp, without belay, struggling stubbornly downward in the eery moonlight. A single wrong move could mean death.

I switched on my headlamp and grabbed my ice axe. In too much of a rush to rope up, our lungs burning, we climbed steadily up the ridge toward the descending figure.

* * *

The moment we started up the ridge, Chris slipped from sight. I craned my neck without luck. I swung my headlamp in broad arcs, dizzy, hoping she'd see my light and climb down toward it.

Two hundred feet up, we paused in the lee of a serac, exhausted. "Do you think we imagined it?" I asked.

"Let's hope not," Dave said. We climbed onward.

As we rounded the serac, a seemingly frozen block of ice rose, then teetered. It was Chris. She had been sitting on the opposite side of the serac, gathering her strength. In my harsh headlamp beam, she looked like a Hiroshima survivor. Her face was scorched red from sun and wind; dime-sized strips of frozen flesh hung from broken blisters on her cheeks. Her eyes were swollen nearly shut. Her glacier glasses, useless in the dark, dangled around her neck. She still wore her headlamp, its batteries long spent.

"It's high time you lads showed," she said. She brushed the snow off her knickers. "I rang Room Service hours ago. Where's that magnum of Prosecco I ordered?" Dave and I hugged her so hard she nearly stumbled off the ridge.

Dave planted a noisy kiss on her blistered cheek. "We heard you saved the day."

"Nonsense," Chris said. "I was just trying to save my crusty old arse."

"How was the view from the top?" I asked.

"Can't rightly say," Chris said, "seeing as how I never made it. You boys can have a fresh stab at it tomorrow."

"How far did you get?" Dave asked.

"There's an ice wall less than a hundred feet from the top. I spent four blasted hours beating my noggin against it. I couldn't get up or around the bloody thing without a belay. Especially with night falling. And then I thought about Sarah, and had quite the attack of bad conscience for not helping her down."

"She'll be fine," I said. "She just needed to get down fast."

"You did what *she* would have done," Dave said.

"Precisely," Chris said. "That's the problem. That's why I feel like a turd. And I'm not so sure she *would* have. Eugene, yes. But Sister Sarah has surprised me lately. I need to get down this hill to her tomorrow and catch up on our girltalk."

"I'm not bad at girltalk," Dave said.

"Stuff it," Chris barked. "Get me to camp, lads." Chris took each of us by the arm.

* * *

Chris shared a tent with Laslow that night. As I lay in my sleeping bag, drifting off, I could hear Laslow laughing riotously. Chris, despite her fatigue, was telling him a bedtime story. It had something to do with three lost and benighted travellers, a very lonely forest troll and his hot buttered kidney pies. I wished I could have heard the whole tale, but the wind swallowed it.

As Dave began to snore beside me and my eyelids grew heavy, I realized how relieved I was that nobody had been lost that day. I realized how unprepared I would have been to deal with the loss of a single life on this mountain. I had been through that once before. And that was one time too many. I slept well for the first time in several nights.

* * *

We gathered before dawn. Chris, looking revived, did us the honors of cooking breakfast. She whipped up a huge mountain of freeze-dried eggs and hash browns, and then brewed several pots of tea. We gulped down as much of the tea as we could, then filled our water bottles with the rest.

A strong wind blew from Tibet as we stepped out into the grey of dawn to rope up. Chris helped us get organized. Dave asked if she wanted to tie into the rope and give the summit one more shot. Chris said that her solo try, even though unsuccessful, couldn't be topped. She would descend on her own after she had seen us safely off. "Okay, lads," she said, like a mother sending her boys off to school. "Everybody have their lunch pails?"

Finally, as the sun peeked over Lhotse's crown, we were on our way.

* * *

We moved slowly but steadily up the relentless ridge. At the front of the rope, Dave was absorbed in his duties as leader. He followed the frozen tracks of the A-Team as best he could. But there were stretches where not even the faintest of crampon nicks could be seen in the hard ice. We came to a halt while Dave peered above.

Laslow, in the middle, plugged on. I could hear the loud whistling of his forced exhalations. He was religiously practicing the pressure-breathing technique Dave had taught him.

Only one thing worried me: his video camera. I glanced up in time to see Laslow stumbling along, not looking where he was stepping, his video camera to his face, taping some cloud over Tibet. I could imagine him walking off the ridge just as Sarah had, pulling Dave and me with him. I shouted angrily; Laslow waved guiltily, lowering the camera.

After only three hours, we reached the spot where the A-Team had fallen. I could see the hole where Sarah had plummeted straight through the cornice. The gaping hole was tinged with frozen blood. Through the hole I could look down thousands of feet to a glacier in Tibet. Nearby was the belay platform Chris had hastily cut into the icy slope after her self-arrest. It was astounding that she had been able to stop herself—let alone the rest of the team.

We paused to sip from our water bottles. The tea had been steaming when I poured it into my bottle after breakfast. Now, I had to break ice out of the neck of the bottle. Then we were off again.

No matter how much I concentrated on my breathing, I still felt as if I were sprinting a marathon. I tried to take my mind off the pain by watching my shadow. I studied its lines, and the contrast between its darkness and the surrounding light. The more I studied, the more the shadow began to move with grace and fluidity.

Only an hour after leaving the spot where the A-Team had fallen, the shadow in front of me came to a halt. I snapped out of my trance. Dave and Laslow stood below the final ice wall that had stymied Chris.

"You okay?" Dave asked me, coiling the rope. "Don't go zombie on me."

"I'm fine," I said. "Just a little spacey from the altitude."

We sat on our packs, our backs against the towering ice wall. I didn't even want to look at it. We sipped more tea and shared a chocolate bar. It was so hard I almost cracked a tooth.

It was finally time to face our final challenge. I had to crane my neck to look at it. The wall, at least forty feet high, was so vertical it seemed to overhang. I had an attack of vertigo and began to pitch backward. I flashed on myself rolling all the way down the ridge, catapulting out across the Khumbu Glacier, creating a massive impact crater somewhere near the solar outhouses of the *Summit 8000* camp. Dave grabbed my elbow and steadied me.

"Definitely the crux pitch," he said.

"We don't have a single ice screw," I suddenly realized. "Butch has them. You're going to have to lead without protection."

Dave stared at the wall, scratching his icy beard. "I'm bushed. I've been leading all morning."

The idea of leading the ice wall made my knees weak. "I haven't led technical ice in years," I protested.

"I didn't have you in mind."

The color drained from Laslow's windburned cheeks. He began to sputter. ""Eugene's right. You're *nuts*, Dave. There's no way I can lead that. I'm not even sure I can follow on it."

"You've been climbing like a tiger today," Dave said. "Don't forget the promise we made to each other."

I had the suspicion once again that Dave was playing a game with Laslow. I couldn't figure out Dave's agenda.

Laslow stared up at the ice wall. I saw a muscle twitch in his neck. "Okay. I'll give it a shot."

"One shot is all we have," Dave said, grinning. He patted Laslow on the back. "One favor," Dave said to Laslow. "Stow your video camera. You won't have time to tape yourself."

Dave stomped a platform beneath the wall. He sank his axe as far as it would go, then stomped down the head. He looped the rope around the axe, then over his boot. "Ready when you are, Laslow," Dave said, taking in the slack.

Laslow needed a second tool. I lent him my axe. He wrapped the slings around his wrists and gripped the shafts. He tested his swing. His aim was uneven; the pick glanced off the ice, showering him with shards.

"*Gently*," Dave said. "Just hook the ice."

Laslow turned to Dave. Laslow gulped; I could see his Adam's apple bob up and down. "Climbing," he rasped.

"Climb away, partner," Dave said. He prepare to feed out the rope.

Laslow swung one axe, then the other, high over his head, hooking the ice. He tested them with his weight. I could see his arms shake. He hadn't even left the ground yet. It didn't look promising.

"Remember," Dave said. "Keep your weight on your crampons. Don't try to hold it with your arms. You'll get pumped out."

"Right," Laslow said. He sounded miserable. Finally, he kicked the front points of one crampon into the ice. He stepped up, pulling on the imbedded axes above him. He kicked at the ice with the other boot. His heels were too high. The front points of one crampon—and then the other—popped out of the ice. Laslow fell right back where he had started.

Still clutching the axes hooked high over his head, his arms painfully stretched, Laslow looked back at Dave. "I'm not sure this is a good idea," Laslow gasped.

"Give it one more shot," Dave said. "What if you don't at least try? The rest of your life you'll wonder if you could have done it."

Laslow faced the looming ice wall. He yanked out the axes and hooked them once more into the ice. He tested them. He liked what he felt. He kicked one crampon, then the next, into the ice. This time, he kept his heels level with his toes.

He closed his eyes and cringed, waiting for something to splinter out of the ice. But—after a long pause—he realized he was solidly anchored to the ice. Surprised and pleased, he grinned down at Dave.

"How's it feel?" Dave asked, holding the rope firmly.

"Solid."

"You look great," Dave said. "Nice tush for a middle-aged man, by the way. Just remember: always keep three out of four points of contact firmly planted. Never have more than one in motion. Stick with those rules, and it'll be a piece of cake."

Laslow inched upward. I stood out of his fall line. I watched until the shower of ice shards drove me into the lee of an overhang. From then on, I watched the angle of Dave's neck to judge Laslow's progress. Dave had to squat low to see all the way up to where Laslow hung from the ice.

"How's he looking?" I asked. If Laslow were to fall, Dave's belay would be utterly useless. Without ice screws placed in the wall, Laslow would bore a crater into the ice beside Dave. The belay would only make sure his battered corpse didn't slide all the way down the mountain.

"He's looking like a champ!" Dave shouted. He held a hand up to shield himself from falling ice, casting a shadow on his face.

Twenty minutes passed. I had been sitting under the ice

overhang out of the sun. My fingers were frozen. Just as I started banging my mittens together, Laslow's voice floated down: *"I'm up!"* I clapped so hard that blood raced back into my fingertips.

"Great job, Doc," Dave yelled. "First, tie one of those axes onto the rope and lower it for the next climber." A face appeared over the top of the wall, then a hand gripping an axe. In his excitement, Laslow forgot to tie the axe to the rope. Dave and I ducked. The axe sailed down end-over-end toward us, whistling like a boomerang. Snow sprayed my face. When I opened my eyes, the axe stood perfectly upright, stuck in the snow between Dave and me.

"Thanks, guy," Dave shouted, wiping snow from his face. "Get back from the edge and rig a sitting belay. When you're set, send us a smoke signal."

I moved to Dave's side. He was feeding out a few more feet of rope to Laslow. "How did you know he could do it?" I asked.

"I didn't. I was worried he'd take a screamer of a fall. But, as they say, nothing ventured, nothing gained."

"With friends like you," I asked, "who needs enemas?"

"Laslow needs to go home knowing that for at last twenty minutes on this mountain, our success depended on him."

An excited shout boomed down. Laslow had his belay set up. Dave offered the two axes to me.

"You next," I said. "Tell Laslow he did a fine job."

Dave hefted both axes. "Belay on, Doc?" he shouted upward.

"Belay on," Laslow shouted down.

"Ready to climb." Dave held each axe loosely.

"Climb away," Laslow hollered.

Dave turned to me and winked. Then he faced the wall. He hooked one axe, then the other, into the ice. Hanging effortlessly from them, he kicked at the wall and scampered upward. When his body was almost doubled over, he scissored his torso upward, placing all his weight on the firmly planted crampons. Now, his two axes were level with his chest. Removing them one at a time, he again hooked them into the ice as high as he could reach.

In less than five minutes Dave was up. He exchanged whoops with Laslow. Then Dave's face appeared at the top of the wall. "Heads up," he shouted. He lowered the axes with the rope.

Once I had the axes loose, Dave and Laslow hauled up the packs. Finally, I tied in. I inhaled deeply. I swung the axes into the wall.

I found myself working way too hard. After catching my breath, I decided to lose myself in my shadow again. I studied my shadow's movements, and focused on making them more graceful. In a few minutes, I was at the top. Dave grabbed my arms and helped me over the edge. "Just like a spider monkey," he said, patting my head through the hood of my parka.

After a sip of icy tea, we roped up again. We were perhaps fifteen minutes from the top. The culmination of weeks of backbreaking effort was within sight. Yet I felt utterly empty. There was nothing ahead but lifeless ice and rock and wind. Why had I left Robin for this? I realized what a fool I had been.

Laslow started to clip into his usual place in the middle of the rope. "*No*," Dave told him. "Up front." Laslow eagerly took the lead. Dave got behind him; I brought up the rear.

Unaccustomed to leading, Laslow had a difficult time finding the proper pace. Dave shouted for him to relax. The pace slowed. Still, it was uneven. I began to lose patience. "Settle down!" I bellowed.

When Laslow looked down, Dave and I saw the problem. Laslow had his video camera lifted to his face. He was taping us.

Dave stormed up the ridge. He ran so fast the rope almost dragged me off my feet. I had to race to keep up. My lungs were on fire. It was as if I'd just inhaled flaming napalm.

Dave caught up to Laslow. Laslow had his camera trained

on him, merrily taping. When the rope to Dave finally went slack, I collapsed and puked up the eggs and hash browns Chris had so painstakingly cooked us that morning.

"Dammit!" I heard Dave shout. On my hands and knees, I looked up from the steaming eggs and potatoes melting a crater in the snow. Dave had grabbed the camera from Laslow. The blow almost knocked Laslow onto his back.

Dave clutched the camera. His sprint up the ridge had finally caught up with him; he was gasping almost as hard as me now. But he found the energy to lift the camera over his head and fling it off the ridge. It arched outward, its lens glinting in the sun, then shot like a rock downward, disappearing into Tibet.

"That was a fourteen-hundred-dollar Sony," Laslow said.

"I'll pay you greenbacks at Base Camp," Dave gasped, collapsing to his knees.

*   *   *

Laslow paused just below the point where all ridges converged. He motioned for Dave and me to come and take the last few steps with him. Dave clambered up beside him. Exhausted, half a rope below them, I leaned over my ice axe. I waved for them to go on. But they insisted on waiting for me. Angered, I trudged upward.

Laslow stood on one side of me, Dave on the other. They both put an arm around me. I resented their sentimentality. "Let's do it," Laslow said.

Side by side, we stepped onto the snowy point from which one could—at last—climb no farther. We collapsed onto our packs. I was too tired to do anything but close my eyes and suck in lungfuls of thin air.

"I'll remember this the rest of my life," Laslow told Dave. "Sony or no Sony." He grabbed Dave's mittened hand, then mine, squeezing them both tightly. I was happy for Laslow. I knew how much he needed this.

We sat facing eastward. The sun was high overhead. It's modest warmth on my face, despite the frigid air temperature, lulled me. Miraculously, the wind had stilled.

I could see the whole sweep of Everest's West Ridge. I could see the cleft of the Hornbein Couloir—its deepest, most secretive recesses brightly laid bare in the midday sun. I could see the mountain's South Summit, less than 300 feet below the true top. We sat for twenty minutes, soaking up the sun and the view, too tired to talk.

Finally, Dave broke the silence. He patted Laslow on the back, bringing him out of his reverie. "Whatcha think, Doc? Time to hit the road?"

Laslow seemed to be staring off into the distance. Without looking at us, he spoke, as if recalling a dream. "I was volunteering in Senegal just before I went to Denali last year," he said, watching clouds. "The clinic was a mess when I took over. A mother and her newborn daughter bled to death in delivery the first day I was there because I couldn't find my equipment. I haven't been able to talk about it until now." Laslow turned his head away from us, ashamed to be crying.

"The Ziplocs," Dave said. "I get it." Dave reached over and put both arms around Laslow. He whispered something to Laslow that I couldn't hear. He rubbed the top of Laslow's parka hood. When Laslow turned toward me again, it was almost as if nothing had happened. He wiped tears from his windburned face and then pointed southward. A high wall of cumulus soared upward on the afternoon thermals, slowly creeping our way. "We should go before the weather poops out on us," he said.

Laslow and Dave began to pack. I bent over to tighten my crampon straps. Something in a shirt pocket poked me.

I fished inside my layers of clothing. It was a photograph of

Robin. I'd carried it all the way from Montana. I scooped a hole in the summit snows of Daughter Peak and placed the photo in it. Then I carefully tamped snow over the hole. Dave and Laslow stood waiting. "I'm ready," I said, standing. "Let's do it."

The other two were clipped into the rope. I grabbed the one vacant figure-eight knot and clipped into it. Something didn't make sense. They had left the middle position on the rope for me. Traditionally, the middle is for the weakest climber. Stunned, I said nothing.

We began our descent. In moments we came to the ice wall. Laslow began to chop a bollard in the ice for a rappel anchor. I peered over the wall to figure out the best rappel route. Dave barked at me to sit down. The harshness in his voice confused me. I silently complied. Laslow finished chopping the bollard; Dave untied the knots in the rope. I began to fume with anger.

When the rope was looped around the bollard and both ends had been tossed over the wall, Dave fed it through his descender. He walked backwards over the edge and disappeared. In seconds I could hear his voice drift upward: "Clear!"

Laslow tapped me on the shoulder. "Your turn," he said. "We should keep moving." I straddled the rope and threaded it through my descender. I was about to step backward when Laslow lunged toward me. He grabbed my harness so violently I almost fell backward.

"You forgot to lock your carabiner," he said. He twisted the locking sleeve, making sure the descender wouldn't disconnect from my harness when I put weight on it.

It was an error that should have embarrassed even a beginner. I looked up blankly at Laslow. It wasn't embarrassment I felt, but panic. It dawned on me why the middle spot on the rope had been left for me.

"Easy does it," Laslow said, "and we'll get down this hill just fine."

Jim Fairchild

I stepped back over the edge and leaned out, concentrating on my balance. I kept my feet spread wide, making sure my crampon points had maximum contact. I walked down the wall slowly, trying to focus clearly on the task at hand.

Halfway down the wall, a shadow darted across the ice, just beyond the toe of my left boot. I swung my head. I caught a glimpse of something black.

It was the gorak, circling on the thermals.

There: circling in front of the sun, keeping a watch on me. Even with my glacier glasses, I was blinded. I took my hand from the rope above, leaving only the brake hand on the rope at the small of my back. I shielded my eyes with the free hand.

"*Jeff!*" a voice below me shouted.

The bird's circle broadened until it soared out of sight behind me. It was playing hide-and-seek.

"Jeff! Get your hand back on the damned rope." It was Dave.

If I could only lean back a little farther, I could see it clearly.

"*JEFF!*"

And then my crampons slipped. My legs shot upward, my head downward. I slammed upsidedown against the ice. All of my weight came to bear on my brake arm, pinioned behind me. I opened my eyes. I realized what had happened. *This could be serious*, I told myself.

"Get your other hand on the rope!" Dave hollered.

Panic filled my mouth with the taste of pennies. My pack pulled down around my neck, choking me. So much blood rushed to my face that my eyes were swelling shut. But I was wide awake now, aware of what had been happening to me, determined not to give in. I reached up with my free hand and found the rope above me. I pulled as hard as I could and kicked wildly.

Finally, I was right side up again. I heaved more eggs. My brake arm, behind me, spasmed crazily. I didn't think I'd broken it,

238

but I'd sure banged it up pretty good.

"Get down here before you give me a coronary arrest," Dave yelled.

I slid down the rope. I collapsed beside Dave on my knees, trembling, fighting for breath, wiping eggs and bile from my chin.

Dave pulled the rope through my descender and yelled "Clear" to Laslow. Then he pulled me aside so we would be out of Laslow's way. I fell again to my hands and knees, sucking in lungfuls of thin air.

"You okay?" Dave asked. "You almost made me piss myself." Above us, Laslow leaned out and began to rappel smoothly downward.

I laughed hoarsely between gasps. "I scared myself, too. I should get down fast. I want to get home with a few brain cells left."

"Aw, heck," Dave said, pleased to hear me sounding more rational. "I'm living proof of how much mileage you can get on a handful of brain cells."

Roped up again, we plunge-stepped down the ridge. Camp was already in sight. Although I felt better now, I couldn't understand why Laslow was racing so fast. He almost pulled me onto my face with the rope. Dave was on my heels, coiling up more rope, until he was just a step or two behind.

The rope tugged at me. Suddenly, I realized I was staring at a cloud over Tibet. I had no clue how long I'd been standing still.

"Come on, partner," Dave said, directly behind me. I felt his hand on my shoulder. It had been there for quite some time. We continued downward.

I stopped in my tracks.

"What now?" Dave asked, almost bumping into me.

"Don't forget your promise."

"*What* promise?" Dave studied me carefully: my eyes, my lips, my balance. I knew he thought my problem was the altitude.

Jim Fairchild

How could I explain to him what was really happening—that I had thought reaching the summit of Pumori would change things—and that, having reached the top, I had found nothing but emptiness? Even at 23,000 feet, I had reached a depth from which I doubted I could climb back.

"*What* promise?" Dave asked again. He nudged my pack. "We need to keep going, partner. We need to get you down."

"You promised to talk to Naomi." Getting the words out exhausted me.

Dave squeezed my shoulder. "You're my best friend," he said. "Let's keep going. I want you to live to be my best *old* friend."

I had lost all sense of time. It probably only took a couple of hours to descend from the summit to Ridge Camp. But it could have been days, or weeks, or months. The terms meant nothing. I had a watch on my wrist, but the numbers on its face looked like hieroglyphics.

"Look," Dave said. "The camp's just below. Another hundred feet."

I could tell by the tone of his voice that I should feel relieved. But I didn't know if "another hundred feet" was good or bad, if we would cover the distance in seconds or weeks or years.

I stumbled into Ridge Camp between Laslow and Dave. Watching them for cues, I unclipped from the rope. I watched the others drop their packs. Laslow went to his tent; Dave crawled into ours. He'd disappeared from sight when he realized I was still standing outside, clueless.

"Pack your gear," Dave said from the tent. "Get your sleeping bag. We need to head down."

I waited for Dave to finish inside the tent. He crawled out in a moment, dragging his gear with him. "Your turn," he said. "Hurry up."

I crawled into the tent. I stared at my sleeping bag. *Get it,*

Dave had said. Or had he said *Get into it*? I unzipped the bag and climbed in, still wearing crampons. A cloud of goose down billowed out. I was snoring in seconds.

Something grabbed my foot. Dave slid me—sleeping bag and all—out of the tent and onto the ice. I tried to extract myself from the bag, indignant, but before I could get my hand on the zipper, Dave yanked it open.

"You told me to get into my sleeping bag," I complained.

Dave took my arm and pulled me upright. When I was sitting up, the bag around my waist, Dave looked at my arm. He let go of it.

"How bad does that hurt?" he asked, staring at my right arm.

I looked down. My parka sleeve had a jagged rip tinged with blood. It was from the rappel: when I'd fallen, my right arm had taken the impact. A chunk of ice had ripped deep into the muscle. The blood had finally soaked through the layers of clothing.

"I hadn't noticed it until now," I said. I found that ridiculous, and laughed. I suddenly realized that my mitten felt soggy. Pulling it off, blood trickled out onto the snow.

Laslow grabbed his medical kit. He peeled off my parka and fleece jacket, then slit my longjohn sleeve. Working silently, he cleaned and bandaged the wound. Dave was on the radio with Base Camp. Although I couldn't understand most of it, I could hear him mention my name.

* * *

After an endless slog down the icy spine, we glimpsed Shoulder Camp. As Laslow reached the tents and coiled in the rope, I looked backward. The sun was hidden behind the summit of Pumori. Fingers of light radiated from its high point like a crown. I looked at my watch: 4:32 p.m. For the first time since leaving the summit, I was able to decipher the numerals. I felt a wave of relief.

During my more lucid moments, I'd worried that I'd suffered a stroke.

We climbed into a tent. Dave cranked up the stove while Laslow fetched a kettle of snow. We watched the snow melt over the roaring flame, too tired to speak. I occasionally caught the other two staring at me. I began reciting Saint Louis Cardinals statistics until both groaned.

"All right, already," Dave implored, dumping packets of instant rice and soup into the kettle. "I pronounce thee cured. Let's hoover this slop so we can get home before curfew."

While Dave and I began to eat, Laslow pulled out the radio. He reached Chotari at Base Camp and told him of our whereabouts. When Chotari asked if we were all okay, Laslow looked at me and winked, then told him all three of us were as strong as tigers.

Laslow asked how John was doing. He seemed so in control of the situation—so in control of himself. Laslow was not the same man I had met that first night in the moss-draped woods near Lukla.

Laslow signed off the radio. "We need to get going," he said. "With all due deference to Doctor Dave, I'm the only real doctor on this mountain, and there are two people down at Base Camp who need my help."

By 6:30 p.m. we were midway down the serac field. The sky bled with the first reds of evening. Laslow came to a halt ahead. "We're not moving fast enough. I need to get down to John and Sarah."

"Why don't you head down on your own?" Dave asked. "Without Jeff and me to slow you down, you could be in camp in an hour."

Laslow unclipped from our rope. He smiled broadly, then headed down on his own. I watched him recede below us, moving with startling gracefulness.

Dave and I continued down through the serac field, the terrain growing gentler, the rope between us losing tension. Dave, behind me, was finally able to relax. It dawned on me how much weight he'd been carrying on his shoulders looking out for Laslow and me.

The sky faded toward purple. Dave began to patter enthusiastically. The tension between us evaporated. I coiled in the rope until there was only ten feet separating us.

Dave said that when he got back to Namche Bazar he would start building a big house of stone and timber for Karma and Mingma and himself. He would see to it that Mingma got the best education possible. Someday, perhaps, Mingma could stay with Emmett and go to high school in Missoula. Dave said he'd keep busy helping Chotari run the Sherpa co-op. If need be, he would hire out as a trekking guide, leading people to the foot of the Goddess Mother for a peek at the Roof of the World—but only if they were reverent guests.

As I stepped onto the rocky moraine and stopped to unrope, Dave still rambled effusively. He said he had kept aloof from his father far too long. The first chance he had, he would put through a call to Emmett. He wanted his father to come to Nepal: to meet Karma, to meet Mingma, to see the icy mountains and high valleys and ancient temples that had so stolen his heart.

Dave bent down to remove his crampons. As he raved on, I listened skeptically. I wondered if he had a clue how much his disappearance had hurt those who cared about him. Putting it back together seemed simple to him.

A part of me hated him for disappearing those sixteen years. He hadn't been there when I had needed him: to help me make sense of what happened on Foraker, to help me make sense of what part I'd played in the loss of those three young lives. A part of me believed that he'd brought me to Pumori as some easy way of making up, far after it would have done me any good. That part of me believed he'd brought me there simply to assuage his own guilt.

Dave lashed the coiled rope to his pack. We began to

243

clamber through the boulders toward Base Camp. Already, we could see the tents. I could make out Pasang's kitchen fly, and wondered what majestic yak concoction he had bubbling beneath it on his stove. My knees creaked. We were perhaps fifteen minutes from camp. I was relieved that I was again able to arrive at such estimates.

The last of the color was gone from the sky when we reached camp. Nobody saw us approach in the dark. Despite the clatter of rocks under our stiff double boots as we staggered under our loads, they hadn't even heard us.

I could see three figures hunkered in front of a tent. I made out their faces in the glow of a candle lantern. Sarah sat cross-legged in the middle. Laslow knelt on one side, adjusting a blood pressure cuff around her arm. Chris was yanking a brush through Sarah's tangled hair.

Dave's shoulders drooped. The spike of his ice axe clanged against a rock. Startled, the three figures turned.

Chris dropped the brush. "My wayward lads!" She ran to us and gave us busses. "You were getting your Mummsie worried."

Sarah was right behind. She gave Dave a hug while Laslow belatedly removed the pressure cuff from her arm. "Congratulations," she said. "It's great to have you two safely back." Then she hugged me. Her ribs were like washboards. Her attempt on Pumori had exacted a mighty toll.

Laslow stepped forward, the pressure cuff in one hand. With the other, he shook Dave's hand. "You got us all back in one piece. Good work."

Dave and I dropped our packs. "How's your patient doing?" Dave asked Laslow, rubbing his shoulders where his old pack had dug grooves. Sarah blushed at being called a patient.

"Her pulse is down, her color is rosy. Her coordination is back, too—but I think she should wait a day or two before tackling any 5.13 boulders."

Laslow turned to me. "How about you? Feeling like yourself again?"

"Nothing three days of sleep won't cure."

Sarah laughed. She crossed her arms. "I wanted Pumori *so* badly. It was the first step in my grand plan. But after I took that dive off the ridge, it finally sank in that people get killed playing this game. Suddenly, all I could think about was curling up at home with my old cat and a good book."

"That sounds like the grandest plan of all," Dave said. Laslow helped Sarah to her tent.

Pasang's lantern glowed brightly under the fluttering fly. Chris escorted Dave and me toward the light, her arms linked around ours. "What's gotten into Laslow?" she whispered. Her peeling nose wrinkled. "He used to be afraid of his own shadow. Now, he's not even afraid of Butch."

Laslow, carrying his medical bag, passed us, heading briskly toward John's tent. A candle lantern burned inside. Judging by the shadows, two figures were inside: one lying down, the other sitting.

Laslow flung back the door. A thick cloud of blue smoke billowed out. He batted away the smoke and climbed inside.

"Young Johnny has placed great stock in your medicine," Chris told Dave.

"An innocent diversion of youth," Dave said. "And it does wonders for the appetite."

"John's been eating enough to feed a team of Shetland ponies," Chris said.

We peeked into the tent. John lay on his back, his head toward the door, still sporting his towel mufti. Although it was dark outside, he still wore his glacier glasses. Laslow knelt beside him, ducking to avoid the swinging candle lantern. He listened to John's lungs with a stethoscope.

In the back of the tent, clutching a pipe trailing blue smoke, sat Pasang. He followed Laslow's every move. It was young

Pasang who had at first been left alone in Base Camp to cope with John's brush with death. The responsibility had weighed heavily on him. Now, Pasang couldn't let go of his charge.

"How's the young scoundrel doing, Doctor Laslow?" Chris asked.

John, on his back, pulled off his glacier glasses. "Doctor Dave! Monsignor Jeff!" He reached up. Dave and I each gave him a high-five. "I wouldn't let Chotari's hired goons haul me away until you got back. Congratulations on making the top. Wish I was there."

"We wish you were there, too," Dave said. "The rogue's gallery was incomplete without you. What's the prognosis, Doctor Laslow?"

Laslow put away his stethoscope. "His chest sounds substantially better. He's putting back on some weight."

"I owe it all to Doctor Dave's medicine," John said. He motioned to Pasang to pass the pipe. He took a mighty hit; Laslow swatted at the smoke.

"Your medicine has helped him to eat," Laslow told Dave. "But the Furosemide and oxygen pulled him back from death's doorstep. Chotari and Pasang did well."

"What about evacuation plans?" Dave asked.

"Chotari has two strong porters lined up for the morning," Laslow said. "They'll carry John down to Namche Bazar in double stages, getting him there ahead of us. John's stabilizing nicely. But his body has taken a terrible beating. I'd like to see him get down even sooner."

"Shucks," John said, handing the pipe to Pasang. "I can handle the altitude long enough for the post-summit celebration."

We left John alone so he could rest. On the way to the kitchen fly, Laslow stopped and grabbed Dave's elbow.

"This is difficult for me to say," Laslow started.

"Say it with flowers," Dave suggested.

"I want to thank you. This mountain was important to me. And without your encouragement—and your occasional shameless gameplaying—I never would have made it."

"Likewise," Dave said, grinning.

"Blow it out your butthole," Laslow said. "The time to patronize me is over. It served its purpose, but now it's irritating. Back to my point: you were kind enough to take me under your wing. You showed me things I'd forgotten were within me."

"You're ready to tackle Everest now," Dave said.

"*Wrong*," Laslow said. "Thanks to you, this is my last mountain. I don't have anything left to prove to myself."

"Maybe we're all looking for that one last mountain," Dave said.

"I have a practice to get back to in Muttontown," Laslow said. "Patients who need me. And I have a beautiful wife who's been crazy enough to put up with me while I've been off climbing mountains. She must love me."

"Love is a powerful and mysterious energy," Dave said. "Promise me you won't stop your volunteer work."

"I promise." The two men shook hands. Laslow went to his tent.

As Dave and I approached the light from Pasang's kitchen lantern, Chotari stood with his back to us, steam rising from a mug of tea. Butch stood behind Pasang, trying to hurry dinner. Pasang glanced sideways at Butch as he stirred his kettle and muttered. Eugene stood, plate and spoon in hand, impatiently waiting on Pasang.

Dave and I stepped under the fly. Chotari turned. A broad smile grew across his weathered face. He tossed the last of his tea into the darkness. "Good to see you, brothers!" He slapped each of us on the back. "Outstanding work. You feeling better, Jefferson?"

I didn't have a chance to answer. Butch had come up behind us, putting a gangly arm around each of us. "Congratulations, gentlemen. Laslow told me all about it. You make me look good."

"Nonsense," Dave said. "How can we make you look any better? You can't improve on perfection."

"I suppose I have that coming, Dave. I've had it pointed out to me that I cold bone up on humility. It's a common affliction of my profession. I want to thank you. You took over the rope when John and Chotari fell out. You got your folks safely up the hill and back. You went above and beyond the call for a client. I'm sending off a cable to see if the home office will consider a discount toward a future trip for you."

Eugene stood beside Butch, his plate and spoon still in hand. "I'm glad at least *somebody* made it up the mountain."

"Easy, Eugene," Butch warned. "Remember what I told you."

Butch turned toward the tents. He cupped his hands and shouted: *"Hey,* everybody! It's time to party!"

Everyone but John circled around. Chotari ran to his tent and fetched his last two bottles of arak. He poured monster shots into everybody's mugs.

The first bottle of arak was already polished off when Pasang clanged his kettle to announce dinner. Eugene sprinted to the stove; famished, I was close behind. Butch reached over Pasang's shoulder and stuck a finger into the yak chow mein. He tasted it, then smacked his lips. "Primo. Let's get these people fed." Pasang glowered at Butch, then took the ladle and served Eugene. Eugene took his plate and went to his tent to eat alone.

Laslow stepped up to the stove without a plate. "I need to speak with you, Butch."

"What's up, Doc?" Butch leaned over Pasang and grabbed a biscuit.

"I want a helicopter for John."

Butch lowered his biscuit. "You told me he's over the worst of it."

"He's worn out. He needs to get to Namche Bazar first thing tomorrow—not in a day or two."

Butch tossed the biscuit onto the table beside Pasang. It rolled off and hit Pasang's foot. "I'm sorry, Laslow. You told me he's out of the woods. I can't afford to have an apprentice guide flown out when I can have porters carry him out for a thousandth of the cost."

Chotari spoke up. "Tell me, Butch. Which medical school did you graduate from?"

"*Excuse me*, Chotari?" Butch's diplomatic veneer vanished.

"I asked you which medical school you graduated from. Unless you've had a secret life I don't know about, Laslow is the only doctor here."

"Let's discuss this in private, Chotari. This doesn't need to be vented in front of the clients."

"By all means," Chris chimed in. "Vent away. I'm not bashful."

"Chotari's hit the nail on the head," Dave said. "There's only one doctor on this hill."

Butch fidgetted. "Let's all relax. We're tired. Tempers are short."

"*Time* is short, too," Laslow said. "To hell with your profit margin. I want you to get a chopper to take John down at first light."

"I can't do that," Butch said. "With this cloud cover, it could take two or three days for a chopper to get here from Kathmandu. By then, if the porters take John, he'll already be recuperating in Namche Bazar."

Laslow pointed into the darkness—off toward Everest Base Camp, two miles to the northeast. "Two choppers are sitting over there," he said. "Get on the radio, or walk over there. A chopper may not be able to get up from Kathmandu. But one of those two can certainly make it down."

Jim Fairchild

"Even if one of the *Summit 8000* choppers *is* available," Butch said, "I don't have enough cash on hand to pay for a flight."

"I'm sure they'd take a promissory note from your guide service," Laslow insisted.

"And the *Summit 8000* choppers *are* available," Chotari said.

"How do you know?" Butch fumed.

"Because," Chotari said, grinning, "every climbing Sherpa in the Khumbu Himalaya is on strike as of one hour ago. The *Summit 8000* team is going nowhere."

"*What?*" Butch asked, incredulous.

"As of one hour ago, Surfer Boy, I no longer work for you. As of one hour ago, the Sherpa people are taking charge of their own lives."

Pasang took off his apron. He tossed his ladle into the kettle. Yak chow mein splattered on Butch's back.

Butch turned angrily. "What do you think you're doing, Pasang?"

"Pasang on strike, too." He threw down his Big Mountain Guides ballcap and stomped on it. "Keep your cheap hat. Keep your three dollars a day."

"I don't believe this," Butch said. He put his hands on his hips like an 18th-century British naval officer staring down a mutiny. "You two must be kidding."

"Nobody's kidding," Chotari said. "You're speaking to the strike leader."

How are you Sherpas going to survive without climbing?" Butch asked. He pointed to Chotari's gold Rolex. "What about that watch? An expedition gave that to you. Can you afford to bite the hand that's fed you all these years?"

"I'm not a dog, Surfer Boy," Chotari said. "You can't toss me a bone and expect me to wag my tail. I am a *man*." He unfastened the Rolex from his wrist and threw it to the ground. He crushed it under the toe of his boot. Pasang gasped at what was left of the watch he'd always admired. It had been presented to Chotari by Bonington's 1975 Everest Southwest Face expedition.

"There," Chotari said. "That is what I think of the bones you've always tossed the Sherpa people."

Eugene reappeared from his tent, plate in hand. Unaware of what had just transpired, he stepped up to Pasang, still behind his kettles. "Hey," Eugene said. "Who's a guy got to bribe to get some seconds?"

Pasang, his arms folded defiantly across his chest, glared at Eugene. "What you want, Eugene?"

"Seconds on chow mein, if that's not too much to ask. I was under the impression you were our cookboy."

Pasang's nostrils flared. "Sorry, Eugene-sahib. I your boy. I get you seconds." Pasang picked up his crushed ballcap and cocked it sideways on his head. He fished the ladle out of the bubbling chow mein.

Eugene held out his plate. "A little more yak this time, too."

"Gotcha, sahib. More yak." Pasang stirred the chow mein, then lifted the dripping ladle over Eugene's plate. "Enough yak, Eugene-sahib?"

"Fine, little buddy. Sometime today would be jim-dandy."

Pasang flicked the ladle. Yak chow mein sailed into Eugene's face.

"Enjoy your seconds, Possum Boy," Pasang said, his eyes twinkling. He tossed the ladle, and then the ballcap, into the kettle. He sat down and poured himself a mug of arak, grinning victoriously. Eugene, still clutching his plate, his face dripping with yak chow mein, stared into the kettle at the sinking ballcap.

"I'd like to get back to the matter of the helicopter," Laslow said to Butch. But Butch didn't have a chance to respond. From out of the dark came a scraping sound. It was John, supporting himself with two trekking poles, their tips rasping against the rocks.

He entered the light. His glacier glasses hung around his

neck. The omnipresent towel was wrapped around his head; on top of the towel sat his Big Mountain Guides ballcap.

"You should be in bed," Laslow said.

"I hope I'm not too late," John said. He turned to Butch. "I suppose Chotari's told you about the strike by now."

"How long have you known about it?" Butch glared.

"Pasang told me a couple of weeks ago."

"This is going to have a bearing on your job evaluation," Butch warned.

"Bear down on *this*," John said, offering his middle finger. "I quit." He chuckled at Eugene, busy wiping chow mein from his face. "Yak becomes you," John said. John looked into the kettle and saw Pasang's sinking ballcap. He took off his own ballcap and added it to the kettle of chow mein. Then he hobbled back toward his tent.

Chris began to applaud. Soon, Sarah, Dave and I had joined in. John lifted a cupped hand and waved like the Pope bestowing blessings upon his adoring throng.

"Now," Laslow said to Butch. "About that helicopter."

"Okay," Butch said. "I'll check into it tomorrow morning. If the *Summit 8000* people don't want too much, maybe I can work it into the budget."

"You're going to check on it *now*," Sarah said, "or you'll never work as a guide again."

Butch looked stunned. "What's that mean?"

"It means that when I get home, I'll slap a lawsuit against you and your guide service that will make your head spin."

"For what?"

"For recklessly endangering John's life. For recklessly endangering the lives of clients by making the first summit push when a storm was coming."

"You know you can't prove that," Butch said.

"It doesn't matter what I can prove," Sarah said. "That's the beauty of the American legal system. I can keep you and your employers tied up in litigation for years. I can bleed them dry in the process. First thing they'll do is fire you and file a cross-suit against your spindly ass. You'll never guide again."

I smiled wistfully at Dave. The old Sarah was back.

"Fine," Butch said, raising his hands in surrender. "I'll head for Everest Base Camp right now. I'll pay for the chopper myself if I have to. Just give me a minute to get my gear together." He departed for his tent.

"I don't know about you," Dave said to me, "but I'm still awfully hungry." He walked over to the kettle and lifted out a ballcap coated with chow mein. "This might be pretty good with some Tabasco."

Pasang jumped up, a little wobbly from the arak. "Sorry, guys. I whip up something tasty real fast."

"You're on strike," Dave said. "Chill out, little brother. We can cook for ourselves." Dave started to rummage through food boxes for something to throw on the stove.

"Hey," Pasang said, pushing Dave out of the way. "Strike or not. This Pasang's kitchen. And Pasang *always* happy to cook for friends."

Soon Pasang had thick yak rib steaks, smothered in onions and peppers, sputtering in his cast iron skillet. While he cooked, Dave and I went back to our tent to get cleaned up. We peeled off our crusty climbing clothes. Chotari brought us a big kettle of hot water, a bar of soap and a stiff brush.

It felt incredible to be off the mountain, to be clean again, to be headed home. I reached for my towel. Dave still stood naked on the other side of the steaming pot, scrubbing earnestly behind an ear with the sudsy brush. Two figures walked up in the darkness. The first was Pasang. The second was a stranger.

"Somebody here to see Dave," Pasang said nervously. The second figure stepped up beside him.

Jim Fairchild

Dave, still naked as a jaybird and scrubbing diligently behind his ears, peered through the suds and the dark. "The pleasure's mine. Whose acquaintance am I making?"

The stranger reached upward to switch on a headlamp, flooding Dave with light. The face beneath the headlamp was cast in shadows. It was a slender face—not Sherpa, but rather Nepali.

The stranger spoke. "I am Captain Mahavishnu S.J.B. Chandira, of the Royal Nepalese Army." I could hear boot heels click. As my eyes adjusted to the bright headlamp, I could make out the crisply pressed khaki jodhpurs, the immaculately starched field jacket, the impatience of rank. I dropped my towel and hurriedly climbed into my hiking trousers.

"I'm honored," Dave said, rendering a British-style salute with one hand, the other hand still digging vigorously in one ear. He held up the soapy brush in the light of the captain's headlamp to inspect the gleanings. The captain recoiled from the brush. Then Dave squinted at the captain. "Pardon my sloppy salute, but it's too cold to come to a fully rigid position of attention, even for an old trooper like mine." Dave tossed the brush into the steaming pot and searched for his towel. Still naked, he began to dry his hair. "To what do I owe this delightful honor, Captain Mahavishnu S.J.B. Chandira?"

"I am here to arrest you, good sir," the captain announced. He reached into a jacket pocket and pulled out a pair of handcuffs. Their chrome gleamed brightly in the light of the headlamp. "As soon as you have done me the honor of putting your garments on, I shall be obliged to place these implements upon your wrists."

* * *

Chapter Ten:
Burning Bridges

Dave was under arrest for the beating of the French trekker. The victim had given a detailed description of his attacker to the investigating constable. The constable, one of Ang Dorje's cousins and a chang-drinking partner of Dave's, had dutifully taken down the description and then promptly and purposefully misplaced the report. It was after prodding from the French Embassy that Nepalese Royal Army Captain Mahavishnu S.J.B. Chandira had been dispatched from Kathmandu to track down the crazed attacker.

Chotari insisted that Chandira allow Dave and me to dress in privacy. He led the captain to the kitchen fly, where Pasang brought out his best Darjeeling tea and sugar cookies.

As Dave and I finished dressing, we listened to Chotari and the captain argue—first in English, then in Nepali. In moments, Chris, Sarah, Laslow, John and Pasang had joined Chotari. They had the increasingly defensive captain surrounded, and were roundhousing him with staccato questions, demands and, eventually, insults.

"It could be worse," I said, finding my hiking boots. "You could be under arrest for smuggling hash."

"I have a confession to make," Dave said, hastily braiding his wet hair.

"What now?"

"There never was a smuggling operation."

"That's a relief."

"Not really," Dave groaned. "The truth is worse. I scammed the generals. I passed word to them that I was setting up an operation, and offered to split the profits in return for their logistical help. But I said I was short on start-up funds. They put up a quarter-million in crisp American currency. I took the satchel of cash and split. I left a trail to the airport that made it look like I'd left Nepal. If Chandira hauls me back to Kathmandu, I'm puppy chow."

I zipped up my jacket. "I always wondered why you brought me here on a guided climb, instead of getting a permit to climb a peak on our own. You didn't want your name on a climbing application at the Ministry of Tourism."

"Bingo," Dave said. He pulled on hiking shorts, despite the cold.

"I'm going with you," I insisted. "I can contact the American Embassy legal section."

"*Sometime tonight*, please, gentlemen," Chandira called to us.

Under the kitchen fly, Sarah leaned into the captain's face, demanding to see an arrest warrant. He calmly replied that we were in Nepal, not in a *Perry Mason* re-run.

Dave and I joined the others. "Your hands, please, sir," the captain said to Dave, holding out the cuffs disdainfully. The captain ratcheted them around Dave's hands. Dave was shown the small courtesy of not being handcuffed behind his back. "It is late," Chandira said. "The sooner we get started, the sooner we can get back to civilization."

"All that starch in your britches has gone to your brain," Chris huffed. "You can't expect a man to hike through the dark with his hands manacled."

"Madam, I certainly do not intend to spend the night *here*," the captain said. Clearly, he was a man of the city, perchance a fan of featherbeds, and found this foray into the wilds a distasteful part of his sworn duties for the kingdom.

The captain agreed to let me come along. I got the feeling he thought he'd be safer that way. He would not be hiking alone in the dark with a crazed man who had a proven propensity for Yeti-like violence. I ran to our tent and packed our daypacks with jackets and a few essentials. Pasang brought me our yak steaks wrapped in waxed paper. Blood ran out of the package. When I thanked him, his eyes brimmed with tears.

Dave and the captain both sat on a boulder waiting. I strapped on my headlamp, then helped Dave with his. "Well, then," the captain said. He dropped his tea mug to the ground and rose, checking his watch. It was after nine o'clock. "If we march quickly, we can catch breakfast and passably drinkable tea in Pheriche." He cinched the shoulder straps on his spotless military rucksack. Pasang, glowering, bent down and retrieved the tea mug the captain had dropped.

"Wait," Chotari shouted. He ran from his tent. In his hand was a piece of white cloth. It was a silk friendship scarf. He placed it carefully around Dave's neck. "Ang Dorje gave me this *kata* a few days before he died," Chotari explained. "I have worn it ever since under my jacket. Its power saw us safely up Daughter Peak and back. Now, it must go with you, David." He held Dave tightly, kissing him on both cheeks. "For the journey that lies ahead."

Pasang, too, stepped forward. He handed Dave his old ice axe.

Dave took the axe in his shackled hands. "Be good, little brother. Thank you for everything."

"You will not need the ice axe," the captain said impatiently. "There will be no more climbing for you."

Dave explained that his father had given him the axe. The

257

Jim Fairchild

captain relented, but told Dave he must place it on his back, where it could not easily be employed as a weapon. Reaching awkwardly back with both hands, Dave stuck the axe spike-first between his back and the shoulder straps of his pack, so that the head came to rest behind his neck.

While the captain stomped his boots, the rest of the team said their good-byes to Dave. "Give a bloke some starched khaki and polished brass," Chris said tearfully, "and he starts behaving like an imperious goon." Sarah kissed Dave's whiskered cheek and promised to follow any legal avenues she could find once back in Namche Bazar. John gave Dave a high-five and promised the party of the century when they met again. Laslow promised to make sure the rest of our gear got carried out for us.

And then, the captain's patience exhausted, we were off. In moments, the glow of Pasang's lantern had disappeared into the night behind us. The captain set a brisk pace; Dave was close behind. I brought up the rear. As we followed the rutted moraine, rain began to fall. It soon soaked my fleece jacket. The captain was moving too fast for me to pull out raingear.

Soon, the rain changed to wet snow. Huge flakes flitted past in my headlamp beam like glowing moths. Their spinning made me dizzy. Shielding my eyes, I stumbled along.

We had to cross streams draining ridges to our right. On our approach, they had been tiny rivulets. Now, as summer neared, they were raging torrents. At the first stream crossing, the captain leapt sprightly from one stepping stone to the next, not even pausing on the far bank for Dave and me to catch up.

And then we crossed a second, and a third. Each time, I watched fearfully as Dave jumped from one wet boulder to the next, swinging his handcuffed arms awkwardly in front of him. The swirling waters threw my balance off. I felt lost without my ice axe. Even though I'd watched Pasang give Dave *his* axe, I'd been too shocked by events to grab my own. Now, it sat with the rest of my

258

gear back at Gorak Shep.

An hour and a half below Base Camp, we reached the fourth stream crossing. It was only perhaps fifteen feet wide, but it raged so fiercely that I could hear rock grinding on rock. Below the churning surface, small boulders were being pushed down the channel.

The captain couldn't find the place where he'd crossed earlier that evening. He began to hop from boulder to boulder along the bank, moving farther downstream, scanning the far side. I didn't recognize any of it. It had been weeks since I'd passed this way, and then it had been in daylight. But the stream was dropping into a deep defile that I certainly should have remembered. I didn't like the look of it. I was sure we were dropping too far down the flank of the moraine.

At last, the captain came to a halt. He pointed toward a narrow gap between boulders on the far bank. It seemed he knew where he was going after all. It looked like the trail continued on the far side.

But one thing had changed. The last time we'd crossed there, a series of tall stepping stones provided an easy crossing. Now, their tops were barely visible above the seething waters. Indeed, some were now submerged. Ahead, the captain stepped onto the first barely-visible boulder. Spray soaked his khakis. He leapt to the next boulder. The ground shuddered as a rock shifted somewhere in the stream bed. My knees began to shake.

This was madness. Somebody was going to get killed. After safely climbing Pumori, it would be ridiculous to die in a stream crossing. The captain leapt onto a third boulder. Foaming water surged to his knees. Dave had one boot on the first boulder, testing it. He obviously didn't like its feel.

I began to shout for Dave to wait. The captain would have to unlock the handcuffs if he expected us to follow. Out on the third rock, waves crashed against the captain's leg; he, too, was finally

Jim Fairchild

having second thoughts.

Suddenly, the captain was gone. A huge surge of foaming water had knocked him down. Dave began to dash downstream, chasing him.

I raced behind. Ahead, I could see the glow of the captain's headlamp bobbing up and down in the raging stream. The glow was sucked between tall boulders; at times, it disappeared beneath the surface, casting a soft green luminosity. Dave, his balance thrown off by the manacles, careened down the bank, crashing from boulder to boulder, in hot pursuit.

The captain had been washed perhaps fifty yards downstream when he was caught in a dizzying eddy. His head was barely above water; the beam of his headlamp pointed down into the frothing pool. His rucksack, bobbing behind him, kept pushing his face into the water. His face ran with blood. I couldn't tell if he was alive.

Dave reached the edge of the eddy. With his hands locked together, he would not be able to pull the captain out of the water by himself. I rushed to help.

In the light of my headlamp, I saw Dave reach back with both hands. He pulled the ice axe from behind his back. He let the shaft slip downward between his manacled hands until he grasped it just above the spike. And then, swinging back, he raised the pick over his head.

I stumbled over a boulder; Dave turned toward me, axe poised over his head. In the beam of my headlamp, the old axe's pick gleamed. I knew how sharp Dave kept it, how many hours he worked on it with an old bastard file, honing the point until it was as sharp as a dagger. And then it crossed my mind—if only for a fraction of a second—that Dave might *kill*, rather than rescue, the captain. I didn't know him well enough any more.

The axe arced downward. The pick plunged toward the captain's neck. Then I heard the sound of ripping canvas. Dave had driven the old axe into the captain's bobbing rucksack—precisely where he had aimed.

Heaving mightily, his boots slipping on wet rocks, Dave pulled at the limp body hanging from his axe. He slipped again, crashing to his knees. With his hands manacled, he was unable to stop his fall. Struggling to keep his own head above water, he was losing the captain. I was paralyzed.

Dave turned toward me. *"Give me a fucking hand! I'm losing him!"*

I had control of my knees again. I plunged into the icy water. I grabbed the captain's shoulder straps. We dragged the captain out of the water just as Dave's axe ripped through the soggy canvas.

We lowered the captain to the ground. Dave knelt over him, an ear to his mouth. I could see that Dave's knee had been gashed on the rocks. Blood coursed down into one boot. Dave looked at me. "He's breathing. But he bashed his head pretty badly." By the light of my headlamp I found a deep cut under the captain's matted hair.

"We need to find shelter," Dave said. "He'll freeze to death if we don't get him dried out."

"Wait here," I said. "I'll look around."

Dave pulled off his wool tunic. He wrung water out of it and spread it over the captain. While he bandaged the cut on the captain's head, I stumbled through the boulders, looking for an overhang out of the blowing snow. A hundred yards back up the trail I found a tall boulder, much like the one Sarah and the Sherpa boy, Sonam, had scaled. The overhang's underside was blackened by smoke. In the overhang's farthest recess I found an armful of dry wood, stashed by some passing porter. We dragged the captain to the overhang.

The adrenaline began to wear off; I realized how wet and cold I was. If we didn't get a fire going, not just the captain, but all

261

three of us, might be dead by sunrise. I took off my fleece jacket and wrung it out; before I could put it back on, Dave grabbed it for the captain. He pulled off the officer's knee-high riding boots and poured out the water. Then he unfastened the captain's pistol belt. He rolled the belt and set it on a rock beside the captain.

The captain opened his eyes. He saw his pistol beside him. It was an ancient break-action Enfield No. 2 with a lanyard ring at the base of the grip. It had probably seen service in World War II. He pulled it to his chest under the jacket. As I broke up firewood, I turned to Dave. "Tell him to unlock your cuffs," I said. "He owes you."

The captain shivered convulsively, then looked at me. Through blue, quaking lips, he formed the word "No."

Soon, the overhang flickered with the glow of a fire. I tried not to stoke the blaze too high, knowing how little wood we had. We dragged the captain as close as we could to the fire, propping his head on his wet rucksack. Then, watching the steam rise from the shivering officer's khakis, Dave and I huddled on either side of the flame, our knees tucked to our chins. The heat of the fire started the blood flowing again on Dave's gashed knee.

I dressed Dave's wound. "You saved him," I said. "And he's going to pay you back by throwing you in jail."

"Nobody needs to die," Dave said. And then, still soaked but too exhausted to care, the two of us managed to doze off.

*　*　*

I awoke. My watch said it was almost two in the morning. Someone had spread my fleece jacket over me.　It was dry now. Then it dawned on me that I'd been awakened by the smell of food.

Dave was still asleep. He was curled on his side, knees nearly to his chin. His clothes were dry now, but he shivered in his sleep. His face and hair were matted with sand.

A military mess plate sat on a rock beside Dave. The plate held a feast: a stack of steaming buttered chapatis, and Pasang's two yak rib steaks, freshly reheated.

The captain sat at the edge of the firelight, his back to us. He was dry now, too, and had a military poncho pulled around his shoulders. "Thank you for the use of your jacket," he said. "It was kind of you. But you were shivering in your sleep, so I gave it back."

"How's your head?" I asked, pulling on my jacket and zipping it.

"Please," he whispered. "Call me Noddy. That is how friends address me."

"Certainly, Noddy," I whispered. "After what Dave did, the least you could do is unlock his handcuffs."

Noddy stared out at the falling snow. Most of it was melting as it alit. "I am sorry, my friend. But my solemn oath to the King of Nepal prohibits me from doing so. It is my duty to return him to Kathmandu to face justice."

Noddy pulled an arm from under his poncho. Finally looking at me, he pointed to the mess plate. "My wife made the chapatis, and I took the liberty of heating the steaks in Mr. Porter's pack. Be sure to avail yourself of my special condiments. I left them beside the food." He smiled cleverly.

A small pair of salt and pepper shakers sat beside the plate of food. A plastic bag held dried chili peppers. Next to the peppers lay the key to Dave's handcuffs.

Noddy turned away again. "My report shall state that a dreadful accident occurred while crossing a swollen stream on the way back to Namche Bazar. I fell into the stream, nearly drowning. I lost charge of Mr. Porter at that time. I do not know what became of him. Perhaps he drowned in the same stream. If so, the chances of finding his remains are nil. *Yes.* I believe my report will stress that possibility."

I unlocked Dave's handcuffs. He roused, eyes wide. "Thank Noddy," I told him. "After he fell in the stream, he never saw you again." I tossed the cuffs and key beside the food.

Dave sat up. He rubbed his wrists. "I hope Captain Noddy made it out of that stream. He was a damned fine man. A credit to his uniform."

"*Eat*," Noddy said firmly, looking away. "And then be gone. I simply ask that you not let me see in which direction you go. In that manner, I shall be able to honestly report to my superiors that I do not know what happened to you."

Dave and I wolfed down steak and chapatis. We left an equal share for Noddy, who insisted we eat first. We grabbed our things. "Thank you, Noddy," Dave said, patting the captain's shoulder. "Safe travels." Then we stepped out from under the overhang.

When we reached the trail, we had two choices: back up to our camp at Gorak Shep, or down toward Namche Bazar. Dave was officially a fugitive; I wondered which path he'd take. Without speaking, he headed toward Gorak Shep. I followed.

We recrossed the lesser streams. I was still short of sleep, and we'd summitted a 23,000-foot mountain the day before. But, all things considered, I felt pretty decent. Soon, though, the snow and drizzle had soaked me again; my headlamp shorted out. Chilled, I stumbled through the dark after Dave.

*   *   *

Dave's pace grew faster the closer we got to Gorak Shep. I barely managed to keep up. The light from his headlamp fell too far ahead to help me. I stumbled along, tripping over rocks.

The snow and drizzle stopped. The clouds above us began to break up. Through the breaks, a full moon shone down on us, igniting the surrounding walls of ice and rock with an electric glow.

Dave came to a halt. I crashed into him. I sat down on a boulder to rest. Dave remained standing.

I tried to get my bearings. Looking at the lay of the land around us, something seemed out of whack. I looked for the final hump in the moraine that should have remained between us and Gorak Shep. Instead, I could see only the vast fractured amphitheater of the Khumbu Glacier. *How could we be lost?* I looked at Dave. He seemed oblivious. And then, as I was about to speak, I looked to the west.

There, half a mile away, lay the icy tarn of Gorak Shep. We were on the wrong trail. We were headed straight up the valley toward Everest Base Camp.

"We screwed up," I moaned, pointing toward Gorak Shep.

"I thought we'd take one last side-trip before heading home," Dave said.

I was astounded that Dave would lead me through the dark on such a lark without asking me. "It's too late to see Naomi," I said. "You're wanted by the law. And I want to go home."

Dave switched off his headlamp. "If you want to go back to Gorak Shep, I'll take you. But I had a little adventure in mind, *if* you're up to it. And it's not a stroll down Memory Lane with Naomi."

I looked past Dave: past the moonlit glacier and the fluted shoulder of Nuptse—clear up to the leaning pyramid of Everest's summit. The moonlight made Dave's teeth sparkle.

"You're stoned," I said. "We don't have a permit for Everest."

"I'm talking about kneeling on the Roof of the World," Dave said. "And you're talking about a piece of paper. I'll never have this chance again. Even if Noddy files a bogus report, the generals will look for me. I'm going to have to leave the country."

"How do you expect to pull this off?"

"*Summit 8000* already has camps stocked clear to the South

265

Col," Dave said. "Now, they're paralyzed by the Sherpa strike. All of their climbers are back in Base Camp. We just sneak past them, climbing light and fast, without the encumbrance of oxygen gear. We climb their fixed ropes, we sleep in their tents, we eat their food."

"That's theft," I said.

"Look at it as *borrowing*."

"I could get banned from Nepal if we're caught," I said.

"So what? You'll never be coming back. This is your last chance, too. Isn't that old dream still in your heart?"

"You didn't bring me to Nepal so I could have a whack at a childhood dream," I said. "You're using me. You have a hidden agenda."

"There *was* a hidden agenda," Dave admitted. "Ang Dorje and I had planned an attempt on Chomolongma during the Sherpa strike. The two of us—one Sherpa, one Westerner—would show the world that the Goddess Mother could be climbed by a small team motivated by love and reverence for her. It would be a blow against the huge commercial expeditions like *Summit 8000*. We wanted to pull off the climb during the strike, when the whole world was watching."

"Where did I come in?" I asked.

"Ang Dorje and I needed a support climber—somebody to help us through the Khumbu Icefall, somebody to come to the rescue if we got in trouble. Ang Dorje told me the choice was mine. I told him I wanted you."

"I guess I should be honored in a criminal sort of way."

Dave went on. "When Ang Dorje died, the plan went to hell in a handbasket. I tried to get Chotari to take Ang Dorje's place, but there was no way he could climb Chomolongma and coordinate the strike at the same time. I thought about going solo. But I realized my solo days are over."

"So I got a promotion before I even knew I had a job."

"To be honest," Dave said, "when I first saw you in Namche Bazar, I wasn't sure you'd cut the mustard. I could see by the set of your shoulders that you'd lost your self-confidence. But I watched you on Pumori. You had a little problem with altitude, but you still have what counts. Even if you don't realize it yourself."

"The altitude almost *killed* me," I protested. "There's *no* way I could survive Everest—especially without oxygen."

"A lot of folks have problems with altitude—even professional guides. You can't predict it. Hillary did fine on Everest in 1953, then two years later collapsed on Makalu and had to be carried down. You've just been to 23,000 feet on Pumori. You'll never be more ready for Chomolongma."

"How can you be sure?" I asked. "Like you said, you can't predict. Maybe I'll be fine my second time at 23,000 feet. Maybe I'll keel over dead at 24,000 feet."

"We'll climb fast," Dave said. "We won't give altitude a chance to get us. Speed is the key. A day or two up, then a day down."

"That's pushing the limits."

"It's been done," Dave said. "Lorettan and Troillet climbed the north side in forty hours. Marc Batard did the South Col route in less than a day. *And they didn't use oxygen.* The extra weight just slows you down."

"But they're athletes," I said. "I'm a burned-out accountant."

"You don't have to be an athlete," Dave said. "If you look inside yourself, you'll find all you need. The *dream* is what gets you to the top."

A gust of wind blew against my back. I shivered. "What about climbing clothes and gear? All of our stuff is back at Gorak Shep."

"One of Ang Dorje's nephews will meet us at Everest Base Camp. He'll get us outfitted." Dave waited for me to find another objection. When I'd sat silently long enough, he spoke once more: "You'll never have this chance again. You can help make climbing history. You can help make a better future for the Sherpas. How can you say no?"

"This is another fine mess you've gotten me into," I said.

* * *

Turning our backs on Gorak Shep—turning my back on the short way home—we headed up the Khumbu Glacier's lateral moraine toward Everest Base Camp. I could smell it five minutes before the shadowy outlines of its sprawling tent city came into view. The air was thick with the stench of the malfunctioning solar outhouses.

Dave switched off his headlamp. Walking stealthily, we reached the outhouses. Their doors hung open, creaking in the wind. As we stepped past, something jumped out of one and came at us. It glowed neon-green in the dark.

Dave introduced me to Pemba Dorje. He was 23 years old. He wore one of the *Summit 8000* windsuits. This was already his sixth Everest expedition. "Chotari radioed me," he told Dave. "I was expecting you. He said you had a small problem with an Army officer. He said you'd probably bribe your way out of it. I hope you didn't pay too much."

Pemba looked me over. "You have been given a great honor. The prayers of the Sherpa people go with you."

The sound of footfalls came toward us. A belching figure in neon-green stumbled toward the outhouses.

"We must hurry," Pemba said. "I'll take you to the supply tent, where you can get your gear. You must be through the icefall by sunrise, so that nobody will see you, and so that you are safely above it before the morning sun loosens the ice." He led us through the camp, off past the charred remains of the Bierhaus tent that had been set afire by porters. The sound of snoring came from countless tents. We avoided the few tents that were lit from within by lanterns.

Pemba stopped outside a big wall tent on the far side of the camp. He peeked inside the flaps, then motioned for us to follow. He found a lantern and lit it, keeping the flame low.

"Help yourselves," Pemba said, motioning around the tent. "The expedition keeps plenty of extra clothing and gear for emergencies. You should find everything you need."

Dave and I rifled through duffel bags and boxes. Shivering, I peeled off my soaked hiking clothes and climbed into borrowed longjohns and a fleece suit. Dave did likewise.

Pemba, whispering, filled us in on the strike. "The *Summit 8000* leaders didn't think we were serious at first. They thought they could bribe us with a few extra rupees a day and a few more pairs of wool socks. I think it's just sinking in. They called the Sherpas into a meeting last night. They threatened us with a lawsuit. I told them they watch too much *People's Court*. They have forgotten whose country they are in. We Sherpas laughed and walked out. The organizers threatened to make sure we never work on a mountain again. They went from tent to tent with fistfuls of cash, trying to bribe enough Sherpas to get them up the mountain. There were no takers."

I dug through the duffels looking for a pair of double boots that fit my size thirteen feet. The closest I found were size twelve. I squeezed into them. They pinched my toes; they would have to do.

Pemba told Dave that not all of the climbers had been freaked by the announcement of the strike. Naomi and two Poles announced that they supported the Sherpas. The three were summoned by the *Summit 8000* organizers, who invited them either to take back their statements of solidarity or forfeit their salaries and pack their bags for home. All three refused to yield. They would be flying out to Namche Bazar as soon as weather permitted.

269

Jim Fairchild

Dave and I pulled on new neon-green windsuits. I needed an ice axe. I found an old one in the corner and hefted it. A name was engraved on the pick. I looked closely: NAOMI YOKOMURA. I took it. I hoped Naomi would forgive me.

Dave and I grabbed a couple of climbing packs. We stuffed in borrowed gloves and socks and goggles while Pemba left for a few minutes. When he returned, he carried sausage and cheese, hard candy and four water bottles filled with hot tea. Dave and I divided it between us.

Pemba checked his watch. "You must scoot now," he scolded. "You must reach the Western Cwm before sunrise." He picked up our borrowed packs and helped us on with them. Mine felt awfully light for an attempt on Everest. Suddenly, the enormity of what we were doing sank in. Despite the warm, dry borrowed clothes, a shiver ran down my spine.

"Thanks for everything," Dave said to Pemba. Pemba handed Dave his ice axe. Dave led the way to the tent's rear door. He turned again to Pemba. "With any luck, we'll be back in two days."

"That is all the time you have," Pemba said. "A low pressure system will be moving in by then. You must be off the mountain before it arrives."

Pemba lashed a borrowed rope under the flap of Dave's pack. Then he pulled back the tent door. We looked out. The tents around us cast stark shadows against the blue snow. The sky was nearly clear; a full moon over Pumori shone on us like a searchlight. High above the summit of Lhotse, tattered tendrils of vapor danced in the jetstream. I shivered again.

"*Be gone*," Pemba whispered, a hand pushing each of us out the door. "The Goddess Mother awaits you. Give her my love."

* * *

Everest's South Col route is not as difficult as, say, K2's Abruzzi Ridge. Of course, one must cope with the unrivaled altitude, the wind and the cold—but the difficulty of climbing is not as bad as that of many routes on far lower peaks. Still, even those who belittle the route respect the history of the first obstacle beyond Base Camp: the Khumbu Icefall.

The icefall is a frozen chaos of teetering ice blocks that rises from 17,000 feet to nearly 20,000 feet. It is formed where the glacier grinding down the gently sloping Western Cwm suddenly flows over precipitous cliffs in the underlying rock strata. The thick ice slowly breaks apart into a precarious jumble of truck- and house-sized blocks.

It is in this one stretch of the South Col route that most deaths have occurred. It is the truly fortunate expedition that goes home without having a brush with disaster in the icefall. No matter how safe-looking a path an expedition might blaze through the jumbled chaos, there is no way to predict when the glacier might lurch, and some seemingly stable ice wall might collapse onto a team of climbers.

As a boy, reading and re-reading the journal of Dyhrenfurth's fabled 1963 expedition, I became familiar with that icefall. Now, twenty years later, I stood at the foot of that frightful cascade of ice, roping up with my old friend. Before I had my knot finished, Dave was tugging on the rope. It was a good 2,500-foot vertical climb through the icefall; the meandering route covers perhaps four horizontal miles. We had to get through it before dawn: once sunlight hit it, fragile fingers of frost holding together massive leaning blocks would soften. Walls could collapse, crevasses could expand. The icefall was a faithful old watchdog lying at the foot of the Goddess Mother: by night it slept, and the stealthy might sneak past. But once daylight awoke that faithful old dog, it eagerly snapped its jaws at any trespasser.

The *Summit 8000* team had strung miles of rope through

271

the icefall, anchored to countless pickets and bamboo poles. The rope snaked through the chaos: around ice blocks, other times over and even *under* them when a path to either side couldn't be found. Each time I had to get on hands and knees and crawl through some tight tunnel of ice under a leaning serac, I held my breath and recited Robin's name over and over. Her name became my icefall mantra. Dave looked back in the dark and wondered what I was mumbling about.

When we weren't climbing over or under or around ice blocks, we were leaping across crevasses. On the narrower crevasse crossings, there was simply a handline to help steady us. The handlines were often anchored to flimsy bamboo poles at each lip, and I doubted they would have held a fall.

Sagging aluminum ladders had been laid across the larger crevasses. Dave stepped quickly across, his crampons scraping against the rungs. I scooted across on my butt. Gazing down between the icy rungs at the bottomless blackness beneath me, I realized I didn't have the courage to cross any other way. This was no childhood game of Chutes and Ladders. I swallowed, trying to clear the cottonmouth, and recited my mantra: ROBINROBINROBIN.

We took no breaks. We had been on the go for more than 24 hours, descending and then re-climbing many thousands of feet. Somehow, exhaustion had sharpened—rather than dimmed—my awareness. I not only saw, but *felt*—in the core of my being—the disappearing greys in the ice around me, and the usurping opaline tints. I knew what that change of hue meant for my chances of reaching the top of the icefall before it began to shift, of reaching the top of the mountain, of returning home in one piece to Robin. It would be a race against time.

I just needed a brief rest. If I could only take a break when we got to the top of the icefall—if I could only curl up for a few minutes or hours or years—I would be able to keep climbing. I realized, though, that I felt strong in one crucial way: thanks, perhaps, to our Pumori climb, my body had grown accustomed to the altitude. Unlike my first trip to the saddle on Pumori, I wasn't breathing so hard that I feared cracking a rib.

We had been climbing for nearly two hours. Looking as high as I could—up toward where the summit of Lhotse should be, obscured by the jumbled walls of ice ahead—I could see a rosy streak of cloud. It was almost dawn.

Finally, the rope went slack. I looked ahead. Dave stood at the base of a huge ice wall, perhaps ninety feet high. A precarious aluminum ladder was anchored to the wall with pickets and ice screws. The ladder curved and buckled where it surmounted bulges in the wall. It looked like a remnant from some misguided Erector Set project. My knees trembled. It was only the insistent tug of the rope as Dave coiled me in that forced me forward.

When I reached Dave, he grinned. "This is the final wall at the foot of the Western Cwm. The icefall's almost behind us."

Looking at the deep seams in his whiskered face, I saw the toll our escapades had taken on him. No, it was more than our jaunt up Pumori and through the icefall that was etched into his face: just as drawing ever closer to the object of our lifelong dream was making Dave look frighteningly older, it was, I suspected, beginning to unmask his secrets. The lines in his face reminded me of the intricate facial tattoos adorning the mummified remains of ancient Inuit. If I could only decipher them, the tattoos might reveal Dave's whole life: they might be a veritable diorama illustrating his trials and travails. Awestruck, I realized what a wondrous deathmask such a web of tattoos would make. And then I realized how this entire flight of fancy must have resulted from lack of oxygen. Standing beside Dave, looking from the lines in his face to the lines of the ladder above us, I laughed.

"We can do it," I said.

"We're in like Flynn," Dave said. He offered me the lead,

Jim Fairchild

but I declined. I took the coiled rope from him. Dave began to inch his way up the ladder, an ascender securing him to a fixed rope looped through the rungs. When the rope connecting us was fed out, I, too, clipped into the fixed rope. We climbed simultaneously. I tried to synchronize my movements with his to minimize the ladder's wild vibrations.

I tried not to look up—concentrating, instead, on the icy rungs directly in front of my nose. Once or twice, though, my crampons slipped on the rungs, and I involuntarily looked down. The base of the ladder seemed miles below. And then I looked behind me. I could see that the sun would be up in minutes. The entire icefall was visible. In the greyness I could even make out the unkempt sprawl of Base Camp—where, no doubt, its occupants were already arising to another day of argument and acrimony. Just a few feet more and we would be over the edge: up into the Western Cwm, up into the high, hidden, ice-covered valley that leads to the Lhotse Face and Everest's South Col. I felt a shower of ice shards and looked up. I glimpsed the cramponed soles of Dave's borrowed boots, disappearing over the edge of the wall.

"I'm up!" Dave's voice drifted down. The cascade of ice had stopped. The top of the wall split the world in two: below, darkness and ice; above, lightness and dreams. Even though I was still reciting my ROBINROBINROBIN mantra, I had no doubt about which direction to take.   The route home—the route to my daughter and to my future—lay upward.

I hauled myself over the top of the ice wall. Dave sat nearby, belaying. He grabbed me by an arm and helped me forward. "Take a look," he said, pointing behind him. The Western Cwm rose like a gentle ramp toward the base of the steep Lhotse Face. "From here, we're on Easy Street."

My eyes followed the steep rise of the Lhotse Face—up past the Yellow Band, up past the steep couloirs leading toward its summit, up past the jagged fan-like summit itself. The rosy lines of cloud had disappeared, and a brilliant white flame haloed the peak. The sun would be peeking over the edge any moment.

We caught our breath, then stood. Just a couple of hundred yards away sat a solitary orange tent, surrounded by piles of tarp-covered supplies. This was *Summit 8000's* 20,000-foot Camp I: it served primarily as a supply dump, where Sherpas cached loads after humping them up the icefall. Climbers normally didn't stay at Camp I unless they'd been caught out unexpectedly late.

"I could sure use a nap," I said, gazing longingly at the tent.

"We'll crash for a few hours," Dave said. "We'll head up in the evening."

I felt a wave of relief. I was eager to head for the tent, but Dave was busy with something at the top of the ice wall. He was on his knees, twisting an ice screw out of the snow. Too tired to ask what he was doing, I leaned over my ice axe and watched.

I assumed he was collecting gear for our climb. He pulled out another screw, then chopped at a rope anchoring the ladder. Then he sat and put a boot against the top of the ladder. He pushed. Metal groaned. He pushed harder.

I finally realized what he was doing. The ladder pitched back from the wall. It stood in the air and wavered. Then it shuddered. The ladder buckled backwards. I could hear it pop out one anchor after another down below, faster and faster, like an opening zipper, as it peeled off the ice wall and crashed in a twisted heap far below.

Dave turned toward me, grinning. A cloud of ice rose from below. He stood up, brushing off his rump with his mittens.

"That was ignorant," I rasped.

"I'm buying time," Dave said. "It'll slow down anybody following us."

"It'll also slow us down if we have to bug out," I said.

Dave coiled the rope. "We can rig a rappel. We don't need a ladder."

Jim Fairchild

I was too tired to argue. On a short rope, we trudged toward the tent. Suddenly, the sun crept over Lhotse and blinded me. My glacier glasses had been in my windsuit all night; I had to dig to find them. In seconds, the heat of the sun had warmed my frozen face; in a few more seconds I would be able to get some much-overdue sleep. Still, something gnawed at me. It was watching Dave destroy the ladder—that final bridge that connected us to safety, to our pasts. It brought home to me just how serious this game was, just how much that fragile link had meant, and how alone we now were.

* * *

Chapter Eleven:
Two Thieves in the Valley of Silence

We were snoring inside two sleeping bags courtesy of the *Summit 8000* team. We should have lit a stove and melted snow for water. We knew that dehydration encourages mountain sickness. But there was no fighting sleep.

I awoke in the late afternoon. My tongue was stuck to the roof of my mouth. The sun had been beating on the tent all day. It felt like an oven. I fought my way out of my sleeping bag and tossed it behind me. It fell on Dave's seamed face. He kept snoring without missing a beat.

I ripped open the door and dove outside. I planted my face in the snow. It had been softened by the sun's rays; I lapped at it greedily. Finally, when I could swallow again, I squinted at my watch. It was almost 4:30. I needed to crank up a stove and melt snow. But I laid there one or two blessed moments more, sandwiched between the warmth of the sun and the coolness of the snow.

I must have dozed off a minute. A shrill noise pierced the crystalline sky. I opened my eyes and looked up. Something black soared across the deep azure of infinite space. High, high up, reeling and playing on the thermals rising off the reflector-bowl of the Western Cwm, was my old friend, the gorak. Don't ask me how

I knew, from that distance, that it was the same gorak I'd met on Pumori. But then how do you know, sometimes, that it is an old friend knocking on your door before you've opened it? I waved an arm skyward. But the soaring speck had already disappeared into the blinding backdrop of the icy Lhotse Face, headed somewhere up the mountain.

I found a food bag in the cache and dragged it into the tent. I dug out a stove and a kettle. Dave had pushed my sleeping bag off his face, but he was still snoring. When I had a pot of tea ready, I awoke him. We drained the kettle quickly. We were too tired to speak. Dave dozed off as I melted more snow. Finally, after the third kettle of tea, we spoke.

"You look bushed," I said, filling Dave's mug. "You feel up to it?"

Steam swirled around his haggard face. "Never better," he said.

I suppose that if he'd said he wanted to head down, I would have followed, glad that somebody else had made the decision. And yet, something inside was drawing me upward. It was vector addition: the logical sum of everything that had ever entered the equation of my life.

Dave slurped his tea. It dripped down the whiskers on his chin and hung a moment before falling. For the first time, I noticed that some of his whiskers had turned grey. It was funny that I had never noticed before.

* * *

When we stepped out of the tent at eight o'clock, I looked toward the west. Pumori's pyramid soared upward through a low blanket of dark clouds. The final crimson ribbons of daylight flickered about her shoulders. I remembered the photo of Robin I'd left on the summit of Daughter Peak and wished I still had it.

We were now at an altitude even with Shoulder Camp on Pumori. I remembered my first trip to the shoulder when I crawled through gale winds to the edge of Tibet, trying to get a glimpse of Art's beloved Mount Kailas. It was only a few weeks earlier, but it felt like a decade ago. I had even imagined Art's presence beside me as I'd peered into Tibet. It had been an acutely electric sensation. I chuckled aloud now as I realized how crazy the altitude had made me. I forgot Dave was beside me, stepping into his crampons. He watched me chuckle, an eyebrow raised. He said nothing.

I zipped shut the tent. If all went well, we would be back down here in no more than two days, and might need to stay here one last time. We roped up.

We followed a line of frozen bootprints. The Western Cwm is so gently inclined that it seemed we weren't even climbing. We followed a looping path through the frozen valley, the way marked by sporadic red flags tied to bamboo wands. The flags whipped noisily in the downslope wind. Their presence assured me that humans had, indeed, traversed this alien landscape before. The frequent piss stains and PowerBar wrappers frozen into the snow provided backup reassurance.

Crevasses were now far less frequent than in the icefall. But, because the glacier was under less tension here, they were also far better hidden. Dave moved carefully, a full rope-length ahead.

Soon, a halo began to grow behind Lhotse. All at once, the full moon leapt upward. Headlamps were unnecessary. I was transfixed by the reflections of moonlight in the icy flutings on either side of the Cwm. To the left, the Southwest Face of Everest rose in a series of steep cliffs and snowfields to the summit. Tendrils of ice were blasted off Everest by the jetstream and spun pell-mell in front of the moon. The wind down in the Cwm suddenly ceased; the flags on the bamboo wands hung motionless, as if time had stopped.

Jim Fairchild

And then, for a few seconds, angles of incidence and reflection aligned perfectly. The spinning vortex of ice particles blowing from the world's highest point was set afire from behind by the moon; the heavens pulsated with spectral iridescence. Geometry shifted once more, and the swirling rainbow whirlpool returned to monochrome.

I thought about Mallory's first glimpse into this icy valley. His biographers have always mentioned his literary bent. Yet the name he'd given this awesome expanse was pathetically inexpressive. The Swiss, who attempted Everest via this route the year before Hillary's and Tenzing's successful climb—blazing most of the route they later followed—chose a much more appropriate name for the Western Cwm: The Valley of Silence. This night, hunched over, too intimidated by the soaring walls and the silence of the night to make a peep, I appreciated the name given this wild place by the supposedly stodgy Swiss.

* * *

It was a quarter before eleven when the tents of Camp II, at 20,960 feet, came into sight. This was a big settlement compared to Camp I: I could see, in the bright moonlight, a half-dozen tents surrounded by caches.

Camp II was situated at a critical juncture in the Valley of Silence. From it, climbers could depart on any of three routes toward the summit. They could continue plodding straight up the Valley of Silence toward the South Col. They could hang a sharp left and angle up onto the West Ridge, as the team led by Hornbein and Unsoeld had done in 1963. Or they could frontpoint straight up a series of dizzying ice chutes and crumbling rock terraces and give the treacherous Southwest Face a try.

We climbed into the first tent we came to. Dave started a stove to melt snow. My first concern was my feet. My toes had grown icy during the slog from Camp I. My borrowed boots, a full size too short, were cutting circulation. I pulled them off and warmed my wooden toes between my bare hands until some degree of feeling returned. Having read enough stories about frostbite and amputation, I was concerned. But I was too afraid to say anything to Dave, despite his occasional glances. It wasn't that I was afraid to upset our plans. I was almost incapable of speech: it was as if I had fallen under the spell of the Valley of Silence.

* * *

Dave and I shared a kettle of tea, then one of hot chocolate, then one of lemonade. When I had my borrowed boots laced back up—looser this time—we clambered out into the moonlight again. It was just shy of 1:00 a.m. We roped up quietly and headed farther into the Valley of Silence.

The Lhotse Face loomed nearer and nearer. I glanced past Dave, trying to judge how far it was to the base of the steep face. I had come to be enamoured of the high shelter of the Valley of Silence, and knew that—once we started ascending the face—danger would again soar. Although this icy valley was higher than the highest point in North America, it seemed a sweet shelter compared to what I knew awaited us higher up.

* * *

All too soon we reached the bergschrund at the base of the Lhotse Face. We clambered up a steep aluminum ladder that spanned the black abyss below. A knot grew in my stomach as the ladder shook under our weight.

We clipped into a fixed rope at the top of the bergschrund. Dave, ahead of me, began to climb steadily. The Lhotse Face was far steeper, far more broken, far more ugly than I had imagined. The fixed rope led up steep, dirty ice, around leaning seracs, and zig-zagged between crevasses. The soaring crown of Lhotse reared directly over our heads, swallowing stars. The Yellow Band, an ancient layer of limestone in the otherwise dark rock of the Everest massif, writhed like a golden serpent above, its scales glowing in the moonlight. The wind whipped down the face and blasted our exposed flesh with ice crystals. They felt like thousands of tiny knife blades—until my face grew too numb to feel them.

I obsessed about my feet. Starting up the fixed ropes on the Lhotse Face, they burned fiercely. Every step I kicked sent a flare of pain clear up my shin. But I figured the pain was a good sign: where there was sensation, there was circulation. As the hours crept onward and the pain in my feet subsided, I should have thought about the flip side to that rule. I assumed my pain threshold had simply crept upward.

I lost track of time. We climbed rhythmically up the fixed rope, our eyes on the ice directly before our boots. Neither of us had spoken since leaving Camp II: too absorbed in our own thoughts, and too tired to shout over the ever-increasing roar of the wind.

Something tugged at my waist. It was Dave, above me, leaning back on the fixed rope. "Take a look," he shouted, pointing upward. Somehow finding the energy, my eyes followed. Perhaps fifty yards up the slope loomed the dark ice wall sheltering Camp III.

We dragged ourselves into one of the tents. Despite the bright moon outside, it was dark enough under the ice wall to require a headlamp. Dave immediately collapsed backward onto a sleeping bag, exhausted. He had pushed a steady pace through the icefall and the Valley of Silence; then, when the going got steep on the Lhotse Face, he had pushed even harder. By the light of my headlamp I could see the pain etched on his face as he lay on his back, breathing deeply, eyes closed, beard caked with rime. Looking at the deep lines in his face, I could see that another design had just been added to the curious dioramic mask that told his life. I could see that there wasn't much space left on his mask for more designs—that some awesome, climactic design was imminent, which would reveal to me—in all its translucent light—the ultimate secret of Dave's life.

I dug around in the tent until I found a stove and kettle. I scooped snow from outside and started the stove. While the snow melted, I climbed back outside to forage for food.

Close by our tent, I thought I spotted a cache. But when I got near, I realized it was a pile of garbage: cardboard boxes, empty fuel cannisters, old wool socks, garbage bags overflowing with frozen turds and used toilet paper. By the glow of my headlamp, I looked farther along the ice wall—past the dark piss stains, past the shredded remnants of old tents sagging amidst their mangled frames.

Far back under the wall, I thought I could make out a large tarp frozen into the ice. Perhaps it was a *Summit 8000* cache. I began to hack it free with Naomi's ice axe. The tarp seemed badly weathered. Steadying myself, I yanked hard with both mittened hands. The ice clutching the fabric gave. I almost reeled backward down the face.

Instead of a *Summit 8000* cache, I had uncovered a decades-old A-frame tent. Its contents—disintegrating rubber air mattresses, a jumbled sleeping bag, an old Primus paraffin stove and blackened kettle—were all caked with frost and frozen into a veneer of ice covering the tent floor. I poked through the debris; though it wasn't a cache, any food found here might still be perfectly edible, locked in a permanent deep freeze.

I prodded at a large stuff sack with the spike of Naomi's axe. I kicked it free of the ice. The bag held antiquated clothes: a frayed Shetland sweater, a wool unionsuit, a Scottish balaclava, and a Sherpa's white prayer scarf, still carefully folded.

I could see no food. I had almost turned to look elsewhere when I decided to check the old sleeping bag. It was obvious something was inside it. Perhaps it had been filled with supplies, then zipped shut.

Hefting Naomi's axe high, aiming at the frozen zipper, I hacked at the bag. Its old cotton shell split brittly; goose down swirled up around my face. After I'd waved the down from my eyes, I took a look.

Frozen into the old sleeping bag were the mummified remains of a Sherpa. His face looked like tooled latigo leather. He had probably succumbed to injury or mountain sickness, and had been left behind by his Sahib employees. He had been used and then discarded like any other piece of expendable equipment.

I tried to cover him, as best I could, with the tattered piece of cloth I had torn away from the tent. I tried to remember a prayer, but had to make one up. It was something about finding one's way safely home to loved ones.

At last, I found a *Summit 8000* cache. I dragged a food sack back to the tent. Dave was sitting by the stove, brewing tea. I was too sickened—too numbed—to explain what I'd just found. I pulled off my boots and warmed my feet until circulation had been restored. They burned as if set ablaze. We drank a kettle of tea, then gnawed on frozen sausage and cheese. We tried to thaw the food over the stove, but ran out of fuel. I was too exhausted to look for another cannister; food barely interested me. Dave said we should be going soon, anyway.

As I pulled my socks and boots back on, Dave coughed harshly. It was a rough, brittle sound deep in his chest. When I had my boots on, we climbed out of the tent.

Dave and I began to rope up; I checked my watch. At first, the liquid diodes seemed to display hieroglyphics. In a moment, though, they reconfigured into recognizable digits. It was half past four in the morning. We were at about 23,600 feet—almost two hundred feet higher than the summit of Pumori. The fact that I'd broken my own altitude record meant nothing; my mind was too busy running an internal systems check for signs of hardware damage or software corruption due to lack of oxygen.

Our next stop would be the South Col, the windswept saddle lying at 26,200 feet between Lhotse and Everest. The South Col is just below the 8000-meter mark—the beginning of the so-called Death Zone. The upper slopes of the world's 8,000-meter peaks are littered with the frozen, wind-tattered corpses of those who have lingered too long in the Death Zone.

By the time we'd progressed a few hundred yards up the fixed ropes beyond Camp III, Lhotse had become backlit by a halo of grey. We wound our way from beneath the last of the seracs on the broken Lhotse Face and cut upward across wide, benign snow slopes.

The fixed ropes led toward the Geneva Spur, a prow of rock angling down from the South Col. In the first pinks of dawn, I could see the Yellow Band draw near. It wriggled across the face, intersecting the Geneva Spur.

The sky was now aflame. I had to fight against the buffeting wind. But, between rest-steps, I could glimpse the view. The Valley of Silence and the icefall, both still sheltered in shadow, had receded far below us. It was hard to believe I'd passed through them. Beyond, to the west, Pumori's summit was already awash in the dazzling white light of morning.

The Geneva Spur drew closer. It had been in shadow just moments ago; the sun hit its crest now, and the yellow rock running through it glowed brilliantly. I fumbled for my glacier glasses.

The South Col was hidden behind the spur, but I could see the snow slopes that led beyond it to the Southeast Ridge. Just where that ridge disappeared into the snow plume was the South Summit, at 28,750 feet. Beyond the South Summit, out of sight, the ridge climbed to the final summit, at 29,029 feet.

We began climbing the rocky spur. The *Summit 8000* fixed rope ran beside a dozen older ropes—some so old they had been frayed by the wind and bleached white by the sun. The route had long ago become a well-travelled highway.

The crest of the spur was bathed in sparkling light; the light crept steadily down toward us. Up ahead, Dave neared the sharp line of light. I fought to keep up. I remembered my icefall mantra. ROBINROBINROBIN: with one syllable I breathed; with the next, I kicked a step upward. I climbed faster toward Dave, taking in a coil as the distance between us shrank.

I felt an odd vibration in the rope. I glanced upward. Dave had reached the crest of the spur, where the wind was so violent he'd been forced onto all fours. The wind whipped the rope so hard it hummed. Crawling, Dave disappeared over the top.

I crouched low. I stepped across the terminator into the bright light. Reaching the top, I was hammered by the full fury of the jetstream. It knocked me off my feet. I fell across my ice axe in the self-arrest position. The jetstream pushed me six feet back before my axe finally bit into a patch of crusted snow.

After I'd caught my breath, I lifted my head. Dave waved to me from the rubble-strewn slope leading down to the South Col. He had unclipped from the fixed rope. It looked like the wind was not quite so bad where he was. I crawled downward toward him.

Dave coiled in the rope. Through cupped mittens he shouted over the wind: "Let's find a tent and get the hell out of the wind. If it's not better by morning, we have to get off the mountain."

I stood and brushed off the shredded knees of my borrowed windsuit. I could feel bruises rising from crawling down the rocky spur. We unroped; Dave slipped the hastily coiled line over his head. We walked side by side, leaning into the wind, searching for *Summit 8000's* Camp IV.

The South Col is a broad, rubble-covered saddle. It's been called "The Windiest Place on Earth." It's also been called "The Highest Junkyard in the World." Every few yards we passed the remains of some old camp: the skeletal poles of tents, tatters of fabric hanging from them; weathered cardboard boxes and plastic bags wedged between rocks by the wind; piles of empty oxygen bottles, faded by the sun. It seemed the ground underfoot was equal parts shattered shale, rusted cans and broken bottles. Even more alluring were the countless frozen turd piles, some no doubt originating from the colons of the Col's first visitors 38 years earlier.

We dropped our packs outside the first *Summit 8000* tent we could find. I weighed down my crampons and ice axe with rocks so they wouldn't blow away. Dave though I was silly. But—when a blast of wind sent him sprawling—he did the same. We hurriedly crawled into the tent and shut the door.

We were out of the wind at last. But the wind shook the tent walls so hard it sounded like a jackhammer, and we had to shout to each other to be heard. We got a stove going and made a pot of tepid tea. Every motion—even opening the door to scoop a kettleful of snow—required a supreme summoning of willpower. The effort left me breathless. Dave, too, was in the same shape. We should have melted more snow, but we didn't have the strength.

Too tired to talk, we climbed into the *Summit 8000* sleeping bags. The icy nylon sucked the heat from me. No matter how much I shivered, I never warmed up. Dave was snoring immediately. I laid on my back, bone-tired, short of breath, listening to the incessant drumming of the tent walls. Occasionally I would drift off. But I would soon jump up panic-stricken, thinking I had stopped breathing. When I had my breathing back under control, I would doze off again, only to repeat the cycle. It was called Cheyne-Stokes respiration, and was a common affliction at high altitude.

The sun beat on the tent—but, unlike at Camp I in the reflector oven of the Valley of Silence, it didn't warm the inside. Our breath froze on the tent ceiling, then fell on us in a miniature blizzard. The falling ice tickled my nose and woke me. At last I

Jim Fairchild

managed to truly fall asleep. I dreamed of a meadow beside a river half a world away.

* * *

I awoke in the dark, my tongue thick, my throat dry, gasping convulsively. I bolted upright. The wind still roared outside, beating the tent. A lower roar came from the stove, cradled between Dave's legs.

"We need liquids," he said. "I can't swallow."

I looked at my watch. The digits floated wildly, like transmuting runes, before settling into recognizable numbers. It was 10:30 p.m. We had rested far longer than we should have. And yet merely looking at my watch left me exhausted.

I glanced out the door at the moonlit saddle. Glittering spindrift blasted past. Nearby sat *Summit 8000's* neat stockpile of oxygen bottles. Of course, all of their regulators and masks were with their climbers' personal gear in Base Camp. Although we were climbing without oxygen in order to avoid the weight, I wished I'd snagged just one regulator and mask for when we were holed up in the camps.

Dave offered me a mug of instant cider. I downed it in two gulps. Although the drink steamed, it was only lukewarm. Fluids boiled at a much lower temperature at this altitude. Dave poured me a refill.

"How are you feeling?" he asked. He started melting more snow.

"Like a chainsmoker running a marathon," I said.

Dave sipped his cider. "Even farting requires the strength of Hercules up here. Just concentrate on your breathing, even when you're not exerting yourself." He adjusted the stove flame. "How are your feet?"

"They were pretty cold earlier. But they feel fine now."

Dave put down his cider. "Let me take a peek." He unzipped my sleeping bag and reached in. He frowned quizzically at me.

"What?" I asked.

"I'm holding your right foot. It feels like a frozen Butterball turkey."

At first, I thought he was joking. I couldn't feel his hands. My foot was totally numb. Dave wrenched my legs out of the bag and ripped off my socks. My toes were steel-grey. We sat up the rest of the night, my feet beneath his shirt, against his bare flesh. Dave was careful not to rub them; rubbing frozen flesh could cause severe tissue damage.

After two hours, I could feel again: a searing pain that radiated from toes to knees. I yanked my feet away, but Dave pulled them back.

"Easy!" I howled.

"No pain, no gain," he said, pressing my flesh closely against his. I could feel the heat of his body flow once more into mine.

*   *   *

Jim Fairchild

Chapter Twelve:
The Final Ridge

At four o'clock, we looked outside. The winds across the South Col had slackened. The snow plume blowing off the summit had shrunk. Automatonlike, we agreed to head up. The decision was devoid of emotion.

By the time we crawled out of the tent, the black sky was fading to grey. We clipped into our borrowed rope, which had frozen into stiff spaghetti during the night. While Dave adjusted the hood on his windsuit, I looked up the mountain. The plume had, indeed, receded. But a lenticular cloud was forming over the summit—a sign that the wind still raged higher up. I looked down into the Valley of Silence. It was carpeted with dark, roiling clouds. A storm had blown up the Khumbu Valley. Whichever way we went—up or down—we would be heading into storm. My stomach churned.

The rope tugged at me. Dave was moving upward. I waited for the icy rope to stretch out. Then I followed in my borrowed boots, my feet in agony.

The rubble of the Col was almost behind us; ahead, an icy slope climbed steeply toward the Southeast Ridge. A cluster of boulders lay to my left; beyond them, I could see the remnants of another old camp. Ancient tent poles creaked in the wind, bent wildly by countless snows.

Just as we were almost past the old camp, something made me jump. A rock had moved. I turned.

There, beside the skeleton of an old tent, pecking at some old tin can, was a gorak. Not just any gorak. This was *my* gorak: far from its winged companions, following two silly humans up into this windswept domain. When the bird saw me, it froze, tin can in beak. It stared a long, strange moment. Then it tossed the can down. The can skittered across the ice in the wind.

"Look!" I shouted to Dave. He couldn't hear me over the wind.

My shouting startled the bird. Flapping its huge black wings, it shot off with the wind. A blast of ice hit my face, and I lost sight of the bird.

We followed the frozen path upward into a series of gullies. Deep in their shelter, the wind hadn't compacted the snow. We found ourselves wading through waist-deep powder. My lungs burned as if filled with molten lead.

Just when I thought I could take no more of the exhausting, snow-choked gullies—just when I had gripped the rope at my waist with both mittened hands and was about to pull on it, signalling to Dave that I'd had enough—we emerged onto the ridge itself. The wind hammered us full-force again. On the right, slabs of crumbling rock rose to a snow cornice hanging over the Kangshung Face. To the left, the Southwest Face plummeted 6,000 feet to the Valley of Silence. Dave picked out a careful route where rock and snow met. The snow on the ridge was far firmer than in the gullies. Although we were climbing ever higher, I felt better—at least for a few minutes—now that I was again on firm ground.

Our next goal was the South Summit, some 2,550 feet above the Col. Back in the Bitterroots, I could have climbed that far in two hours. Now, with luck, we would need six.

I tried not to look up. I concentrated on my breathing and kick-stepping, taking my cues from the rope in front of me. It

Jim Fairchild

slithered upward each time Dave took a step. All I had to do was keep up with the rope, to keep the tension between us a perfect mathematical constant—not too tight, not too slack.

We surmounted several rock outcrops and snow domes. To my left, the Southwest Face grew steeper. I felt a vacuum pulling me in that direction, and overcompensated by straying to the right of Dave's crampon tracks. When I'd strayed too far, I could feel the equally fearsome pull of space sucking at me from out over the corniced Kangshung Face. My equilibrium dissolved. Focusing again on my mantra—ROBINROBINROBIN—I wiped everything from my mind but the rhythm of lungs and feet, and realigned myself with Dave's track.

It had once been routine for expeditions to place a final camp somewhere on this ridge below the South Summit. Dyhrenfurth's 1963 expedition had placed a camp at 27,450 feet; Hillary and Tenzing had left for the summit from a camp 450 feet higher. Three hours after leaving the Col, we began to encounter some of these old camps, the frames of their decayed tents twisted against the snow.

At each site, Dave coiled in the rope until I'd caught up. We breathlessly fell onto our packs, gulping air like fish out of water, while the bright morning sun began to set the Valley of Silence aflame. I searched for my glacier glasses and stuck them on my face. They were crooked, but I was too exhausted to straighten them.

We climbed on. Somehow I found the courage to look upward. An arching ridge of snow-streaked rock on the left skyline converged in the sky with the ridge we were climbing. Where they converged would be the South Summit. From there, we would be two hours from the top. I doubted I could last.

I needed to divide the remainder of the climb into a series of intermediate goals. High above, I caught sight of a tiny red speck on the ridge, halfway to the South Summit. I figured it must be the remnants of one more ancient camp—perhaps even Hillary's and

Tenzing's. That which I could see, I could attain. Forgetting all else, I concentrated on closing the gap.

After two hours, the red speck sat perched just up the ridge from us. I could see the tattered red tent fabric. A gold banner tied to the top of the tent had frozen in the direction of the perpetual wind. In minutes, I would be there. In minutes, I would be able to pick out my next goal, and start the mental game again.

Up ahead, Dave reached the old tent. He flopped down on the steep slope, leaning against his pack. He coiled the rope as I made the last slow, painful steps to the tent, my eyes focusing on Dave's tracks.

Finally, I looked up. Dave was sprawled out in front of me, smiling fiercely, watching the light of morning sparkle on the summit snowfields of Pumori. They were far below us now. With one arm, Dave hugged the remains of the old tent.

Something seemed askew. Dave's teeth radiated an eery white in the brilliant light of morning; I could see my reflection in his glacier glasses. The convexity of the image threatened my balance. In the crystalline image reflecting back at me, I could see my own puzzlement.

And then I realized why I was puzzled. All this time I'd thought I'd been looking upward at a red tent. Instead, I'd been looking at a climber sitting in the snow, clad in red. Dave sat beside the climber now, his arm around the stranger's shoulders. *Who could this be?* We were supposed to be alone on the mountain thanks to the Sherpa strike. I shook my head, trying to clear the fog.

Dave began to laugh. In the thin, crisp air, his laughter crackled like breaking glass. He hugged the climber beside him; they rocked together. The other climber must have been cold; he rocked stiffly. I could see that the other climber had long, blond hair. The climber had lost his hat; his hair had frozen stiff as a straw broom in the jetstream. Dave, laughing hoarsely, poked the other climber in the side.

293

Jim Fairchild

Looking where Dave poked, I saw a hole in the climber's parka. I could see a white sweater through the hole; Dave seemed to be pinching the knitted ribs of the sweater. I shook my head again. The fog at last cleared.

The climber sitting beside Dave was—or had been—a woman. She had been dead many years. And it was not a ribbed sweater Dave was twisting: it was one of the woman's bleached ribs, visible through the hole in her parka. I focused on the shredded hole. It slowly dawned on me that something had been pecking at the frozen corpse.

"Goraks," Dave said.

The joke was over. Dave helped me sit down. Over the roar of the wind, he told me that the corpse was that of a German woman who had died on the way down from the summit in 1979. Exhausted, she had sat down a moment to catch her breath. She never got up. Dave pointed up the ridge to three other bright dots in the snow: others who had paused too long in the Death Zone. Now, their corpses served as route markers.

* * *

We crawled onto the South Summit. We fell onto our packs, huddling out of the wind, surveying the route ahead. The ridge dropped for thirty or forty feet below us to a saddle, then began to climb again. Although less than 300 vertical feet remained to the final summit, I was shocked by the steepness. I ignored the wind and concentrated on the sun hitting my face. I imagined the sensation of heat, although there was none. It lulled me toward sleep.

Something tugged at my waist. I opened my eyes. I expected to see Dave coiling the rope, ready to leave. But he, too, was still collapsed against his pack, his face lifted toward the sun. I was shocked at how decimated he looked. I close my eyes, happy to wait for him.

Something tugged the rope again. Roused to anger, I tugged back. Then I opened my eyes. Dave sat bleary-eyed, wondering why I'd yanked the rope. I muttered an apology. He almost immediately began to snore.

I checked the rope. Something had certainly tugged at me. And yet it couldn't have been Dave. He looked too wasted to tug his own bootlace.

I closed my eyes again. As a boy, I'd read countless tales of climbers who had ventured into the Death Zone. Many had described a phenomenon that—for want of a scientific label—might be called the "Phantom Climber Syndrome." Exhausted climbers had sensed the presence of an unknown partner. Sometimes they could actually see the phantom climber; sometimes they felt the strange tug of an unseen person tied into their rope; sometimes it was simply the eery sensation that somebody was nearby, watching them—or *watching out* for them. The syndrome had always been laughed off as anoxia-induced hallucinations.

I breathed deeply, then stood. I tried to coil the rope strewn about us. I tugged at the end running to Dave. He was having a hard time waking up. I studied his face. His cheeks were burned; blisters had peeled away and hung flapping in the wind. His lips were cracked and bloody. Ice caked his beard. "*Dave*," I shouted over the wind. I shook him by the shoulder. "Time to go."

At last, he awoke. He pulled his glacier glasses onto his forehead and squinted at me. "Good morning, Ethel. My usual triple espresso, please."

I pushed his glacier glasses back over his eyes. I helped him to his feet. At last, we were ready to head up again. Dave began to lead. I grabbed his shoulder.

"Let me take it from here," I said. "You've done too much already."

There was no argument. I handed Dave the coils, then

295

stepped past him. He paid out the rope as I plunge-stepped down to the shallow saddle. The drop was only thirty or forty feet, but it was steep and deep with unstable snow.

When I reached the saddle, I stood hip-deep in powder. I glanced toward the final summit, hidden behind a series of cornices and rock aretes. I waved at Dave, watching me from the South Summit. Before I could coil in the rope, he began to plunge toward me. In a moment, he was sliding. In another, he was cartwheeling. I could make out a flailing boot or a mittened hand sticking out of the wave of snow.

I braced for a collision. The wave subsided at my feet. Dave sprawled out in front of me, plastered with snow. "Body-surfing," he explained. He wiped snow from his eyes.

We had less than 300 vertical feet to go. But I knew I was near the end of my physical and mental rope. Sitting, catching my breath, I studied the steep slope leading back to the South Summit. Perhaps—*just* perhaps—I might still be able to summon the energy to get back up it, if we turned back now.

Dave rose to his feet, surrounded by a snarl of icy rope. Suddenly, he lost his balance and collapsed in the waist-deep snow. Only his head stuck out, rolling from side to side as he gasped for breath. In a flash of pity that both sapped and emboldened me, I saw just how drained he was. I saw—with diamond clarity—that our roles had reversed. It was now Dave, and not me, who was the passive accessory. As heartless as it sounds now, I knew that my way led upward, with or without Dave. He would have to keep up.

I moved up the steep ridge toward the main summit. I needed eight rasping breaths for each step. Rock walls dropped away to the left; snow cornices rose to the right. I was tempted toward the right, onto the smooth snow. But just as I started to stray, the rope ahead of me tugged me back.

I shook my head. *There was no rope ahead of me.* And yet, when I glanced out of the corner of my eye, I could sense a rope running upward. Yes: although I couldn't see it when I looked directly—no doubt due to an optical phenomenon unique to high altitude—there was a line running upward from me, snaking along the juncture between snow and rock.

I could feel that line tug at me now. I looked up. There, barely visible above the next rise of snow, stood a tiny figure. I looked back at Dave; he was fighting so hard for oxygen that he was oblivious. For a fleeting moment I thought about getting back to the South Summit and down the other side before I suffered permanent brain damage.

But then I looked upward again. There could be no doubt: we had picked up another partner who had taken the lead. Perhaps Chotari had joined us. I could see the distant figure wave an arm aloft. I could hear a soft voice drift down over the wind: "*Come on!*" Was it Sarah?

The burden was off my shoulders. Somebody else was leading again. Relieved, I could simply follow. I stepped upward again. I had to tug on the rope to get Dave going.

We came to the Hillary Step, the last true obstacle to the summit. Each year, thanks to the vagaries of weather, the forty-foot step takes on a different look. One year, the step might be a daunting rock cliff; the next year, a wall of rotten snow. I could see that the winds had been strong this year—they had blown most of the snow from the step, exposing the underlying rock.

In so doing, the wind had also exposed a dozen fixed ropes. Some were at least a quarter-century old, and would be too weakened by sun and abrasion to carry a climber's weight. I would have to decide which to climb. If I picked the right one, it would get us to the highest point on Earth. If I picked the wrong one, we might do a 10,000-foot backflip.

I collapsed at the base of the Hillary Step. All of the swaying ropes looked the same. I couldn't tell which was newest. I thought about asking Dave if his vision was any better than mine.

Jim Fairchild

But he was far below me, collapsed in the snow.

Suddenly, one of the ropes began to sway more than the others. At the top of the step, a small figure was just slipping from view. She had found the right rope. I yanked the rope running back to Dave. He stumbled upward.

I watched the gargantuan heaving of his chest: ten gasps between steps. The higher we climbed, the slower. I wondered if we were locked into some cosmic, slow-motion carrot-and-stick game: if no matter how hard and high we climbed, our goal would always recede tantalizingly out of reach.

When Dave at least reached me, I started up the appointed fixed rope. Coiling in the rope that linked us, he shouted something about a belay. I ignored him. I knew that the climber above would be belaying me. Clipping into that fixed rope, I hauled myself up the broken rock.

* * *

When I reached the top of the Hillary Step, the lead climber had already started up the final snow slopes. I wanted to thank her for her firm belay, but saw that I'd have to wait until we were on top. I sat down and belayed Dave, inching his way up the step on the fixed rope.

Waiting on Dave, I watched the lead climber recede up the final ridge. Her progress was so quick and so sure; Dave's so tedious and uncertain. I thought about cutting the rope between Dave and me. I tried to remember where my pocket knife was. It dawned on me it was deep inside my windsuit somewhere and digging it out would take energy I didn't have. I knocked my borrowed boots together to keep the circulation going in my feet. I was pleased that they were no longer in pain.

Dave's head finally appeared. He hauled himself over the lip and collapsed, chest heaving, at my feet. *"What the hell were you thinking?*" he gasped, his purple-splotched face pressed against the snow.

"What do you mean?"

"You started up the fixed rope before I could belay. The rope was rotten. We could have both bought the farm."

I looked down at him, has face in the snow. He was obviously losing his faculties. I could barely make out our lead climber, leaning into the wind-driven snow half a rope-length up the ridge. I rose and followed.

The final stretch to the summit was a series of snow humps. To the right, each ended in fantastically shaped cornices. Through gaps in the cornices I saw snow whip past, and—farther out—the deep cobalt of space.

The rope from Dave tugged me. I collapsed: first onto my knees, then onto my side. The impact stunned me. Looking down the ridge, I could see Dave, too, leaning on his side against the slope, trying to prop himself up with his ice axe. At last, giving up, he dropped his head against the snow. Looking ahead, I could see three or four more snow humps. I could see the arc of the West Ridge rising on our left to meet the ridge we were on. Although I couldn't see the point where they met, I knew it was wondrously close.

I felt another tug and looked upward. Out of the corner of my eye, I glimpsed our lead climber. She signalled me to follow. Strengthened by her constancy, I struggled to my knees, then to my feet. I yanked on the rope behind me until Dave, too, rose. I kicked one foot, then the other, into the slope. Like efficient, uncomplaining tools, each foot swung in a perfect arc and found purchase. I took ten rasping breaths. Then I mechanically kicked a wooden appendage upward again. I staggered upward against the wind, on feet no longer burdened by sensation.

* * *

Jim Fairchild

We had climbed into the lenticular cloud. The winds must have been eighty miles an hour. I was forced to crawl, my head turned, fighting for each breath. The wind sucked the air from my lungs.

The rope to Dave seemed impossibly heavy. When I looked back, I could see it arching tautly in the wind as if plucked by celestial fingers. Where its arc met the ridge again, I could see Dave, collapsed against the slope on his side. He had not given up. He slowly lifted the knee beneath him and planted the edge of his boot a few inches higher, pushing himself up. But our progress was maddeningly slow. From somewhere far back in my mind came the certain knowledge that we would soon be dead at the rate we were going, even with the top just one or two more rises away. I would have to make a decision.

The rope leading upward tugged gently. I crawled another inch or two before collapsing. Who was our lead climber? Chris? I tried to see her through the ground blizzard. She stood atop the next rise, waving for me to follow. I could see her white dress whipping in the wind. She tugged again, refusing to let me stop.

We were so close. And yet, despite the insistent tug from above, I collapsed against the snow. I concentrated on its coolness against my cheek.

I'm not sure how long I had been resting when the hairs rose on the back of my neck. I had the distinct sensation I was not alone. Of course, I knew that Dave was collapsed below me, and I knew that our lead climber was waiting patiently just ahead, on the final rise. But I had the queer feeling that there were still others. I was too tired to open my eyes.

And then I sensed a shadow soar past. I opened my eyes this time. I saw that the winds had suddenly relented. A huge black bird soared up the ridge past us. It alit on a rock ten yards up the slope from me.

300

The gorak! It settled onto the rock, its back toward me. It stretched its jet-black wings, then folded them. It began to turn toward me.

As it did, the bird changed. The black of its feathers turned brown. The feathers of its head became white. It was not a gorak at all, but an eagle. It cocked its head and stared at me through a fierce, unblinking eye.

"I know you!" I shouted hoarsely.

As I spoke, the bird changed again. It became a young man, perhaps eighteen years old. He wore an olive drab parka with a white fur ruff around the hood. As he began to stride down the slope toward me, I could see that he was wearing thin leather combat boots. He was limping.

"Emmett!" I rasped.

The young man stood beside me. Smiling gently, he bent down. He touched my shoulder. He started to speak. At first, his voice was like the sound of a wild river. After a moment, I could understand. "You can make it," he said. "Just seven more miles to the sea." And then the young eagle-man moved up the snowy slope. Despite the limp, his stride spoke of strength and grace.

"Emmett!" I warned. "Your feet!" I didn't have the heart to tell him that as an older man he would look back bitterly on the day he froze his feet.

The young eagle-man stopped and looked back. "It's *your* feet you should worry about," he said gently. "When we meet again, you will have lost them both." And then he turned his back once more. I watched, dumbfounded, as he moved up the slope. When he reached the top of the final snowy rise—near where our lead climber still awaited me—he was an eagle again. He lifted off into the cobalt sky and disappeared.

I pressed my face into the snow, trying to bring myself back to my senses. I could hear the fierce wind again, could feel the windblown ice cutting my face. Again, the rope tugged upward. I

Jim Fairchild

dug the toe of a boot into the snow and crawled a few more inches before collapsing.

A shadow passed over once more. The wind had calmed again. When I opened my eyes, a huge butterfly carrying a bullhide briefcase flitted to a landing on the same rock the eagle had chosen. The butterfly flexed its wings before folding them. They were radiant with the colors of the rainbow.

Beneath its feathery antennae, the butterfly's face was that of my father. Upon its silky chest the butterfly sported a pocket protector outfitted with mechanical pencils. The butterfly carefully set its briefcase down. It reached up with the tip of one gossamer wing and pushed at the horn-rimmed glasses that had started to slip down its nose.

"*Dad?*" I asked incredulously.

"My name is Teinopalpus imperialis," the butterfly answered, a bit imperiously. "Of the family Papilionidae. Of the order Lepidoptera. Noted for the minor miracle of metamorphosis."

The wind picked up for a moment; the butterfly's delicate wings quivered. It braced itself against a gust. "What are you doing up here?" I asked.

One of the butterfly's antennae drooped. "I'm here to ask you to turn back. Your choices affect others. On the day that I learn of your death on this mountain, my world will experience a diminution of colors—a gradual shifting of the visible spectrum toward the bleaker frequencies."

And then the butterfly turned. It stretched its rainbow wings, then retrieved the briefcase. With a flick of its delicate wings, it was aloft. It circled upward on the currents, disappearing somewhere beyond the farthest rise.

The rope tugged at my waist; I fought a few inches higher. But I had to stop again. I closed my eyes. I knew I had lost my mind.

Again, I sensed somebody watching. I looked. There, on the

302

same rock upon which the eagle and the butterfly had alit, crouched a young red-haired man. He radiated an unbearable sadness that I was unequipped to comprehend.

"*Art?*" I asked.

"Hello, Jeff."

He rose. He was wearing a crisp white naval officer's uniform. The buttons and the braid were of gleaming gold. His chest hung heavy with many-colored ribbons. The gold was so bright I had to look to one side. When I did, Art's uniform blended into the wind-driven snow.

He stepped down the slope to my side. "You're almost to the top," Art said. "You can't stop now."

"What ever happened to you?" I had wondered and worried for two decades.

"I got to Tibet. I snuck over the border, disguised as a yak herder."

"What about the freckles?"

"I smeared yak dung on my face."

"Did you make it to your holy mountain?"

"Yes," Art said. "I made it to Mount Kailas. I crawled around the mountain with the other pilgrims. It took me ten days. I didn't have any skin left on my knees and elbows. But it was worth it."

"I'm happy for you. What happened to you after that?"

"I was washing my wounds in a stream," Art said. "I had left my clothes on the bank. A gang of bandits who prey on pilgrims stole my things. Then they snuck behind me and slashed my throat. One of them severed my testicles and made a coin purse from my red-haired nutsack. He shows it off in teahouses. They tossed my body down a gully. It still lies there unburied."

"Oh, no," I sputtered. I thought my chest would burst.

"Then again," Art said, "I might be alive and well, an overweight alcoholic Allstate agent, living in Cleveland in a '50svintage split-level on top of an unmarked toxic-waste site, with six freckled kids and a wife with her own Amway business. Don't believe everything a hallucination tells you. But—speaking of Mount Kailas—there's a great view of it this very moment from the top of this mountain, if you hurry." He began to stride up the slope.

I tried to crawl after him. I wanted to tell him how much he had changed my life. I wanted to tell him how much I had worried about him. But he was moving fast. He reached the top of the final snowy rise, where our lead climber had just been standing, and paused.

"*Hurry*," he said. "Kailas will be hidden by clouds soon."

I tried to follow. But something tugged firmly at my waist. I looked down the slope. Not one, but *two*, ropes led downward. I saw that the wind was blowing again; the two ropes danced wildly against the snow. One rope led to Dave, collapsed on his side. The other rope ran to a girl dressed in white. Her long blond hair blew in the wind. She tugged on the rope connecting us.

"*Robin?*"

"It's time to go down, Daddy. It's time to play by the river."

"I'm so close to the top," I said. "I can't quit."

"You can always come back in your heart," Robin said. "The river will always bring you here."

I dug my heels into the snow, fighting her pull. I turned to look for Art. But he had disappeared over the rise.

The rope tugged again. "If you don't start down right now," Robin said, "your friend will die." She touched Dave's shoulder. He barely stirred.

It dawned on me just how serious a predicament we were in. I remembered the decision I had to make, and made it. Turning my back on the world's highest point—just yards away—I slid down the rope. After I reached Dave's side, I turned to thank Robin for bringing me to my senses, to promise her that I would never leave her again. But she was gone. The rope that had connected us had vanished. There was just one rope now: the one connecting me to Dave.

I shook Dave's shoulder. He mumbled to himself, eyes closed, his face against the snow. I shook harder. Finally, he opened his eyes. "Morning, Stella," he grimaced. "Mocha java, please."

I helped Dave sit up. His face was splotched with blue, his lips purple. Spittle clung to his beard. When I wiped it away, I saw that the spittle was tinged with blood. I wiped my mitten on the snow, then grabbed Dave by the shoulder. "Come on," I said. "Let's get down this mountain."

"Wait," Dave said. He fumbled with the zipper of his windsuit. Finally, he reached in and pulled something from around his neck. It was the tiny gold Buddha given him by the abbot of Thyangboche.

"I guess this is the end of the ride," he said. He crawled a few feet to the lee of a boulder and began to dig in the snow. I looked at my watch. The squiggles on the face were hopelessly indecipherable.

"Hurry up," I yelled, fighting back panic.

Dave dropped the tiny Buddha into the hole, tamping snow over it. On his knees, he said a short Buddhist prayer. And then he crawled back to me. "Let's get off this hill," he said. "It's a long hike back to Montana."

With me in the lead, we careened down the ridge, the wind buffeting our backs. Finally—together—we were heading home.

* * *

Chapter Thirteen:
Longest Night, Brightest Dawn

I staggered onto the saddle between the Main and South Summits. Dave, straggling behind me, dragged heavily on the rope. We were wallowing again in waist-deep powder. I coiled in the rope as Dave teetered toward me; I squinted through the blizzard at the steep slope leading up to the South Summit. Dave reached my side. He began to totter; he fell facefirst into the snow.

I knew there was no way we would make it back up the South Summit: not as drained as we were, not with the snow as deep as it was, not with the wind still howling at what must have been seventy miles an hour.

There was only one answer: a bivouac. I couldn't read my watch; it must have been four or five in the afternoon. If we could dig a snow cave and get out of the wind until morning, perhaps we'd have the energy to make it up the South Summit and the rest of the way down the mountain the next day.

I told Dave we must bivouac. He shook his snow-plastered head in agreement. We would be spending the night at over 28,700 feet without bottled oxygen, sleeping bags or stove. We both knew that the chances of surviving such a night were perhaps fifty-fifty. And yet—without having to talk about it—we both knew that neither of us had the strength to battle any farther through deep snow and hurricane-force winds. We would certainly be dead in hours if we didn't seek shelter.

Dave and I unroped and dropped our packs. We searched for a spot to dig. Ten yards away, through the blowing snow, I spied a large boulder. Perhaps we could burrow up against it. I waded through the snow toward the rock.

I could see that the boulder's face plunged vertically—perhaps even concavely—into the snow. The snow would be deep against it. It was perfect.

A frozen tatter of nylon poked from the snow. It looked like a multi-colored parapente canopy. Someone had already used our perfect bivouac site. Perhaps there was already a cave below, its entrance drifted over.

Dave staggered over, a pack over each shoulder, clutching our ice axes and frozen rope in his hands. I began digging while he collapsed in the snow. Down on my knees, I dug like an ice-encrusted dog, flinging the snow behind me. When I paused to catch my breath, I saw that I had covered Dave from head to toe. I apologized, and reached back to brush him off. But he raised a hand, grinning, and motioned for me to keep digging. Then, with a supreme effort, he brushed himself off.

When I had dug two feet into the slope, I suddenly fell forward. I wiped the snow from my eyes. I was inside a low-roofed snow cave. The big boulder formed the back wall. The abandoned parapente lay rolled up and frozen against one wall. Soft opaline light filtered through the scalloped digging marks on the roof.

Inside, the raging wind was only a hushed whisper. I crawled outside and told Dave what I'd found. The hole was a bit tight for both of us; but, within a few minutes, I'd enlarged it enough for us to stretch out comfortably. Dave, his teeth chattering uncontrollably, climbed in stiffly after me, dragging the packs and axes with him.

Once we'd stuck our packs in the doorway to block spindrift, the storm was just a muted sigh. Our body heat warmed the cave to a degree or two above freezing. Drops of condensation began to drip onto our heads.

I dug out what food we had. We had taken what was left in the tent at the Col, but had been too exhausted to search outside for a cache. We now had one small salami, a half a wheel of Edam and half a stick of chocolate. We had pushed all day without stopping to eat. The altitude had thwarted my appetite, but I knew my body needed fuel. The handful of food before us looked like a feast.

Our two water bottles were frozen solid. Without a stove, there was only one way to make water. Gritting my teeth, I placed the bottles inside my windsuit, hoping to melt a few ounces of water with my body heat. I didn't have the heart to ask Dave to put a frozen water bottle inside his windsuit. He lay on the snowy cave floor, legs crossed tightly, arms folded, like a snowy mummy. He had already begun to snore.

In his sleep, Dave's shivering lapsed toward convulsions. I knew we would die of hypothermia before morning in our borrowed clothes. Our plan—such as it was—had assumed we'd be staying in *Summit 8000's* camps, amply stocked with warm sleeping bags. We hadn't carried even one. For that matter, we hadn't carried down parkas. We assumed that by staying on the move we wouldn't need them. I looked beside me at the frozen folds of the old parapente. I figured we could at least wrap ourselves in the canopy.

I tugged at the fabric with both hands. I tugged again, harder. It gave slightly. Then I realized that something heavy was wrapped inside it.

It was quite obvious what was inside it. Another climber had dug this cave to escape a storm, and had wrapped himself inside the parapente for warmth. I felt, for just a second, as if I were desecrating a grave. And then I decided that Dave and I needed the canopy far more than an old, frozen corpse.

I tugged harder; it was like pulling heavy carpet off a roll. I braced my boots against the cave wall and yanked at the sheer fabric and its hidden weight. It gave so suddenly that I fell back against Dave.

I sat up. I was looking at the icy corpse of a young male Caucasian. His frozen eyes stared upward; his hands were folded across his chest. He looked no more than 25 years old. Frost clung to his sparse whiskers. I remembered reading about a young Frenchman who had disappeared high on Everest the year before. He had the audacious plan to launch a parapente from Everest's summit and land first on Lhotse, then Nuptse. It looked like his flight had been cancelled.

Dave stared casually at the corpse. "I hope we get a break on the room rate," he said. "I don't like sharing with strangers."

I pulled the last of the parapente out from under the body. We laid down on it, pulling its billowy folds around us. "As comfy as the Sarajevo Super Eight," Dave said, happily ensconced.

I tried to think of a few wise words to say for our frigid roommate. And then I realized how silly that was. Words of wisdom would do him no good now. Planting a boot against his side, I rolled his body so that he faced the wall.

"Look," Dave said. Beyond the corpse, beside the cave wall, sat a butane stove, a kettle and a mug. A small backpack lay nearby.

I reached over the body and grabbed the stove. Icy metal stuck to my bare fingers. I shook the stove. Fuel sloshed inside the cannister. I tossed the stove to Dave; skin ripped from my fingers. My fingers were too frozen to bleed. I reached into my windsuit and yanked out the two frozen water bottles, tossing them aside.

I handed Dave the kettle and mug. "Hot toddies on the way, Sahib," he chimed. He scooped a kettle of snow from the cave wall and put it on the stove.

I inventoried the contents of the dead man's pack. There were three more cannisters for the stove. We would not die of dehydration. And we would not starve to death: the pack held

another stick of salami, some hard candy, and a can of anchovies.
Together with our larder, it looked like a Thanksgiving feast.

* * *

We drank kettle after kettle of lukewarm water. Taking turns
with the mug, we drank until our cheeks glowed red. I was glad to
see color again in Dave's face. We drank until—for the first time in
a day and a half—I had to urinate. I parted the two packs propped in
the door, leaned back on my knees and tried to pee between them.
The raging wind blew the stream back inside, all over the dead
man's leg. I muttered an apology to the corpse. Dave chuckled.

We ate half of the salami and cheese, saving the other half
for the morning. Dave ate the anchovies after politely offering them
to me. I passed. Then, thanks to Dave's genius, we melted the hard
candy in a kettle of tepid water. While we watched the candy—
cherry and butterscotch and licorice, all thrown together—bob up
and down in the convection currents, Dave turned toward me.

"I think my feet are frozen," he said quietly. Then he stared
back down at the rising and sinking candy.

While Dave watched the kettle, I pulled off his icy boots,
then peeled off two layers of wet socks. What I saw—by the blue
glow of the stove's flame—shocked me. Dave's feet, from toes to
ankles, were the waxy grey of cheap candles. I didn't tell him how
bad they looked.

I zipped open my windsuit. I pulled up my fleece jacket and
longjohn top. I lifted Dave's feet, as cumbersome as frozen hams.
Holding my breath, I placed his feet against my bare stomach.

After half an hour, I checked my work. It had grown darker
outside; I had to use my headlamp. I could see that color was
returning to Dave's flesh. He flinched as I handled hs feet, but he
didn't complain.

We both sat silently in the dark for a long time, listening to the purr of the stove and the dripping of water from the cave ceiling. It could have been half an hour; it could have been two hours. I couldn't judge time any more. Dave's feet were still against my stomach; he turned off the stove after melting another pot of snow. I could see him only by the fog of his breath and the steam rising from the mug as he lowered it from his lips.

He spoke in the dark. "I'm ready to head home. Back to Montana. I have to figure out how to get Karma and Mingma out of the country with me." He erupted into a spasm of coughing. He wiped blood-tinged spittle from his lips.

"Let's get some rest," I said. Soon, Dave was snoring. But there was another noise—like rustling dead leaves—coming from deep inside his chest.

I pressed his feet against my belly as long as I could. Sitting in the darkness, staring at the icy walls, listening to the noise in Dave's chest, I started seeing black spots swimming across my eyes. I blinked, trying—without success—to make them go away.

I began to drift off. I could hear the steady sound of breathing nearby; my own lungs began to keep time with the susurration. Then I realized that the sound did not come from Dave.

I opened my eyes in the darkness. Something glowed faintly beside the frozen corpse. By the dim glow of the full moon filtering through the cave roof, I could make out a tiny figure. She wore a white dress, and sat against the dead man's legs. Her arms were folded about her knees. She watched me intently.

"*Robin?*"

"Don't fall asleep," she commanded.

I searched beside me and found my headlamp. When I turned it on, Robin was gone. But I took her advice. I checked Dave's feet; they were completely pink again. I tugged his socks and boots back on for him. Once I had the stove purring again beneath a pot of snow, I shut off my headlamp.

In the dark, I could hear Robin's gentle breathing again. I

Jim Fairchild

could see her dress once more in the moonlight. I didn't look directly at her, afraid I might scare her away. Her company meant more to me than life itself.

I adjusted the stove. I could't keep silent any longer. "If anything happens to me," I told my daughter, "I want you to know I love you."

Something stirred in the dark. I could hear joints creak; there was a hoarse cough, then a prolonged salami fart. It was Dave.

He switched on his headlamp and shined it in my eyes. "I love you, too," he rasped. "But I'm too tired for a bro-hug." He switched off the light.

I blushed in the darkness. I handed Dave a mug of water. He took a noisy sip, then handed it back. And then, in a moment, I could hear his snoring—and the disturbing counterpoint welling up from within his chest.

I sat in the dark, sipping water. Dave was showing symptoms of pulmonary edema. The only cure was descent. And it would have to wait for the light of dawn. I began to feel myself drift off again. Just as I nodded, something kicked my leg.

"*Don't fall asleep*," a small voice insisted. "You'll never wake up."

I roused. I offered some water to Robin, but she was gone.

I woke Dave and made him drink. As he dozed off, I scraped more snow from the wall of the cave and lit the stove again. Finally, the fuel cannister ran empty.

I managed, by the light of my headlamp, to change the cannister. But I was too tired to start the stove again. I looked at my watch. I couldn't read the numbers, but it must have been well after midnight, judging by the height of the moon—a faint brightness backlighting the scalloped ceiling.

I switched off my headlamp again. I turned toward where Robin had been sitting. Out of the corner of my eye, by the glow of the moon, I could see she was back again, clutching her knees patiently, her back against the dead man. *"Please,"* I begged. "Let me sleep."

"All right, she sighed. "But only a little while. I'll wake you."

"Thank you," I said. "Oh, thank you." I closed my eyes.

I slept fitfully until dawn, awakened punctually every half hour by a swift kick to the ribs. Robin was determined to make sure I didn't drift too far away. Once or twice, as I begged her to leave me alone, Dave switched on his headlamp and stared at me. Robin would disappear somewhere behind the dead man; Dave would say nothing, and switch off his light.

Once, perhaps two hours before dawn, I took a particularly mean kick to the kidneys, and turned to complain to Robin. Peering through the dim blue glow, I could see that Robin had company. Sitting beside her were three figures clad in orange. I could see that their clothes had been savagely shredded and bloodied. I rose up on an elbow to get a better look.

They were the three young climbers who had fallen on Foraker. A rope was tied to their waists. It had been slashed between two of them. The frayed ends sat on the snow, their inner white core gleaming like some ugly truth.

I sat up. "I'm sorry," I said to the three. I wanted to tell them how their deaths had haunted me all my life, and to ask for their forgiveness.

"Don't be sorry," Dave's voice rattled in the darkness. *"Just shut up."*

I apologized to Dave, then looked toward the dead Frenchman. Robin sat against his legs, her dress glowing in the moonlight. But the three Japanese climbers were gone. I laid back down. Although dawn was just an hour or two away, time seemed to slow down. The closer we got to dawn, the slower time crawled. And whenever I was about to fall asleep—which might have helped time pass more swiftly—I received a kick to the backside. It was

Jim Fairchild
the longest night of my life.

* * *

Robin must have finally taken mercy on me. I had actually fallen into a deep sleep. I was awakened by someone singing "Guajira Guantanamera." The voice was Dave's; his chest rattled so much as he sang that it seemed he was accompanying himself on maracas.

The cave was suffused with gentle white light. Scallops in the roof shone soft turquoise. The sun had risen. Dave sat near the door, his back toward me. I could hear the hiss of the stove, cradled between his legs.

"How are you feeling?" I asked.

"Like a million rupees," Dave rattled. He started another verse of the song.

I sat up and coughed. It felt like my lungs were on fire. "We have to get down," I said. "Let's get packed."

"Ay, amigo. But first, drink up. I've whipped up some of my famous *agua caliente*. *Muy bueno*. Hope it isn't too spicy for your *Yanqui* tastebuds." He handed me the kettle. The water was not hot at all. It was icy. Chunks of snow still bobbed in it.

I asked Dave for the mug. He said it was near the wall, where he'd been sleeping. When I looked, I found the mug. I also found a dozen clots of bloody mucus frozen into the snow. Dave had coughed them up during the night.

"Forget about water," I insisted. "We have to get down *now*."

"The stove's out of fuel," Dave said groggily. "Grab another cannister, will you?"

"It can't be out," I said. "I changed the cannister less than an hour ago." I listened to the steady hiss. It slowly dawned on me that spindrift had completely blocked the cave door during the night.

314

There was no longer enough oxygen in the cave to sustain the stove's flame. The stove was spewing unlit butane in Dave's face.

"You're breathing gas," I yelled. "Turn off the stove." Dave didn't respond. he was still humming; his head bobbed with the melody.

I lunged for the stove. Before I could reach it, I felt as if I'd run headfirst into a brick wall. The air was so full of carbon monoxide and uncombusted butane that my knees buckled. I collapsed, gasping.

Something pushed at me. When I looked back, it was Robin. She was bent over in her white dress, grunting, pushing frantically. "*Get up*, Daddy. Your friend is dying."

"I can't," I protested. Robin kept pushing. I rose onto one elbow. Then, as Robin shoved mightily, I got up on hands and knees. As she pushed, I arched my back and sucked in a chestful of carbon monoxide and butane. I almost collapsed again. But Robin, summoning all her strength, shoved upward.

With her help, I staggered to my feet. My head crashed through the thin snow ceiling. The cave collapsed. Snow cascaded down my hood and filled my clothes to the waist. I gulped in lungfuls of crisp, clean air: containing barely a third of the oxygen of air at sea level, but better than the poisonous gases in the snow cave.

Robin, beneath the collapsed snow somewhere, tugged at my waist. I could hear her muffled shouting: "*Find your friend!*"

I was buried to my waist. I dug with my bare hands, groping in the direction I thought Dave had last been sitting. I could find nothing. I dove facefirst into the snow.

Finally, I felt something. It was Dave's shoulder. Blinking away snow, I rose, pulling his limp body after me. I found a level spot near the cave's former entrance and sat Dave down.

His face was plastered with snow. When I wiped it away, his skin was as blue as it had been near the summit. His head rolled like a marionette on slack strings. A bloody string of spit hung from his mouth. I wiped it away.

"You going to make it?" I asked.

"I'm *bueno*," he said. "I hope you have homeowner's insurance."

I made sure he wouldn't slip from the spot I'd put him. Then I waded back into the snow, digging until my hands were numb. Dave watched, curious.

I found only the dead French climber. Accepting, at last, that Robin was gone—a figment of my imagination—I dug for our gear. I found our packs, ice axes and crampons. But I couldn't find the rope.

I dug into my borrowed pack for a spare pair of mittens. "Dave," I said, pulling them on over my wooden fingers. "What did you do with the rope?"

Dave sighed, his eyes closed. "I cut the wrong one." His chest rattled.

Squatting beside him, I looked at the lines on his face. An odd new illustration had appeared in his tattooed mask. I tried to decipher it; it seemed pivotal. "Breathe deeply," I said. "Try to remember. What did you do with the rope?"

"I cut the wrong one, my friend." He was too exhausted to open his eyes.

The sun was climbing up just past the South Summit. It was the brightest morning I had ever seen. *"You mean on Foraker,"* I said, my hands steadying Dave's shoulders.

"I couldn't hold both ropes," he said. I could feel his shoulders sag—as if something had collapsed down deep inside. "I thought my back was broken. So I looked at the numbers. I could save three lives by cutting your rope. Only I missed. I cut the wrong one. *You* were supposed to go down that gully."

I looked up at the gleaming sky. Dave was crying, the tears freezing on his blue cheeks. He told me this was why he'd dropped out of touch all those years: from the moment he'd made the decision to chop my rope, he would never be able to look at me again without seeing the corpse I was supposed to be. He would never be able to look at me again without seeing the three young men mistakenly sent hurtling down that gully.

"It's okay," I said. I rubbed Dave's head fondly. Black spots still swam across my eyes, but I could see the path leading to the South Summit. And I could see that the wind had ceased—the wind that had beaten at us on Everest for days, the wind that had beaten at me ever since Foraker.

I helped Dave pull on his mittens. I never could find the rope. We would have to make it down to the Col without it. I helped Dave with his crampons and his pack. I helped him get his hand through the leash of the old ice axe Emmett had given him.

Before I stood, I bid adieu to the dead man buried in the rubble of the cave. I turned my back on him. He had chosen his fate; I would leave him to it. My fate lay somewhere down this mountain, somewhere across an ocean, somewhere beside a river that ran through a meadow near my home. Nothing on Earth would keep me from it.

"Let's go," I told Dave. I lifted him and held him against me until he found his balance. Then, without another word, we began to climb the steep slope to the South Summit. Every muscle in my body was cramped from the endless night in the cave. Behind me, I could hear Dave's wheezing and rattling. We still had a long, long way to go before we were out of danger.

And yet, laboring up the South Summit, I found the energy to lift my face toward the sun. For the first time in my life, I was truly happy. For the first time in my life, I was truly free. Every day since the fall on Foraker had been an incredible gift. And home was just a downhill away.

* * *

Chapter Fourteen:
Severing the Rope

I didn't pause atop the South Summit. I knew that Dave showed symptoms of pulmonary edema—and I, of cerebral edema or even a stroke. Survival meant getting down the mountain *fast*. I had already started down the jagged ridge toward the South Col when Dave pulled himself onto the South Summit. I could see that he wanted to stop and rest. But I waved him onward; he followed, staggering downward like a drunk.

I led, since I was stronger, and because I didn't trust Dave to follow the route. I tried to keep my pace slow enough for him, but soon I had to stop every few minutes for him to catch up. Then I'd have to wait several more minutes for him to catch his breath. I watched the sun climb higher. We had been on the go for a couple of hours, and were still only perhaps 300 feet below the South Summit. It would be well into the afternoon before we even reached the Col.

There was no avoiding it: we would have to glissade down the ridge. Dave agreed. "Lead the way, Sahib," he said. I took off my crampons and strapped them to my pack. Then I helped Dave with his.

I took the stance for a standing glissade. I stood bent at the waist and knees, feet apart. I held my ice axe to one side, the pick in the snow, for braking and steering. Taking several deep breaths, I looked down the ridge. It dropped steeply in a series of rocky terraces toward the South Col. I would have to glissade down the fine line between the rock to the right and the snow to the left, careful not to curve too far up onto the cornices.

I was pleased to see that Dave had the clarity of mind to use a sitting glissade. It would be a little slower but more controllable than standing. The heels of his boots and the pick of his axe were dug into the slope, waiting to go. It seemed crazy to glissade: certainly one us would plummet through a cornice over the Kangshung Face or take a header down the Southwest Face. But I was absolutely certain that we would die if we continued plodding down the ridge at the rate we were going.

"Ready?" I asked.

Dave held up a thumb.

And then we pushed off.

I hurtled down the winding ridge, leaning on my axe, the edges of my borrowed boots digging into the icy slope. I arced as high toward the cornices and as low toward the cliffs as I could to burn off speed.

In moments, Dave had shot past me in a straight line downward. He grinned wildly, snow spraying in his face. Instead of using his axe to brake, he waved it in both hands over his head. He looked like a child on an amusement park rollercoaster. The frozen corpse of the German woman appeared on the slope below. Dave flew past her, inches away, spraying her with his snow wake.

*   *   *

At the edge of the South Col, Dave misjudged the runout. He took a tumble in the rocks, and was just getting up, face bloodied, when I swooped down. The wind was still uncannily calm. I helped him into the tent we'd used on the way up. It felt like a lifetime ago that we had rested in it. I bandaged the cuts on

319

Jim Fairchild

his forehead and nose and chin. Although they were so deep I could see connective tissue, they hadn't bled too badly. I found it odd. Then, while Dave collapsed onto a sleeping bag, I started the stove. I made a pot of heavily sugared tea, which we used to wash down some frozen salami. Our lips were so cracked it was almost too painful to chew. When we finished the tea, Dave wanted to sleep.

But—barely an hour after reaching the Col—I made him wake up. We climbed out and strapped on crampons again. It seemed to take forever to struggle up the short slope to the top of the Geneva Spur. We clipped into the fixed rope and began to move downward.

At the bottom of the first rope, I stopped to unclip. Dave was still midway down. I tried to read my watch; the shifting digits still meant nothing to me. Judging by the sun, it must have been shortly after noon. When Dave reached me at the bottom of the fixed rope, he unclipped, and promptly slipped. I grabbed his arm. If I hadn't, he would have plummeted down the mirror-smooth couloir that runs between the Geneva Spur and the Lhotse Face.

It was obvious we were going to have to rope up again. Although we would have been able to move faster descending separately on the fixed ropes, I couldn't trust Dave to safely clip and unclip himself from each of the fixed ropes without a belay. I stomped a platform in the snow and told Dave to sit down. Then I toiled back up the last fixed rope. When I'd climbed perhaps fifty feet, I fumbled in my windsuit for my knife, then cut the rope. I coiled the severed line, looping it around my neck. Then I free-climbed back down to Dave.

Tied together on the short rope, we headed across the Lhotse Face. Dave led, staggering unsteadily; I followed, keeping the rope tight. At first, the fixed ropes angled gently downward across a broad, snowy amphitheater, the top of Lhotse high above.

The fixed ropes began to zig-zig down between the increasingly frequent seracs and crevasses. I kept my belay tight. I knew I could have covered this stretch quickly on my own. My lungs at last felt clear of the fumes from the snow cave; my legs felt strong, the cramps gone. I though about leaving Dave behind and going down for help. But I knew I would be too tired to climb back with a rescue party. And I knew Dave wouldn't survive one more night out.

Finally, at what must have been three or four in the afternoon, we came around the corner of an ice wall and found Camp III. We crawled into the same tent we'd borrowed before. While Dave collapsed onto the sleeping bags, his chest laboring, I cranked up the stove and made a kettle of bouillon. Once again, within an hour, we headed downward. This time, I moved out ahead of Dave, even though I should have been behind him to belay. I had to tug constantly on the rope to keep him from collapsing.

* * *

It was growing dark by the time we staggered into Camp II, in the heart of the Valley of Silence. We limped past frozen hillocks of trash and found the tent we'd visited on our way up.

Dave tottered beside the tent door while I helped him off with his crampons and pack. Down the Valley of Silence, beyond the Khumbu Icefall, the perfect pyramid of Pumori was backlit in orange and purple.

Kneeling beneath Dave, unclipping his crampons, I had to steady him so he wouldn't collapse onto me. Pumori's deep hues reflected in his exhausted eyes.

"I heard you talking to her," he said.

"You're tired. We'll rest for an hour, then head down again."

"Last night," Dave insisted. "In the cave. You talked to your little girl."

"That's ridiculous," I said. I tossed his crampons beside the tent. I was nearing the limits of my patience. I wanted to get down this mountain. I wanted to make it home. And—as horrible as it is to admit now—I saw Dave as the biggest hindrance to me getting there. I zipped open the tent and crawled in.

Dave stood outside. The fading light from Pumori was slipping from his eyes. "Don't let anything keep you from getting home to her," he said.

"Get in the tent," I barked. I reached outside and yanked him in. He collapsed into the sleeping bags; I lit a stove to melt snow. As I watched bubbles start to roil, I listened to the gurgling and rasping in Dave's chest. I helped him to drink his half of the water. And then, feeling a wave of pity that threatened my resolve to get home, I gave him my half of the water, too. Once again, within an hour, we were on our way down again.

* * *

We wandered by the light of the full moon through the meandering Valley of Silence. Dave, behind me, dropped into the snow every minute or two, no matter how hard I tugged on the short rope.

Finally, disgusted with our slow progress, I stopped. The moment I did, Dave fell again. Sighing deeply, I headed back to his side. I untied both of us, then lashed the short rope to my pack. I took several breaths, then pulled Dave to his feet. Swinging one of his arms over my shoulder, I stumbled onward, studying the moonlit snow carefully. I knew that even this gentle terrain was laced with hidden crevasses, and travelling unroped was a desperate gamble.

Up ahead, nestled in a gentle hollow in the glacier, sat the single lonely tent of Camp I. I felt an uncanny certainty that if we stopped there to rest, we would never leave. I left the deeply rutted path and skirted wide of the camp; Dave, hanging onto my side, never saw it.

It took what must have been an hour to cover the last hundred yards to the bergschrund overlooking the icefall. Dave fell over and over again; lifting him up each time had drained the last of my reserves. Now, lying on his back at the top of the ice wall, Dave's eyes reflected the light of the moon. He watched every move I made. He seemed afraid to miss anything: as if he were watching a movie he'd paid far too much to see, and wanted to get his money's worth, even if he didn't care much for the finale. I crawled on my belly to the edge. I peered down through ninety feet of empty space.

At the base of the ice wall, the bergschrund yawned in the darkness. Something lay limply across it. It was part of the crumpled aluminum ladder that Dave had kicked down. I clambered back to Dave. I took the rope from my pack and tied a bowline in one end, then clipped it to Dave's harness. "I'm going to set up an anchor, then lower you down the wall," I explained. "I'll have to pendulum you across the crevasse at the bottom."

"Aye-aye, Skipper," Dave said. He threw me a weary salute.

I tried to sink the shaft of my axe into the snow, but it had frozen steel-hard in the cold of night. I would have to dig a trench and bury one of our axes for an anchor. I chopped at the snow, showering Dave with shards. After just a few whacks, I had to stop to catch my breath. Sitting beside Dave, listening to his rattling lungs, I knew that time was short.

I thought about the rappel bollard Laslow had dug on Pumori. "Where's the Ziploc King when we need him the most?" I asked. I tried to smile, but my lips were too cracked.

Dave cupped his hands to his mouth and shouted downward into the night: "*Is there a gynecologist in the house?*" He was rewarded for the effort with a bout of coughing.

I was shocked by the strength he had mustered. His shout echoed off the walls of the Valley of Silence and reverberated down the serpentine back of the icefall. At last, the sound faded.

Jim Fairchild

"This has been one heck of a vacation," I said. "I wanted to thank you."

"You're welcome," Dave said. "But maybe we should do Barbados next time." His shout for Laslow had reduced his voice to a whisper. He coughed, then managed a pained grin. "I suppose you want to get down this wall." He absently wiped bloody phlegm from his mouth.

"Yeah," I said. "My hands are freezing. Pretty soon I won't be able to handle rope."

"Wouldn't you rather get some rest and wait for dawn?"

"I don't know if I'll have the energy by then," I said.

"You've been working hard. Give the ponies some rest, Kemosabe. There's no wind. We'll be warm enough. We'll saddle up and hit the trail at first light." He crossed a hand over his chest like a solemn Tonto.

If I had been less exhausted, I might have realized what Dave was doing. I sat down with my boots dangling over the edge of the wall, my head against his hip. I felt the rough rise and fall of his breathing in the back of my neck. In moments I was asleep, unburdened by dreams.

* * *

When I awoke—my head still against Dave's hip—the black of night was softening to grey. Out past the icefall, I could see the golden moon settling onto Pumori's shoulder. I tried to read my watch. The squiggles meant nothing. I guessed it was an hour or two before dawn.

And then I realized that my neck was no longer rising and falling in time with Dave's breathing. I thought at first it must be due to the stiffness in my neck.

And then I realized the obvious. Sometime during the night, Dave had stopped breathing.

It hadn't happened like in a movie. There had been no stoic farewell speech. There had been no revealing last words to help me make sense of the way our lives had become so chaotically entangled. Dave had simply passed away in the middle of the night, after conning me into falling asleep. Bitter tears ran down my cheeks and froze.

Sitting up, I looked at him. His face was purple; his lips black and bloodied from sun and wind. His beard was encrusted in ice; his eyelashes were frosted by what may have been his final exhalations. His eyes were frozen open, covered by a thin film of feathery frost. I bent down and blew gently into them. The warmth of my breath melted the frost; for a second, his eyes were clear and watery again. For a fleeting moment, I was in a dream, and had the power to give him back his life with the warmth of my breath. But the cold won out; his eyes froze once more into a final frosty gaze. I relinquished the dream.

I could see, by the moonlight, how the intricate lines tattooed in his face were now wondrously whole; how his curious dioramic mask was now complete. It radiated a balance and a fullness I have never seen in any work of art. If I hadn't left my camera at Gorak Shep, I would have tried to capture its marvelous design, so that I could spend the rest of my life deciphering its meaning.

Then I cursed him aloud: for having tricked me to follow him up this mountain, for having tricked me to pause at this ice wall, when we should have kept moving downward. If it hadn't been for him, I might have saved his life. And then—feeling as if the Earth had just spun away from beneath my feet—I emitted a howl that echoed off the icy fluted walls of the Valley of Silence. I listened to the echo subside, stunned by the stillness that followed.

I finished hacking the trench for an anchor. I tied a loop in the free end of the rope and slipped it over the shaft of Dave's axe. I buried the axe in the trench and stomped snow over it. Struggling with frozen fingers, I fed the rope from Dave through the descender on my harness.

I was ready to lower him down the ice wall. All I had to do was push him over the edge. But first I unzipped his windsuit. Reaching around his neck, I found the silk friendship scarf that Chotari had given him. The scarf was supposed to ensure safety for whatever journey lay ahead. I figured it couldn't do me any harm. If I made it home, I would give it to Emmett.

And then, reaching into his hood, I found his ponytail. I lifted it out of the hood, laying it on the snow beside him. I could smell the yak butter pomade. The ponytail was still immaculately braided.

I fumbled in my windsuit once more for my knife. It was a struggle to open the blade with wooden hands. Finally, by the dying light of the moon, I severed the ponytail.

This would be for me alone. I coiled it neatly, then tucked it into my windsuit. Finally, I clipped myself into the anchor. Looking straight out, I could see the first greys of dawn hitting the very top of Pumori. The moon's pale face peeked over her shoulder. I looked down at Dave. I kicked with all my might.

His body stubbornly refused to roll. I replanted my cramponed boot firmly against his backside. I pushed once more. Finally, his body rolled over the edge.

The rope yanked at my waist. But the anchor held. I began to pay out the rope through the descender as smoothly as my frozen hands allowed.

Suddenly, the rope lurched to a stop. I peeked over the edge. By the feeble light of the moon, I could see Dave's body dangling. The ice wall was concave; his body spun slowly. For the first time, I realized the short rope from the Geneva Spur was not long enough to reach the bottom of the wall.

Still, I didn't know why things had ground to a halt. I looked at my descender. The icy rope had kinked into an incomprehensible snarl, jamming into the device.

I pulled off my mittens. With frozen fingers, I tugged at the snarls. Each time I unravelled a loop, the rope lurched jerkily downward under the weight of Dave's body, putting even more tension on the next knot. I worked with my teeth, too: biting and pulling at each snarl that refused to let me lower my dead friend.

After fifteen minutes, I had managed to lower Dave another five feet. And still, I knew that the rope wasn't long enough. I reached into my windsuit.

I lifted out my knife once more and raised it to my mouth. Biting the back of the blade with my teeth, I pulled at the handle with both frozen hands. Somehow, I managed to open the blade. In the process, it slashed my right palm, exposing rich red meat. Like Dave's wounds on the South Col, my flesh was too frozen, my body too fatigued, to bleed much.

Suddenly, welling up behind me, there came an insistent sigh. For the first time that night, the wind had picked up. I looked around. Ahead, the moon was finally gone. Behind me, watching from above, was the Goddess Mother, her veil pulled back, her elusive face bathed in the first pink blush of dawn. It was difficult doing what I had to do with her watching me.

I pressed the blade against the tangle jamming the descender. I sawed with one hand, holding the rope beneath the descender with the other. As the sheath parted, I could see the bare, white core beneath.

Suddenly, the bight I'd been sawing parted. I heard a sonorous *TWANG*, like that made by an archer's bow. The rope beneath the descender slipped through my hand; it ripped frozen flesh from my fingers. I fell backward. The rope shot downward, pulled by Dave's weight, then was gone.

* * *

Chapter Fifteen:

In An Instant, They Are Separated

I sat with my feet dangling over the edge. I closed my eyes. At first, I saw the arc of the severed rope as it whipped from sight. But then I saw the arc of the river that runs through a meadow near my home. I became aware of the faint sensation of heat on my face. When I opened my eyes again, the upper ramparts of Pumori were sparkling in the brilliant light of morning. I had never seen a prettier sight. Pumori's gleaming ridges met in a perfect pyramid against the pristine sky.

I looked downward. The jaws of the icefall were still cloaked in greys. The light of morning had not quite reached its chaos. I almost closed my eyes again, called back by the river. But something caught my eye: a procession of light was snaking toward me through the madness of the broken ice. I realized that the light came from headlamps on eight figures—after several attempts I was able to count them—moving slowly but surely, linked together by taut ropes.

I closed my eyes again and leaned back on my pack. I let the sun warm my cracked face. I swung my legs over the edge like a child on a bus headed home after a humiliating day at school. I must have been banging the ice with the heels of my boots, judging by the vibrations. But my feet could not feel.

My eyes had been closed perhaps ten or fifteen minutes. I'm not sure how much time had passed; I'd given up on reading my watch. I would have already flung it over the edge, but my fingers were too frozen to take it off.

I felt a welling of wind. I opened my eyes, certain the shockfront of an avalanche was sweeping toward me.

It was not an avalanche. It was the gorak. It had alit so close beside me that I could have reached out and touched it if I'd had the energy. Its inky black wings glistened in the morning sun. It flexed its wings twice, warming them in the heat of the morning sun, before folding them, only a feather or two out of place.

The gorak never looked at me. It had spied the lights moving through the icefall. It watched as alertly as if the lights were prey.

Down in the maze of the icefall, the procession of light had paused. Arms were raised in different directions. A section of the icefall had subsided since Dave and I had passed through. I could see a few arms gesturing downward—back toward the safety of Base Camp. At the front of the procession of light, I could see one arm pointing insistently upward.

And then a shrill shriek split the stillness of the morning. It was the gorak beside me: its sharp beak raised to the sky, the muscles in its neck rippling. The single sustained shriek reverberated so sharply off the fluted walls of Nuptse that a small powder avalanche started in one narrow chute high up. The avalanche played itself out before reaching the Valley of Silence.

I could see the procession of light begin to dance. The puddles of light transformed into wildly swinging arcs, seeking the source of the sound.

And then the gorak—without once looking at me—beat its glistening wings. It launched off the edge. It plummeted down at first, straining with its wings. Just when I thought it might plunge into the crevasse holding Dave, the bird began to climb. It rose

Jim Fairchild

above me in a tight helix.

I looked down into the icefall again. The arcs of light were all aimed toward the wall upon which I sat. I could see eight arms raised, gesturing excitedly. And then the figures began to climb swiftly toward me.

When I looked up, the spiralling bird had disappeared. I'll never know if it flew up the mountain or down, although I often wonder. I closed my eyes again, knowing help was on the way.

* * *

The sound of metal striking ice roused me. Someone was headed up the ice wall. I peered over the edge, down between my useless, frozen feet.

I could see six figures milling about, peering into the crevasse. The beams of their headlamps were swallowed by the black depths. The figures gawked at the remains of the collapsed ladder; they gestured silently at something farther down in the crevasse—something barely visible, wrapped in a tangle of severed rope. I thought I heard a collective sigh as they peered downward, although it may have been just a gentle updraft from the crevasse.

One of the figures leaned against an ice block. He was belaying someone who had started up the wall where the ladder once rose. The climber swung two ice tools rhythmically over his head, moving up on the front points of his crampons. He paused every fifteen or twenty feet to swiftly place an ice screw.

It was Naomi. He climbed toward me with a gracefulness that moved my heart. I waved down to him. "Morning," I croaked.

Already halfway up the wall, Naomi paused, hanging from his tools. He returned the greeting. "Jeffrey-san! What about those Cards!"

"What *about* those Cards?" I repeated, confused. It took me a moment to remember that the Cardinals were a baseball team.

"What was that '74 season record, Jeffrey-san?" Naomi continued upward with his ice tools.

I thought a moment. "I don't know," I croaked. "I'm having a hard time with numbers."

Then I could see Naomi's head. First one, then the other of his tools swung over the lip of the wall. Their picks sunk firmly into the ice beside me. Naomi, his neck muscles like steel cables, hauled himself over the edge.

He rolled onto the snow beside me and pulled on the rope, getting slack. He sank the shaft of an axe into the snow. He wrapped a bight of the rope around the head, then shouted "Off belay." He slapped me on the leg. He examined my burned and cracked face. He lifted my icy hands from my lap. He cringed at the torn flesh hanging from them, and the deep knife gash. He asked me where my mittens were; I didn't know. They must have dropped over the edge when I was lowering Dave's body. Naomi took off his own mittens and slipped them over my hands.

"And where is our friend David-san?" Naomi asked hesitantly, blowing warm air into his cupped hands.

I pointed over the edge—down toward the dark, gaping crevasse below. "He died last night. I dropped his body into the bergschrund."

"Ah," Naomi sighed. "I was afraid of that." He closed his eyes a moment, nodding slowly. His sadness was a palpable weight on his shoulders. "The mountains have lost a good friend." Then he forced a smile. "Pemba Dorje told us this morning what you two scoundrels had been up to. He was afraid you were lost."

"We always knew where we were." My voice was a fatigued monotone.

"Of course," Naomi said. His eyes narrowed; I could see deep crow's-feet at their corners—from age, from fatigue, from grief. "This morning—an hour or two before sunrise—the big gorak landed beside my tent. It began to shriek. I threw rocks, then cans,

331

then bottles at it. I threw a kettle, a stove, a bag of dirty clothes. I even threw my boots. But still, the big bird would not budge. And then I had the strange feeling that this crazy bird had come for me. I sat in the door of my tent, with all my belongings thrown outside like a trailer park yard sale, and tried to fathom the bird's cry.

"Finally, Pemba Dorje came to see what the racket was about. He said the bird was an omen. He shared with me the secret of your climb, and sent word throughout the Sherpa tents that David-san might be in trouble. Every Sherpa volunteered to come. I had to limit the search party's size. We started up before the sun had risen. The icefall has grown unstable in the last few days. We almost turned back where the route had collapsed, fearing the worst. But the bird called us again, from this very spot." He pointed to the snow beside me. "It was only when the bird soared upward that we saw you."

I looked at the snow where Naomi had pointed. I could see no talon marks. Perhaps my eyes were too burned by wind and sun. I tried to point out this oddity to Naomi. But my words came out as gibberish. Naomi began to construct a rappel point with pickets he'd carried up the wall. "If you will be patient, Jeffrey-san, I will soon have you down this wall. You will soon be on your way home."

When he had the anchor set up, he sat down again to rest. He dug a water bottle from his pack and offered it to me. I drained it while Naomi, amused, looked on, warming his hands again with his breath.

I handed him back the empty bottle. Both of us stared at it. I finally spoke. "Dave told me something."

"Yes?"

"About Foraker," I said. "About the fall."

"It is okay, Jeffrey-san." Naomi gently squeezed my arm.

"Dave cut the wrong rope. Your three friends weren't supposed to die."

Naomi tousled my hair. "I know, Jeffrey-san. David told me sixteen years ago, when I climbed down to him in the gully. You were unconscious. David-san was devastated. It was too much weight for a young boy to bear."

"It's funny," I said. For the first time since I'd cut the rope, I began to cry. "I feel better knowing it was supposed to be me."

Naomi patted me on the back. "You are *free* now, fellow accountant. You are guilty of no primordial crime."

"I'll miss him," I said. The tears in my eyes began to freeze my eyelashes together. I wiped ineffectually at the ice with Naomi's mittens.

"We all will miss him." Naomi gently dabbed the ice from my eyes.

"Where do I go from here?" I asked. I had been haunted half my life by an erroneous self-inflicted myth. Now, though free of that falsehood, I was left empty and hurting somewhere deep, deep inside.

"Home is where all downhills lead," Naomi said. "There's nothing more to it than that. I will strap you to my back and rappel down. You can sit back and enjoy the view." He wrapped a rescue harness around me. I was too weak to help. Just before he was ready to clip me to him, I stopped him.

I pointed to the anchor I'd used to lower Dave. I asked Naomi to retrieve Dave's old axe. I wanted to give it to someone. I handed him the other borrowed axe—his own—to dig out Dave's. Naomi's eyes twinkled.

"I apologize," I said. "But I took good care of it."

"It is yours," Naomi said. "Think of it as the game bat. When you look at it in years to come, let it fondly remind you of the friend we leave here."

Naomi sat near the edge. I scooted behind him. When I was clipped securely to him, he lowered the two of us slowly down the wall. I clutched him around the shoulders as strongly as I could

Jim Fairchild

with my frozen hands.

At the bottom, countless mittened hands reached upward and grabbed our legs, swinging us across the crevasse and onto the lower lip. I rolled onto my back helplessly, Naomi on top of me, until somebody helped unclip us. When I looked up, seven goggled Sherpas smiled down on me. After the night spent alone, the close press of faces was overwhelming. But then I recognized Pemba Dorje, who'd helped outfit me for the journey, and who had recognized the gorak's message that morning. And then I recognized Pasang. This trip into the icefall was the first time Pasang had ever tied into a rope. As Naomi was being pulled free from me, I reached a wooden hand toward the young Sherpa. Happy to see me, Pasang grabbed it; Naomi's mitten, uncinched, fell off.

Poor Pasang grimaced at the sight of my wounds. He gingerly placed the mitten back on my hand. He was wearing clothes borrowed—like mine—from *Summit 8000's* supply tent. They were huge on him. "When you get down to Base Camp, I make you big pot of yak Tetrazzini. Then you feel better."

The Sherpas lashed together two packs to make a travois, then zipped me into a sleeping bag and strapped me on top. Pasang dug into his pack and fished out a Walkman; he carefully tucked it into the sleeping bag with me and placed the yellow headphones on my ears. The Walkman was playing a tape of resonant Tibetan chants. I looked up at Pasang.

"The *Five Rembrances*," he explained.

Then, with three men pulling on each side and Naomi and Pasang dragging from the front, we began to thread our way downward through the broken ice.

The rocking of the travois lulled me. Lying on my back, I looked up into the faces of the men toiling on each side of me. They were working too earnestly to notice my stare. I felt amongst old friends. I felt safe. I fell asleep, the heat of the sun on my upraised

334

face, the gentle men on each side carrying me downward, my heart dreaming of that meadow beside the broadly looping river back home.

*   *   *

It must have been ten or eleven in the morning when the Sherpas lowered me into Naomi's tent. Naomi brought me four water bottles full of heavily sugared, steaming-hot tea. He made me drink. Then, when he had zipped me inside his sleeping bag, he went to look for the *Summit 8000* doctor. Through the thin tent walls, I could hear the big camp aswirl with activity: Sherpas jesting and laughing, clients cursing and arguing. The sounds were like the rapids and eddies of a rushing mountain stream. And then I realized the Sherpas throughout the camp had fallen silent. Those returning from the icefall had spread word of Dave's death. Wind whispered like a sigh against the tent. I could smell juniper burning. I drifted asleep.

The tent door pulled back perhaps fifteen minutes later. Naomi crawled in, followed by the sullen salaried French team doctor. Although I was too tired to follow the entire conversation between the two, it seemed Naomi had caught the doctor as he was packing his gear, preparing to abandon camp. Only a few days into the Sherpa strike, the organizers of *Summit 8000* had disappeared in one of the expedition helicopters toward Kathmandu, taking what remained of the payroll. The Italian chef had strong-armed his way onto the helicopter, too, one hand holding his toque blanche to his head. According to Naomi, most of the paid climbers had already departed on foot, hoping to catch flights from Lukla for the capital. The doctor had been getting ready to hike out, too. Naomi had caught him just in time. Naomi had to sign a personal promissory note for the doctor's services. He would not attend to me without guaranteed payment.

Jim Fairchild

The doctor reeked of cigarettes; the tips of his right thumb and index finger were stained yellow. He warmed a large kettle of water over a stove while Naomi tried in vain to refresh my memory of Cardinals statistics. Then, while Naomi held my hand, the doctor soaked my feet, one at a time, for twenty or thirty minutes. The doctor apologized brusquely for any pain, and gave me Demerol. And yet, below the ankles, I could feel no pain. When the soaking was finished, the doctor wrapped my feet in gauze. My hands had already started to thaw on their own and escaped the hot water immersion. They burned as if held over a blowtorch. The deep gash from the knife started to bleed profusely. The doctor closed it with sutures, then wrapped both hands in gauze.

Naomi and the doctor helped me back into the sleeping bag; the doctor handed me two capsules of chloral hydrate to help me sleep. As I began to doze off, the two men rehashed, in hushed tones, the doctor's fees. I could hear the disgust in Naomi's voice. He told me later that this was the doctor who had impatiently paced about while Ang Dorje's brother died on the Lhotse Face.

I don't remember much of that day. Naomi and the doctor came to the tent several times to check on me. Naomi made me drink more tea; sometime after dark, the doctor removed the bandages to check my feet. Holding them by the ankles, he whispered glumly to Naomi. Then he rebandaged them.

I awoke the next morning, still groggy from the drugs, my tongue thick, my eyes feeling as if they were full of sand. Soft light streamed through the tent walls; a gentle breeze made the canopy flutter.

As my head cleared, I sensed movement outside. I gingerly unzipped the tent door with a bandaged hand. Light reflecting off the glacier blinded me. Squinting, I saw that the tent's guylines had been adorned with dozens of gaily colored prayer flags. During the previous day and night, those Sherpas still in camp had each tied one there, saying a prayer for my speedy recovery.

Naomi appeared, followed by Pasang. Pasang carried a tray laden with buttered tea, boiled eggs and—true to his promise—yak Tetrazzini. Although my stomach wasn't quite ready, I dug in. Naomi filled me in on the news. He was trying to make arrangements to get me evacuated to Kathmandu. He wanted to get me flown out on *Summit 8000's* remaining helicopter, but there were complications.

First, another storm was moving into the Khumbu, delaying an evacuation until the next day at earliest. Second, the remaining pilot—like the doctor—had been stiffed by the expedition organizers, and would not fly without a promissory note for an exorbitant sum. I told Naomi that I would, of course, sign the note. He told me that he had already signed it himself. It was the third complication, Naomi said, that could really delay things. It seemed that after the expedition leaders fled with the payroll, someone had removed the fuel pump from the remaining helicopter. Nobody knew who the monkeywrencher was; both Pemba Dorje and Naomi were busy now, going from Sherpa to Sherpa, pleading for the return of the pump.

I fell asleep again after breakfast. The doctor came at noon to check my dressings. A smoldering Gitane cigarette dangled from his mouth as he worked. Outside, I could see that low clouds had moved in. Two more chloral hydrate capsules knocked me out until nine or ten o'clock that night. When I awoke this time, light cast from tall flames danced on the tent walls. Naomi climbed into the tent. He told me that the Sherpas were burning trash and equipment abandoned by the fleeing climbers. They had piled it up around the perpetually malfunctioning solar outhouses and had soaked it with aviation fuel before igniting it. I could hear cymbals and drums and chanting—and somewhere, through all the noise, an old Booker T and the MGs tune: "Green Onions."

"Pasang," Naomi explained. "He had the helicopter's fuel pump. He traded it back to Pemba Dorje in return for the *Summit*

337

8000 cassette tape collection. Pasang thought he might be able to use the pump to supercharge his Primus stove. The helicopter will be able to fly you out tomorrow, if the clouds have lifted."

* * *

Pasang awoke me the next morning. He reached inside the tent with a big mug of steaming tea. Naomi sat in a sleeping bag beside me, sipping his own tea. Outside, grey clouds still hung low.

"Perhaps you fly out today," Pasang said. "Perhaps the clouds lift."

Then Naomi told me about the icefall. While I had been asleep the previous afternoon, during the heat of the day, the glacier lurched. Much of the route through the icefall had been obliterated. The crevasse bearing Dave's body had been buried under thousands of tons of ice. The crevasse would be Dave's final resting place.

Naomi began packing his own gear that morning. He said that Pemba Dorje had radioed Chotari, asking for porters to be sent up. They would carry down personal gear belonging to the Sherpas as well as the climbers sympathetic to the strike. The porters would arrive by noon.

Naomi told me he would be busy the next few weeks. He and a few other veteran climbers had offered to help Chotari coordinate the strike. Naomi and the others had already been sending word to alpine clubs in Europe and North America and Japan, pleading for understanding and support. Chotari had been organizing human chains across the trails leading to the major Khumbu peaks. The chains, comprised of both Sherpas and Western sympathizers, would block all outsiders from entering the mountain domain.

"There is no turning back," Naomi said. Then he left me alone with the chain-smoking doctor, who once more checked my feet and plied me with chloral hydrate.

I awoke at midday. From outside the tent came the clamor of arriving porters. When I looked outside, I could see Pemba Dorje and Naomi assigning loads. Under the gloom of the overcast sky, I recognized several of the porters who had carried loads to Gorak Shep for our Pumori climb. I recognized the young boy who had bested Sarah at rockclimbing—Sonam the Smokechaser. When he saw me in the tent door, his face lit up. He waved gaily. I waved back.

Naomi came to the tent with an old canvas day pack. "We found this in the supply tent," he said. "It was David's. Do with it as you see fit."

When Naomi left, I opened the pack. A pair of motheaten socks tumbled out. There was more: a bundle of yellowing envelopes, held together with a rubber band. They were all from the Department of Veterans Affairs, addressed to Dave: at general delivery addresses all along the West Coast of the United States, at the Hotel Habana in Mexico City, at the Plantacion Abrego in Santiago. Many bore cancellation marks and forwarding instructions in more than one language. Inside each envelope was an uncashed Treasury check for $788.75, with the notation at the bottom: SERVICE-CONNECTED DISABILITY. There was an envelope for almost every month since 1984.

And, lo and behold, there was a Ziploc pouch. Even Dave had not been immune to the seductive powers of the polyethylene pouches. By its grease-pencil markings—SOCKS, LINER, DAYS 7 – 10—I could see that the pouch had once belonged to Laslow. It contained a roll of American and Nepalese currency as big around as a fist, tied tightly with scratchy twine. My state of mind made counting impossible, but it must have been ten or fifteen thousand dollars.

There was another envelope at the bottom of the pile. It was larger than the rest, and bore, in Dave's impatient, scratchy cursive, these words: TO WHOM IT MAY CONCERN, IN THE EVENT

OF A SCREW-UP. I opened the envelope, my fingers trembling. It was a simple, hand-written will, leaving everything Dave owned to Karma. I didn't know if the will would be legal back home. But here—in the Land of Light he loved so much—I was sure it was sufficient.

Something remained at the bottom of the pack. It was a book: *The Tibetan Book of the Dead.* I had seen this book before: Chris had carried a copy. As I began to open it, several dog-eared photographs fell out.

One of the photos made my heart leap. It was of Art and Dave and me, standing beside the shining shore of Enchantment Lake. Art had a hand on each of our shoulders. In the distance, out across the shimmering turquoise water, rose the sun-baked granite of Ghost Spire. The picture had been taken on a summer afternoon two decades ago.

The next photo was of Dave and his parents. They were sitting on Emmett's Harley trike. Dave must have been five or six years old. They had been a happy family then. This picture had been taken on a warm summer day, too. Emmett was facing partially away from the camera, and his shirt was off. I could see the tattooed eagle on his shoulder flexing its wings.

The third photo, less dog-eared than the others, was of Ang Dorje and Dave. They knelt beside a rock cairn. They could have been father and son. Behind them soared Makalu's West Face. They had just buried a friend.

I could not decide whether the photos should go to Karma or to Emmett. I flipped open the book to stash them away. The book fell open to the title page. An inscription had been scrawled in ink: "Give my regards to the Goddess Mother. Take good care of little Jeffie. Love, Chris."

So. This *had* been Chris's book. She had known Dave's plan. I dropped the book and laid my head back. No matter how many times it happens, it hurts to find out how naïve one can be. I closed my eyes and wept.

* * *

Naomi's soft voice roused me. He stooped in the tent door. "Somebody's here to see you, Jeffrey-san. Rise and shine, my friend."

When I looked out, I could see Karma and little Mingma. They were both tying prayer flags to the tent's guyline.

I didn't know what to say to them. Pemba Dorje helped with the translating. It seemed that Karma and Mingma had hastened toward Gorak Shep when Captain Noddy returned to Namche Bazar with his tale about Dave vanishing at a stream crossing. Not understanding that it was a ruse, they had searched for Dave—or his corpse—at every stream along the way, and had then spent several lonely nights at Gorak Shep—by now vacated by our Pumori team. They had huddled between boulders under thin blankets, burning incense and praying resolutely that Dave would reappear.

Finally, porters descending from Everest Base Camp shared with them the story of our surreptitious attempt on the peak. Karma and Mingma had just now crossed the glacier from Gorak Shep. They were exhausted and hungry and fearful. Although they'd heard rumors, they had not yet been formally told of Dave's death. It fell upon me, with the help of Pemba Dorje, to break the news.

I don't know how good a job I did. I was still groggy from the chloral hydrate. But maybe—thanks to it—I was able to speak from the heart. Mingma stood in front of the tent in his long wool tunic, his jaw quivering silently, his fists clenching the tunic's hem. He was too confused to cry. Karma stood behind him, holding his shoulders. She was not confused. In her short lifetime she had already received the news too many times that a loved one had died on the heights. Tears poured down her soft brown cheeks.

I found the bundle of cash, the stack of disability checks and

Jim Fairchild

the will. I handed them to Karma, and instructed her to see Chotari
back in Namche Bazar. He would be able to straighten out the legal
details.

And then I reached back and found Dave's ice axe. I handed
it out the door to Mingma. The old wooden-shafted axe was almost
as long as the boy was tall. As he clutched it, his eyes blazed. He
bowed deeply; I nodded back wordlessly. I prayed to myself that
Mingma would not have to risk his life hauling tourists up the peaks.
I prayed that the axe would serve simply as a reminder of the sad
way things in the Khumbu had once been, and as a promise of better
times to come. I knew Emmett would be pleased with the axe's new
owner. It was getting late, and Karma and Mingma had to be going,
headed down-valley before dark. Pasang insisted that they stop at
the kitchen for all the yak Tetrazzini they could eat before their
journey home. I wished them well, not knowing when I'd see them
again, but promising that—someday—we'd sit around a fire and
share tales about Dave.

* * *

The clouds never lifted that day, making a flight out
impossible. Pungent smoke still hung over the camp from the
previous night's outhouse bonfire. Despite the vast quantity burned,
much *Summit 8000* gear remained. So, in the afternoon, Pemba
Dorje divvied up more amongst the throng of curious Sherpas who
had swarmed to the campsite since the strike. Porters in tennis shoes
headed home with coils of generator cables and microwave ovens
and cases of bucatini in their wicker backpacks. Base Camp was
now stripped almost bare. Naomi's tent remained, along with a tent
for the doctor and the helicopter pilot, a larger tent for Pemba Dorje
and two of his Sherpa companions, and the kitchen tent—manned by
Pasang, who had volunteered his services.

Pasang—wearing a crisp white jacket abandoned by the

fleeing Italian chef—delivered dinner, as usual, to my tent. It was yak Puttanesca, washed down by hot arak in the company of Naomi and Pemba Dorje. When we were done with our drinks, we sat in the gathering gloom and talked about the strike's chances for success. The *Summit 8000* organizers had held an impromptu press conference at the Kathmandu airport minutes before leaving the country. They had blamed the strike on the usual bogeymen: *outside agitators*. At the kitchen tent, Pasang washed dishes by the light of his lantern, his clean white jacket lovingly hung from a tent pole. I could hear voices above the hiss of the lantern. Finally, Pasang called for Pemba Dorje.

When Pemba Dorje came back to the tent, he stooped low in the doorway and spoke softly to me. "A stonecutter is here," he said.

I looked at him. I didn't comprehend.

"It is tradition," he said. "Whenever a life is lost on the mountain, the name of the dead one is added to the monument below Base Camp. The name is carved on the rock—along with a simple epitaph, if desired."

"What kind of epitaph?"

"That is up to you. You were David's best friend."

How do you sum up a lifetime in a few words etched in stone? I thought of the book Dave had been carrying. It was somewhere behind my sleeping bag. I reached back and dug around, aided by the light of Naomi's headlamp.

When I found the book, I held it closed between my bandaged hands. I studied the edges of the pages, looking for dog-earring—for signs that one page, more than any other, had been a favorite. But I could find no such clue. Finally, I closed my eyes and let go, letting the book fall open where it may. When it had flopped open, I stuck a finger onto the page. I opened my eyes and read the passage under my fingertip.

I read it again. *Yes*. This would be perfect.

"Here," I said, handing the book to Pemba Dorje. "Carve this on the stone." Pemba Dorje and Naomi read the passage. Both smiled broadly. Pemba Dorje began to leave with the stonecutter.

"Wait!" I shouted. I began to dig through my things for cash. "What do I owe him?"

"The Sherpas took a collection," Pemba Dorje answered, standing in the glow of the lantern outside. "It is taken care of."

* * *

In the morning, the skies were a brilliant blue. The prayer flags tied to the tent hung limply. It would be a fine day to fly. And none too soon: Naomi told me that news crews were on the way, looking for me. I wanted to be gone before they arrived. Pasang served up a final breakfast to those of us remaining. He was wearing a chef's toque blanche as well as the white jacket now, a spotless white towel folded over one arm. After a feast of fried eggs, yak liver and onions—and a couple of Demerol washed down with buttered tea—I was on my way.

The pilot had calculated that the density altitude was insufficient to take off directly from Base Camp with passengers. Instead, he would fly solo to a spot a thousand feet down the glacier, where he could safely pick me up.

Naomi, Pemba Dorje and his two Sherpa friends carried me down to the rendezvous site. They took turns carrying me on their backs in a seat fashioned from a porter's wicker basket. We wound down through névés penitentes and ancient leaning boulders, and chronologically ordered hillocks of debris from different generations of sloppy climbers. Finally, an hour or two below Base Camp, we came upon a broad, sloping rock wall.

As the others set me down to take a rest, I could read the names carved in the wall. I could see the first inscription, at the top—weathered, but still legible, in big block letters:

344

IN MEMORY OF
JOHN E. BREITENBACH
AMERICAN MT. EVEREST EXPEDITION
1963

There were other names after that, too many to count: so-called sahibs from Europe and America and Japan, and *far* too many Sherpas. I was shocked by the lopsided ratio. And then, at the bottom of the list, freshly etched into the dark rock, was the inscription I was looking for:

ALL WHO PASS HERE, PAUSE TO HONOR
DAVID PORTER (1956 – 1990)—
FRIEND TO THE SHERPA PEOPLE
AND TO THE GODDESS MOTHER OF THE WORLD:
IN AN INSTANT, THEY ARE SEPARATED;
IN AN INSTANT, COMPLETE ENLIGHTENMENT

*   *   *

PART THREE:

Return to Earth

Chapter Sixteen:
Blossoms on the Wind

I am almost home. The 737 is on the final approach to Missoula. It makes a broad loop, following the gently snaking Bitterroot River northward. I am sitting alone near the tail galley. I can tell that the plane is slowing and dropping. I can feel the plane's wings flex like a mighty bird's. My eyes are closed, thinking of what I will say to those who are awaiting me.

And then I feel the presence of someone beside me. I open my eyes. It is one of the attendants, standing by the galley window on the port side, studying the view. It's her first flight on this route. Pure, brilliant light is pouring in the window, framing her face, and I can see the awe in her eyes. Realizing I'm watching her, she turns.

"I've never seen such beautiful mountains," she gasps.

I smile. I can't see them out my starboard window, and can't stand on my bandaged feet to catch a glimpse out the other side. But I don't need to. I know these mountains: they are the mountains of my youth. I can sense each of their radiant spirits as they pass: Trapper, Sugarloaf, Castle Crag, Lolo. As a boy, I knelt, out of breath, upon each of their summits. I know that they are deep in snow right now. (What month is this? May? Yes, this must be May. But I have no idea about the day of the month. How long have I been gone? I haven't a clue.) Somewhere down there is a lake named Enchantment, and a rock named Ghost Spire. The lake will still be icebound, the spire heavy with snow. But—with patience—summer will come.

* * *

We have landed. I am so nervous I can feel my palms sweating inside the bandages. I am the last passenger off the plane. The attendant who had admired my old mountains wheels me down the ramp to the gate. The other passengers have long since met those awaiting them. There is just one cluster of faces left. I see them all, and am overwhelmed: my parents, Emmett, my wife, my two daughters.

I am surrounded. I am surrounded by love. I surrender to it. I am inundated with hugs and kisses and flowers and countless simultaneous questions. I evade the questions, and turn to thank the attendant. She wishes me luck, and is gone. She was my last connection to the Dreamworld, to Dave's Range of Light. I feel a door shut irrevocably behind me.

There's nowhere to hide now. I must face Emmett first. This moment is more difficult than anything I faced on the entire climb. This moment is more difficult than anything I have ever faced in my entire life.

How can I explain to this good man why I couldn't bring his son home? What can I say that will ease the pain of losing his only child? But Emmett beats me to the draw. He squeezes my shoulder and tells me he understands. He knows Dave died doing what he loved most. Emmett is glad that his son died in the company of his best friend. I reach inside my jacket and find the silk friendship scarf Dave was wearing when he died. I hand it to Emmett. He drapes it proudly around his neck, over his grey tweed jacket. The jacket has suede elbow patches, and its grey tweed matches his beard, which is neatly trimmed nowadays. He reminds me of one of my old accounting professors, although I never saw my professor cry. My mother pats Emmett on the back.

Emmett clears his throat. He studies my bandages. "Looks like you've been in a bar fight in Butte, Kiddo."

"You must feel like Dorothy," my mother says, straightening my hair, which is tousled from almost two days in airplanes.

"Dorothy?"

"Judy Garland," she explains. "In *The Wizard of Oz*. When she wakes up and finds herself back in Kansas."

I point to my bandaged feet. "I've been clicking my heels awfully hard." We all laugh.

My daughters have been waiting patiently for my attention. I turn first to Gretchen. "Come here, Toto." I gingerly wrap a bandaged hand around her, holding her as tightly as the wheelchair allows. She squirms from my grasp and retreats to her mother's side. She was always the effusive one. Now she stands away from me, glum. I am saddened by the change.

And then, as I hug Robin, I understand why Gretchen acts this way. Robin, in her tiny voice, is telling me about a new box of crayons she has just gotten, and is reciting the colors to me. She is bubbling with excitement. Except for the two words whispered in my ear as I was leaving for Nepal, she has never spoken directly to me. Poor Gretchen scowls, knowing she is no longer a necessary intermediary.

I am astonished. I look at Robin, then up at my wife.

"Something happened while you were gone," Jen says. "The first few weeks, Robin hardly slept. Then, two weeks ago, she started talking a blue streak. She made up the funniest stories about your climb, and drew pictures to illustrate them. She would come to me in the middle of the night with the latest chapter. Thank God you're back. Maybe I can get some sleep now."

Robin yanks on my sleeve, and I look down. She hands me a

Jim Fairchild

piece of gold construction paper that has been folded several times.

"What's this?" I ask.

"Part of the story I wrote," she says. "Read it."

As the others look on, amused, I unfold the paper gingerly, trying not to tear it on the folds. When it is open, I hold it between my bandaged fingers. What I see makes my hands shake. Her story is told in pictures instead of words. But I catch the drift.

It can't be.

"This is the mountain you climbed," Robin says, pointing to an inverted V drawn in black crayon. And then she points to three sky blue stick figures connected by a thin red line. "That's you, and that's your friend, and that's me. And that's my jump rope, holding us together."

She points to a huge upright V with concave sides. It is drawn in black, soaring in the sky just above the three climbers. "That's Mister Bird," Robin says. "He came to me at night. He told me stories about you. I made him promise to watch out for you."

And then she points to a lower corner of the paper. A crude oval is drawn in raw sienna. It is filled with squiggly Byzantine patterns in plum and blue-violet that seem to tell a story, despite their waxy, juvenile clumsiness. "That's your friend," Robin says. I know this drawing. It is Dave's odd death mask.

Jen pats Robin on the head. "She's got quite an imagination," Jen says apologetically to the others.

I thank Robin for the picture. I fold it carefully and put it in my jacket. Robin is playing with the braid of hair hanging from the arm of my wheelchair. She asks where the hair came from. I tell her it is from a yak's tail. Then I explain to her what a yak looks like, and what it smells like, and what it tastes like in the hands of an expert chef like Pasang. My father begins to push me toward Baggage Claim, my entourage in tow. Robin stays by my side. She and I will have much to talk about in the coming years.

*   *   *

On a sunny Sunday in mid-June, Emmett pulls up outside the small apartment I am now renting. When I answer the door, he is dressed in a white tuxedo; the matching friendship scarf hangs around his neck. He has come to take me to the memorial service for his son. Emmett wheels me out to his lawn care truck. The doors are emblazoned with the green logo GROMORE. He helps me into the cab, then folds my wheelchair and stows it in the back beside the sacks of fertilizer and mulch and pine bark. We drive down the Bitterroot Valley, the jagged ridges and soaring spires rising to our right. We pass the spot where Emmett surprised Dave and me with shiny new ice axes twenty years ago. And then we turn off on the dirt road to Enchantment Lake.

The road is rutted and muddy from the melting snows of winter. Two miles from the lake, we pass a school bus mired in the mud. It is the bus carrying much of the local orchestra. The bus driver is attempting to rock the bus out of its ruts while the bass drummer and tuba player lever the rear bumper with stout lodgepole limbs. Mud sprays their white gowns, but they are laughing. Much of the orchestra has already taken off on foot for the lake.

We overtake them, strung out like tired but smiling Boy and Girl Scouts. Many carry their instruments: French horns and oboes and bassoons and bass clarinets slung over their shoulders, one hand lifting their white gowns in futile efforts to save them from the mud. They hop onto the GROMORE rig. Emmett climbs out to help the harp player load her huge instrument onto the safety of the bags of fertilizer and mulch and pine bark.

We catch up, at last, with the piccolo player. He reminds Emmett that he has walked a mail route for 32 years through wind and rain and sleet and snow and, yes, *mud*, and declines a ride. He leads the procession, piping "Tipperary," while Emmett lumbers along in first gear behind him. The bus has caught up behind us.

Jim Fairchild

Soon, most of the orchestra is playing along, filling the woods with their sweet notes. Tiny black squirrels flit from branch to branch to get a look at the commotion, chittering in alarm. I bang out a rhythm line on the steel dashboard. Emmett hangs his head out the window, watching for potholes. "Just two more miles to the lake, gang. We'll make it yet."

* * *

Finally, everyone has assembled under the tall lodgepole pines beside the lake's gravelly shore. It is quite a crowd: the orchestra, still smiling despite their muddied gowns, is ensconced in a semi-circle of lawn chairs. There is a contingent of Emmett's friends from the Fallen Angels—his old biker club—decked out in worn leathers over beer bellies, buckled engineer boots and jeans caked to the knees with mud. Their mud-covered bikes are parked in a perfect circle under a Ponderosa pine. The Fallen Angels have already screwed the caps off their jugs of Paisano, but they act as dignified as church ladies. Happily mingling amongst the bikers are the women from the botanical club—who, indeed, look like church ladies, their soft hair dyed the radiant hues of spring's first lilac blossoms. Emmett, the club's sole male member, has recently been elected president in a landslide vote. The botanical club members have brought a five-gallon insulated jug full of Margaritas. They have obviously gotten a healthy headstart on the Fallen Angels, and are squinting broadly—not just from the sun reflecting off the glassy lake. They wave gaily and bat their eyelashes at Emmett whenever he walks near. Emmett also introduces me to several friends from his prison tenure. They hand me their business cards: public relations, advertising, political consulting.

My daughters are by the water's edge, skipping stones. My mother has brought them. Emmett leaves me now to tune up with the rest of the orchestra; I sit back from the water under a sap-

352

streaked Douglas fir, watching my girls. They are enthralled by the lake. Someday I will bring them camping here.

Dave's mother is here, too. Emmett paid for her to fly from California, where she now lives. She is remarried. They don't have much to say to each other. There is still too much pain. As the discordant sounds of the tuning orchestra rise up across the lake and echo off Ghost Spire, I see my mother and Dave's walking beside the lake. They both wear black dresses hemmed with mud. They walk barefooted, their highheels in hand. My mother has her arm around Dave's mother's waist. I realize how much I have kept my mother out of my life, and resolve to change that. It is one of many resolutions I have made since coming back to Earth.

*   *   *

The service starts. Emmett stands at a rented podium, speaking into a microphone with a feedback problem. The guests sit under the pines. I sit in my wheelchair several yards behind the last row of guests. I am embarrassed by the smell emanating from my dying feet.

Emmett speaks with dignity. His beard is not as wild as it once was, and he has lost weight, now that he doesn't drink. His face glows. "I'll keep this short," he says. "My son loved the mountains. He found something magical each time he reached the top of one. I can't say that I understand it completely. But I think it isn't too far from what I used to find on a flathead Harley with the throttle wide open, the wind in my face, and miles of open two-lane ahead of me on a fine spring day. I think maybe it has to do with freedom: freedom of the body, and of the heart, and of the soul." And then Emmett lifts a toast. I can see that his cup is filled with lemon-lime Gatorade. The guests under the trees hoist high their Margaritas and Paisano and Prosecco.

"*Here's to David,*" Emmett shouts proudly. He smiles

fiercely—but even from where I sit, I can see the tears streaming down into his beard. And then he drinks. The crowd cheers. When the Gatorade is drained, Emmett throws the cup over his shoulder. I think it might hit the harp player, who cowers behind her instrument, but it soars past her. Luckily, the cup is plastic. I drain my cup of Prosecco. Dozens of empty cups fly everywhere. I pity the clean-up crew.

Emmett had asked me some weeks earlier to say something at this point in the service. But it is too soon. Someday, there would be much to say—perhaps a bookful. Instead, Emmett introduces the orchestra's presentation. It is Strauss's "Death and Transfiguration," Opus 24. Emmett will conduct. First, he props his half-frame reading glasses on his nose and reads a poem written a hundred years earlier to accompany the opus.

I can't remember much of the poem. It has to do with a young man's struggle to realize a high ideal, and to make that ideal even higher by his effort. But—just as his goal is finally within reach—death overtakes him. Only in death does he finally reach his goal: deliverance and transfiguration. I think about Dave, and I think about myself. I think a better name for the opus might be "Death and Disfiguration."

And then Emmett is done reading. He turns his back to us and raises his baton. There is a moment of electric silence that even the squirrels honor. I am amazed at Emmett's pent-up energy, by the way his body swells in anticipation. I can imagine the eagle on his shoulder flexing its wings; for a second, I am a boy again, glimpsing that eagle for the first time in the last red rays of a sultry summer evening. I shudder from vertigo. The baton drops sharply downward; the opus begins. I pour another cup of Prosecco for myself with my bandaged hands. Trembling, I spill most of it in my lap.

When the orchestra is done, it takes a bow. The crowd claps and cheers and lifts drinks high in salute. Emmett steps to the podium again.

"Before we start the party," he says, "I have a special surprise for all of you." And then he explains that my father will be flying over the lake in his Ag-Cat, making a special airdrop.

"As many of you know," Emmett says, "I have recently opened Emmett's Green Thumb Nursery. I've been developing a new variant of the Bitterroot, the state flower of Montana. I had planned to present it to the governor on Statehood Day. But today seems more appropriate."

From somewhere behind Ghost Spire I can hear the droning of an airplane. Emmett pauses to speak into a walkie-talkie. Then he addresses the audience again. "*Lewisia rediviva* is known for its amazing powers of resurrection. I am pleased to present to you this new strain, which I call *Lewisia rediviva Davidum*. Those of you interested in wholesale terms may see me after the service. I'd like to thank the fine boys at the Drug Enforcement Administration for providing me the leisure time to explore my interest in horticulture."

And then the sound of the airplane grows still louder. From somewhere just behind Ghost Spire I can hear the wailing of its straining pistons.

Emmett speaks into the walkie-talkie, then turns to us. The cropduster appears from behind Ghost Spire. "Ladies and gentlemen," he announces with a grand sweep of his hand, "*Walter Parson and his amazing flying machine.*"

The biplane roars low over the lake—so low that its mirror-smooth surface is broken by a wake, just as if the plane were a dragonfly whose wingtips have touched the water as it skitters past. The plane circles once more behind Ghost Spire; when it emerges again, it is flying upside down. The crowd gasps and applauds. My father circles around Ghost Spire for a series of passes, each sporting a different acrobatic move. Emmett describes them: a barrel roll, then a full loop, then a hair-raising Immelmann turn. I beam with pride for the creature my father has become.

Jim Fairchild

Finally, it is time for the finale. "Ladies and gentlemen," Emmett says, as the plane roars back into sight at the far end of the lake, "it is my pleasure to introduce *Lewisia rediviva Davidum.*"

The cropduster buzzes low over the lake. As its throaty roar reverberates off Ghost Spire, I can see a belly panel slide back. Just a hundred feet above the lake and a hundred yards away from us, a rivulet of pink blossoms begins trickling, then raining, out of the belly of the aircraft. The blossoms blow back wildly in the propeller wash. And then, as the plane disappears, the blossoms float gently downward.

The audience applauds wildly. Paisano and Prosecco and Margaritas are raised. Gretchen and Robin, who have sat impatiently through the service until now, jump up and down in the front row. Like a gentle spring shower, whole blossoms and single petals begin to patter onto the mirror-smooth lake. As they strike, they create thousands of concentric ripples; I can see hundreds of other concentric ripples formed by rising trout, driven into a frenzy by this odd shower. The still lake has become alive. A gentle breeze blows down from Ghost Spire, and blossoms and petals begin to drift down onto the heads of the ecstatic crowd.

"Let the party begin!" Emmett shouts triumphantly, as a blossom comes to rest on top of his head.

I see Robin run down to the water's edge. She has an old Zebco spincast rod borrowed from the piccolo player. She frantically casts her lure amongst the hundreds of rising cutthroat. I sit back under the pines by myself and pop another bottle of Prosecco.

* * *

The breeze is picking up again, and pink blossoms are washing in toward shore. Robin, leaning into the breeze, her white dress fluttering, the butt of the borrowed rod against her hip, is

356

reeling in her line. Suddenly she pauses, eyes wide, staring at something just beneath the surface.

I have to admit that I am, by this time, quite under the influence. But there can be no mistake about what follows next.

The wind pauses. An eery stillness falls. It reminds me of the way the wind fell on Everest just before the winged creatures appeared. My heart races. Knowing this is irrational, knowing this adrenaline rush is nothing more than a post-traumatic stress-induced flashback, I nevertheless know that something is about to happen that will change someone's life.

The blossoms floating on the water in front of Robin begin to stir. Something is agitating the water just beneath the surface. I see Robin taking in the slack on her line. Her eyes are big and unblinking, like a cat watching a mouse; she watches the water, then the tip of her rod, then the water again. Time begins to expand; what follows next is like a slow-motion movie.

The water explodes.

Robin yanks sharply on the rod. Although she hauls back on the grip, the tip doesn't come back. It is, instead, bent over in a tight arc, pointing straight down toward the water. The rod is bent so tightly it seems impossible the old fiberglass doesn't shatter.

I begin to sputter, then shout to those nearby. But I am too excited to get out intelligible words. Instead, I begin to race toward Robin in my chair. I careen off rocks and fallen limbs. I race through a huckleberry thicket in my wheelchair; the ponytail beside me almost snags in the branches. I am shouting for Robin to keep tension on her line.

And then—just as I reach the water's edge—the fish leaps upward. There can be no mistaking what I see: a giant cutthroat— at least a yard long, at least twenty pounds in weight—leaps heavenward out of the water, its back arched. It is the biggest trout I have ever seen. Brilliant light glistens off its back. Robin furiously reels in the sudden slack, but the line whips upward through the air

Jim Fairchild

in a double curve.

And then, dumbfounded, I realize that the fish is an albino. The chances of catching an adult albino cutthroat are infinitesimal; born blind, most die as fingerlings. But this is, indeed an adult albino: it is a sleek white, with the exception of the blood-red gills, and the ridge of its back, which is faintly splashed with the gentle gold one sees at dawn in the mountains.

In the slow-motion unreeling of events, the huge fish is now hanging in mid-air, at the top of its leap. Its back is arched, its tail tucked. Gravity is about to suck it back down under the surface, where it will disappear from the realm of reality and enter the realm of myth.

This is no mere fish. This is a fearsome prehistoric beast. This is a creature that exists outside of time. This is the freaking Loch Ness Monster!

And then the fish drops. Robin has taken in too much line. The light tackle gives. As gravity sucks the monster downward, the air is split asunder by a shotgun-loud TWANG. The line explodes. Robin collapses backward, the rod still in her hands. The fish crashes with a mighty implosion back into the depths—as if a burning comet has just crashed into the lake.

As the boiling water subsides, I roll forward and help Robin to her feet. Her elbows are bleeding. I expect her to cry. But, ignoring her wounds, she stares silently at where the water is still foaming and fizzing. Her eyes burn with a mysterious inner flame. Together, in silence, we watch the waters calm.

* * *

So let me tell you what I dream of now:

I dream of visiting Naomi, when I am feeling better—when I am back on my feet, so to speak. We leave Tokyo as night falls over the teeming city, headed for the summit of Mount Fuji. We take a bus, then a tram. And then we rent donkeys from a grizzled farmer for the final leg of the journey: because I can't walk, and because Naomi doesn't care to. The gentle animals carry us slowly up the perfect slopes, their hooves crunching carefully over the volcanic rubble and then the snow. We ride upward through the crystal night, braced by the cold, mesmerized by the glitter of the thousand stars above, and by the thousand lights of the city below. We reach the top just as morning breaks far to the east across the fog-shrouded sea. We tether the donkeys, give them soft words of thanks and sugar cubes and gently rub the sweat from their backs. Then, at the Shinto shrine on the summit, we say prayers for those we have lost on other mountains. Afterward, sitting on an ancient volcanic summit rock, we toast the dawn with hot sake Naomi heats on his battered old Primus stove. On the way down the volcano, the jostling of the donkey makes me sick; I mark the way upward for other pilgrims.

And I dream of visiting Nepal again. I take Emmett with me: to meet his grandchild, and to meet Karma, and to meet Mingma. In Namche Bazar, I look up friends. Pasang owns a restaurant now, specializing in yak fusion dishes. No visitor has truly experienced Namche Bazar without trying his famous Tetrazzini. Tourists gladly wait in line for hours to sit at one of Pasang's six tables. Reviews in travel magazines say the wait is worth it. Pasang refuses to let us pay the bill.

I look up Chotari. He is busy now as director of the Sherpa co-op, but he is delighted to see me, and even more delighted to meet Emmett. Chotari has let his hair grow long. It is now braided and pomaded with yak butter, as Ang Dorje's once was. He still loves his Vuarnets. As we walk to Chotari's house, the village children follow us. They take a liking to Emmett. He is soon carrying two of them, who are tweaking his beard; others pull at his sleeves, clamoring for a ride. I am worried about his heart. But Chotari chides me to let him be.

Jim Fairchild

Together, Chotari and Emmett and I rent yaks for an overnight ride to Everest Base Camp. I want Emmett to see the Valley of Silence. I want him to see where his son rests. When he has done so, neither of us can speak, but we both feel better. The three of us tie fresh prayer flags to a pole by the rock bearing Dave's epitaph. As we prepare to leave, a shriek resounds off the low clouds. We look up. It is a gorak, headed somewhere up the mountain. And then, saddling up, we ride gently downward through the mist.

* * *

Epilogue:
Back to the Bitterroot

I've been down to the river again today. I go there with my two daughters on the weekends I have them. They play King of the Mountain on the boulders at water's edge and dance in the meadow beside it. They spin my wheelchair around until I'm dizzy, and grab at the braid of hair on the chair arm that I tell them is from an old yak.

And then the three of us play a game. There's an old concrete boat ramp that leads into the water, and the girls ease me down it with an ancient length of borrowed rope tied to the back of my wheelchair. As I roll downward, I can look out across the river shimmering in the August sun, out at the mountains that bear the same name, and make out what remains of last winter's snow—sad traces hidden in the northern shadows. They ease me down so that the icy waters reach past the stumps where my feet were. The girls laugh and giggle, threatening to let go of the rope. I holler and plead, pretending to be afraid of the river.

When the waters are midway up my bare calves, I can feel my feet again. They feel the way they felt just below the top of Everest, just before I lost feeling in them forever. For those brief moments in the river, my daughters holding me by the rope, I am on Everest again, and Dave is beside me. I holler, and whoop, and sometimes cry from the pain of my ghost feet and my ghost friend.

Jim Fairchild

And then I laugh, and signal with the wave of an arm, and my daughters pull me up.

My wife and I are going through a fairly amicable divorce. Her lawyer is asking for the house, the children, most of the community property and the bulk of the savings. I haven't fought. My daughters deserve no less. My lawyer swears I'm crazy, that I suffered brain damage on Everest. Maybe he's right. I just don't care about the money. In fact, since I've been back, I haven't had much interest in numbers in general anymore. It's funny. I think about that and laugh aloud. Me, the accountant. Me, the boy with the endless lists of expedition gear with its weight and cost. The numbers just don't matter now.

I've been talking with the investigators. I've been telling them everything I know about EarthCorp, about how I cooked the books and abetted—all right, *orchestrated*—its tax scam. The investigators have assured me I will be immune from prosecution in return for my testimony. Again, I just don't care. I just want to make things right.

As for walking: I still face another round or two of surgery to snip away the last bits of dying flesh. With any luck I'll be fitted with prostheses in a couple of months—just in time to cope with the first slippery, snow-dusted sidewalks that can come to Montana in October. But that, too, doesn't really matter. I don't really miss my feet. If I ever do, I'll always have the river game. And I'll always have the dancing of my two little gold-maned divas. And I'll always be dancing in my heart: because I've knelt before the Roof of the World, and I've glimpsed inside the gates of Heaven.

* * *

ABOUT THE AUTHOR

Jim Fairchild earned degrees from the University of Montana in journalism and English. He worked in Antarctica for seventeen seasons as a heavy equipment operator, cargo handler and fuelie. He has also worked as a wildlands firefighter, an Army infantry squad leader, a golf bag assembler, an aluminum can inspector, a graveyard clerk at a convenience store, a janitor and an editor. He once changed tires at a J.C. Penney Automotive Center for three hours, and was a driver-trainee at a Domino's Pizza for 47 minutes.

He started backpacking in 1967 and climbing in 1972. His dreams have always included climbing Mount Everest and holding a steady job—both increasingly unlikely at this point in his life. His most recent novel is *Europa Awakens*, a science fiction story set on the Jovian moon but loosely inspired by his Antarctic experiences. He lives in Missoula, Montana.

Made in the USA
Columbia, SC
13 February 2022

56147949R00217